DISTURBANCES IN THE FIELD

Lynne Sharon Schwartz

"The triumph of *Disturbances in the Field*, Lynne Sharon Schwartz's luminous third novel, is that it faces the most relentless loss without sacrificing its humanity. . . . The power of the story is undeniable, but what makes this novel more than cathartic is its intellectual range and depth."
—*The Village Voice*

"Prepare for an uncommonly intelligent novel of contemporary life. . . . Schwartz leads us through a devastating personal tragedy with breathtaking skill—maintaining a relentless confrontation with pain, yet steering clear of all cliches and bathos. The unexpected ways in which Lydia thinks and reacts demonstrate how thoroughly Schwartz has entered the complex and unique character she has created."
—*San Francisco Chronicle*

"With unfaltering intelligence and compassion, Lynne Schwartz demonstrates what a good realistic novel can do: give us another's life with all its similarities and differences. . . . A deep sense of humanity illuminates this involving book."
—*Publishers Weekly*

"Life, we learn in the opening pages of this relentless work, is a field of needs and fulfillments repeated cyclically unless there is a disturbance of great magnitude. . . . [Lydia's] journey from resignation to a grudging reaffirmation of living, of returning to the field, disturbs the reader's own field with its unmistakable ring of truth. Highly recommended."
—*Library Journal*

Bantam Windstone Books
Ask your bookseller for the books you have missed

DISTURBANCES
IN THE FIELD

Lynne Sharon Schwartz

BANTAM BOOKS
TORONTO • NEW YORK • LONDON • SYDNEY • AUCKLAND

DISTURBANCES IN THE FIELD
A Bantam Book / published by arrangement with
Harper & Row, Publishers, Inc.

PRINTING HISTORY
Harper & Row edition published October 1983
Serialized in M. magazine, March 1984.

Bantam Windstone Trade edition / October 1985

Library of Congress Cataloging in Publication Data

Schwartz, Lynne Sharon.
    Disturbances in the field.

    I. Title.
PS3569.C567D5   1985   813'.54   85-6000
ISBN 0-553-34128-6 (pbk.)

Published simultaneously in the United States and Canada

PRINTED IN THE UNITED STATES OF AMERICA

CW   0 9 8 7 6

Contents

The name of the bow is life, but its work is death.

HERACLITUS

DISTURBANCES
IN THE FIELD

Prologue: The Field, 1980

The object cannot really be separated from the field.
The object is in fact nothing else than the systematically adjusted set of modifications of the field.

ALFRED NORTH WHITEHEAD, *The Concept of Nature*

George remarked that he has trouble working with patients who complain of overbearing mothers. His mother died when he was four. He was brought up by men. To have a mother, even a suffocating one, is to him enviable. Luxurious.

He said, "It's difficult to respond appropriately because of disturbances in the field."

I was struck by that phrase. While George went on about how private history persists like static in current encounters, I brooded over it, the way a plane caught in fog hovers longingly over a blurred landing strip.

"Could you say that again, what you just said?" I asked.

"What, you mean 'reluctant to live in the present reality'?"

"No, no, before that. About the field."

"Oh. Disturbances in the field."

"Ah!" Incomprehensible but tantalizing, the words excited me. It was the sort of excitement you might feel when a veil is about to be lifted—the excitement preceding revelation. And revelation—of order, meaning, purpose, what have you—was what I had always hunted. I was nearly forty-two and still seeking to understand. Not that anything very drastic had happened to me to spur my quest, nothing apart from the ordinary

1

failures and miseries life passes around from time to time like a
tray of bonbons, just so we know we have not been overlooked.
I tended to exaggerate even those disturbances—to imagine that
a child's cough would never end and he would languish his life
away on some magic mountain, or to assume, years ago, that
Con Edison's turning off the lights for nonpayment hinted at a
much more profound darkness descending on us. I was not a
stoic, though in college I had studied *The Golden Sayings of
Epictetus:* "God has . . . given us these faculties by means of
which we may bear everything that comes to pass without being
crushed or depressed thereby. . . . Though possessing all these
things . . . you do not use them . . . but sit moaning and
groaning." There had indeed been times in my married life
when I moaned and groaned. I did not use adversity as a means
of strengthening my character—what Epictetus calls the rod of
Hermes: "Touch what you will with it . . . and it becomes
gold. . . . Bring sickness, bring death, bring poverty and
reproach, bring trial for life—all these things through the rod of
Hermes shall be turned to profit."

Even though I gave up studying philosophy early in college—
those revelations were so stiff and formal, so abstract—and
studied music instead, George's phrase, with its allegorical
overtones, touched a live nerve.

"What does it mean?" I asked.

"It's a term from field theory." Field theory! I stared with
anticipation. "It means that something intrudes between the
expressed need on the one hand and the response on the other.
So the need doesn't receive the proper response and the transaction remains unfinished. What intrudes is the disturbance. I'll
give you an example."

But first he reached across my coffee table for the bottle of
wine and poured us both some more. We were drinking Chianti
to warm us, for outside the wide uncurtained windows it was
February in New York City, and my living room, in an old,
high-ceilinged apartment building, was spottily heated. Often
in winter, our family of six huddled around the radiator rubbing their hands, the way Stone Age families must have huddled around the fire.

"Supposing," he said, and paused. "Supposing a baby cries."
He smiled at his example, tailor-made for me: I had had four

babies and knew all about their crying. "The usual response would be for the mother to run and comfort it, right? But—" He paused again for drama. "But the telephone rings."

George is a psychotherapist, eclectic, but roughly of the school they call ego psychology: first a philosophy student, then a social worker, he narrowed his concerns, attracted to ever more subjective woes. On the walls of his office he has such inspirational and dubious sayings as "Be the Dream," and "Anything worth doing is worth doing badly," which really do not do him justice. Knowing his principles and dedication to his work, I once teased him with the gift of a lovingly hand-lettered poster quoting Epictetus: "A philosopher's school is a surgery: pain, not pleasure, you should have felt therein." He accepted it with good grace, but I don't think he hung it up. George crossed his corduroy-covered legs nimbly on the sofa. He had always been nimble, and boyish; even now, at forty-six, with gray patches in his hair and opulent eyebrows his round face radiated energy, he looked younger than he was. Only once in a great while, when he was still and thoughtful, could I see his years in the lines on his cheeks, traced by a kind of heavy resignation. George is a dear friend of more than twenty years, Victor's as well as mine, though Victor doesn't wholly trust him, with some reason. We met at college: George was older, political—a rarity in the 1950's—a self-styled proto-ombudsman for the student body. He didn't last long in student government— he slept with too many of his constituents, for one thing—but our friendship with him lasted. He became a stocky man of medium height, with a coppery mustache and shrewd hazel eyes; he moves with the slyness of an elf or, as those who distrust him say, a satyr. At first glance he looks as though he might turn blustery—those full lips—but in fact he is mild, almost self-effacing, maybe because no mother ever made him feel like the axis of the universe. George's combination of erudition and naiveté makes him lovable. His tendency to use jargon when he is on shaky ground detracts from his lovability. He is the sort of exasperating friend who now and then drives you to ask, Is he worth it? but the answer is yes. Adept as he is with other people's dilemmas, he has made his own bachelor life a series of narrow escapes from amorous and professional mis-alliances. Now at last in private practice, he has attained some stability. George is sentimental and loyal, like a dog, and almost feminine in his absorption in the drama of personal emotions. Motherless, he confronts the world and its people, especially women, with an attitude of seduction, sometimes charming, sometimes irritating. He has brought over countless women for Victor and me to meet, as though we were parents who had to approve. Each one is presented as a marvel, a prodigy of beauty or talent or goodness. Through them our horizons have stretched; we have learned about astrophysics, travel agenting, poetry therapy, computer programming, urban design, dental technology. Weeks later I will say to George, "How is so-and-so? We really enjoyed meeting her," only to learn she has withdrawn to the world of urban design or poetry therapy whence she came. But his enthusiasm is unflagging.

"The telephone rings," he repeated, "so the mother can't respond right away to the child's need. Actually she chooses to answer the phone rather than attend to the infant"—George sounded a bit severe about this. "Well, never mind her needs. From the child's point of view, assuming he could have one, the telephone is a disturbance in the field. He feels his need unanswered and experiences frustration."

My enthusiasm was ebbing. "I thought there'd be more to it than that."

"There is. That was a simple example because first of all the field of an infant is, well, limited. Also he has very little control over getting his needs satisfied. To complicate it, let's say the mother hears the child cry but she's preoccupied with an argument she just had over the phone with her own mother. Let's say she's feeling unloved and rejected; she may resent the baby momentarily, for being loved and expecting her attention so imperiously. So she doesn't respond right away."

"Shameful. Plus if the telephone rings again on top of that."

"Look, Lydia, you asked in the first place. The point is, her relationship with her mother becomes a disturbance in the field. Unfinished business prevents her from handling new business."

"Business?"

"It's a convenient term," George said apologetically. "Anyway, that's what I meant about my patients. If my private reactions require them to detour, well then, I'm not helping." He took another sip of wine and dug a handful of gorp out of the bowl on the table.

Gorp is an addiction my son Alan, eleven, brought home from his socially aware camp two years ago. Even though it is undeniably a health food, it tastes very good. Gorp is a mixture of unsalted peanuts, raisins, currants, coconut shreds, granola, and sometimes figs. Alan made the best gorp, the ingredients most evenly balanced, but by now we all made it quite well, dumping everything into a big blue ceramic bowl (made by Phil, fourteen and a half, in some shop class) and running our fingers through to mix it up. I always insisted they wash their hands first, even Althea, who was offended that I should tell her this at her advanced age, sixteen. Nevertheless whenever I ate gorp I sensed it bedewed by warm, sweaty child hands. I took some myself and said, "Have you noticed, George, that all your examples are about mothers?" I could tell immediately it was the gorp of Vivian (nine), heavy on the raisins.

"Yes, I have." He chuckled in his boyish way. "That just proves my point—the tendency is always to try for some sort of equilibrium in the field. To complete an unfinished transaction. Or if that word is too crass for you, Lydia, an action. Then the field can take on a new shape and we start all over with the next need. But I'll give you something without any mothers in it. They've done experiments with children, offering them chocolate but setting up obstacles to getting it, to see what effects disturbances have on behavior."

"But what if they don't like chocolate? Vivie and Phil don't."

"That's one of the variables. A child will pursue the chocolate according to the strength of his need. Or, to put it another way, the chocolate has a valence indicating how strongly it's desired. You know, whether the kid is hungry, what the obstacles are, whether he's a passive or aggressive type . . ." He saw me laughing and gazed with mock pomposity at the ceiling. "I'm sure you'll be happy to know all this can be expressed mathematically. B equals behavior, P equals the person, E the environment. . . . You know, what I need"—he held up his glass—"is a little ice in this. It's kind of warm."

The telephone rang. "There is our disturbance. You'll have to satisfy your own need. Try the freezer." I heard the soft, innocently murmuring voice of my youngest child, the whimsical Vivian, reporting that on the way back from her friend's house both her tokens, primary and spare, had fallen into the snow from separate holes in her pockets. She was standing on the corner of Seventy-second Street and Broadway and it was getting dark. It was cold. She had spent her last dime to call me. What should she do? I told her to browse in the nearby Pakistani dress shop while she waited.

"I'm sorry to cut this short," I told George, "but I have to pick her up. Can I drop you off?"

"Sure. I've got to go anyway. I have a patient. Then I'm having dinner with this terrific woman I just met. I must tell you about her sometime. She's into biofeedback. But why didn't you have Vivie take a cab? You could pay when she gets here."

I hesitated, feeling foolish. But George has heard from his patients, as well as committed, so much folly that he inspires candor. "I'm afraid to have her take cabs alone. Frankly, I'm afraid they'll drive her off and rape her." It was one of his redeeming features that he didn't laugh. "Anyway, she'll enjoy the personal service. She's feeling kind of down. Alan is off on this school ski trip today and she didn't get to go because she's too young. She's pining with envy."

"Poor Vivie. She's so lovely, she should never have to be unhappy."

The old Volvo slid scarily onto Broadway. I dropped George at his combined apartment and office on West Eighty-third Street where, he told me, he would shortly be seeing a man who had terrible problems with his father. The father, a renowned neurologist, snubbed his son's achievements in real estate, which drove the son to bigger and better deals, verging on illegality. "I'm very good on fathers," he said.

"What's her name? The biofeedback woman."

"Elinor."

"Elinor. Romantic. Have fun."

He kissed my cheek and climbed off over the piles of snow. "Give my love to Vivie," he called. "Tell her there'll be snow next year too." As I pulled away I almost skidded into a waiting taxi—there was a treacherous film of ice everywhere.

A few days later I telephoned him. "George, hi, it's me. I've been thinking. What is the field, exactly?"

"I'm sorry, I'm with someone. Can I call you back in half an hour?" I knew that tone: no proper names, no endearments, nothing in the voice to hint at relationship or emotion. Nothing to cause gratuitous disturbance in a patient's field.

"I'll have a student then. Can you call around two-thirty?"

A far cry from our college years, when we could knock on doors at any time; friends were instantly available when needed. Nina, Gabrielle, Esther, and I would lay aside books or plans at the slightest provocation. Now we live under the dominion of daily calendars—we have discovered it is the way to get things done. In twenty years we have become the ones who move the world along. The graduation speeches predicted this would come to pass, and so it has. And yet, in our overheated dormitory rooms, when we took up the ancient philosophers' debate over the active versus the contemplative life, there was hardly a contest: " 'If reason is divine in comparison with man,' " Nina read aloud with approval, " 'the life according to it is divine in comparison with human life. . . . We must . . . strain every nerve to live in accordance with the best thing in us.' " God's activity is contemplation, and God is surely the most blessed being. Therefore, " 'those to whom contemplation more fully belongs are most truly happy.' " To question reason's divinity did not occur to us, but then it did not occur to Aristotle either. No, with the laser light of thought, we would pierce the skin of the world to get at the nucleus.

And now we strain every nerve not "to live in accordance with the best thing in us" but simply to live. Telephone calls are disturbances. Gabrielle, who welcomed interruption when she was a housewife, has become editor of an arts magazine. She is serene at last and her right eyelid has stopped twitching; her actions impinge visibly upon the world—her magazine is on every downtown newsstand. Her husband Don treats her with deference because she brings in steady money. Her children respect her because she goes to an office daily, where they can visit occasionally after school and receive the red-carpet treatment. But she is often too busy to come to the phone, and is guarded by a gruff-voiced male secretary who makes me give my phone number, as if Gaby didn't know it after all this time.

Nina, who is frequently out teaching chemistry or in her lab, or stealing precious hours with her married, civil rights lawyer lover, has a machine on which her voice, low and pleasing, an excellent thing in woman, recalls Muriel the fine cigar on the radio of my childhood: "Why don't you pick me up and smoke me sometime?" I can't help laughing into the machine, thinking of how discreet Nina really is. "This is Lydia," I murmur. "I too am very sorry you're not able to take my call. . . ."

And Victor. Victor is the worst. In his studio downtown he takes the phone off the hook when he needs absolute concentration. The world, presumably what he is painting, must not disturb, so that he can better envision it. I or any of our children could perish and he would not hear of it for hours.

George called back promptly at two-thirty. "I'm sorry I couldn't talk. I was very involved. This guy is going to get himself investigated by the Housing and Development Agency if he doesn't watch his step. He's really acting out."

"Acting out? Does that happen in the field also?"

"Lydia, don't you even know what acting out is? I mean, where have you been?"

"I do know what it is." My voice had the injured tone Phil affects when Victor and I suggest he spend more time studying. "I mean, I think I know."

He cleared his throat pedantically. "Field theory is an approach, a way of thinking. Acting out is a label for a certain kind of excessive behavior—when you mistake your fantasies for reality."

"All right. But what is this field? I keep seeing a meadow. Peasants dancing."

"Well, you might say the field is the general area of physical and emotional operation of all the people in the situation."

"George, really."

"Okay, okay. It's not a place or anything static. It's the sum total of the organisms and the environment—no, rather the organisms in the environment, as a unit. The field is everything that made the people what they are, that affects their needs and responses at the moment."

"But what about accidents? Say the mother is on her way to the crying infant but she trips over a roller skate her older kid left in the hall and breaks her leg. Is the roller skate part of the field?"

"Sure. Everything that happens happens in the field. The field is constantly being created and altered. Look, imagine experience as a succession of needs and fulfillments, or nonfulfillments, as the case may be. Ideally, once a need is satisfied it recedes to the background. Say you come home hungry, cold, and tired—you'll take care of one thing at a time depending on which is most urgent. Now beyond merely physical needs—one adventure gets completed and you're ready for the next. New needs arise, the whole thing repeats itself. Unless, you see, there's a disturbance you can't get past. A particular need is not satisfied. You can't move on. You get stuck."

"Do you mean to tell me life is just a string of these little transactions? With built-in obsolescence?"

"I prefer to think of them as adventures," he said a bit huffily. "It doesn't preclude more, uh, high-minded things, Lydia. It's simply a methodology. They have it in physics. Listen, could we continue this later? I only have ten minutes between patients and I'd like to wash up before the next one."

"I thought you only talked to them."

"A euphemism, sweetheart."

"All right. I'm sorry I bothered you. It just makes life sound so acquisitive. Like those kids who collect shells and string them together to make a necklace. If you have lots of adventures that's a long necklace. If you die young all you've got is a bracelet."

"It's easy to dismiss something you're not familiar with. Oh, hi, Jerry," he called. George runs an informal practice. "I'll be with you in a minute. Good-bye, now," he said in his bland public tone. I had become a disturbance in George's field, and in Jerry's. Jerry needed George's undivided attention, George needed Jerry's money. They were ready for their next adventures, so I hung up.

I was one of those children who collect shells on the beach. I always hoped to make a beautiful necklace but I never did, because I didn't know how to make holes in the shells without breaking them. We spent our summer vacations at the beach, my parents, my younger sister Evelyn, and I. My father had three weeks off from the insurance firm. Each twilight for three weeks, after a day on the beach, Evelyn and I emptied the pockets of our sweatshirts and piled our shells in two separate mounds. Evelyn was three years younger. She gathered shells of all sizes, some big enough for ashtrays, a few suitable for a necklace, the rest good for nothing, only beautiful. I sometimes made fun of her motley collection and she didn't know how to defend herself, turned away and retreated into a shielded privacy, and I was instantly sorry. Except for one summer, when we lived, inexplicably, in near-perfect harmony.

Back home I kept my shells in a bowl on my nighttable. It irked me to see them so useless, never to be linked into a design, through my own ignorance. Yet I never asked how the holes were made. I imagined it to be a delicate process, and even though my fingers were agile enough on the piano, I probably feared they would break the shells. I remained attached to them, though, and took them with me to the college dormitory, then to the apartment I shared for two years with Gabrielle, and then, when I married Victor, to our ramshackle flat with the cracking plaster on East Twenty-first Street, where once I found a roach in my hair and cut it all off. Victor liked the shells: he sometimes arranged them on the chipped porcelain table in the kitchen and drew them. He didn't see them as a thwarted necklace. Some twelve years ago, during a massive housecleaning following the death of my father, I tossed out my childish shell collection. I wasn't renouncing, metaphorically, the hope of making order and continuity out of random acquisitions. I think I was simply trying to show myself how much I could do without.

My next adventure was coming up too. It was time to coach my twice-weekly chamber music trio of high school students. They were doing Haydn, who is hard to ruin and always a pleasure to hear, even with amateurs. Although I had been on the faculty of the venerable uptown music school for seven years, I still felt a secret thrill walking through its corridors and being greeted as if I belonged there; sitting around with other musicians and arguing over whether or not to modernize the repertory for advanced students, or what should the programs be for the spring concert series, or should we start an evening chamber music group for amateurs. This last was my private cause: I was sure lots of good pianists would jump at the chance to do chamber music with professional coaching. I was willing to organize it, but I needed to win over Irving Bloch, our sixty-five-year-old martinet of the strings. His standards were impossibly high and his pedagogic manner intimidating, but for those who could tolerate him he performed wonders. Naturally

I didn't tell anyone of my secret thrill, especially not Irving; part of the thrill was in appearing to take my position for granted, like a man.

The trio gave me another sort of thrill; despite their wrong notes and occasional fumblings, this afternoon they captured the measured buoyancy of Haydn. Life was bountiful; I congratulated them and treated us all to hot chocolate in the cafeteria before the cold trip home, where I fried chicken and set Althea to peeling potatoes. I was about to call Nina when Vivian appeared.

"I need to do an experiment to weigh air for science. How do you weigh air?"

Weigh air? "I have no idea, sweetie. Althea, did you ever weigh air?"

"In a lab. With water, balloons, tubes, all sorts of stuff."

"Ask Daddy when he comes home. He might know."

She looked at me gravely, assessing my ignorance. "How about a palindrome? Do you know what that is?"

"Yes. So there. A palindrome is something that reads the same way back and forth. Anna. Level. Otto."

"Madam, I'm Adam," said Althea.

"Able was I ere I saw Elba."

"Wait, wait a minute," cried Vivian. "You're going too fast. Onion?"

We laughed. "No no no, not onion."

"Onion," Vivian repeated thoughtfully, playing with the potato peelings. "On-ion. Why not onion?"

"Althea, my hands are all greasy. Write onion and show her." Althea did. I turned a few pieces of chicken, wiped my hands, and dialed Nina's number. Althea wrote in large block letters, "A man, a plan, a canal, Panama." She took each of Vivie's forefingers and moved them from opposite ends of the phrase, towards each other, making them jiggle at each letter. Vivie was giggling.

"This is Nina Dalton," a voice said slowly, bemused. "I'm very sorry I'm not able—" Then the real voice of Nina, or the real Nina, cool and wide-awake, sounded over the recording. "Hello? Hello?"

"Nina, it's me."

"Hi. We have to let it run its course." After the beep she said, "Sorry about that. I just got in. How are you, Lydia?"

"Good. I have to dash to a rehearsal, but I wanted to ask you a quick question. Something George mentioned. In physics, do you have the field?"

"The field? Of course. Magnetic, electrical. There are all kinds. Which one do you mean?"

"None in particular. The Field. George says it's a way of thinking, not a thing."

"Field theory. Well, that's a pretty basic concept. Relativity. Einstein? Surely you've heard of him?"

"The name does sound familiar."

"In field theory, instead of having matter sitting out in space like lumps, you concentrate on the way things interact. The relationships of matter and energy and time are what's determinant. Nothing is static, everything is dependent on and defined by the movements of everything else. The field is not so much a place where all this happens but the conjunction, the interaction itself. As if the universe is recreating itself, moment by moment."

I turned over a few more pieces of sizzling chicken. "Is it like Heraclitus? Everything in flux?"

"Well." She had that kindly, enigmatic tone scientists use, suggesting complexities too vast to broach. "Broadly speaking, I guess you might say that."

"It sounds a lot better than the way George described it, but still it makes me edgy."

Nina laughed. "You don't have to have a subjective reaction. Life goes on exactly the same with or without these notions."

"I'm never sure about that."

"Even Einstein was convinced of the harmony of the universe."

"Was he? That's encouraging. Anyway, thanks. You sound tired. Are you okay?"

"I'm all right, but Sam's wife is in the hospital."

"Again?" Sam is the civil rights lawyer. His wife has diabetic comas periodically, and attendant complications. "Is it very bad?"

"No." Not bad enough, she might have said were she not Nina, brought up by stern midwestern Presbyterian parents to tread the paths of righteousness. She is totally miscast in the role of other woman. She wishes Sam's wife no harm; she merely thinks about her as little as possible. "Time-consuming. He needs a lot of solace, I get resentful. Same old thing. I won't bore you with it."

When I hung up, Althea, faithful galley slave, said in her self-possessed manner, "What would you like me to do with these potatoes?"

"You can fry them or mash them. I'll leave it up to you."

Vivie was sitting at the table studying the palindromes Althea had written out, her long black hair (my color) in two bunches falling over her cheeks. I decided not to ask her to help with the salad. She did everything in such a dreamy way. Telepathic, she looked up at me. "Aren't you going to eat with us?"

"I'll eat later. I don't have time."

Her face clouded, but she allowed me to hug her passionately, the only one of the four who still did. There was a familiar clutch of guilt in my chest but I ignored it. Four nights a week I conversed with her about the foibles of the Greek gods, the nurturing habits of wolves, could chimps really be taught to speak and if so, was it speech as we know it. I promised to come in and kiss her good night when I returned.

"I hope Daddy can figure out how to weigh air." Her parting shot.

"Is it okay if Darryl comes over? He's going to help me with physics." Althea brushed back her fair long hair, pushed up her sleeves, and edged the potatoes expertly into a saucepan. Neat and efficient; beneath the jeans and sweatshirt, voluptuous. Not shy about the boyfriend but aware of cleverly managing me.

"Sure. Thanks for the help. And watch out for that hair over the flame," I kidded her. Months ago, Althea's French teacher had invited her prize students to tea in a dim Victorian-style apartment lit by half a dozen candles in brass candlesticks. "*Attention aux cheveux!*" Mlle. Riviére cautioned, waving her waxy hands nervously. "You have the kind of hair that easily ignites!" Althea came home with an unusual fit of giddiness and a French accent. "Did you know I have the kind of hair that easily ignites?" Her brothers have adopted the joke. Phil lights matches and holds them perilously close. Alan brandishes scissors; he wants to send a sample to the *Guinness Book of World*

Records. Vivian stares at her own wistfully and says, "Do I? Do I have the kind of hair that easily ignites?"

I kissed Althea's cheek and went to see the boys. Rather, I wanted them to see me. My visibility was like money placed in the collection box at church, overtly to maintain a worthy institution, covertly to buy a share of safety and salvation. For outside I was an unregenerate sinner, impassioned by my work.

Phil was sprawled on his bed eating gorp and reading *Sports Illustrated*. He looked like a television-comedy version of the typical teen. In his room, the only soothing place to rest the eye was the wall opposite his bed, where he had hung four large posters, close-ups of each Beatle. Phil himself had something of the intelligent, defiantly insecure look of George Harrison, only he was not quite so dark or so gaunt. My efforts at small talk evoked mostly grunts. "I have to go out now." "So I see." "Althea is cooking, so would you help clean up, please?" A grunt of concession. I took a step forward, but no, he did not look as though he wished to be kissed good-bye.

In Alan's room, on the small phonograph Victor got him for his birthday, the Beatles' *White Album* played: "Blackbird singing in the dead of night, Take these broken wings and learn to fly . . ." Alan, at his desk, glanced up, smiled gallantly, and sniffled. His nose was still running from the ski trip. I smiled back and rested my hands on his shoulders. Before him were problems with fractions of the most unwieldy kind. "All your life," Paul McCartney sang, "You were only waiting for this moment to arise. You were only waiting for this moment to arise." "Are you sure you can concentrate with that on?" "I can't concentrate without it," he said, tolerant and undefensive. We had this dialogue all the time. "That's a pretty song," I said. "Yes, but it's not my favorite." "What is your favorite?" " 'Why Don't We Do It in the Road?' " I nodded. Alan was suave beyond his years, and very deadpan. Sometimes it was hard to recognize a joke. At the door I changed my mind about interference. "You can't subtract those until the denominators are the same." He clapped his hand to his forehead, widened his eyes, and let out an exaggerated "Ah!" of discovery. He has acted in several Victorian melodramas at school. "Odds bodkins! Thanks, Mom." "Don't mention it."

Downstairs in the lobby I met Victor lugging a twenty-four-inch TV set. The sight of him, as always, brought a flicker of elation. He looked good to me even in a blue down jacket which could make a well-shaped person shapeless, and a brown wool cap pulled over his ears. His cheeks were ruddy from the cold; flakes of snow glistened on his lashes and in his sporadic beard, where some gray hairs had lately shown. He kissed my cheek under the amused eye of the doorman, pretending to doze in a corner.

"So, how does it work?"

"It was fine in the shop. The guy said if it doesn't work here it's because nothing works here unless it's hooked up to the cable. We're due north of the twin towers."

His sister Lily urged this used TV set on us last week, when we made our semiannual visit to Westchester. She led us into the wood-paneled den where it sat neglected on its wheeled metal stand. "Take it, please," she breathed in a smoke-filled voice, bobbing her lacquered head up and down. "Believe me, you'd be doing me a favor." Lily can seem to be breathing down your neck though she is four feet away. Like Victor she has forceful presence, and like their mother, Edith, she is well-polished, but the presence is suffocating and the polish sticky. "Let Vivie or Alan have one of their own. My family is so spoiled, they won't look at black-and-white any more." Lily's munificence surprised me, but when we got the TV home the mystery was solved. All we could coax out of it were parallel lines and snow. "I thought so," remarked Alan. But Victor, defending the family honor, said all it needed was a minor adjustment.

"How much was the minor adjustment?" I asked.

"Forty bucks."

"If it doesn't work, it's eleven seventy-five a month to hook it up to the cable. That's a lot of money, considering they don't watch that much."

"Well, we'll see when I plug it in. It's awfully slippery out there, Lyd. Maybe you should take the bus and I'll pick you up."

"No, I'll be careful." I held the elevator door for him. "By the way, you're going to be asked how to weigh air."

"Air?" His face, as it vanished upwards, was turning pensive. His children's needs were serious business to Victor. Suddenly

I felt guilty again—I could have asked Nina how to weigh air.

It was impossible to go more than fifteen miles an hour along the curving, icy Drive. I thought about George's illustrations of the mother and the crying infant. It didn't seem to have occurred to him that the child might be a disturbance in the mother's field. When my infants cried, particularly the first two, my impulse was not to run and comfort them but to hide my head under a pillow, which I sometimes did. Of course most of the time I went to comfort them, but I didn't run. Well, all that was beside the point; George idealized mothers. The point was the word "need."

I couldn't see how any need worthy of the name was ever fulfilled once and for all. Everything from that infant's first unanswered cry is unfinished business. New needs may arise daily, as George said, but we still must keep placating the ancient ones, like jugglers who set a dozen plates spinning, then dart up and down the line frantically keeping them all awhirl. Sure, the old needs can be temporarily quelled (what George airily termed "receding to the background"), but only to rise again, tyrannical. Alan says, after eating lasagna, "I don't want to eat for a week," but the next morning rises ravenous. Grown-ups feel the same way about sex; certainly George does, or did when we were intimate, more than twenty years ago. (Love, though, may be a luxury. At least I have seen people—my old friend Esther—live for long periods without it.)

Needs are deceptive, too, the bark worse than the bite. When my father died and I painfully threw out the shell collection and other clutter, I saw that one could do without a lot and remain the same person, whole and intact. And yet there must come a point. . . . Supposing the stripper, after removing the G-string and the rosettes on her nipples, peeled off the patch of hair and the breasts themselves?

I parked the car on 120th Street opposite Riverside Church and made my way through the snow humming the Beatles song I'd heard in Alan's room. "Blackbird singing in the dead of night, Take these broken wings and learn to fly. All your life . . ." It was one of those brilliant, glittery snows that ought to emit some glorious sound with each crystal falling to earth, something transcendent like a Bach cantata. I turned to watch it falling on Grant's Tomb, that dumpy monument made grand at night by floodlights, in whose aura the snow drifted with a golden tinge. It was covering the layer of ice and the older, blackening snow, softening the silhouettes of cars and dampening the intermittent sound of crunching tires. I stuck out my tongue in a sudden craving for the cold, ran it across my lips and swallowed. Then I shivered. I had so much. Better to reason not the need. Adventures, shells on a string, were nothing: all that mattered was the essential impulse of the surf that swept them to shore for us avid collectors.

I got into the building feeling high on snow. I brushed it from my coat, stamped it off my boots. Jasper, our trio's violinist, was standing near the elevator. I felt like throwing my arms around somebody, but shy, angular Jasper, his face austere as a hermit's, was definitely not the one. Even my exuberant greeting seemed to alarm him. He shrank into his narrow pea coat and gestured to me to precede him into the elevator. "Jasper," I cried, "we really must do something grand and passionate next, something like Brahms or Shostakovitch." He frowned and nodded, as at a zany stranger, and I became subdued. Those moments of spiritual plenitude, induced by extreme heat or cold, never last long anyway.

Rosalie, the cellist, early and tuning up, welcomed us with a wild wave of her bow. I could have thrown my arms around Rosalie—I had in the past, in appreciation—but the moment was gone. Appreciation: for nine years Rosalie's rich talent and gypsyish air had flavored our West End Trio and kept us invigorated. An ample woman of about fifty with coarse dark hair, dark skin, and large, classically shaped features, Rosalie claims her maternal grandmother was an American Indian married to a Polish Jewish immigrant. How this could have come to pass I do not know. Rosalie is full of unlikely stories made credible by her vibrant narrations. Her deep voice billows through the air—I envision a wave bearing Rosalie's voice aloft. She gestures with her bow for emphasis, so it is dangerous to get too close.

We were doing Mozart tonight, preparing for the spring Friday evening series. During her pauses in the music, Rosalie, as always, bit her lower lip and listened keenly, hugging the warm amber cello between her knees like a lover. When I first

met Rosalie I worried that such a woman would lavish sentiment on every phrase, but she plays with nuances of restraint,
with powerful understatement that can bring tears even to our
eyes, Jasper's and mine.

Mozart went well. We barely needed to talk—we three had
been together so long. When we took a short break Jasper
struggled out of his turtleneck sweater and left the room, as he
frequently does during breaks. Jasper, a young thirty-five, enjoys playing with Rosalie—anyone would—and as he plays, the
accumulated suppressed emotion of his private life, to me
unknown, oozes deliciously into the music, to be drawn back in
abruptly at the final note. But he is wary of her sensuality and
her careening bow. Left alone, Rosalie and I lit up. Smoke
makes Jasper cough. I went to peer out the window at the
snow, while she hitched up her voluminous peasant skirt, rubbed
an edge of the cello absently against her inner thigh, and continued the ramifying story of the demise of her marriage. She was
recently separated from a psychiatrist who appeared unobjec-
tionable in public.

"Everything I did, for fifteen years, he said it was acting
out."

"Acting out! Someone else just mentioned that to me. What
exactly is acting out?" Of course I knew: outlandish behavior,
based on distorted images of reality, but I wanted a fresh slant.

"Acting out," said Rosalie bitterly, flicking ash from her
small black cheroot, "is what the rest of us call living."

I

FAMILIES AND BEGINNINGS

The Brown House

> Even in early youth, when the mind is so eager for the new and untried, while it is still a stranger to faltering and fear, we yet like to think that there are certain unalterable realities, somewhere at the bottom of things. These anchors may be ideas; but more often they are merely pictures, vivid memories, which in some unaccountable and very personal way give us courage.
>
> WILLA CATHER, *Obscure Destinies*

Happy families are not all alike. I have belonged to three, now all families of the past, families no longer in existence, and they had little in common except for my membership.

The family my parents made was secure and practical and loving and staid. It sent my sister Evelyn and me off looking for excitement, in our diverging ways. During the steamy hot summers in Hartford we were restive. Late at night in bed we whispered about the exotic and cool places we wished we lived in: Norway, Alaska, the South Pole. And each morning as we watched my father set off uniformed and dapper in a business suit to peruse numbers and charts, we longed for our three weeks at the beach. We always had a good time at those rented houses, the same sort of good time every year, so that the summers run together in my mind, making one continuous summer, like a Platonic Idea from which any single beach vacation can draw its individual identity.

Except for the one summer, so idyllic that it stands apart

with all the sensual detail of reality and none of the annoying abstraction of Plato. I don't know why it was so perfect: some magic in the brown house itself, where we stayed, maybe, or some special concatenation of weather and internal chemistries. No rain. No toads in the garden. There must have been toads, but I have forgotten them. I did sometimes wake up at night terrified of the dark, but that was such a familiar panic, already a grudgingly admitted part of me, that it didn't count.

Our life at the brown house moved in a cycle of order and harmony, a hypnotic rhythm which worked its way so deep in me that years later, it is still hard to accept that order is an anomaly, not to be expected any more. Hard to accept that the close harmony I shared in with my sister, she high on the dunes and I grappling below in the surf, will not come again. My sister is in Switzerland now, high in the mountains, as I might have foreseen. She was always a bit other-worldly, like Vivian. Evelyn too would have been capable of losing both her primary subway token and her spare in the snow, from holes in different pockets. Like Vivian too, she was overpoweringly sweet-natured, weaving a spell of entrancement wherever she went, and yet unabashedly selfish: younger daughters both, they looked out for themselves first and thought that only natural. Their refusals were final, while Althea or I can be coaxed into almost any favor. Evelyn spent her junior year of college abroad, met a Swiss businessman fifteen years older and married him, just like that, not to return except for rare visits. I felt deserted.

But that summer. The night before we left I watched my father undress when he came home from work. My father was a man who could not be rushed. And because his every move was slow and deliberate, the simplest gestures would assume a weight and texture of high significance. First, from the pockets of his navy blue suit he took out keys, wallet, handkerchief, loose change, several folded envelopes, a package of Chiclets, pens, pencils, cigars, matches, a little packet of business cards. It was like the tiny-car act in the circus, but in slow motion. He took off the suit and placed it carefully on a hanger. "Stay right there," he addressed it, then me: "I won't have to be wearing that for three weeks." In his shorts and undershirt, he leaned toward the mirror and began clipping his mustache in neat, jovial little snips. I went to examine the suit, hanging on a

doorknob. "What do you need all these pockets for?" "Pockets?"
He came over, and with a hand resting on my shoulder he
revealed the secret lore of men's pockets. Upper left hand: the
handkerchief folded in a triangle. Upper right hand: pens,
pencils, cigars. Those inner breast pockets, layer upon layer of
grownup business—cards, letters, mysterious slips of paper with
numbers and names. Back pants pocket: wallet ("But don't you
sit on it?"), crumpled handkerchief (for use, not show). Front
pants pocket for loose change and keys, rattling against the leg.
And a strange little square pocket up near the belt loops.
"Watch pocket." "Watch what?" "For a watch, silly Lydia." He
rumpled my hair. "Dresses don't have all those pockets," I said.
My future looked bleak and sparse. "No, but you ladies have
your pocketbooks. They hold even more." Pocketbooks were an
appendage. Pockets were part of the suit, inseparable. Well, if I
couldn't have a suit I would have a man, at least, and I would
know what wondrous things were in each of his pockets.

The next morning we set off for the Cape, unwrapping our
pastrami sandwiches when we were barely out of Hartford.
Hours later, nearing our goal, we were tired and full of
trepidations, even Evelyn, wise for her six years, because my
parents had taken the house sight unseen and paid in advance.
We were relieved as soon as we saw it. More than relieved.
Enchanted.

A rangy, gray-haired man called Mr. Wilson had built the
brown house and rented it out for part of every summer. I
regarded him as a kind of God or prime mover, to have been
able to create such a paradise. Squarish, solid, and warm-
looking, it might have sprung up as part of the natural landscape,
an inevitable design against woods and sky, figure and ground
merging. I also marveled that something so large as a house
could have been built by one man. But Mr. Wilson had managed it all—walls and floors and windows, long brown beams
on the ceilings, front and back porches with stairs of dark
red-brown wood. Once when we met him in the drugstore I
couldn't resist asking again if he had really built it by himself.

"Well, like I told you before, I had some help with the
kitchen and bathroom pipes, and with the electrical wiring. But
otherwise, sure, I did it myself." So nonchalant about his
miracles.

The bedrooms in the brown house were downstairs and the kitchen and living room upstairs. When our mother told us to come up for breakfast or go down to bed, Evelyn and I laughed. Was it possible Mr. Wilson had made a mistake, or had he reversed the floors on purpose, for some deep reason beyond our imagining?

Evelyn and I slept in two small beds with a nighttable in between and two low chests of drawers opposite, where we piled our daily gleanings of seashells. The door was diagonally across from my bed: Evelyn liked it shut and I liked it open. Each night I yielded, and then after I was sure she was asleep I got up and opened it. The floor was tiled, a rare infelicity on Mr. Wilson's part, for it was cold setting our feet down first thing in the morning. My mother mentioned buying a couple of scatter rugs in the five-and-ten-cent store a few towns away, but she never got around to it. A high window overlooked the woods; peering out at night I saw the dark tops of trees, like a comforter placed against the house. Over the right-hand corner of my bed was a tiny wall lamp, which meant I could read at night while Evelyn slept. I felt it had been provided especially for me, as if Mr. Wilson had anticipated my presence and understood my habits. There were those times when I woke in the middle of the night seized by panic—it was so densely black in the room. The worst thing about darkness in a new place is how it annihilates distances and proportions. I felt blind. I couldn't orient myself in the space, couldn't tell how near or far the walls were. The room might have been a cell or a cavern. But I remembered to reach up and switch on the lamp, and immediately all was well. This panic and its relief I also felt had been anticipated by Mr. Wilson, with the lamp.

Flowers were arrayed outside the brown house, with seashells around them in orderly protective rings. It was no easy task to grow flowers in that dry terrain, but somehow, miraculously, Mr. Wilson's thrived in big clusters of red and gold and purple and pink, their faces turned up to the sun. There was one enormous sunflower, almost as tall as my sister, with which she held private converse every evening at dusk. I longed to know what they said to each other but had too much pride to ask. If I lingered nearby she would lower her voice to a whisper and soon stop altogether. I was pained by her secrecy but pretended not to care. Perhaps this was a small toad in my idyllic garden, but far greater than the pain was my admiration for Evelyn's ability to keep her inmost thoughts to herself. I was a talker; my thoughts never seemed quite real till they were aired and acknowledged by someone else. Much later, when I took Vivian to the Children's Zoo in Central Park and watched her face to face with the Shetland ponies, just about her height, I wondered what was being exchanged, and thought of Evelyn.

Mr. Wilson asked that we water the flowers generously, and so every evening we did, watering ourselves as well, with a long green hose. He told us to pick the vegetables as soon as they were ripe or else woodchucks would get them. Every morning before breakfast, while my father slept past his insurance company hours, we went out to the vegetable garden in our nightgowns, our mother carrying a long sharp knife. It was odd to see my mother wielding that glinty instrument outside of a kitchen. I knew a fairy tale in which the wicked mother takes her children out to the garden and lops off their heads in a trice. Of course I was aware that my mother, gentle and placid, could not possibly do such a thing. Nevertheless I behaved very well when she had the knife in her hand.

We were city people, ignorant of vegetable gardens, but Mr. Wilson had shown my mother how to cut the zucchini from their stems without hurting them. How fastidious a God, his care extending even to the lowliest of his creatures. My sister and I, his minions, helped twist and cut them off in the special way. We were not fortunate with the tomatoes; woodchucks mauled them every night. When we reached the stringbean patch my mother, a lover of raw vegetables, would say, "There really aren't enough of them to bother cooking. We might as well eat them now."

They were crisp and tart, the first juice on our tongues. They were born in the soil and grew up slowly in the sun, she told us as we munched; that was why they tasted so good. She said this so wistfully, I wondered if she was making comparisons. I knew how we were born. It sounded far better to be born in the soil and grow up in the sun. Once she personified the stringbeans that way, locating them in a natural cycle, it struck me that our chewing must be their death, and I had a queasy feeling. But I suppressed it and bit in as eagerly as before.

Down a hilly narrow path through the woods in back of the house was a clearing, and in it was something that looked like a seesaw, except it spun horizontally, describing a circle parallel to the earth. Evelyn and I loved to ride it, but our parents insisted it was dangerous—if we stood in the wrong place it could saw us in half—and we must not go down there alone. They took us, and stood out of range as the plank spun like a planet with us, shrieking for joy, aboard.

Each day at around eleven we set off for the beach. Evelyn would wave and call from the back window of the car, "Goodbye, brown house. See you later." I found that infantile, yet I envied her freedom to say it. Usually we went to the ocean, which my parents and I loved; occasionally to the bay, for Evelyn's sake.

Endlessly, late at night in bed, in soft whispers, my sister and I discussed the rival qualities of ocean side and bay side. She liked the gentle, warm water of the bay since she was not yet much of a swimmer; I liked water that was rough and cold. The bay beach was covered with stones and shells that stung the soles of our feet, while the ocean floor was velvety. Plus the ocean side had those huge sand dunes she loved to climb, I reminded her. Yes, she said, the dunes were very important. But the bay side had that prickly grass to hide in. And at the bay we could walk far out before the water reached our chests. We could dig for hermit crabs on big muddy islands. But at the ocean those fierce waves attacked the moment we set foot in the water. She shuddered under the covers. There was also the question of sand. I pointed out that the sand at the bay was dark and coarse; it stuck to our palms and wasn't good for building. At the ocean side the grains were fine and soft and packed well. We could play ball at either side, but it was often so windy at the ocean that the ball blew away and we had to chase it down the beach. Evelyn was inordinately afraid of losing things; she was afraid of wind because it blew things away. We once lost a kite at the ocean and she cried, until a stranger appeared from far off carrying it back to us. She ran to the stranger with outstretched arms. It was beautiful, like the enactment of a myth. Lost and found.

I didn't like the wind either—the only imperfection of the ocean side—but not because it blew balls away. It was a disturbance that spoiled the stillness and harmony of the scene. The dependable rhythm of the waves was all the motion I wanted. Once in a while, for an instant, the wind did stop. A strange lull of absence fell on the air, and for that instant the tableau was fixed, levitated out of time. But only for an instant.

At the beach, my father would open the trunk of the car and announce, "Everyone has to carry something." We were not a family who traveled light: blanket, pails and shovels and balls, plastic bear, towels, kites, rubber rafts, umbrella, sweatshirts, Band-Aids, suntan lotion, books, picnic basket. But the bearing of our burden was orderly too, each according to his abilities.

To get to the beach we had to climb down an enormous dune, which I believed must be the highest dune in the world. It would still seem high to me, high enough, not being a mountain person, but Evelyn has since found much higher places. We stood at the top for a moment to contemplate the world below. Three wide stripes were all the world: blue sky, black ocean, white sand. On the stripe of white sand, little figures like dolls moved about. Evelyn and I glanced at each other and smiled: soon we would be four more dolls on the stripe of white.

We raced headlong down the dune, dropping things along the way and climbing back up to collect them. Our parents more sedately took a path that arched sideways down the hill. When I asked how the path first got there, my father said it was made by the feet of people, all summer long, climbing down the dune. And each summer the path was in a slightly different place. During the fall and winter, when the beach is virtually deserted, he explained, the wind blows the sand around and resettles it over the old path, and sometimes snow covers it up. In spring, when the snow is gone, the path is gone too. Then summer again; people who love the ocean return, and a new path is made by their feet. "Do you understand?" he said. "Everything in nature goes in cycles."

That wind, always. I nodded, and ran off down the beach.

"If you ever get lost on the beach," my father told us, "look for the yellow and white umbrella with the blue rubber slipper on it." The corner of one canvas triangle had come off its metal spoke, and my father would hang his slipper on the bare tip so it wouldn't poke out any eyes. A number of times we did get lost. There were many yellow and white umbrellas; from a distance it was hard to see the blue slipper. I had to hold Evelyn's hand and pull her along as she whimpered, assuring her we would spot it any minute. I liked the role of older sister. Two or three times I pretended we were lost, just for the chance to soothe her with that exquisite, knife-edged condescension.

Evelyn was a dune climber. Once she had cooled off perfunctorily in the waves, she would run back across the wide beach and start up the dunes. The slope was steep. She had to take deep breaths and use her hands to help her. When she got to the top she waved both arms above her head in semaphore fashion, celebrating her feat, and called to us to see how far away and solitary she was.

She felt very big and wonderful up there. She whispered to me late at night in bed that I shouldn't ever tell anyone, but up there she was really the Princess of the Beach. I never did tell. Much later, watching Vivian running down sand dunes, bronzed and glowing, her thick black hair dripping iridescent sparkles, I wanted to fold her in my arms and dub her Princess of the Beach, but I felt it would be a betrayal of something. I hugged her and said it in my mind, but I wish I had out loud. Even though I am a talker by nature, I kept my word. Occasionally when I type those flimsy blue air letters to Evelyn I have the urge to address her as Dear Princess of the Beach, but I hold back. I still feel she deserted us.

After she finished waving like a semaphore she would run back down. Together the wind and the slope of the dune carried her, feet barely touching the hot sand. She couldn't have stopped. I know how it felt because I did it myself, but without her sense of magical flight. She flew faster and faster. She zoomed. The ocean and shore rose closer. Near the bottom she let go and rolled in a heap the rest of the way. She dashed into the water to wash off, then dashed back to the blanket to ask our mother for something to eat.

I was a surfer. While she tried uselessly to resist the breakers, I welcomed them, then pushed farther on to jump over the crests or dive through them. Once in a while a wave would catch me unawares, churn me so hard in its roil and spin that I lost all sense of up and down, but I had survived before and knew enough not to struggle. I got up laughing, flung the muddied hair off my face and ran in again. I would wait for a really big one, stretch out on top and let it waft me in to shore. I was a mermaid cast up in a strange land, and I gazed around in wonder: what are these alien objects—towels, umbrellas, picnic baskets, humans? Since I was older and obliged to be more sensible than my sister, I never whispered this secret identity to her late at night in bed. Besides, I wanted to hold something back to get even for her private conversations with the sunflower.

When we tired of dunes and waves we built castles, tunnels, bridges, and with our mother's help, a naked woman, larger than life, who lay on her back like a sleeping statue. She looked powerful—full thighs and belly and breasts; our mother had a very solid conception of the essential female—but benign. No sooner was she completed than a huge wave washed over her. Instantly she was hollowed out at the peripheries, diminished, like someone who has aged tragically and prematurely. I kicked in her remains. My sister was sad and wanted to rebuild her; even my mother was downcast, but I laughed and said she was only sand. I kicked at her with exultation. Since she was half ruined, she might as well be all ruined. What use was half a woman?

We stayed so long at the beach we could watch the tide change—it has a six-hour cycle. At low tide we waded out to mud islands where we huddled, shipwrecked, scanning the horizon for a sail. High tide, late afternoons, we sat on our blanket watching the waves inch their way up the sand, and measuring time by their growing reach. Waiting. Every few waves, our parents would drag the blanket farther back, but not much. I didn't know it at the time, but they were playing a silent waiting game too. Sure enough, a stupendous wave would come heaving up out of the sea and rumble towards us. We sat excited but immobile as in a dream, daring it to wash over us, inviting it, teasing the power, accomplices in our own downfall. Till the very last second, I thought its impetus might stop just short of our blanket, our blessed island. And then the game's great climax: a phony, belated scramble to escape, an assault of cold force. Our things were drenched, our pails and shovels gone. Evelyn and I ran to rescue them, while our parents wrung out wet towels and moved farther up the beach, this time in earnest. We pretended irritation but we were enraptured.

My father could have stayed at the beach forever. His great pleasure was being the last family, all alone against the three stripes. It was the waning, melancholy time of day when sandpipers arrive to brood and peck over stones at the water's edge. Gulls swooped low over the crests. Our mother made us change into jeans and sweatshirts. "Come on, Danny. It's getting cold." He would not be rushed; he did not answer right away. Finally, "All right," he would sigh, with one last gaze at the water. As before, everyone carried something. At the top of the hill my sister turned and waved. "Good-bye, beach. See you tomorrow." I thought this talking to the beach was as silly as talking to the house, but silently I echoed her.

When we got to the brown house we would clamor for a ride on the dangerous plank that could slice you in half if you stood in its whirling path. Not now, our mother would say. First a bath, then a ride. And in the twilight, scrubbed clean, Evelyn and I sat on the polar tips of the world as it spun wildly, and when my father muttered that it was a dangerous toy, we felt the secret contempt children feel for caution. Every night we dropped into bed half dizzy with pleasure.

The three weeks went quickly. Mr. Wilson, who would be staying at the house next, appeared as we finished packing. Holding our hands, he walked around and examined his flowers.

"Thank you for taking care of them. You two really did a good job." He was a benevolent God, provided you met his few simple demands.

We passed each other by, loading and unloading the cars, and I remarked to my father that this coming and going was like a cycle too. Mr. Wilson gave Evelyn and me an orange each for the trip home, culled from his giant bag of groceries; we hunted through our depleted supplies and gave him an apple and a cupcake. He said, "Did you ride on that plank back in the clearing? Did you like it?"

Oh yes.

"But you were careful?"

We were careful.

He shook hands with us gravely and patted our heads. A benediction. "See you girls next year."

"See you next year," Evelyn called to the house from the back window of the car.

But we never did see it or him the next year. In most ungodlike fashion, Mr. Wilson got sick and retired to the brown house year-round. We rented other houses near the beach but they were never as good. There were never flowers or vegetables either, just barren dusty miller. My sister grew older and stopped saying hello and good-bye to inanimate objects, out loud at any rate. Late at night in bed she no longer whispered things on the order of, I shouldn't tell anybody but she was really the Princess of the Beach. Soon we moved to a larger apartment so Evelyn and I could have separate bedrooms. When our parents began leaving us alone without a babysitter, we would go to sleep in their big bed for comfort till they came home, and once again we whispered secrets. That was good but not quite the same.

I went to college and met the people who became my adult friends: Nina, Gabrielle, Esther, George. I married Victor and we whispered a lot in bed, on all sorts of delicious as well as grueling subjects. The unexamined life is not worth living, Victor quoted to me as we were falling in love. Impressive. But is the examined one? That is what I wonder.

My parents, who carried so many heavy things in their arms, in time weakened and died. When I think of them now, it is mostly their last years I remember, the specific declines in their bodies. But once in a while, in an unlooked-for flash, I see them as they were that summer at the brown house, my mother short and soft in her long yellow nightgown, barefoot, her cheeks ruddy and her straight cropped hair—dark like mine, dark like Vivian's—still rumpled from bed, her face unlined and clear-eyed, her suntanned hands bearing the knife to the vegetable garden, deftly twisting the zucchini on their stalks without hurting them; my father, lean and hairy in his navy trunks, beginning to have a bald spot in his light brown hair but still able to awe us with a taut bicep, poised on top of the dune effortlessly holding umbrella, kites, rubber rafts, beach towels, paying tribute to the ocean he loved so well. These flashes are given to me, simple gifts, as in the Shaker song my son Alan used to play by ear: "And when we find ourselves In the place that is right We will be in the valley Of love and delight."

I understand now why Evelyn liked the gentleness of the bay, and I marvel that I should have been so intrepid so young, inviting those rough waves to tumble me and rising laughing and ready for more. My sister crossed the ocean to live among mountains. I wish she had never left. I have never felt such rightness as I did that summer, when our proclivities and declivities complemented each other as neatly as the broken halves of a bowl. I would like to go back to that time. Not to the brown house itself, but to that condition, which though it partook so thoroughly of the natural cycles seemed utterly static and safe; a condition of harmony vastly inclusive yet lived against three broad, clear stripes; a condition of being intact and guarded by a wise and providential power. I can still see the brown house and those twenty-one days like one long sandy day, and hear my father explaining about the paths and the cycles. I suppose new paths are still being made every summer by the feet of people climbing up and down. I suppose nature is a cycle to which we contribute our lives and deaths and should do so willingly, but sometimes I just don't want to be a part of it at all. Everything had the chance to be so beautiful, and look what has happened.

Schooling, 1957

In college we took for granted our private distortions and perversities. They were not yet called "hang-ups." We might deplore them as we deplored a birthmark or a thickness of the ankle, but that they were ours no less inseparably we never doubted. The fluid issues, open to constant reexamination, were ideas. They drew our fervent emotions like pipers charming rats. Over chocolate chip cookies in the small hours, we thrilled to Plato's parable of prisoners in the cave, sadly debarred from the light of true wisdom. Through the grimy glass of iron-grilled dormitory windows we too—Nina, Gabrielle, Esther, and I—watched shadows, cast by intermittent traffic under Broadway's street lights, and nodded sagely. Girlish still, we played with our ideas like jacks, feeling their cold hardness, pressing our fingertips against their sharp points and round protuberances, testing how many we could scoop up at once and cradle in our palms—twosies, threesies, foursies! Thales, Anaximenes, Anaximander, Heraclitus—their names as exotic as their accounts of the nature of the universe. The earth is made of water. The earth is made of air. No, the earth is made of the four elements mingling, crowding each other out in a struggle for preeminence. No. "This universe, which is the same for all, has not been made by any god or man, but it always has been, is, and will be—an ever-living fire, kindling itself by regular measures and going out by regular measures. . . . The sun is new each day." The earth is fire. Heraclitus, sagest of all.

Other girls might pick up and drop the boys across the street at Columbia. Our way of being fickle was switching allegiance from Plato to Aristotle. For two weeks we thought Plato the last word, and prematurely believed the adage quoted by our winning Professor Boles, disheveled and abstracted as a philosophy teacher should be: that all the rest of philosophy was merely a footnote. Till Aristotle, who came dragging the reputation of a plodder. He even looked dull: the pages in his text were thinner, the lines of type closer together. But Eureka! The whole material world Plato had left behind returned incarnate, every seed, every egg with an earthly destiny to fulfill. Other girls might aspire to diamond rings or posts in student government; our mission was to locate Truth on whatever library shelf it might be found. And to see, as some hope to see God, entelechy: essence unfurling itself in the passage from potential to actual reality.

We slipped into middle age and a turnabout occurred. We have seen so many ideas come and go; they appear on the horizon as fleetingly as rainbows, they rise and fall and rise again like hemlines. They are our cast-off familiars, we keep them in the attic with our inappropriate dresses, too sentimentally valued to throw away, worn now and then in a frivolous mood. There is a place for Heraclitus and the notion of genesis in fiery strife, a place for patient Aristotle and even for the weightless Bishop Berkeley, a place for the existentialists and the masters of Zen. They coexist in tranquillity as they would in an afterlife; they drift in space as insubstantial ghosts do, and parlay their differences without rancor.

We still try to understand and look for truth. But without the same urgency. Paradoxically, our quest has become academic though we are long out of the academy. Urgency now is reserved for ourselves. In the midst of life, our children, husbands, work, money, aging parents, and shall we take lovers are the daily ontological quandaries. What a falling-off, from that grand fire of Heraclitus that sparked the universe, to our small fires within. And yet to demean the personal is a form of sophistry (Professor Boles was harsh on sophistry), as well as a form of self-deprecation, feminists say. In any event, what we discuss with fervor today is our lives, their inner workings. This is a tedious sort of fascination, a fascinating sort of tedium. A casuist's labor. When we have thoroughly dissected our aberrations from some Platonic Idea of ourselves, parsed our neuroses,

we move on to a more pragmatic question, just as Greek
philosophy, Professor Boles tidily summed up, moved from
scientific to epistemological to ethical: What do we know, How
do we know it, and What are we going to do about it? What are
we going to do about our own perversities? Ignore them where
possible? Exorcise them? The patients of the better sort of
doctors come away not so much purged as mellowed. Esther
had herself analyzed. It did not change her noticeably but
maybe she finds life and herself easier to tolerate. Shall we
accept them, even love them? Surely if we can be exhorted to
love our neighbors and love our enemies, we can attempt to love
ourselves. Or shall we exploit them for professional advantage,
like politicians and military men, high-class whores and artists?

On the topic of friendship Aristotle says, "It is well not to
seek to have as many friends as possible, but as many as are
enough for the purposes of living together." We were a family
of sorts, a family of sophomores, sophomoric. We switched the
roles of parents and children, depending on the need. After
studying alone till eleven or eleven-thirty, we gathered in Nina's
and Esther's second-floor dormitory room with the beige institu-
tional curtains and brown bedspreads on the twin beds. Esther
and I were the restless ones, changing our places nightly—the
beds, the floor, the windowsill. Nina and Gabrielle were always,
reliably, where they were. Gabrielle sat on the new amber shag
rug that was losing its glow from absorbing Esther's cigarette
ash. She would have preferred a bare floor but she made do.
Long-legged, hard-muscled, and ponytailed, Gaby did warm-
ups in second position, flexing and pointing her bare feet,
widening nightly the angle between her thighs till by graduation it was close to a hundred eighty degrees. In our freshman
year she had directed a modern-dance performance illustrating
the myth of Prometheus. That was how we became friends. We
were in the corps, cavorting after her as she leaped magnificently across the gym, a living torch, even her flying hair one of
the deeper shades of flame.

Nina took the single armchair, rust-colored. She fit in it best,
neatly combed and neatly dressed in tweed skirts and nylon
stockings that she didn't remove till bedtime. She always looked
impeccably like a lady. Her oval face, with its straight, clean

features, was never shiny; her dark hair never escaped its pins. Everything about her face and body was fine and understated, so that later, when she deliberately cultivated glamor, it was like adorning a neutral base. I didn't room with Nina, so I never saw her in morning disarray. But even in the required swimming course she remained herself, tall, slender, and composed in the regulation tank suit which made the rest of us anonymous. Our lockers were adjacent; as she undressed she folded away every light and clean undergarment. She never complained about menstruation, as everyone else in swimming sooner or later did; there was never a sign of it; she was unspotted and strove to believe the world was likewise. The years to come would unravel her beliefs and blot her purity, but leave her ladyhood intact.

Earth, water, air, fire, Professor Boles told us the first day of The History of Philosophy 101. The story began simply. The second week they were all three out with flu. I was delegated to take good notes and report back without fail, as if the course were a serialized detective story. I went to the sickroom around midnight, fixed them tea and handed around the notes. Esther and Nina huddled under blankets, Nina in a bathrobe for once.

"She's still wearing that gray tweed suit but she changed the blouse. And her hair wasn't so wild today, and she had lipstick on. Maybe she was going out to lunch. The best thing she said isn't even in the notes. You know how she tosses out these little gems? It's not really philosophy, I guess. Thales, the one who said everything was water, also figured out how to measure the height of a pyramid. If you were ancient Greeks and had to measure the height of a pyramid, what would you do?" Silence. I crossed the room and paused a moment, for suspense. "He waited until that time of day when a man's shadow became equal to his height. Then he measured the shadow of the pyramid."

They didn't seem very interested.

"Actually," said Nina, "he could have measured a man's shadow at any time of day and then applied whatever proportion he found to the pyramid."

"God, she's so smart," said Esther despairingly from her bed. It was true, Nina was extremely smart. I certainly would not have thought of that. Did Thales? And yet it did not have the same poetic rightness.

"For some reason," I said, "that little story fills me with wonder. Why is that?"

"Because," said Gabrielle. She was lying on the floor groaning with muscle aches but flexing and pointing her feet so as not to waste time. "Because it's based simply on the measure of a man. Or it could be a woman just as easily. From the size and scope of one human body you can discover immense secrets of the universe. That's what you like, Lydia. Your pride likes it." Gaby had an odd and rare feature—one blue eye and one green eye. Most of the time there was only a shade of difference, but at moments of strong emotion or insight they flared up, each gleaming its own color. I used to stare, and then I got used to it.

Earth, water, air, fire. The way up and the way down. I remember all about Heraclitus though I haven't much memory for ideas. I do have an ear for sound. I remember Nina's and Esther's voices playing counterpoint, a canon of repetition in shifting keys. Nina's was clear and subdued, with a narrow range that dipped lower when she got irritated—one of the few visible signs. She also blinked when she was disturbed, and smiled. Esther's voice was deeper and coarser, with an alluring crack in it, like some magisterial old woman who has smoked all her life. And Esther's voice had amazing degrees of expression; it could travel from its natural deep tone right up the scale through a series of querulous, astonished, indignant, and facetious notes, and she hit every one of them, every night.

Nina: "Wisdom consists in speaking and acting the truth, giving heed to the nature of things." That's what Heraclitus says.

Esther: Big deal. So what else is new?

Nina: Now, the basic principle of reality is change. One element slides into another. Earth, water, air, fire. Fire starts in the sun, then becomes smoke, vapors, clouds, mist, rain, earth, rock. A gradual hardening. That's "the way down." Do you see?

Esther: The way down. Righto.

Nina: Then you have the way up. It goes in the opposite direction, a melting instead of a hardening. Rock, earth, dew, mist, rain, clouds, vapors, smoke, fire.

Esther: Rock, paper, scissors. Scissors cuts paper, paper covers rock, rock breaks scissors.

Nina (her voice getting lower and very calm): Do you want to learn this or not?

Gabrielle (from the floor, flexing and pointing, her book open between her spread legs): Leave her be. That's her way of connecting. I do the same thing myself.

Nina: But you got ninety-two on the last quiz and she got sixty-two. The way up and the way down are going on eternally and at the same time, Esther, do you get it? There's a rhythm in their opposition. The two main features of the way up and the way down are continuity and reversibility. She'll definitely ask that next time. And the principle, remember, is change. "Everything flows and nothing abides; everything gives way and nothing stays fixed."

Esther: But is that true?

(That worried me too, silent in a corner with my book. *Everything* gives way? *Nothing* stays fixed?)

Nina: That's not the point. Repeat to me, now, about the way up and the way down.

Esther: Continuity. Reversibility. Earth to water to air to fire and vice versa. Listen, I'm not dumb. I can remember. I want to know if it's real.

Nina: First pass the test. Then you can worry about whether it's real. That was very good. Also remember about strife. "All things come to pass through the compulsion of strife." He means strife between the way up and the way down.

Esther (grabbing the book from her): "Fire lives in the death of earth, air in the death of fire, water in the death of air, and earth in the death of water." That is pretty grim. Everything lives through something else's death? I don't think I like that.

Nina (ever calm): It's not a hostile sort of strife. It's an objective description of a cycle. Nature is that process. But I do think he had a preference. I think he liked the way up better. He says, "A dry soul is wisest and best."

Esther: You ought to know.

Nina was hurt. She was doing her best to save Esther from failure. Back home in Indiana, if Nina had failed a test she would have been sent to bed without her supper for a week. Back home in Indiana, her duty was to excel, to obey, and to agree. Independent inquiry was rude and criticism was morally suspect. She had attended Sunday school in starched dresses every Sunday of her childhood, and curtsied for visitors, and if they asked how she was, was expected to reply, "Fine and dandy, just like sugar candy." By the age of four she was trained to pick up all her toys and put them away each evening, and then her mother would supervise her prayers, said aloud, kneeling alongside her bed. She became a math and science whiz kid; she could remember anything schematic. Admissions offices wooed her. Though we tried to take her in hand, Nina could not help behaving, the first couple of years, as though she were a house guest of the college, too well-bred to question any of her hostess's offerings. And when she felt she had failed to meet anyone's highest expectations, she developed a slight stammer, which gave me a pang in my heart. It still does, though she has long ceased to blink and to smile, and has even learned to leave her living room strewn for days at a stretch. It was when she discovered passion that the careful surface began to alter: her parents had never shown or alluded to sexual passion, and so she thought adults, having outgrown the vagaries of childhood, were guided by reason.

We sat up late, talking of how we ought to spend our lives. Gabrielle aspired to Martha Graham's company. A few Saturday afternoons she had urged me downtown to see Martha Graham as a violent Greek heroine or a goddess, swathed in fabrics that possessed a life of their own. Gabrielle said that with enough work she could bridge the gap between flesh and spirit, and we all nodded admiringly. One night I saw her toss down her copy of *Père Goriot* (in French!) and scrutinize her body in the full-length mirror on the closet door. "À *nous deux, maintenant!*" she muttered. She would master it by force of will. What was flesh, what was spirit, and what was the nature of the gap, if indeed there is one, she didn't say, and no one thought to ask.

Nina wanted a happy home life: happy children, happy husband, happy happy. I found that sickening. "Talk about received ideas! If you've never seen the ocean you think a lake is the greatest thing there is. I mean, who knows, you might find more happiness being . . . oh, a madam in a brothel. It might do you good." I had just read *Mrs. Warren's Profession.*

"But why on earth would I want to be that?" she gasped.

"Especially with a degree from here," Esther added.

"I would say that's a puddle." Gabrielle stood up to attempt a slow backbend. Her long fingers reached down for the rug behind her.

"The point is to make it new," I snapped at them. I was reading Ezra Pound.

"That is true about the ocean, though." Esther opened a box of Lorna Doones wistfully. "I remember the first time I ever saw the ocean, last year. And I had seen pretty big lakes. The Great Lakes, you know, are not exactly ponds. But still. It was at Coney Island. I met this guy Ralph at a freshman mixer. I didn't like him that much and he was an inch shorter than I was, but I was lonesome. He came from New York and knew his way around. He had—"

"Esther, we're in the middle of something." Gaby made it to the floor—a high arc, a strip of olive-skinned concave middle exposed between sweatshirt and tights. In a strained voice she asked, "Is this going to be another saga of masochism?"

"No, no. I just must tell you. . . . It's not all that irrelevant— we're talking about what we want most. He had a car, and he asked me what I would most like to see in New York City, and I said, The ocean. He laughed when he heard I'd never seen it. He had a nice laugh, sort of a low chuckle. His face improved when he laughed. When he wasn't laughing it was very square and bony. Anyhow, he said it was especially beautiful in the fall, and the water was still warm from summer—you could dip your feet in. So, he told me to meet him the next Sunday afternoon at Alma Mater and he would take me. I didn't even know what Alma Mater was but I figured I'd find out by Sunday—I didn't want to sound completely . . . you know. Well, Sunday came, and I waited at that goddamn statue for an hour. I was so furious I kicked it. It was cold, too, not one of those gorgeous fall days when you'd want to get your feet wet. After fifteen minutes I was ready to leave. I mean, who did he think he was? Then I thought maybe something happened and I ought to give him a chance. Can you believe that for forty-five minutes I stood there debating with myself, Should I stay or should I go? I do have some pride, but on the other hand I really wanted to see the ocean. Well. Just as I was about to leave, his little form trotted onto the horizon. What had happened was . . ."

The ocean made it all worthwhile. Esther got her feet wet. They ate hot dogs, rode the carousel, seized the brass rings, shivered on the boardwalk, necked in the car. She caught a cold. He phoned several times but she refused him since she hadn't liked him very much in the first place.

"Did you know there's a club, the Polar Bear Club, of people who swim all year round? While we were freezing on the beach this troop of people, mostly old, I mean middle-aged, forty, fifty, came running past us and raced into the water. They splashed around for a couple of minutes and then raced out. He told me it was the Polar Bear Club. Can you imagine? It couldn't have been much more than forty-five degrees."

We talked about what we would change in the world, if we had the power. Stupidity, I said. And chaos. Her parents and her legs, said Esther. In general she would prefer to be a Modigliani rather than a Rubens. Nina said timidly that she would not keep Richard Nixon as Vice-President. There was something about his face she didn't trust.

And what we feared most. Our fears are touching, like old family photos of our grandparents as babies, swaddled in lace gowns and bonnets, overstuffed, innocent of life and death, and absurd: sexual frigidity, being locked in a closet with mice, mental stagnation, childbirth, failure, public humiliation. Today I would gladly suffer public humiliation if in return I could change the course of one specific afternoon. Any of the other things too. Even the mice.

"I can't believe it! I really can't believe it!" Esther stomped through the room in her blue baby-doll pajamas, flapping her notebook around. She had the soft, pink-tinged skin of a strawberry blonde, and she was rosy with vexation. "First they say everything is in constant flux. The basic principle is change. 'Everything gives way and nothing stays fixed.' Remember? So okay, I figure I'll have to live with that. And now they say that nothing ever changes? Everything is fixed? Never began, never will end? An arrow can't even hit its target? What kind of nonsense is that?"

The Eleatic school, very uncharming. "What is unthinkable is untrue." "Movement is impossible." Parmenides and his henchman Zeno poured reason like molten lead into the veins and arteries of the universe, and the system stiffened into paralysis.

"You're not supposed to take it literally," Gabrielle told her. "It's just another phase. The other ones were poetic, these are intellectual. They're trying to think clearly."

"But why would anyone want to think such things? Look, are you going to deny what you see with your own eyes? Can I or can I not walk across this room?" She demonstrated, stepping over Gaby.

"Not in the abstract, you can't," Nina said. "Between one step and the next is an infinity of little steps. You can't get through infinity."

"Are you trying to tell me you believe this garbage?"

"Well, uh, I wouldn't say I believe it in the sense you mean, no. But I do, uh, understand it," Nina stammered. She could be imperious drilling Esther by rote. When it came to defending a position, she had to blink a lot. "It has to do with a kind of relentless thinking, Esther. Carrying something to the very end, like a clue in a mystery, even if you don't like where it leads. It's more honest that way. It seems to me, at least." She cleared her throat and recrossed her legs.

Esther stared out the window at the November rain; she was silenced, braiding the fringes of the beige curtains. She rarely carried any clue to the very end. "I'm cold," she said finally. "Where's my bathrobe?"

"I put it in the wash. I was doing my own things and I thought you wouldn't mind," said Nina.

"I don't. Thanks. But it doesn't help the fact that I'm cold. Unlike some people, my body temperature moves, hot to cold, cold to hot."

"Close the window, then, and wear mine."

A truly Christian gesture, seeing that Esther was such a slob. She had grown up with three generations of messy, uncommunicative family living under one creaking, leaking roof in Chicago. "You bourgeois types wouldn't believe them!" she told us condescendingly, and we couldn't. There were a senile maternal grandmother, an incontinent paternal grandfather, aunts and uncles who dropped in and out, besides her parents and three

older brothers. Like a commune? Gaby suggested. No, no, not
at all like a commune. No Brook Farm. No principles. Just a
collection of people, barely a family. There were vague invest-
ments they shared; living under one roof made the money go
farther.

Esther's people, as she called them, took their own meals at
odd hours, nodded cursory greetings in the halls, and lived for
the most part in pajamas. There were cats, her mother's. "Her
warmest feelings were reserved for the cats. She held them all
the time. Me, never." It was like a poorly run hotel, she said,
no one minding the front desk. "And I. I was an afterthought.
An accident, I mean. I'm sure they weren't still doing it. He
probably fell on her in his sleep, or somethlng like that. I was a
grown man's wet dream."

Her father didn't talk much to his children, but he would
sometimes warn her brothers against the corruptions of capital-
ist success. (Not much danger of that, Esther noted with relish.
One was in the army and one worked as a garage mechanic.
The third built sculpture out of debris.) "My father was a leftist
when he was young. An organizer." A twinge of pride seeped
through, like light through a slit in a curtain. "He got disgusted,
I guess, in the thirties when the war came. He gave it up."
When, wearing her baby-doll pajamas, she ran into him in the
kitchen at midnight, both in search of leftovers and surprising
the water beetles into a frantic scurrying, he hardly gave her a
glance. "But he shared the food. You've got to give the devil his
due. Anything he found, he gave me half. Each according to his
needs, you know."

On warm days, atavistically, Esther might wear bedroom
slippers to class if she could get them past Nina. It was Nina
who reminded her diplomatically to get her shoes reheeled, to
hang up her skirts so they didn't crease, to buy new bras when
the old ones lost their shape. Nina was uncomfortable seeing
large breasts flop around. Perhaps she reminded her about
taking showers too: whenever I met Esther ambling down the
hall in her ancient green flannel robe, a wet towel slung over
her shoulder, pinkish skin aglow and golden curls dripping, she
would announce with a certain belligerent pride, "I just took a
shower," as if I couldn't tell, or needed to know for the record.

"I am a product of will over chaos," she declared every so

often. "How else do you think I got here?" Leafing through a *Guide to American Colleges and Universities*, she had liked the sound of the small women's college abutting the great university, and she liked the distance between New York and Chicago. After a few bitter remarks about private education under capitalism, her father agreed to pay the bills, though he considered the venture pointless. "If you think you can find a better husband there than here, be my guest."

"That wasn't so bad. That I could take. It was my mother who nearly did me in. 'New York! My, my. Do you really think you can manage? I wonder who looks after you girls.' Looks after! I don't think she looked after me from the first morning she deposited me at kindergarten. 'But if you feel you must, dear, I certainly wouldn't stand in your way.' Stand in my way! She wouldn't stand, period. She was always lying down. Reclining, you know, on one of those old-fashioned chaises, sort of like Mme. de Staël awaiting her guests. She took naps on and off all day long and never bothered to comb her hair when she got up. She would powder her face, though. She was overpowdered. She had a powdery look, you know what I mean? Like you had an urge to sort of dust her off." Esther could keep us laughing, but it was unwilling laughter. I hoped she was exaggerating. " 'Be sure to take good care of yourself out there, Essie. The change of air . . . You were such a delicate little thing when you were a baby.' Nine pounds four ounces. Delicate! And she only nursed me for two weeks. Two goddamn weeks. She said I bit. She said I was born with teeth. 'Remember, if you don't like it you can always get on a plane and come back home.' Home! Sure, so I could join her and we could rot together. Of course she wanted me home—who else would do the shopping and cooking, such as it was."

"Esther, I didn't know you could cook."

"Will over chaos." She ripped open a sample pack of cigarettes. "I'd be happy never to see a pot again for the rest of my life. The kitchen positively reeked of cats, the garbage piled with all those open cans. I tried, believe me. But you can't get rid of that smell. It's an indestructible smell. No one else seemed to smell it except me—they were inured." Nina shuddered. She loathed cats, like her mother before her. "Well, anyway, then she would turn back to her needlepoint. Discussion of my education is finished. She was always doing needlepoint: cats, horses, zebras—she hung them all over her bedroom. Her big excursions were going out to the needlepoint shop. She'd get all dressed, and powdered, naturally, and put on this dark green coat with little foxes' tails hanging from the collar that made her look like something in those cases at the Museum of Natural History. She would come home all atwitter with a new piece of burlap or whatever the hell it is. Take a plane home! I would rather have died than gone home. Do you remember—well, I guess you wouldn't; I hardly knew you all then, except Nina— that first semester I spent three weeks in the infirmary? Every- one thought I had mono, I had all the right symptoms. But I think I was having some kind of collapse. I wouldn't let them call home. I threatened to hang myself if they did. But they made me compromise. I would call my mother and say I wasn't feeling too well and just sort of chat, so Dr. Peters wouldn't be in any trouble, I guess in case I died or something. Peters must have listened in on the extension, because after that she didn't bother me any more about calling. She gave me pills."

"But why was your mother like that?" Gaby asked. "What happened to her?"

Esther was surprised by the question. "I don't know that anything special happened to her. That was how she was. I never really thought much about why." She shrugged and lit another sample cigarette. "Her sister was like that, her mother, maybe I'll get that way too. Maybe it's in the genes."

It was Nina's and Esther's room we gathered in because my roommate had to go to bed at eleven-thirty; she claimed her brain cells could not function on fewer than eight hours of sleep. Until eleven-thirty she sat hunched over her desk in her flowered flannel pajamas with feet, like Dr. Dentons, winding her lank brown hair around her fingers and squinting over thick biology textbooks whose colorful diagrams of inner organs were unsettling. Particularly unsettling was the female sexual and reproductive system, viewed in profile section. To me it was a woman bisected vertically. I have seen that profile many times since, in gynecologists' offices and in those booklets that explain sex and menstruation to little girls, and still it appears so remote from what some writer called felt life.

My roommate, who came from Denver, ate bananas while she studied. In her open, easy accents, she told me the virtues of potassium. Like me, Melanie was always hungry and always slim. She let the peels pile up on her desk, so that the studious evenings unwound in a sensuous banana aroma, like incense. Mornings brought the bittersweet smell of rot. To offset the banana peels I ate oranges, the large, thick-skinned kind. Orange peels left out overnight do not stink. But sometimes I ate the peels as well. The fleshy white part kept some of the sweetness of the pulp; the closer I got to the outside, the more tart. I loved the bumpy texture but I took very small bites because of the acid. Melanie never thought this slow, luxurious nibbling at the rinds was at all peculiar. She also never seemed to mind my turning on the light in the middle of the night, if I chanced to awaken and panic at the dark.

We were not together in the room very much: for hours every day I used a piano practice room on campus, while she peered into a microscope. Weekends I went to free concerts or lay on my bed reading, eating oranges and an occasional banana; she was out with her boyfriend. Each May we chose to room together again. After graduation we said good-bye warmly, embracing through our identical commencement robes. I think it was the only time we touched. She still sends me Christmas cards from Maryland, where she is a professor of gastroenterology at Johns Hopkins. From Melanie I learned about coexistence, and since then, when Victor and I have had bad spells, thwarting each other's groping efforts at contact, I have suggested that we try simply to coexist till things improve. I envision us like Melanie and me, for four years sleeping, eating fruit, working, dressing and undressing, demanding little, feeling the mild good will which Aristotle says does not involve intensity or desire yet is a kind of inactive friendship: the parties wish each other well but would not go out of their way to do anything for each other. Victor has no interest in coexistence, though. Victor wants all or nothing.

Gabrielle's roommate was quite a different matter. An anachronism, years ahead of her time, Steffie Baum slept guiltlessly with the boys across the street. She even stayed out overnight. Apparently a network of Columbia students rented some cheap apartments nearby for their rendezvous, and worked out careful schedules, but I knew nothing yet of the details. Steffie was a small, curvy girl with a pretty face and large, unapologetic blue eyes that could hold a steady gaze longer than anyone else's; Steffie was never the one to avert her eyes first. Her other impressive feature was her hair, satiny and long enough to sit on. She changed its arrangement each day as if to demonstrate her infinite variety: loose and flowing, a tight bun, two braids resting on her bosom. Whatever the hairdo, she moved through the dormitory halls and in and out of the shower with an enviable easy languor. We assumed this easy languor came from the carnal knowledge we lacked. We may have mixed up cause and effect.

(Technically I didn't lack it. There had been a boy in high school who pushed his way through once, quickly, in the dark. He offered me a challenge and I accepted, to show I was afraid of nothing, at fifteen. But in spirit I was still virginal. I hadn't felt much except shock at my own daring.)

Steffie was the sort who could do everything well and remain likable. She got excellent grades (a history major), though she cut classes to the legal limit. She sang in the Gilbert and Sullivan Society. She wrote for the school paper. The year she did theatre reviews she asked friends along on her pair of press seats. I got to see *The Threepenny Opera* and studied the musicians while Steffie took notes with a little pen that had a flashlight on top. She tried to organize a tutoring program for children in the slums bordering the college, and when her recruiting failed, since it was hardly an era of activism, she tutored on her own. And yet with all this, she managed to tiptoe down the corridors long after signing in for the night. In sneakers and ponytail she looked like a runaway child, a bag over her shoulder containing a toothbrush and comb, the next morning's books, and a nightgown—she didn't wear pajamas like the rest of us. Some boy had taught her how to unlock the door to the emergency exit with a pair of pliers so the bell wouldn't ring. We shook our heads with worry. She was never caught, though, and for that we called her lucky.

She might have been one of us, but we kept her just outside our inner circle. That world would claim us all too soon. We deferred it. It was not an era of voluptuousness, either; it was the late fifties, a quiescent time. Except when Steffie appeared mornings after, unchanged, efficient and alert in class, I felt a bit of a fool. I was always competitive, and the sight of her gave me a vague physical unrest.

"Aha! So there is change after all! Everything is not so static. I knew it. I knew it," Esther cried in triumph. It was nearing Thanksgiving and fittingly, we had reached the Pluralists: Empedocles, mystical poet, Professor Boles announced, as if he were about to enter from the wings. And Anaxagoras, prosaic man of science. Thank goodness they happened along—Parmenides had brought matters to a dead end with his fixed and eternal universe. *Ex nihilo nihil fit.* Nothing can come of nothing, she quoted. Speak again. And these two spoke, clearing a middle path. All was not constant change, they concurred. But nor was all immutable. Beneath the undeniable evidence of change was something enduring, something that abided. No power could take it *all* away. A vast relief eased through me as Professor Boles unraveled the plot, grinning like a master detective, her wild gray hair afloat.

Back to the beginnings again: earth, water, air, fire. But not as simply as before. The four elements are the roots—and how we loved that word, roots; it gave us a sense of getting intimate with truth. Every mortal thing is made of the immortal elements in diverse combinations. An intricate dance, the four roots forever mingling and separating, cleaving and riving, world without end. And what propels this fantastic parade? Ah, Empedocles, what a romantic. Love and Strife. Love joins together, Strife axes apart. "And I shall tell you something more." Oh yes, Empedocles, by all means speak again. "There is no birth in mortal things, and no end in ruinous death. There is only mingling and interchange of parts, and it is this that we call 'nature.'"

And as if this were not enough, Anaxagoras, prosaic man of science though he was, went him one better. Not Love and Strife, but Mind "took charge of the cosmic situation. . . . Mind set in order all that was to be, all that ever was but no longer is, and all that is now or ever will be." That suited me fine. No death, and Mind in charge.

Nina did not share my relief. "It's not any ultimate truth. It's only part of an ideological sequence, and naturally it gets a little more sophisticated as it goes along." She paused to light her weekly cigarette. "All of this has been completely superseded by modern science, of course. It's only of interest historically, and maybe poetically."

I wanted to protest but I didn't know how. Nina was admittedly the smart one, and already she was stammering less.

"I'm not so sure they've been superseded," said Esther. "Look, Anaxagoras says there's a little bit of everything in everything else. Black and white have the seeds of gray. Food has the seeds of the blood and bone it's going to help make. That's pretty clever. It's not so different from your periodic table of ninety-two elements or however many there are. Everything starts from—"

A neighboring door snapped brusquely shut. Loud, ponderous footsteps.

"Oh-oh, the witching hour," Esther moaned. "Honestly, we ought to make a scarecrow some night, just to make Mrs. Ramsey's job more exciting. She hardly ever gets the thrill of discovery."

The college had lately adopted the progressive policy of allowing males—presumably the boys from across the street—to visit in the dormitory rooms till midnight Thursdays through Saturdays, provided the doors were kept ajar. This was an advance over the former policy of allowing males only in the small ground-floor rooms known as beau parlors and equipped with floral-upholstered sofas, provided, again, that the doors were kept ajar and all four feet remained on the floor. (Nothing specific about feet was enjoined in the new rule.) For enforcement, Mrs. Ramsey, a short squat woman, made the rounds at midnight in her tight black rayon uniform and black oxfords. Mrs. Ramsey was wasted on us: her face was so impassive that she might have policed on a much grander scale, in a sheikhdom, a sultanate. Fortunately for some, her heavy tread gave a few seconds' notice. She granted a warning knock before flinging doors wide. I wondered if anything could jar that face—a naked male, maybe with an erection, maybe inserting it into willing flesh . . .

"Hi there, Mrs. Ramsey," Esther called brightly, springing from the bed. "Not a thing here to worry about! See?" She yanked open the door of the closet. One half was an orderly array of dark smooth clothes obediently on their hangers; the other a jumble of stripes, prints, peasant skirts swirling into each other, shoes heaped on the floor like abandoned auto parts, a green slicker painfully lopsided on a hook that pierced its shoulder, two enormous straw hats sliding from the top shelf. Esther dashed back to lift the bottom of the bedspread, inviting Mrs. Ramsey to have a peek, but the woman, unfazed, had turned to go. Maybe beneath her face she was contemptuous. Her toneless words trailed after her: "Please keep the noise down." Esther leaned out the open door and called down the hall, *"Cherchez l'homme!"*

"Listen, listen to this." Gabrielle had been reading all the while. She would not object to such antics, nor would she take part. "Empedocles says some wonderful things. This is very *à propos:* 'It is in the warm parts of the womb that males are born; which is the reason why men tend to be dark, hairy, and more rugged.' "

"I guess that has been superseded by modern science," I said, and Nina smiled faintly.

" 'Abstain entirely from laurel leaves,' " Gabrielle read on. "Oh, and this one is very passionate: 'Wretches, utter wretches, keep your hands away from beans.' I wonder why. Oh dear." She sighed and fluffed out her long hair, just washed and drying at the open window.

"What's the matter?"

" 'I wept and mourned when I discovered myself in this unfamiliar land.' "

She looked up, her eyes filled with tears. She had been brought to this strange land as a child of five. Her parents were French, her father in the diplomatic corps. Could a small child really feel that kind of pain? Or could she summon tears for Empedocles?

"That's how I felt," said Esther, "when I came to New York, even though I was glad to leave home. That's why I went to see the ocean with a boy I didn't even like and let him paw me. I was so lonesome. That's why I got mono, or whatever that sickness was, and the only thing that kept me here was imagining the satisfaction on my mother's face if I gave up and went home."

"So you're glad you stayed?" asked Nina.

Esther looked around at all of us. "Now? Sure! Sure I'm glad I stayed. I'm fine now."

We all went home for Thanksgiving, and on the first day back Nina tucked in the lower right-hand corner of her mirror, the place where some girls kept photographs of their boyfriends or families, a three-by-five card. On it, typed, were the questions that members of the sixth-century B.C. Pythagorean Brotherhood asked in their daily examinations of conscience: In what have I failed? What good have I done? What have I not done that I ought to have done?

"What is that supposed to be, a mother substitute?" Esther demanded.

Nina smiled. She rarely tried to justify herself.

"You told *us* we took it too personally," I reminded her.

She smiled.

We pointed out that the card was inconsistent in spirit with what was ranged on the dresser top just below it: Revlon Touch & Glow liquid make-up, Jean Naté spray cologne, Nivea cream, Cutex colorless nail polish, an ashtray with tortoiseshell barrettes for her mass of black hair, perpetually bridled, silver-handled hairbrush, five lipsticks. She accepted our teasing and said, "It may be best to stay in balance by keeping one foot in the real world and one foot in the ideal."

"And who said that?" Esther wanted to know.

"No one." She smiled in earnest this time. "I made it up."

On the three mornings we had The History of Philosophy we would meet downstairs at a quarter to nine and walk over together. Nina began not appearing. "She was already gone when I woke up," Esther reported. "That's odd, isn't it?" She would greet us in class, composed as ever, maybe a bit quieter than usual. Since Nina was not the kind you could interrogate, Gabrielle, the ever-resourceful, undertook some research. The Pythagorean Brotherhood, she learned, followed a moral and mystical regimen for purifying the soul and attaining wisdom. " 'They performed their morning walks alone and in places where there was appropriate solitude and quiet; for they considered it contrary to wisdom to enter into conversation with another person until they had rendered their own souls calm and their minds harmonious. It is turbulent behavior, they believed, to mingle with a crowd immediately on arising from sleep,' " she read to me. "Is that what we are, a crowd?" We were wounded.

"She's probably working on her memory, too. Listen to this. 'To strengthen their memory the students began each day, on first waking up, by recollecting in order the actions and events of the day before; after that they tried to do the same for the preceding day, and so on backwards as far as they could go, taking care to make the order of recollection correspond with the order in which the events had actually occurred. For they believed that there is nothing more important for science, and for experience and wisdom, than the ability to remember.' "

I tried it for three days and gave up. I could remember many things, but not in the order in which they occurred. They regrouped themselves in thematic patterns like music, as if memory were coaxing life to make more structural sense than it possibly could.

"Do you really do it?" I asked Nina, alone.

She nodded. "It helps keep things in order."

"I thought you had things in very good order."

"Oh no, Lydia. Inside is all turmoil." Her face was troubled. Unblinking and unsmiling, it seemed to cover webs of complexity. But I couldn't press her further. The others were about to join us; we were having a Chinese dinner on Broadway to celebrate Nina's nineteenth birthday.

The pre-Socratics were superseded. Only in poetry did they remain unsurpassed. Earth, water, air, and fire. The way up and the way down, eternal and reversible. Professor Boles confessed she had lingered too long under their spell; now we must move more swiftly. Past Plato and Aristotle and the medieval schoolmen. The weather grew cold as we progressed in a northwesterly direction to ,encounter three Continental Rationalists, three British Empiricists, and three German Idealists. Cunning minds indeed, to have arranged themselves in geographical triads.

"I think, therefore I am?" It was just after Christmas vacation and Esther, fresh from the homestead in Chicago, was in a querulous mood. "I think, therefore I am? I don't get it. It doesn't sound authentic."

"But it's as simple as can be!" Gabrielle exclaimed. "He

wants to start from scratch. How do you know you're there? Because someone is asking that question."

"Yes," said Esther, "I realize *that* much. But before I even ask the question—not that I personally would ever ask such a question, I have never had such high-class doubts. But all right, suppose I had. Before I would even hear that clever little voice asking that clever little question—God almighty, I feel, I touch, I smell, transitively, that is. I mean, thinking is a pretty advanced thing. If the guy wants to be primitive he's got a long way to go, if you ask me. Throw me one of those cigarettes over there, would you, Lydia?"

Among the chewed pencils, tangled beads, hairbrush crammed with shed gold hair, and crumpled paper on Esther's dresser top, were half a dozen open sample packs of cigarettes. I reached over and picked up a miniature blue box with white and yellow trim, containing six cigarettes. "Hit Parades. Hit Parades are the absolute worst, Esther." I tossed them over.

"I know." She shrugged. "But listen, they're free."

We didn't yet know about tar and nicotine. Once a week blandfaced young salesmen in business suits walked through the smoking section of the library offering free samples of atrocious new brands. Esther accepted them indiscriminately; when the young men pulled out their market-research questionnaires she responded that they were all terrible, but she would take another of each, thank you. She seemed always short of money, and practiced other small and arbitrary economies—denying herself a four-dollar scarf in winter, or a dollar movie at the Student Center. Her father provided a checking account, but she used it as little as possible. I imagine that self-denial made her feel closer to this father who barely acknowledged her existence and also warned her brothers against the corruptions of capitalism.

She lit up a Hit Parade and tossed the match, still aflame, across her bed into the heavy, mud-colored ashtray she had made in high school and brought with her all the way from Chicago. She was proud of it. She said it was the only decent thing she had ever made with her own two hands besides sandwiches and stews.

"Esther, someday you may set this place on fire. I worry

when I get into bed and you're still smoking in the dark. I can see the little orange circle flashing around."

"Sorry." Esther leaned over to reach her ashtray and blew out the match; her breath sent up a black spray that drifted down to settle on the bedspread. "Oh well. Sorry again." She tried to brush off the ashes but they smudged. "Anyhow, there is one thing I like about Descartes. Here. 'To accept nothing as true which I did not clearly recognize to be so . . . nothing more than what was presented to my mind so clearly and distinctly that I would have no occasion to doubt it.' In other words, don't believe anything until you've proven it for yourself."

"Well . . . not exactly," said Nina. "Not in science. It would be absurd to start from scratch every time you devised an experiment. Some things we take on faith, from past research."

"Nothing on faith! Nothing on faith! Isn't that what it says right here? I don't believe there's an unconscious mind. I don't believe there's a God. I'm not even convinced there are little protons and electrons. Give me a microscope, let me see for myself."

"I'll vouch for them," said Nina. "Won't you take my word for it?"

"No. You believe what you've been told. Didn't you believe in heaven and hell for the first fifteen years of your life?"

"This sort of jejune discussion is not what Descartes had in mind," Gabrielle said severely from the floor. "Not what he had in mind at all."

"Jejune?" said Esther with a lively flick of her curls. "Jejune? Is that French?"

I also found the three Continental Rationalists disappointing, but I tucked in the right-hand corner of my mirror the sentence that most intrigued me: "The effort by which each thing endeavors to persevere in its own being is nothing but the actual essence of the thing itself." Spinoza. I didn't really know what it meant, but I hoped that I would in time, and that it would be worth the wait.

Gabrielle, in a royal blue leotard and tights, sat with the soles of her feet touching, her class notes in the parallelogram formed by her legs. She was eating Pecan Sandies. Every few moments her long bare arm would extend mechanically up towards the bag on the windowsill. She rarely indulged that way, only when she was getting her period and craved sweets, but it was the night before the final exam. I was replaying Professor Boles's voice in my head; I heard tones and intervals, with words giving them boundaries and shape. The hard part was restoring meaning to the words. Nina's and Esther's duet was a distraction.

"Entelechy, Esther?"

She was smoking ravenously. "Entelechy. Each thing's essence moves from its potential to realization. Aristotle."

"Very good. What are the four ways? Or she may call it the four causes of a phenomenon. With an example."

"Material, formal, efficient, final. The example in the book is a house. But a house is so unoriginal. If she asks that I'm going to use something else. A shoe."

"Why not start with the house?" Nina cajoled. She was eating too. She had even kicked off her black pumps, and sat curled in her chair, a box of Mallomars on her lap.

"Such a conventional mind, Nina. It's a pity. Material cause: bricks. Or mud, as the case may be. Ice, for an igloo. Formal cause: plans or blueprints. Efficient cause: labor. Tote that barge, lift that bale. Final cause: someone needs a place to live.

"Very good!" Nina's eyes shone with pleasure. Her labor was paying off: Esther was being built. "Of course on the exam you'll leave out the asides."

"But the asides are my essence. Give me a Mallomar, would you? I'm thin this week. Now I will tell you about a shoe. Just to show I can do it on my own. Material cause: leather. More likely plastic, these days. Formal cause: design for a shoe, I suppose. Efficient cause: same thing, labor. No! Elves! Final cause: The foot wants a covering. Baby needs a new pair of shoes. Shall I go on? I could do more complex things. A nervous breakdown. A painting by Picasso. An orgasm. Hey, would you like me to do an orgasm? I've read all about it."

"There really isn't time," said Nina coolly. She licked chocolate off each finger. "I think we'd better go on to his ideas about friendship."

Gabrielle suddenly moaned in agony. I thought she must have pulled a muscle. "Oh, this stuff makes me so sick," she growled. She stood up in one spasm of motion, swishing her hair around, waving the sheaf of notes in her hand. Her voice spiraled; the mellow, sensible girl was left far behind. "Sick! A whole term of trash! I thought there'd be some connection with reality. But all this is nothing but classification. Three grades of faculties of the soul. Four kinds of law. Four cardinal virtues. Is that truth? It's some kind of mumbo-jumbo numerology! Five proofs of the existence of God. Oh sure, first you decide what you want to believe, then you invent the reasoning."

Her face glistened with sweat. She bolted through the room, a jagged path of bright blue, and flung open the window. A gust of air rushed in. With her wide, broad-shouldered stance, every bone and curve articulated in the leotard, hair blowing and head lifted high in indignation, she seemed at last the Martha Graham tragic heroine she longed to dance. Woman confronting the betrayal of the intellect. Her eyes were shadowed; I couldn't see their colors.

"That was wonderful." I applauded. "*Brava!*"

"I'm not fooling around, Lydia. We wasted so much time. Look, the so-called enlightened ones are no better." She riffled through her notes. "Hume. Such an original mind, she told us. But the same old thing—seven different categories of relationships. Would you like to hear them?"

"No!" Esther said. "And could you please stop running around the room? You're making me dizzy."

"Oh, all right." She dropped to the floor and breathed deeply. "Also those fallacies. They made up as many fallacies as truths." She was calmer; we were still transfixed. "Fallacy of ambiguity, fallacy of equivocation," she droned. "Fallacy of composition, fallacy of division—I can't even remember all the fallacies."

"Oh, come on," I said. "The fallacies are fun."

"Aha, speaking of fun—have you run across the Hedonistic Calculus, by any chance? Jeremy Bentham? I know it wasn't in the course but I happened upon it. The Hedonistic Calculus helps you choose between competing but mutually exclusive pleasures." She grabbed a book and leafed through. "I bet you didn't know there were seven ways to measure your pleasure."

"Gaby, really. Talk about jejune."

"I didn't make this up, Lydia. This is the product of a great mind. Number one. Intensity of the pleasure. Number two.

Duration of the pleasure. Three. Certainty or uncertainty—that means how far the experience is guaranteed to deliver the pleasure." Her lips moved tentatively in a gamine kind of smile. The Greek Fury was giving way to a Gallic wit. "Four. Propinquity or remoteness—how close the pleasure is, in space as well as time. Five. This is a good one. Fecundity. How likely is it that the pleasure will lead to subsequent pleasures of the same sort?" She had us laughing, in relief as much as amusement. The impending test was forgotten. "Six. Purity—the absence of any little bits of pain mixed in. And seven. Extent. How far can the pleasure be shared with others?"

"Well," said Esther. "We could go out and share a pizza, at least."

The next morning Professor Boles, looking melancholy in her old gray tweeds, asked us to trace the successive phases of pre-Socratic thought. I think she loved the Greeks and hated to see the semester over. Dutifully, sophomorically, I repeated vision after vision until I reached the mystical poet and the prosaic man of science, who reassured us that there is indeed movement (and with it possibility, and hope), and underneath, the eternal and the immutable. Something abides, I wrote to her in my blue book, like a personal letter, my heart in my pen. Those elemental roots—earth, water, air, fire. ("Good but too literal," she commented in red pencil. B plus.)

I was disappointed that there was no question remotely connected with how Thales measured the height of the pyramid. Even though Nina was right—Thales could have measured a man's shadow at any time of day and applied the shadow-man ratio to the pyramid—I found the appeal of the story lay in the waiting. I imagined him patient and serene, maybe eating cookies and talking to his friends, waiting for that ripe moment when an insubstantial shadow on the sand inches up to a human magnitude that can break down a pyramid's recalcitrance. But it was a no-nonsense exam.

"That was not really related to the course, Lydia," said Gabrielle. "Only of biographical interest. Are you taking the next semester?"

"Sure." I remembered her outburst of the night before. I would take it warily, not expecting truth but simply watching the mind flex and point. (I could never hold on to that correct attitude, though. Not then and not later.) I would devote my better energies to music. Practice more, learn the oboe too, and venture across the street, where the Eastern European professors were playing with computers and electronic equipment.

Naturally Nina was going to take the second semester. Esther also, to our surprise.

"*Mais certainement,*" she said. "I looked through the syllabus and the reading list. It says the world is all blind irrational striving. Someone's will and idea. I mean, even the titles are terrific. *Fear and Trembling? The Sickness unto Death?* Believe me, I'm going to do just fine." (She did. Professor Boles didn't know what came over her. How the tables were turned! In the glow of early May sunshine Esther would try to explain to Nina what Sartre meant by bad faith, and what he meant when he said, "We were never more free than during the German occupation." "How could they be?" Nina sat dulled with puzzlement. "Because they were close to the edge, stupid." Esther was not a patient tutor. "Because they were close to death. *Death,*" she whispered hoarsely. "Everything they did had to be real. No time for fooling around. They had to resist, Nina. Make their lives mean something.")

Meanwhile we sat in the West End Bar sharing a bottle of wine to celebrate the end. Nina said, "I thought it was a pretty easy exam. Did everyone answer that question about Aristotle? I mean the little optional one."

We had all answered the optional question about Aristotle on friendship. We grinned at each other across the table, suddenly shy.

"So what did we all say?" I asked.

"What did you say, Lydia?" Gabrielle's eyes shone blue and green, and she flashed her quizzical, wry look. At those moments I could swear she had the trace of an accent too, or maybe it was only an inflection of the voice. It still happens once in a while. The alien vowel, the sprung rhythm flickers by, almost between syllables, and vanishes.

"I? All right. I said that there are three kinds of friendship. The first two kinds, friendship based on utility and friendship based on pleasure, are transient, and endure only as long as the friend continues to be useful and pleasant." I was reciting Professor Boles's words from memory. "But the third type, which is perfect friendship, is a friendship between equals, and founded in goodness. Each person wishes good for the other just as she would for herself; in fact Aristotle says 'a friend is another self.' The principal virtue of friendship is loving, and since it is a mutual love of character rather than of any passing quality such as pleasure or usefulness, it endures a lifetime as character itself endures. Which is not to say," I concluded, and I poured wine slowly for all of us in turn, the way my father used to do at our Passover Seders with his teasing, maverick expression, "which is not to say that such friends cannot also be useful and pleasant, since whatever is enduringly good cannot be otherwise. I made it short, because after all, it was only worth five points out of the whole term's work."

We drank to it.

And then, slightly drunk, for we were young girls not used to wine, we danced our way back to the dormitory, prodding the reluctant Nina. It was the fire-bearer dance Gaby had choreographed the year before for the Prometheus myth—live torches flaming up Broadway in winter's quick coming of dark.

And then, years later, they tell us that there has never been any such thing as friendship among women, only rivalry, and that it is time to attempt Sisterhood. Sisterhood. The word has a grating sound. A friend is another self.

Simple Gifts, 1980

Heraclitus was right. No sooner is a position established than it erodes. The solid earth under our feet
melts into water, evaporates into air, and is consumed in fire. I
moved from one family to another. I saw the former family
dissolve behind me and went on to the next with the dogged-
ness of a peasant uprooted by a volcano, who insists on making
his new home in the shadow of another active volcano.

My father, hearty all his life, died of a heart attack at fifty-
nine, not on the broad stripe of beach he loved so well, but in
his insurance office, in his suit. My mother spent a year in
Arizona to be near a sister, a year in Switzerland to be near
Evelyn, then came and settled in an apartment near us. She was
tentative about visiting, anxious not to intrude, but needlessly,
for we all loved her, and when she appeared, like a fairy
godmother she cooked and ironed and helped with homework—
my burdens were her pleasures. She died last year, a peace-
loving woman who believed in doing good and not straining the
brain over the fine points or ambiguities. Painlessly and
unambiguously, her heart stopped and she was gone—no more
of her chicken soup, the children's shirts are creased. I try. Phil
eats the soup, puts on the shirts, says Grandma did it better. I
don't mind, but Vivian is offended for me. "Mommy is an
orphan now," she tells Phil. "You shouldn't say mean things to
her." "It's okay, Vivie, I know I don't iron as well as Grandma
did." She puts her arms around me, not quite nine years old,
long thin arms. "Do you mind very much being an orphan?"
"Well, sometimes." "I don't want you and Daddy to die. I
would mind a lot." I promise not to die till she's much older,

and I take the liberty of promising the same for Victor, who's at his studio. "Even if they did, Viv," says Phil, trying to smooth out his shirt by hand, "you'd probably only feel bad at first. Then you'd get used to it." "Oh no! How could I get used to that?" "Phil, for the moment let's just say we won't die, okay?" He skulks out of the room with dissatisfied steps, heels down heavily in protest, so that his shoes are always down at heel. The second of four is an awkward position. His standards are severe. He is troubled by injustice, by white lies and compromises, troubled by the demands of teachers for neatness and coherence, troubled by his long gangly body, and by the contentment of others, which he calls complacency. His recent, man's voice is gruff: perhaps he feels kind words would sound incongruous in so gruff a voice. He approves of his father, whom he resembles: I imagine Victor had that troubled intensity as a boy of fourteen and a half, but Victor also had his painting to absorb the excess. Phil regards me, however, as a frivolous character. Flighty. Airy. A *luftmensch*, as my father called people who had no life insurance. That is because I run the house in a haphazard manner and go out at odd hours to rehearse and do concerts. Phil likes to see me safely drab around the house in his old corduroy pants and no makeup. He looks askance when I dress up in scarves and earrings and colored tights, making up for the years of drabness he cannot remember. When I go twice a year to meet his teachers he says, "Don't put feathers in your ears. Wear something normal." "Come into my closet. Do you want to pick it out?" I shouldn't. I'm the mother. Victor talks to him in his room sometimes, in the evenings. As I pass the closed door, Phil's rumbling voice sounds aggrieved, while Victor's better-tempered tones undulate in waves of limitless, loving patience. Then late at night in bed, Victor tells me what Phil has on his mind. I appreciate his telling me but I resent getting my information secondhand.

"To think," I have murmured to Victor in bed, "that this was a boy who actually baked apple pies. He started making his own lunch when he was ten! Vivie and Alan will never make their own lunch, I can tell. He was so nice," I grumble. "Remember he used to creep into our bed because he was afraid of the dark? He used to bring me bouquets of dandelions in the park. I didn't have the heart to tell him they were a weed." He was a ruddy, easygoing boy, a boy who could be trusted to take care of his younger brother and sister, a bit of a clown—his imitations of a pixilated neighbor talking to her basset hound were wickedly accurate—a boy who left quaintly spelled notes for me in odd places (the breadbox: "Please bye bread"), a boy who made amazing, Gaudi-like constructions out of pieces of metal and rubber that plumbers left behind—friends would save old washers and doorknobs and scraps of tubing for Phil. And his apple pies were splendid, only someone had to light the oven; he was afraid to strike a match.

"All that was before puberty," says Victor. "It will pass. Don't fret. Would you scratch my back? No, lower. Higher. Left. Ah."

Still, I worry that he is lost to me. I have no skill with the taciturn. Althea's adolescence is full of drama too, but above all, communicative. She likes to drag us through her every phase.

"At least suggest that he wash his hair. Those boys with long hair don't realize it has to be taken care of."

Beneath my anxiety is guilt. He was born during a bad time, his first few years spent under a cloud. I was the cloud. I had paralysis of the will, a casualty of a way of life. But I recovered and determined I would not get that way again. I do not want Phil to be a casualty, permanently shadowed though the cloud is gone.

The family from the dormitory dissolved, after graduation, into good friends. I shared an apartment with Gaby until she married Don, who was becoming an orthopedic surgeon. I was bothered by her marriage; I found Don too proper. I wanted to see Gaby become a dancer, and how many proper doctors' wives are dancers? But she made her choices. She got happy children, happy husband, happy happy—what Nina had wanted. Nina did not marry.

Esther was married twice, briefly and disastrously. Once to the boy who made her wait so long for her first view of the ocean and told her about the Polar Bear Club. The first time he beat her up she moved into our dingy apartment in the East Twenties for three weeks, sleeping on a cot near Althea's crib. The second time, the summer she was twenty-six and seven weeks pregnant, she lost the baby and Ralph was taken to the hospital to be detoxified. She also lost her job in the production department of a publishing house because she couldn't concentrate. Driving back from visiting Ralph in the hospital, she hit a truck on the dark wet road. The truckdriver was unhurt, fortunately. Esther suffered whiplash and a shoulder injury, spit out a couple of teeth, and almost lost the sight in her left eye.

"Enough, enough!" she said. "I'm tired. I'm going home."

"Home! Don't you do it. You've said often enough it was no home for you." I had a sickening premonition of Esther taking up needlepoint and cats, lying on a chaise in her green bathrobe, rising only to powder her nose. "You'll be sorry. Please, Esther, you can move in with us again if you like." I was offering her the same cot in the same small room with two babies now, a cluttered household, and my own sour fog, but even so, it was better than home. Her mother had lapsed into premature senility and didn't recognize the members of her family. There was a young nurse who she decided was her only daughter. When Esther visited she had to introduce herself, again and again. "She won't even know you anyway. What do you hope to gain?"

"Oh, she knows, she knows." She paced our drab living room, smoking passionately, while Phil nursed on my lap and Althea banged the piano. "She knows who everyone is, she knows exactly what she's saying, believe me."

"Esther. Even the doctors say it's an illness. The brain cells deteriorate."

"Brain cells, my foot. She's saying what she's felt all along, only now she has the excuse of being sick. Who am I and what am I doing in that house? That was always her message to me. Nothing has really changed."

"All the more reason not to go, then." I shivered inside, for I harbored those feelings too, in secret. Who are these two babies and what are they doing in my house? What am I doing?

"The hell with it. It's a place to relax. Nothing ever changes there, just like those Greeks said in Philosophy 101."

She went. She sat talking to her mother, who was having a lucid spell and seemed to recognize her despite her bound-up shoulder and the black patch over her left eye. In a moment of weakness, yearning for commiseration, Esther confided a little about her recent sufferings. Her mother was attentive; for once her twitching hands fell still. Esther waited, tremulous.

Her mother looked up, her eyes cloudy. "But are you happy?" she asked.

"What!"

"Are you happy, dear?" her mother crooned in a soft singsong. "Because if you're happy, then I'm happy too."

Esther flew back to New York. She began seeing a therapist. She began proceedings for a divorce. She had a bridge made to replace the teeth knocked out in the accident. She got a job in a shelter for emotionally disturbed children and enrolled in social work school. And for a while she did seem happy. For a much longer while, though, she was cured of her yearning for commiseration.

Victor's family dissolved too. His mother, Edith, died of bone cancer in 1972. His father, Paul, is still alive but cannot remember how many children we have or their names—Althea, Phil, Alan, Vivian. He cannot always remember how many children he has or their names, Victor and Lily. He lives in a well-appointed nursing home in Westchester—carpeting and beautifully upholstered furniture and large steel elevators decorated with colorful notices of discussion groups and hootenannies. Lily found it and Victor objected: his father was not going to end his days in an institution—he would live with us if Lily could no longer handle him. Paul was wandering through Scarsdale's rusticities, leaving the door unlocked, gas jets on, bathtub running. And Lily said sensibly, in her smoky voice, But he *wants* to go there. Come and see it. He *likes* the idea, Vic. Lily was right. He sings and eats and strolls, and on the days when he can remember the sequence of cards, plays cards. He likes it more than he likes us, it appears. Victor was hurt at first. Unparented. Did he spend four unwilling years in college to please this man who barely remembers him, he muttered in bed, who, when we visit, keeps us waiting till he finishes sticking tiles in a mosaic ashtray? Oh, there was a time a few years ago, before the walls of Paul's blood vessels got so thick, when he would try to put on a good show. We could see him forcing energy into the lax muscles of his face, straining for the amenities of greeting, casting around for the proper gambits of conversation, so visibly relieved when he found them, so bereft when he exhausted them. We came prepared to entertain him but he wanted to entertain us, as he had done in the days of his health, with a gracious wit. Then after a while he stopped trying. He lost interest in everything except his own maintenance. He retired from being a father, grandfather, adult, as he had retired from being a lawyer. We watched it happen, and Victor came home and drank Jack Daniel's in bed, glared at television, and made love fast, without talking. Then he got used to it.

Amid all this decay here we stand, enjoying our heyday. We are six, flourishing; like the amaryllis the children grow almost as we look at them—tall, lanky children except for Althea, who is small like my mother and perfectly made. Yet she too takes up a great deal of space: her voice carries, her pronouncements are assured. No major defects. The only profound scare was when the pediatrician, after listening intently and for a very long time to Vivian's three-year-old heart, put her back on my knee and told me she had an "innocent murmur." Innocent because it occurs in early childhood, then vanishes. A peculiarity of the heartbeat. "Of no consequence at all"—in his fatherly way, flat honest eyes peering over bifocals, veined hand dangling a rag doll at her. "Now don't go worrying—I see already you're as pale as a ghost." She could play ball, skate, ski, whatever she liked—a perfectly healthy child. Okay, I nodded. Only arrhythmic. Come to me my syncopated baby. That was how she spoke, too, in an innocent murmur. I did what he said, didn't go worrying. Each year when we visit him for camp shots I plan to ask if it is gone yet, that innocent murmur, but I forget—his office is so crowded, he bustles so heartily through the routine examinations.

We are fortunate and we know it, but not being believers we do not know where to address our thanks. Awkwardly, we address them to the void, to some rich source in the void.

It is August and the camp bus has arrived safely once more, bringing Alan and Vivian home from the Quaker wilderness where they slept all summer in open wooden cabins, fed pigs and goats, swam in a freezing lake and partook of a utopian communal spirit. The literature of this camp is mired by virtuous platitudes in hip language, but it is a magical place. On visitors' day the faces we meet on the stony paths are luminous. That is because they have the Inner Light, Alan tells us. Vivie says it is simply that everyone acts nice to each other.

I am in the kitchen with the two open trunks and Alan, who is eating Mallomars and drinking Coke. The Quaker camp's food is virtuous too, and he comes home starved for junk. With thumb and index finger, touching as little of the fabric as I can, I lift clothes from the trunk and drop them into the washing machine. Clinging to some items are twigs, dry leaves, small clumps of Vermont soil. They say the European immigrants, our forefathers, brought over clumps of soil to kiss, but I throw these relics in the garbage. A pungent smell slowly fills the kitchen—dark earth and greenery mingled with children's unwashed clothing. I open the window wider. Alan is describing the various levels of achievement in woodsmanship.

"The highest thing you can do is if you stay out alone in the woods for four days or maybe a week, I don't remember, and you have to hunt and skin and cook your own food—and all you have is the basic equipment, what you can carry on your back."

"I hope you didn't try that. I wonder what they cook."

"I guess squirrel. You don't have to worry. Only one person in the whole history of the camp ever did it. Vivie did well this year. She got her first Woodswoman plaque."

"That's great. Terrific."

As he pauses to eat I listen to Vivie's song, coming from the shower in a pure soprano. She ran to the shower with glee, like a Bedouin to an oasis. In camp they had showers once a week, cold, three minutes long. I listen, because against the background of splashing water like vivid Romantic orchestration, comes the exultant, rising melody from Aaron Copland's *Appalachian Spring*. Her voice always perfectly on key, the mystery of where she learned that melody, the pleasure of having them back, all suddenly swell in me—an instant of joy. The next instant I notice a caterpillar crawling in the T-shirt I'm holding.

"Alan, please remove this since you're so woodsy."

He laughs at me and lets it creep around on his palm.

"That song she's singing. Where did she learn that?"

" 'Simple Gifts.' That was one of our songs."

"It's from Aaron Copland. *Appalachian Spring*. A ballet by a famous American composer."

He is immune to pedantry. "It's just a song. 'Simple Gifts.' "

Copland did use folk melodies, I remember. "Wait a minute." I brush off my hands and go to rummage in my studio. The ancient record jacket of *Appalachian Spring* says, "Its simple beauty and fullness of heart lie partly in the use of Pennsylvania Dutch and Shaker tunes." It mentions "Simple Gifts."

"You're right," I tell him, back in the kitchen. "An old Shaker tune.

"Of course I'm right, Ma. You should always believe me. But it's Quaker." He puts the caterpillar outside on the window ledge. "Maybe it'll find its way to the park."

"Shaker, but what's the difference."

"There is a difference." He starts to explain it to me, a fine theological or maybe historical difference; but in the middle of the explanation Vivian enters, a blue and white striped towel wrapped around her like a sarong, her long dark hair hidden under a white turbaned towel, leaving bare and incredibly lovely her wide-boned face with its satiny, pre-acne complexion burnished by the sun, a face with the look of unearthly purity certain children's faces have between nine and eleven—you have to catch it, it passes fast. I tell them how that is one of my favorite melodies yet I never knew it was a song that could be sung. Of course they don't appreciate my wonder at this serendipity. Vivie plunges her wrinkled-clean hands into the filthy trunk, hunting for her Woodswoman plaque, which she shows me and I admire.

"Would you sing me the song?"

They shrug. Sure, if it's so important. Alan plays the piano. He has played by ear since the age of four, like me. "It kills me that you can do that," says Vivian. "How do you do it?"

"I don't know. I just do." That is true. She thinks he won't tell her the secret, but it cannot be told.

They sing. Vivie knows how to deliver; she sings the words as if she understands what they mean, and who knows, perhaps she does:

'Tis a gift to be simple
'Tis a gift to be free
'Tis a gift to come round
Where we want to be.
And when we find ourselves
In the place that is right
We will be in the valley

Of love and delight.
When true simplicity is gained
To bow and to bend
We shall not be ashamed.
To turn and to turn
Will be our delight
Till by turning, turning
We come round right.

It is like hearing the music of the spheres, for which Nina strained her ears in college on those early morning Pythagorean walks. That these two could be Victor's and my children seems a miracle. The first two I recognize—subtle, urban souls. But these, close and alike, one conceived as an afterthought and one an accident, are simply gifts; their own gifts are simple too— grace and temperance and mildness. I want to possess the song, clutch it to me and drink it in, in a way I would not presume to possess them. I ask them to teach me the words and they do, as we disentangle grass from the dirty clothes and get the first load of wash spinning. They teach me willingly, yet puzzled about why just another camp song should mean so much, why I should want to keep them, their voices, close by in the kitchen after two months of absence.

Later on I play the record for them so they can hear what Copland makes of the melody, what swirls of embellishment, what silvery, streaky qualities he gives it. Alan is interested and listens, but Vivie is not. Vivie goes to sit on Victor's lap, hugging her Woodswoman plaque.

And the next minute it is approaching April and guess who is arriving this time? Evelyn! From Switzerland. Since Mother and Daddy are both dead it must be me, my family, she wants to see. Unless her banker husband is sending her to transact secret business with rich celebrities. No, I doubt that he would use Evelyn for such missions. The children are excited, especially the younger ones. They have seen Evelyn only a few times but I have told them Evelyn stories—the sunflower, the lost kite, the sand woman we made and I kicked in. (Not that she fancied herself Princess of the Beach; that I have told no one.) The advent of the real Evelyn is like a mythical character coming to life.

Alan says we must do something special. He reminds me she is arriving just around Passover. Spring springs and with it Evelyn, a sprite. We should have a Seder, he says. A Seder? I thought Alan had given his soul to the Quakers. The Inner Light. "You used to make them when Grandma was alive." "I did it for her. The season wouldn't seem natural to her without one." "I know. Last year was the first time we didn't have one. It didn't seem natural." "I didn't think you cared. All right, if you care that much, we'll do it." We'll do it right. It shall be a huge feast. Althea, faithful scullery maid, will be called in to dip her capable hands in matzo meal and roll balls. We will have our friends. Evelyn can look everyone over, as she did once before, years ago, when she came to Columbia to hear me play Schubert's "Trout" Quintet with the Chamber Music Society. "Gabrielle's family and Nina are not even Jewish," says Althea. "Do you invite them to a Seder?" "By all means. You're supposed to have outsiders at a Seder—it's a tradition." Who knows, this might even be true. "Maybe I should ask Darryl to come, then." Darryl is her boyfriend of physics fame. "Sure, ask him if you like." "But do you think people would think it's odd to invite a black person to a Seder?" "I'm quite sure no one would gasp, Althea, if that's what you're worried about." "But the Haggadah says all those terrible things about Egyptians. It might make him feel uncomfortable."

Often I wish my mother, who didn't worry about the finer points, were around. My mother would be appalled at Althea's having a black boyfriend, but once she got over being appalled, which she would in due time, having inspected Darryl, she would say: What's all this fuss? You want him there? Then invite him. So I say that too.

"I don't know if I remember how to do it," says Victor. "It's been a couple of years." "I can ask George to do it. He's from a family of rabbis, you know." "No, never mind, I'll manage." I knew any suggestion of George filling his shoes would bring him round.

I have offered Evelyn a bed in the large room Althea and Vivian share, but she stays in a hotel. She is careful not to interfere, to maintain privacy. It is clear that though I am the main object of her visit, she has other interests too. What they are she doesn't say, just disappears. But when she is with us she is one of us. She talks to the children as if she has known them forever; she is one of those people who can talk to children, who remember. She and Victor seem to appreciate each other. It strikes me that she and Victor are alike in some ways. They have little small talk. They speak the truth, their versions of it, directly, without elaboration or justification. They see by their own lights and are unaffected by trends of interpretation, cultural weather.

When we are alone together I feel a touch of that old harmony. We could be in the bedroom downstairs at the brown house again, whispering secrets late at night.

"You were such a good swimmer, Lydia. Weren't you ever afraid of the waves?"

"No. I was a little afraid up on the dunes, though. That height."

Evelyn smiles. Her smile is Vivian's, wise, wide, full of marvel. We are walking, Sunday morning, on the broad mall down in Riverside Park. All around us, groups are playing volleyball on the grass; sweaty joggers pass by, roller skaters, bicyclists—some are little children learning to ride, wobbling, with a parent chasing behind, every few seconds gripping the back of the seat to steady it, shouting encouragement in Spanish and English and French. On our left is the river. Whatever muck lurks beneath, the surface is sparkling cleanly in the sun. An early spring. Cherry blossoms are in premature bloom, their so brief life, and I am glad Evelyn has come in time to catch it. I point them out like a proud landowner; she nods and smiles at their beauty. Then I think, how can this compare to her Alps? Nothing I have to offer could make her stay. That family is over.

Evelyn and I speak in shorthand, eulogizing. Evelyn does not make statements with subjects and predicates. She gives fragments—the missing pieces are inside her.

"Those stringbeans," she says, "at the brown house."

"Born in the soil." I laugh.

"Grew up in the sun. Remember Mother with that knife? She took it so seriously."

"Yes, the zucchini."

"Cut so it doesn't hurt."

"I never liked zucchini. I ate them so I wouldn't hurt her feelings. She was so proud. Seven ways of cooking zucchini."

"Remember when I lost that dragon kite?"

"Oh Lord, Evelyn. I thought you'd never shut up about it."

"A man came along . . ."

"You were always afraid of getting lost."

"The blue slipper on the umbrella."

"Sometimes when I said we were lost we weren't really. I just wanted to . . ."

"I know. Sometimes when I cried I wasn't really crying, either. I figured I'd let you . . ."

"I didn't know that. I thought you . . ."

"I know. I mean, I knew you didn't know. That was part of . . ."

"Oh Evelyn." We link arms.

Oh Evelyn, why did you go so far? Princess of the Beach. Now landlocked.

"That sand woman," says Evelyn.

"Remember how I knocked her in? God, I was a little sadist, wasn't I?" Evelyn doesn't answer. There are so many things I want to know, but to talk with her of the present feels strange. The past is more comfortable. Still . . .

"How are you up in your Alps, Evelyn? Are you happy?"

She smiles. "It's beautiful."

"I imagine René is very busy. What do you do with yourself?"

She shrugs and brushes her hair off her neck. So warm for this time of year. Our necks are damp. "There are things to do. I have some friends. In the winters I ski. Do you go skiing?"

"No. Not enough time."

Why no children, I want to know. She had a miscarriage, a bloody rush to the hospital, but that shouldn't . . . Did they take it all out and no one told me? What about work? Isn't there anything she wanted to do with a passion? I can't ask those things. Those are the kinds of things Evelyn would tell the sunflower. She was the closest person to me once, and I don't understand her at all. I don't understand how to be without doing.

"When they used to leave us alone," she says.

"Yes, in their bed."

"Then I was scared." She laughs. "You too."

"I shouldn't have been. I was eleven."

"Oh Lydia. You're still setting standards."

What do you do in New York when you're not with me? Is it a man? Or the change of flat city streets? Fancy shops? Museums? I don't care, I'd just like to know.

"That time you played the 'Trout' at Columbia," she says. "You were wonderful."

"We had that pizza after. So many of us, they had to push tables together."

"Daddy talked about the concert all the way home. He couldn't get over it. Anchovies, was it?"

"Sausages. But he used to tease me about the piano lessons. Remember? My little Paderewski. It really irked me."

"I know," says Evelyn. "But he was very proud. That George. You were sleeping with him, weren't you?"

"How could you tell? You were only seventeen."

"I don't know. I could tell."

"Do you think Mother and Daddy knew?"

"No. I liked Victor better, though."

"So did I. George will be at the Seder."

"Oh. You don't still . . .? I'm sorry, I shouldn't ask. . . ."

"Oh no. It's all forgotten. We're friends, that's all."

"Yes," says Evelyn. "Sometimes that's easier."

What on earth does she mean? Some love affair? Or with René, nothing? I have seen René several times. A solid, portly, courtly banker, master of four languages and fifteen years older than Evelyn. In his early fifties now. He collects *objets d'art*. Perhaps she is one. He treats her adoringly. Dotingly, in a way that seems to preclude any grownup passion she might return. He has traveled everywhere and seen everything and talks well. After his visits, lying in bed, I try to figure out who he is, for he gives little indication. He uses the passive voice, and the pronoun "one," like an Englishman. Victor reminds me that he's a banker. "So? What is that supposed to mean?" "The mind of a banker," says Victor, "—it's so simple, Lyd, why can't you see?—is on money." But I am always looking for something else in him, what Evelyn sees. Victor says security, ease. "Plus, well, he's a cultivated man, better than your average American banker. Sweetheart, your knee seems to be somewhere in my liver. Would you mind?" "Sorry. Do you like her?" "Sure I like her." "Would you like her, I mean?" He pauses, visualizing. "She's a little airy for my tastes." "Phil thinks I'm airy." "Hah!

What does he know about women, a mere boy." Victor sees into things and I suppose he is right about René. But why? What made her run for cover so early? I study her profile against the passing trees.

"You were always so busy with so many things," says Evelyn, "and I . . ."

"You what?"

"I didn't know how to care about things."

This time I am silent, waiting.

"Maybe," she gropes, "because you did so much, it left me . . ."

"Don't say it left you nothing to do, Evelyn. There are plenty of things to go around."

"I wasn't going to. I was going to say it left me free to . . . As if you would do it for me."

She is persuasive in her fuzziness. I am almost ready to agree. Then I think, Nonsense, Evelyn. You have a poetic vision, but life is not a poem, balanced. "I don't think so. I guess it's just our different natures."

She sighs. "I guess so."

"Why don't you adopt a child?" I say on impulse. "There are so many needy children."

"It's such a big job. Maybe I wouldn't love it enough. And then . . . you have so many."

"Jesus, Evelyn, what does that have to do with it?"

"Don't get angry. Look at that man, Lydia! He's riding a unicycle. Isn't that fantastic!"

Why haven't you come more often? It's easier for you than for me: rich, free. You should be a happy woman. I think all this.

"Lydie." She squeezes my arm. "I'm not unhappy, you know. I wish you could understand."

The night of the Seder arrives. It will be a crowd—the six of us and Evelyn; Nina; George; Gabrielle and Don with their children: Roger, a freshman at Amherst, and Cynthia, who is fourteen. (Esther is not here: she is a social worker in Washington. Darryl is not coming after all; his parents had tickets to *Ain't Misbehavin'*: I asked George if he would like to bring Elinor, the biofeedback woman he mentioned two months ago, but he said,

Alas, she is a thing of the past.) Even so, the preparations have not been burdensome. Evelyn rolled up her sleeves—in a kitchen she is down-to-earth and competent. Althea was indispensable with her lists, crisply issuing directions. Victor helped, and even the little ones. Little ones—they laugh at me. Eleven and nine.

Phil walks around examining critically. "Why do you need so much matzo piled up here? It's really cruddy stuff."

"That's the bread of affliction, kiddo," says Victor, patting his shoulder. "It's not supposed to be any good."

"And the lettuce. Do you have to ruin it, drenching it in this salty gook?"

"Bitter herbs. Because it was bitter, being slaves."

"You have thirteen at the table. It's unlucky. She should have talked Darryl into coming."

"That's okay," says Victor. "We have Elijah. He makes fourteen. There's even a glass of wine for him. Hey, Lyd, aren't we supposed to leave the door open for Elijah?"

"I think in a New York apartment we could get a special dispensation."

We gather. Victor performs in English, gallantly. He goes to hide the matzo for the children to find later on. He says blessings as if he meant them. He looks around benevolently at the crowd, winking handsomely at Cynthia, who is overweight and has acne. He always makes a point of flirting with Cynthia. Watching him, I remember our first real talk, in a bar twenty years ago. He said I could get to love him and I have. He said he would be a painter, he said he saw in me great potential for arrogance, he said we were the same. He was coercive, but everything he said turned out to be the truth.

Vivian, the youngest, asks the four questions. "Why is this night different from all other nights?" She puts down the book and raises her eyes shyly. "Because this night we have Aunt Evelyn with us."

Evelyn, alongside her, draws in a quick breath, hugs Vivie close, and says, "Oh love!" Then she hides her face in her hands for a second.

Victor reads the story of the four sons, one wise, one contrary, one simple, and one who does not even know how to ask a question. When the wise son asks the meaning of the Passover he is told all, down to the last detail. The simple son gets a simple, serviceable explanation. And the son who does not even know how to ask a question is given an even simpler account. Each according to his needs. All but the contrary son. In older editions, I remember, he is called the wicked son.

Victor reads: " 'The contrary son asks: "What is the meaning of this service to you?" Saying *you*, he excludes himself, and because he excludes himself from the group, he denies a basic principle. You may therefore tell him plainly: "Because of what the Eternal did for me when I came forth from Egypt, I do this." For *me* and not for *him*; had he been there, he would not have been redeemed.' "

I cannot look in Phil's direction, but across the table, Victor's eyes and mine meet.

"I have to pause a moment to editorialize. That's what the old rabbis did, you know," says Victor, placing the book face down. He frowns, strokes his beard in an unctuous, rabbinical manner so that the children laugh. "This seems a little harsh, doesn't it? A little vindictive. Those old Jews were tough guys, very fussy. Chosen, not chosen, who's to say? I'll tell you what. At this Seder, in this house, kids, everyone is redeemed whether he likes it or not. No one is excluded."

Victor invites the company to spill a drop of wine for each of the ten plagues God sent down on the Egyptians. Everyone spills, uproarious; the tablecloth is spattered red. And for each plague they bang a fist on the table. What rejoicing at the oppressors' destruction; it has always made me cringe. Blood. Frogs. Vermin. Beasts. Murrain. ("Murrain? What's murrain?" Vivian asks every year. "Cattle disease, same as last time," Phil reminds her.) Boils. ("Ugh!" Alan starts a wave of scratching.) Hail. Locusts. Darkness. (Evelyn glances at me. She remembers I turned on the light after I thought she was asleep.) Slaying of the firstborn.

Don looks dubious. What vengeful people, he may be thinking. How un-Christian indeed. He is too polite to say it, of course. Perhaps it is simply all the spilling and banging and scratching that distresses him. His own well-bred children, Roger and Cynthia, whose ancestors were never slaves, are having a fine time, joining the horseplay with the rest. Gabrielle, at peace with herself at last, looks on benignly. Nina and George look nostalgic, he for his youth, she for the youth she did not have. Maybe they will go back to her apartment afterwards and make love. They had a brief summer affair towards the end of college, and from time to time they revive it, pointlessly, Nina tells me. But it does cheer them up. I can't imagine how it feels, what is called casual sex. Nina says it's not really so casual, with her and George. They are very fond of each other. "Maybe you should get married," I once quipped. "Married! We can't take each other that seriously."

We sing "Dayenu," enumerating God's miracles, among which are blood, vermin, boils, locusts, and so on. Had he merely delivered us—enough! But he delivered us and castigated them. The deliverance, the manna, the Sabbath—all that would have been enough. But he gave us the commandments, the temple, the land of Israel. Enough! Enough! The table is full and rowdy. Is this also a song of fullness of heart? Darkness? Hail? Slaying of the firstborn? Forty years in the desert? Thank you so much for the deliverance. But enough. A little too much, maybe.

"Next year in Jerusalem," Victor concludes, having skipped the boring, holier parts.

"Next year a senior," cries Althea. "Thank God."

"Next year in Paris," murmurs Gabrielle.

"Next year the ski trip," says Vivian. "I'll be in fifth grade."

"Still the ski trip? It's ten months away. That's a long time, Vivie."

"That's why I said *next* year the ski trip."

She will not rest content until the school's chartered bus whisks her off at dawn with the other fifth- and sixth-graders, to somewhere north, three hours out of the city. The ski trip is a hallowed tradition; the children come back at night exhausted and windburned, their noses running. Some stay home and cough for a few days. Then they talk about it for a month. This February was Alan's first time. He spared Vivie no detail of the day's joys—the bumpy, tortuous, singing bus ride, the chair lifts, the hot chocolate, the ever-more-difficult hills. He tortured her with details, in the name of brotherly love. Vivie regained her good spirits after a week or so, but her ardor for the ski trip, marinating in envy, lies simmering beneath. Next year. I only hope she does not break a leg.

Althea and Evelyn and I bring on the feast, and some time

after the last macaroon has been consumed, after the kids have found the hidden matzo and been rewarded, after Elijah has been and gone and the sated company, sprawled on pillows on the floor, begins to think of rising and heading home, Alan announces that at camp to end a celebration they would join hands and do a simple dance while they sang "Simple Gifts."

"Dance?" says Don. "I don't think I can move."

But Gabrielle charms away his inertia and Alan prevails. The dance is so simple, hardly more than a stately, circular parade breaking every few bars into revolving couples, that even Phil agrees to do it. Alan plays the song for us and those who know the words sing. It happens that Nina knows the words from her childhood spent in Sunday school. George knows the words from singing in an amateur group of political activists and pacifists. Roger knows the words from the Amherst chorus. Gabrielle knows the words from having written a college paper on Martha Graham's choreography for *Appalachian Spring*. It astonishes me that so many people have known for a long time what I only lately learned. Dancing in a stately parade around the disorderly, wine-sprinkled table, we repeat the verses till by the end everyone knows the words.

> 'Tis a gift to be simple
> 'Tis a gift to be free
> 'Tis a gift to come round
> Where we want to be.
> And when we find ourselves
> In the place that is right
> We will be in the valley
> Of love and delight.
> When true simplicity is gained
> To bow and to bend
> We shall not be ashamed.
> To turn and to turn
> Will be our delight
> Till by turning, turning
> We come round right.

"I don't know if I like all this talk about bowing and bending," says Don. George tells him genially, "Ah, shut up and keep singing." He looks a bit startled but obeys. And so they all go home. Our Seder may not have been faithful to the letter; we even had dry wine instead of sweet. Nonetheless Elijah came and drank.

"I'm going to become a Quaker when I'm older," says Alan, clearing the table.

Victor, aproned at the sink, looks over his shoulder at me. We telegraph: That would be odd, wouldn't it, but we don't need to think about it now, do we? Plenty of time.

"That's nice, dear."

"Yuk, how could you sit through all those silent meetings?" says Vivie. "They are so boring."

"How would you know? You hardly ever came."

"Well, what's it your business?"

"Kids, please, it's late," says Victor. "We're all tired."

"But it's true. She hardly ever came. The counselors used to go looking for her."

"I can be silent alone," says Vivie.

"Yeah, it's not hard when you're sleeping in your bunk."

"Oh, don't bicker. We had such a nice time. Quakers are peaceful, Alan."

"I might decide to have a bar mitzvah anyway," he adds.

Evelyn and Althea giggle. Even Phil grins.

"That's nice, dear." Plenty of time for that one too. Obviously what he likes is ceremony. Having things. The Seder was his idea.

"Good night," I say to Vivie, tucking her in. "Sweet dreams, sweet Vivian."

"I'm going to dream about the ski trip." And pulls the covers over her head. How can she breathe that way?

More Schooling:
The "Trout," 1958

Gabrielle wanted us to take a course in Chaucer with her. She had decided to major in English—in case the dancing did not work out, she could always be a writer. Chaucer? Nina frowned. Aristotle didn't say whether friendship went that far. We were juniors now, supposed to be serious and focused. Nina had not gone home over the summer but worked in a laboratory in the city. The nervous smile was growing extinct, and in its place was a new species, wry and enigmatic. Chaucer. She smiled doubtfully. "Just three hours a week," said Gaby.

"No one would take Organic Chemistry or Logic with me. No one cares about the beauties of the basic syllogism. Sixty-four permutations!"

"They're too hard for us," Gaby said craftily. "Chaucer is entertainment. *Divertissement*."

The professor's head was large, heavy with the weight of his scholarship, and his body was fleshy, but he moved with a sprightliness befitting his subject. Just as Professor Boles had seemed close kin to the pre-Socratics, Professor Mansfield appeared to live and move and have his being in the days when that plucky band wended on their pilgrymage to Caunterbury with ful devout corage, and to regard us—our strange garb, our unadorned accents—as curiosities. Like the Host of the *Canterbury Tales*, he was bold of his speche, and wys, and wel ytaught; like the Host he praised us for being so merry a company, and offered to guide us on our journey, on which no translations were permitted; we had to learn Middle English. My text was soon dense with scribbled definitions, the pages richly ornamented like a medieval manuscript. We were required to memorize twelve lines from every tale, and each day, to open the class, Professor Mansfield would choose someone to perform. At the back of the room sat a cluster of males who had crossed the street into our domain. I knew two of them slightly from the Gilbert and Sullivan Society, George Silver and Ray Fielding; one of the pleasures of the course was hearing Ray deliver his Middle English lines with the brilliance of a born actor.

Diverting, as Gabrielle had promised, until "The Clerk's Tale" of Patient Griselda, a parable teaching how to submit to the reversals of fortune, to take whatever adversity God sends with "virtuous sufferance." Griselda was a gauntlet tossed down from the fourteenth century; she roused in us something deeper than even the philosophers had done.

The story opens with the young marquis Walter being chastised by his subjects for not taking a wife to ensure his lineage. The idea of marriage does not thrill him. "To that I nevere erst thoughte streyne me. I me rejoysed of my liberte." But he bows to the greater good. The wedding day is set, the feast prepared, and still Walter's choice is kept secret: the lowliest maiden in the kingdom, Griselda, lowly in station but not in virtue. In the home of her father (widowed? no mother is in evidence, and cleverly so), Griselda tends the sheep, picks herbs, and keeps house, never idle, never sheltering a mean thought from dawn to dusk; in the breast of her virginity, says Chaucer, was enclosed "rype and sad corage," which does not mean ripe and sad courage, as well it might, given the circumstances, but a mature and sober heart. In one of her frequent surges of humility, she hopes to steal a moment from her chores to watch the wedding procession pass by. But lo, the marquis stops at her very doorstep! With some distaste, attendants strip Griselda of her poor garments and outfit her as a fine lady. She makes an excellent and unpretentious marquise, appeasing all discord and rancor with her mature and sober heart. Soon she bears a daughter; well, at least she is not barren, and everyone hopes for a better issue the next time around.

Now, Walter is possessed of a strange urge (a "merveillous desir," Chaucer calls it) to test his wife's sworn obedience. He

tells her, falsely, that his people resent her and her daughter for
their lowly birth. He sends a sinister man to carry the baby off.
Griselda agrees with no complaint. She and the baby, she tells
her husband, are "Youre owene thyng; werketh after youre
wille." She asks only to kiss the child, and begs the sinister man
to bury the body rather than leave it to be shredded by wild
beasts. Four years later she bears a son. Again Walter feels the
"merveillous desir" for a test, and the son is snatched away.
"Whan I first cam to yow, right so," says Griselda to her
husband, "Lefte I my wyl and al my libertee." Walter's third
test involves forging a papal bull that permits him to put aside
his wife and take another, of more fitting birth and rank.
Patient Griselda wishes him luck. But she utters a sentiment of
regret:

> O goode God! How gentil and how kynde
> Ye semed by youre speche and youre visage
> The day that maked was oure mariage!

She has one request. Walter has said she may take with her the
dowry that she brought him. But all she brought, she reminds
him, was her body, and surely he would not wish her to leave
the palace naked. In a career of passivity it is her single brilliant
moment. What she says, in modern English, is, "You could not
do so shameful a thing as to have that very womb where your
children lay be displayed all bare, as I walk before the people."
Such moments confounded our indignation. How could it be—a
great poet with an offensive theme! In any case, Walter allows
Griselda a "smok" in fair exchange for the virginity she brought
him but cannot take home with her. Strictly speaking, he was
generous—the smock is much bigger than that membrane he
punctured. We brooded over the smock at length in the dorm. I
thought it must be a kind of nightie, but Esther said it would
look more like a slip. Nina saw it as something sack-like to cover
the naked body; the defining garments of femininity, bodice,
corset, and so forth, would go on top.

The highborn young bride and her little brother are on their
way. Walter needs some woman to straighten up the palace and
arrange the bedrooms exactly to his tastes. Who knows his
tastes better than Griselda? She comes willingly, glad to be of

service. During the wedding feast he calls her away from her sweeping to present his bride: "Griselda . . . How liketh thee my wyf and hire beautee?" Griselda likes her right well. She has a word of counsel, though: that he not "prikke" this young maiden with "tormentynge" as he has done to others. Others! At last, however faintly, the unmistakable note of wifely acrimony. Because, suggests Griselda, a tenderly bred maiden could not endure adversity so well as a creature of lowly birth. A creature!

And lo again, Walter's strange urge, his "merveillous desir," is satisfied! Perhaps it is satisfied because she diluted her saintliness with that note of wifely acrimony. He embraces Griselda and reveals that the young bride and her little brother (twelve and seven years old) are their children, not shredded by wild beasts after all but raised by Walter's sister, a countess in Bologna. When she recovers from her faint, Griselda is dressed once more in garments befitting a fine lady. It does not say what becomes of the "smok." They all live happily ever after. It cannot be without irony that Chaucer opens his Envoi: "Griselda is dead, and her patience with her, And both buried together in Italy."

Esther's wrath was not focused: Chaucer, Walter, God, Griselda, and Professor Mansfield all came in for a share.

Professor Mansfield tried to placate her. "Didn't you read the Envoi, Miss Brickman? Chaucer clearly dissociates himself from the story. 'Don't let humility nail your tongues,' he tells all noble wives. 'Don't give anyone cause to write this kind of story about you.' " He smiled in a conciliatory way. "Now isn't that enough?"

"Too late, too late," she grumbled. "By that point the damage is done. And the poetry's better in the main part anyhow, isn't it?"

"Miss Brickman, the entire tale illustrates a moral thesis. These are not real people. You must try to read with the sensibility of Chaucer's age and suspend your modern judgment."

Esther said fiercely, "I will never suspend my judgment!"

In the privacy of her room she vowed revenge. In the privacy of her room we all vented our disgust. Walter was unspeakable, but it was Griselda who mortified us. I still had the quote from Spinoza tucked in my mirror: "The effort by which each thing endeavors to persevere in its own being is nothing but the actual essence of the thing itself," and I blamed Griselda for neglecting to persevere in her own being. I was wrong, however. The essence of Griselda was what Chaucer calls Patience and we call self-abnegation. She persevered. Not that it makes her any more appealing.

It was Esther's turn to recite her memorized stanzas in class. She was flushed and jittery as she walked to the front, but that was not unusual. She hadn't spoken more than two lines when I began to pay closer attention. I watched Professor Mansfield to see what he would do. He sat at his desk with his customary wys and wel ytaught expression, spinning his swivel chair gently from side to side. His glasses were pushed up and resting on a receding hairline, his fingers raised in a little church steeple, softly tapping, as Esther recited:

> Whan that Grisilde's doghter was ytaken
> She silently devysed hire a planne
> For to revenge swich deed she wold not slaken
> Though Walter bynne a markys and a manne.
> Whil in her veynes the fury swifte yranne,
> To Walter's chambre stoleth shee by nighte,
> And whispred, "Yor dere wyf namoore I highte."
>
> Up reysed she hir axe as up he sterte
> And cleved she his manhood righte in tweyne.
> "Ye be nat fitte to lyve, withouten herte,"
> Said she, whil Walter clutch'd himself in peyne.
> "Next comes yor nekke; the blood will flow like reyne!
> Me liketh not to soffre as ye heste.
> Yor kyngdom now is myne!" She axed his breste.

When the applause died down, Professor Mansfield rose to the occasion. Genial, Chaucerian, he praised Esther's near-faultless iambic pentameter and Middle English delivery. He asked to see her verses and she went and fetched a ragged notebook page. She was awesome standing in front of the class, thin this week, her hair pulled back and lashed into a long ponytail, two splotches of pink on her cheekbones—the stance of a martyr to conscience facing the gallows.

Professor Mansfield inspected her paper and put a few errors in spelling and diction on the board for the edification of us all. Writing Chaucerian verse was a fine way to understand the poet; he recommended it. He also recommended a dictionary and handbook of Middle English usage, of which he was one of the four compilers. However, we must try to understand the spirit as well as the letter. The spirit of Chaucer was not vindictive.

"And now the two stanzas you memorized, if you would, Miss Brickman." She wouldn't, couldn't, having stayed awake for two nights preparing her revenge. He marked her down as unprepared. Esther's mouth opened in shock but she did not protest.

After class she was surrounded. A genius! And she had never let on! Wasn't he a bastard to mark her unprepared! She shrugged that off. As the girls drifted away the boys approached in a phalanx, at the center their evident spokesman, who looked a bit older, with a clever, bearded face. George.

"That was a wonderful addition to a moral tale," began George. "Deeply affecting. But poor Walter. After all, he was only a personification of higher powers."

"Oh yeah?" said Esther curtly and breathlessly. Her chest rose and fell, she was pale now, and her eyes were like emeralds. "Tough luck, then."

So we laughed together, and they induced us to cross to the other side of Broadway, to a retreat called the Lion's Den, where they entertained us with coffee and doughnuts and the brand of wit Columbia men were known for—sharp and supercilious. Great names wafted through the air like badminton birdies. They were mostly seniors, with a year of Contemporary Civilization, CC, behind them—every great book since the world began. A man who has taken CC at Columbia, rumor had it, is, like Odysseus, never at a loss. We kept up as best we could. Our initiatory course, The Individual and Society, had been gossipy, personal, feminine. But we knew our Greeks, and we relied on pure mother wit.

"Don't blame it all on Chaucer," said Ray Fielding. "Griselda started in Boccaccio."

"And then she turns up in Petrarch," said another.

"Evidently," remarked Esther, "she had a certain appeal for all the fellows."

I watched Victor Rowe. In his light eyes was the most critical expression I had ever seen. Anybody who scanned the world that way, I thought, must be the most clever, the most supercilious. And if he knew how striking he was, it would be so much the worse. He was tall and rangy and moved with the coordinated, weird grace of a giraffe. His hair was straight and sandy, his forehead high, and his eyes bluish-ivory and liquidy. Did they weep with disdain?

"The only profitable way to read Griselda," he said, "is as comedy. Chaucer's answer to medieval soap opera. Or a takeoff on Job." His tone was not at all disdainful, only detached in a way I found intimidating.

"Female version," I said. "He ranted to heaven and she keeps her mouth shut."

"Yes," said Victor, "but they both get it all back in the end. That's why it's comedy."

There were hollows around his cheekbones, and a feeling of impatience around his mouth. His whole face was a study in planes and shadows, extra shadows because he needed a shave. He had clean white sneakers on, and red wool socks, and tiny flecks of paint studded his tan chino pants. His hands were flecked with paint too, especially the cuticles: large, hairy hands, strongly articulated. They looked older than he did.

We talked about courtly love, and Victor said the vestiges of courtly love were still with us. "Unfortunately. Knights and ladies, sacred virginity, tests of devotion. It's all part of a structure to maintain the status quo. Falling in love. You don't think falling in love is natural, do you? It's a learned response. Every society in history had lust, sure, but not too many have had falling in love, the way we do."

My pride was offended. I took it as a proclamation of invulnerability. I would have liked to appear invulnerable that way too.

George, on the other hand, loved the idea of courtly love. He was ready to do anything for a lady, he said, provided someone gave him a good horse, and a sharp sword, and a pretty coat of arms. The other boys all laughed, but I wasn't sure why. They were pleasant boys behind the show of cleverness, and George was something more: not quite a boy, for one thing. He had been in the army before college, so was a few years older than the rest. George's cleverness was ingratiating and inclusive. He liked to joke about his shortcomings: couldn't master Latin case endings, couldn't learn to dive, couldn't have three drinks without falling asleep or throwing up. When our little party dispersed he drew Esther aside and asked her to go to a movie that evening.

Once we crossed Broadway all was changed. We made friends, we accepted the company of men. Esther's stanzas inspired a spate of Griselda parodies, recited aloud and with hilarity in the Lion's Den. Steffie Baum published them in the student paper in a special box near the editorials, one at a time for two weeks running. In Ray Fielding's, Griselda chopped up her daughter herself rather than yield her to the sinister man. When Walter reveals that he meant merely to hide the child at his sister's, it is too late. He rends his royal garments. In another, Griselda went mad in the manner of Ophelia, drifting through the palace in her smock, intoning lyrical non sequiturs in Middle English. But these evaded the point. The best, though I hated to admit it, was Victor's. Five stanzas long—he must have labored for days. After the kidnapping of the children, Victor had Walter chop pieces off Griselda—her toes, one each day, then her fingers, hands, arms, legs. In a few weeks she is a stump. With each blow of the ax she repeats, "I am youre owene thyng; werketh after youre wille." Victor asked me to have a beer in the West End Bar, but I was afraid my own cleverness wouldn't fill an hour alone with him. I said I was busy.

I was. I spent hours working on Beethoven sonatas and the prescribed Haydn and Mozart trios. On my own I was practicing Schubert's "Trout" Quintet, which the Chamber Music Society would present at its spring concert. The auditions were not till April; I had begun preparing in September, trying to make it an inseparable part of me. I wanted to be chosen with a passion. The quintet entranced me, most of all the fourth movement, a theme and variations using the melody from Schubert's song about a trout. Aside from its sophisticated pleasures, the melody pierces the heart, and the variations, like prisms, candid and relentless, flash the heart's exposed facets. It may be nothing more magical than the symmetry of the intervals—a fourth up, third up, third down and fourth down, the unexpected fifth, and then the descending, syncopated scale, like someone skipping down a flight of steps. But that explanation sounds like Nina, decanting magic.

A pianist needs another instrument, and the only free time I had to learn the oboe was late at night. Music did not touch Melanie; play away, she said. So, many evenings I sat on my bed piping halting scales, while Melanie slept curled in her Dr. Dentons. We continued peacefully to coexist. And for comic relief I had joined the Gilbert and Sullivan Society, a suitably zany bunch that needed an extra accompanist for rehearsals. The regular accompanist, Henrietta Frye, was a slender senior with milky skin who resembled the lovesick maidens Gilbert and Sullivan immortalized. In fact she was a hiker and tennis player as well as an excellent pianist, better than I. Only if something happened to Henrietta Frye—not something awful, I hoped, but something minor and incapacitating, like spraining a finger on the courts—could I get to play for the performances, *Patience* in the winter and *The Yeomen of the Guard* in the spring. But I suppressed my visions. Henrietta was deserving and I was a bit superstitious, like my mother.

"George is okay, he's very nice," said Esther, "but he's not right for me. Or me for him, either. Lots of times we just kind of miss each other. You know what I mean? Like paper airplanes. At home we used to try to make them crash but it's hard, they're so light."

We were swimming in the college pool, nearly empty at five in the afternoon. Esther swam daily to stay thin, but she found it too boring alone. Nina and Gaby and I took turns. I swam laps to set a good example, but Esther mostly treaded water and talked.

"Too clever. Always has a ready word." She swam a few lazy yards and returned. "He'd be much better for you, Lydia. Much more your type."

I frowned and swam away.

"Oh, and there's another thing," she called after me. "All he cares about, mostly"—she dove underwater to tantalize me, and rising, shook droplets from her face—"is going to bed."

"Aha! Well?"

"What do you mean, aha, well?"

"Esther, you know exactly what I mean,"
She giggled, floated on her back. "I did, once."
"Just once?"
"Yes. He's a little distressed about that, understandably. You remember Fecundity, in the Calculus?" Since Gaby's outburst of last year, Bentham's Hedonistic Calculus had become a dormitory joke. Everyone knew it by heart. Intensity, Duration, Certainty or Uncertainty, Propinquity, Fecundity, Purity, and Extent, how far can the pleasure be shared with others? "It seems if you do it once it's supposed to lead to the next time, and the next, ad infinitum. But frankly, I don't like him *that* much. Oh, he was all right. He did quite well, actually."

She was so blithe—I could hardly believe it. "How do you know? You have nothing to compare him to."

"That's true, but I could tell he put on a good show. Interesting. I just don't have that feeling for him."

"And what makes you think I would?" What did a good show consist of, anyway? Interesting? I swam four laps to seem indifferent, but she waited, paddling around.

"I know you, Lydia. You're so restless. And you could fit him very easily, ha ha, into your busy schedule, I mean. He's diverting. Like in Pascal. A *divertissement*."

"You have to do at least six laps or else it's a complete waste of time. Come on, Esther, your fat cells are multiplying." I swam furiously to elude my fantasies, vivid now that they contained a specific person. Last week she had handed me the new loafers that squeezed her instep. And now this. A friend was another self indeed.

Early December, a still-mild day, a bunch of us were finishing a paper-bag lunch on the boys' campus. One by one people straggled away until only Esther and George and I were left. I gathered up my debris. "Don't rush off, Lyd," she said. "You don't have your quartet till three." George told us how he had enlisted in the army to feel distinct from his father and uncles, who were all rabbis, but now he was a pacifist. "How could you ever think a uniform would confer distinction?" Esther asked. "And now I'll leave you two to your own devices. I have an appointment with my French teacher. Good-bye!" George watched her run down the steps and across the campus till she was out of sight. Then, like a salesclerk shifting to a new customer, he turned his attention to me.

"Esther seems to feel we should get to know each other better."

"You certainly don't beat around the bush, do you?"

"And I thought I was being indirect. . . . Oh good, I made you laugh."

"That's not very difficult. I'm a sucker for silly jokes. At home they used to call me the giggler."

"I've always been curious about you, Lydia. Can I ask you a personal question?"

"What?" I felt leery already.

He pointed to the paper bag on the grass. "You just had one and a half hamburgers, a doughnut, and coffee. How can you eat so much and stay thin? It's phenomenal. You know how Esther is always dieting."

"I burn it up. That's what they told me when I had a metabolism test. You know that Shelley line, 'I fall upon the thorns of life, I bleed'? Gabrielle showed it to me. She says I fall upon the food of life, I burn."

He liked that one. This was a kind of performance too, like the simpler duets in the Chamber Music Society. I studied him, his body, and wondered what it might be like.

"Esther says you can sing. I didn't know. In Gilbert and Sullivan you just play. There are other things I would like to know, but . . . well, I don't like to pry." He looked around at the dry fountains, the concrete, the bare December trees.

"I would tell you most things you would ask. I'm not mysterious, like Nina or Gabrielle."

"Oh, them!" George raised both hands as if fending something off. "They scare me. They would take ages."

"And you think you could know me in a flash?"

"No, it's only that you don't offer so much resistance. You talk. The fact is—" He gave an earnest glance, or perhaps an imitation of an earnest glance. "I could use a person like you."

"Use? What for? Bluebeard?"

"Oh, come on." He reached out and touched my arm. "I only meant to hone my wits."

"Wit, or wits?"

"Exactly. To make distinctions. Either. Both." He paused and smiled. "I might have my uses too."

I tore strips from my cardboard coffee mug. "Oh yes, I remember you would do anything for a lady. But where are you going to get a horse?" I looked at my watch. "I have to go now. Telemann calls."

"Would you like to go to the movies Saturday night?"

"Aren't you still going with Esther?"

"No. She won't go."

"I see. Well, in that case . . . what movie?"

When he kissed me the first time, after the movie, in one of those apartments rented for assignations, what I felt most was the beard and the mustache. In 1958 a beard was an affectation, not yet a political statement. George's was chestnut-brown, small and well-trimmed. When the kiss was over I said it felt like kissing a rabbi. "No," I amended, "more of a rabbi's son. Or a rabbinical student. You make me feel I'm the one leading you into sin."

"My family are not Orthodox rabbis. They have no beards."

"So why, then?"

"For distinction. I feel undistinguished." In fact he was distinguished. The beard and the thick glasses with tortoiseshell rims gave his benign face a highly decorated look. George wore bright colors in a dim age. He was rococo, a bit of a dandy.

"You mean you feel indistinguishable."

"Good girl." He clapped me on the shoulder like a pal, then moved to kiss me again. I backed off.

"I want to look around the place. Do you mind?"

"Go right ahead."

The apartment had two bedrooms. In the other one were Victor's painting things. Most guys came here to . . . relax, George explained, but Victor came to paint. Victor, he said, grinning, was . . . "Aesthetic, did you say?" "Ascetic," he enunciated. It was a square, dusty room with no furniture, only a bare striped mattress on the floor, but it had large windows facing north and west. There were rolled canvases on the floor, a stained easel, jars and rags and the stinging smell of paint. Three stretched canvases, one with a gray shirt hanging over a corner, leaned against the west wall: abstract, blue and brown, dun-colored blotches that seemed to be jostling each other for more space. They were incommunicative paintings, the artist mumbling to himself, and I did not care for them. George said, "He's trying things out. He's very versatile. You would have liked what he did last year better. Melons and eggplants. Come." He took my hand and pulled me towards the other bedroom, which was cleaner, and furnished in a neat, nondescript way. He sat down on the bed. I stood in the doorway. I was having a strange, disoriented sensation. I remembered being blindfolded and whirled around, years ago, at birthday parties.

"I'm not sure why I agreed to come here."

He smiled. "Urgent curiosity."

"Is that it?"

"I imagine, from what I know of you. You don't like mysteries."

"Is that enough reason?"

"Well." He laughed again. "More reason than some people have, and less than others."

"I think I ought to feel . . . well, you know, something more."

"It's not always easy, nine feet away. If you came a little closer, maybe . . ."

George was a cheery epicure, while I undertook it in a spirit of quest, just like The History of Philosophy. Between us there was affection, but not any question of love—we wanted experience and excitement in safety. The caution of the age was deep in our bones. (Only later, as friends, did we come to love each other, without excitement.) We would meet in the apartment two or three times a week, never after curfew hours. I was no Steffie Baum. My daring was all within limits. I was careful also never to miss a session of the Chamber Music Society or cut my practice hours to be with George. I felt my dignity rested in such bargains, because with him I didn't feel I had much dignity at all. Just pleasure and profound confusion.

I was taken with some essential flimsiness about him, in which the intelligence and charm were wrapped like jewels in tissue paper. He was taken with my combination of bold and bashful. Adorable. Adorable was a word I hated, I told him. It certainly did not describe me. "Not all of you, Lydia. Just that particular mix. That careful eagerness. Will you at least allow me my tastes?" "Your tastes! Your tastes are so catholic. If I allow you your tastes everything gets in." "No, it's that I want to get into everything. Could you come a little closer?" "You also make it sound so crude, and I don't like it." "No? I don't see you struggling."

We were both thorough and methodical people. He had read widely on the subject—he liked literary erotica—and he was conscientious too. The certainty of the pleasure became more reliable. Fecundity increased; intensity, extent, all of the categories. But I was unsatisfied in my mind, just as in The History of Philosophy.

"Nice as it is, this is not the answer," I told him one evening, on his smooth sheets. He always brought clean sheets, in a briefcase; he said he didn't know who might have been in the bed before us. He was a domestic creature, even dusted and swept occasionally.

"What is the question?"

"The answer to anything. It couldn't be a religion, for example. It has no content. And it lasts so short a time."

"Some groups have made it a religion. There are cults. . . ." He looked at me curiously. "How long does it last?"

"What, you mean just the momentary . . .?" I was still shy about the words.

"No, no, I know how long *that* lasts. I mean after. The feeling. Aura. How far can it take you? How long can it keep you floating?"

I was taken with that in him too. He pondered over obscure, intangible things. The floating. He was asking about Duration. "Oh, a pretty long time."

"How long is a pretty long time?"

"Eighteen hours, maybe? I'll feel it all evening and sleep in it and when I get up I might still have it. Then gradually it'll slip away and I'll feel alone again, wide awake."

George beamed. "That's very nice to know, Lyd."

It was far nicer than he knew. The feeling I took away with me was a nimbus of warm air around my skin, weather I carried with me, a lush spring in January. I didn't tell him how fine it felt—I was not yet so willing to give. I begrudged him the knowledge because I felt he had made my life bizarre. My friends had what girls our age were supposed to have: flirtatious phone calls in the dorm, leading to dates—movies, walks in the whitened park. Snowball fights. I was almost as bad—or as good—as Steffie, except Steffie didn't think having a sexual life was bizarre. I could keep my eyes wide open in bed, but when I dressed I had to turn away. And when I tossed my book bag over my shoulder and became a college girl again, rushing off to make her curfew, the apartment felt like a sea of confusion I had to fight my way out of.

"But even so," I said, "even if I were part of a cult where you made love so often that the feeling never lapsed—still it wouldn't work. Can you see spending a lifetime? It would be boring."

"I don't think so. Maybe I bore you."

"You don't bore me. Yet. I would like something sustaining and fixed, though. Like an idea. Do you believe in anything?"

"What an embarrassing question. Do you know, that makes me feel the way questions about sex must have made our grandparents feel. No, I guess I don't, really. You can't ever get any notion to stand still. Every configuration changes the minute you fix it in your eye."

"That's only the way things appear, though."

"The way things appear is the way they are."

"George. Four years of being a philosophy major and that's all you've arrived at?"

"I'm not alone. You remember Heraclitus?"

"Yes indeedy. Fire."

"He had a disciple, Kratylus. Kratylus took very seriously what Heraclitus said about everything being in constant flux. When he was asked to explain his ideas he waved his hand in the air. His point was that a statement can't even remain true for as long as it takes to say it." George waved his hand in the air to demonstrate, a graceful, rueful wave; it came down ruefully on my breast.

"But we can't stay with that. The mind instinctively seeks more."

"It may seek, but that's our problem, love. Yes, I know, the structure of the mind reflects the structure of the universe. But that's the epitome of wishful thinking."

"You are nothing but a Sophist. Professor Boles would be scandalized if she knew I was with you."

"I'll tell you something. I think they got a raw deal. They made Socrates nervous, so he gave them a bad name in the agora and nobody's taken them seriously since. Yet what is so terrible about taking money for your teaching? And as far as teaching strategy rather than substance, well, it's presumptuous, in a way, to try to teach anything but strategy. They were right about a lot of things. Change is the only stable element. You're not the same person today that you were yesterday. You especially, kiddo. Six weeks ago you were an innocent."

"This"—I glanced down at our bodies—"doesn't change my basic identity."

"What basic identity, my sweet? Show me where it is. I see everything else, but I don't see that."

"There is something. There's got to be. Something abides, you accumulate a self. By experience, even this, okay. And memory. You endure. The changes you're talking about are on the surface."

"Memory is not a live thing." He slid his hand along my leg.

"Memory is the livest thing of all. Without it you're nobody. An amnesiac. It's too frightening."

"I'm nobody, who are you?" he whispered in my ear.

"George, you are so . . . you're a facade. There's nothing to you. I mean, you won't let there be."

He stopped moving his hands. His whole body seemed to wilt.

"Sorry," I said. "Sorry, sorry."

He moved off so he could see me—without his glasses he was farsighted—and he flashed his wide, ingratiating smile. "You won't have to remember me," he said. "We'll be friends for life. Won't we?"

"Sure. Friends for life. But what hypocrisy. You say it at a moment when you're hating me. You don't even want to touch me because I said that."

"I want to touch you. It was momentary." He touched my face to prove it. Then he rolled over on his side, away from me. A moment later he rolled back, smiling again, and sang, " 'Prithee, pretty maiden—prithee tell me true (Hey, but I'm doleful, willow willow waly!), Have you e'er a lover a-dangling after you? Hey willow waly O.' " They were lyrics we heard three times a week at the Gilbert and Sullivan rehearsals, and we delighted in them. Everything about Gilbert and Sullivan was so gloriously inane—the best possible respite from our studies and our studious sex. "Come on, Lydie. Do it."

I gave him the response. " 'Gentle sir, although to marry I design (Hey, but he's hopeful, willow willow waly!), As yet I do not know you, and so I must decline. Hey willow waly O!' " It made us laugh like kids, and forget for the moment that as a pair we were hopeless.

At the end of January we all went to see *Patience*. Henrietta Frye, the wan slender pianist, having sustained no minor injury, I was free to sit in the audience with Nina and Esther and Gabrielle, with Victor and the other pleasant boys, watching George and Ray in the chorus of Dragoons. They hammed without stint and we cheered them on. But Steffie as Patience was a revelation. It was a comic role and she got her laughs, but she also managed to make the absurdity believable and tender. Her versatile hair shone in two thick plaits; she wore a blue and white checked, ruffled milkmaid's dress, with a milk pail on her arm—a common-sensical maiden baffled by the bunch of heartsick aesthetes—and the image was perfectly credible. Steffie of the shady midnight escapes sang, with the utter sincerity that the inane role demanded, " 'Love that no wrong can cure, Love that is always new, That is the love that's pure, That is the love that's true!' " In the audience were the three junior high school students she tutored, along with their families, the only black faces present. I had had it all wrong—she was far more sensible than the rest of us. She gave herself fully to what claimed her feelings. As a matter of fact she had said no to George—he told me so himself. I felt a sudden twang in my gut, as if a spring had snapped. I wished I were like Steffie. I had been with George only a few hours earlier—quickly, for he had to get dressed and made up. Lying on top of me, he had joked that real opera singers weren't allowed to do this before a performance; he hoped I appreciated the risk he was running. I kept the feel of him, and the nimbus of warm air. At the finale, as he embraced the lovesick maiden assigned to him, I felt his arm around my waist, and that ocean of confusion, salty, dark, fishy.

I passed the rest of the winter dazed, by the love-making and by the music. I shuttled from one to the other, living for the feeling of levitation, like a junkie. Unlike a junkie I worked hard to get it—the same high in both, only one means was sanctioned and reputable. I lived high, ate hugely, and felt my insides burning it up, a revved engine. When I was alone I heard music and felt his body, and those live memories of sensation carried me through the routine drudgeries. I was isolated from my friends, with their approved snowball fights. I could never tell them how I had presented myself to George and that though I was free to walk out at any moment I didn't feel free. I felt wet and waiting for the next time.

"Something is wrong. You don't look right"—Gaby, one night as we stood washing over adjacent sinks. "You're not pregnant, for God's sake, are you?" I brushed her off, hid my face in a towel. "Of course not. I wouldn't be so stupid."

I did feel pregnant, though. I was gestating the "Trout" Quintet, practicing it hours every day. The auditions were in a few weeks. I took Schubert's songs out of the library and brought them to the apartment—George could help. Faltering over the German, which we read only phonetically, we sang the one about the trout, which Schubert borrowed for his piercing fourth movement.

"What does it mean?" George asked. "It's hard to sing without knowing the meaning."

"Oh, it's totally asinine. A pretty fish gets caught, that's all, and the person watching gets very worked up about it. But it's peculiar, with that bouncy music, kind of tongue-in-cheek."

"Can't we sing it in English? Let's see the translation."

"No, the words don't match the music too well."

He insisted, and so I read it to him, though it embarrassed me to be so captivated by a melody with these lyrics:

> The brook was sparkling brightly
> And dancing all about,
> And by me like an arrow,
> There flashed a lively trout.
> I stood upon the brook-bank
> And saw with joyous heart,
> The brook so gaily rippling,
> The fishes dash and dart.
> But soon there came an angler
> With rod and line and hook
> To catch the fish that swam there,
> So happy in the brook.

As long, as now, the water,
I thought, is bright and clear,
The man can never catch him,
The trout need never fear.
But in the end the robber
No more could wait.
He made the water thick and muddy.
The trout snapped up his bait.
He twitched his rod and caught him,
What pity, poor little trout, thought I,
And sad at heart and grieving,
I saw the victim die.

"Well, there. I knew you'd think it was silly."

"It's not silly. The death of a beautiful thing. Too young."

"It's just a fish. . . ."

"But the angler is death, you see. The narrator has seen how death works. He gets his victims by trickery, making the water muddy."

"Oh, you're getting as bad as Gabrielle. Since she's an English major she sees symbols in every little thing."

"That trout was so easy to get. He should have been more alert. Put up more of a fight, at least."

"I just want to put up enough of a fight to get picked. The only real competition is Henrietta Frye. And she never even catches a cold. Healthy as a horse."

"Henrietta's very nice, actually."

"I know. I don't really mean it. . . . You haven't slept with her too?"

"No, Lydia. Can't I say someone is a nice person without—"

"Sure. I was just curious."

"Do you know what that song reminds me of? Freud says somewhere that what we call the instinct of self-preservation might be nothing but an organism's wish to die in its own way, in its own time. That's why it fights off any outside danger. It's funny, isn't it? We like to think we persevere because of the will to live, but maybe it's really the will to die our own kind of death. A fitting death."

"Sometimes I feel if I don't get to do the 'Trout,' I'll die. I

mean it—I'll want to die, I want it so badly. I've spent seven
months—"

"Now *that* is truly asinine." His voice was new to me, harsh.
"How can you even think that? People spend years and years.
There'll be plenty of other times if you don't make this one."

"It's because of you I'm like this. Everything is too . . .
heady. Before, I didn't use to feel I would die if I didn't have
what I wanted."

"Oh, it's a sexual thing? Is that what you're telling me?" He
slammed the book of songs shut and tossed it to the floor.
"Should I apologize for waking you out of your, uh, prolonged
latency? Did I do too good a job?" I had never heard him nasty
either, only rueful.

"George! Take it easy. Sensual, I meant. All cravings are the
same, the object isn't important."

"All cravings are the same, huh? Tell me something. What if
I tied you to the bed and I sucked you, licked and licked, and at
the moment before you were about to come I got up and walked
away. Would you feel you would die?"

I looked away. Those words. "What an awful thing to say.
How disgusting you can be." I moved across the bed, as far
away as I could.

"All right, I'm aware of that. But would you?"

"I don't know. I might." There was an unpleasant, perverse
silence. "You couldn't tell the moment, though."

"Oh no?"

And then he did it. Of course without tying me to the bed.
That was hardly our style, nor was it necessary. I let him. I was
curious. I didn't think he would really stop. He got up and
walked to the window, wiped his mouth on the back of his hand
and lit a cigarette. I said, "I don't believe this."

"Wait it out. See if you die. Or if you're afraid to die you can
do it yourself."

"I'm not Patient Griselda, you know. I don't have to go along
with your strange urges, your marvelous desires."

"You're not tied to the bed either. The door is unlocked."

I didn't die. I put on my clothes and left. He caught up with
me an hour and a half later, coming out of a theory class, and he
apologized.

"Go away. I didn't want a teacher. I wanted a lover." That was hard enough to say. I ran on ahead.

He ran too, and stopped me. "Listen. My mother died. You throw that word around so lightly. But she really died. I was four. I don't think I ever told you. They said she had to go on a long trip. Later, when I understood what had happened, I thought I would die if I couldn't have a mother like everyone else. But I didn't die. It's not so easy to die. I grew up and did without. It makes me very angry to hear people magnify small things, their little needs. Whether you play the 'Trout' this year or next, whether you come today or tomorrow, is of very small consequence, and it's about time you knew it."

That was the most intimate thing he ever said to me. I treasured it, not because I liked it or liked his tone—I hated his tone—but because of its intimacy. I knew that for George it was a great deal to part with.

"I'm sorry about your mother. I wondered, but I didn't like to ask. Still. That is no reason to humiliate a person. Some pacifist you are."

"I'm sorry." He hung his head like a four-year-old. "Are we still friends?"

"I don't know."

"You said friends for life."

"Did I?"

"Yes, in a moment of weakness."

"I guess I'll have to stick to it, then. But for the moment would you just go away?"

The issue became academic. I was chosen to do the "Trout." Henrietta didn't try out for it; she preferred to do Bach. I went downtown to Carnegie Hall to hear what Rudolf Serkin made of it: he liquefied it, gave it fluidity and luminescence. I listened to other pianists in the library till I was mesmerized. Nina would come to fetch me, tapping gently on my shoulder, making me jump in my seat. I moved an earphone aside. "Come on, Lydia. Esther's making a pot of spaghetti." Or chili. Curried chicken. We were tired of dormitory food. Esther cooked every few days, in one of the apartments the boys rented, sometimes in the apartment I slept in with George and in which Victor kept one room for his work. I wondered whom he made love to on that bare mattress, if anyone. He didn't look ascetic. But why should I care? I was hearing the quintet in my sleep, waking to it. I played it on classroom desks and on my pillow, I sang it to the sleeping Melanie amid the banana peels. But when I practiced I didn't allow myself my fill of emotion. I was ascetic. I played the notes slower than their proper tempo, with a metronome, and concentrated on accurate dynamics and fingering and phrasing. I was hoarding it, trusting that on the night of the performance the suppressed emotion would find its way out, steadily and serenely controlled, all the more resonant for having been suppressed. I knew the "Trout" so well I almost felt I had composed it. It was a fertile, exuberant work of perfect balance—the themes were balanced, and the contribution of each instrument. The story goes that Schubert composed it on request, to while away an evening in his patron's drawing room. A diversion, like a romantic novel. And yet it seemed to me the rich exuberance was a screen for its poignancy, a sense of loss and nostalgia amid plenty, of death in the midst of fertility. If you gave in to the poignancy, though, you lost the exuberance, equally important. Neither could exist without a reminder of the other; the two qualities hung in dependency, a mobile. I resolved to remember, also, that lively and beautiful fish, too innocent for the angler, an image I would never tell the other four doing the quintet, all boys and all more experienced performers than I.

Music students dropped in on the rehearsals, mostly to hear Professor Duffy's astute comments. I didn't mind the traffic. I never suffered greatly from stage fright, which I suspect is a form of pretension. I felt unassuming, simply making a small contribution to a vast fund. (Yet Victor called that unassuming feeling arrogance, or pride, the special careless and secretive pride of the anonymous donor.) I didn't mind Professor Duffy's public corrections either—he told me I was a good ensemble player, but I must be sure to stand forth and claim my own in the solos. I was perhaps too comfortable merged with the group, he suggested. I would nod calmly and sometimes mark places to remember. But I did get uneasy the afternoon Victor walked in and took a chair at the back. He was not a music student. I knew quite well he had not come to hear Duffy or even Schubert but to hear me, that self I thought each person accumulated but George said didn't exist.

After the rehearsal he came up and, with a strained smile, asked, "Would you come have a beer with me?" He was wearing a maroon sweater and the usual tan chinos and sneakers with red socks. His eyes were not blue but slaty. He didn't look ascetic, only drawn and tense as if he needed a good night's sleep, but still unnervingly beautiful. I said yes because I didn't know how to refuse smoothly. His body moved with a proprietary sense of space. Walking alongside him, fast, to keep up, I felt I was on his territory.

"Where are we going, the Lion's Den?"

"No, you meet everyone you know there."

"How about the West End?"

"Too crowded."

He took me to a dim, warm neighborhood place on Amsterdam Avenue, near the Cathedral of Saint John the Divine, magnificently Gothic but unfinished. It would remain unfinished, the minister once explained, to symbolize the unfulfilled aspirations of the people in the ghetto it bordered. I was determined, once we sat down, to establish my own territory. But it was not a student hangout—men in work clothes, a couple of stout old women, black teen-agers, Spanish girls with sharp voices. There was a world outside of school, close by. And in it Victor didn't look like a student. He ordered two beers.

"I hate beer. I'll take a coffee."

"Oh. I should have asked."

"It doesn't matter."

"No? Look, I've wanted to talk to you alone for a long time."

"Yes, I remember you did suggest it once."

"I did once, and you said you couldn't. I wanted—" This time the smile was genuine. "I wanted to go out on a real date. Hold hands in the movies, walk in the park, all that kind of thing."

"You like all that?"

"Yes, why not?"

"I don't know. I had the impression . . ."

"What impression?"

"Nothing. It doesn't matter." I paused. "But now I'm seeing George."

"Now you're seeing George." He stopped talking while the waitress brought the beer and coffee. "But not for long."

"What do you mean, not for long? Did he say something to you?"

"Oh no. He doesn't talk about you." My alarm amused him. "All he ever says is that you like to eat. He has to go to the grocery before you come over. No, I just have a feeling. I know him, and you, a little."

"Very little."

"That's the point. I would like to know more."

"Oh. What is this, an interview?"

"No." He stretched his hands out flat on the table. "The position is yours, if you want it."

"Oh Lord! I'm . . . I'm . . ."

"Touched?"

"Touched! No! Just the opposite."

"I'm sorry, then. You must have misunderstood."

"I'm not sure. If George is such a good friend of yours, how come you're doing this?"

"Esther is your friend."

"Oh, but that was different," I burst out. "She said—" I glanced up at Victor. I had a horrible thought.

"It's nothing like that. This hasn't been engineered. I'm being openly underhanded. I got tired of waiting till you got tired of him."

"I see." I had no footing at all, no words. "Do you always operate this way?"

"No. I thought I'd take a chance." He gave a wistful look. He would never be at a loss.

"Well, I don't know what to say. I know even less than you do. Tell me something. Tell me about the painting."

"All right, that's fair enough. There's not a lot to tell, though. I'm going to do it as soon as I'm out. For the rest of my life. I don't care about much else."

"Why did you bother going to school, then? Why didn't you just stay home and paint?"

"I wanted to. But my parents were very insistent, my father in particular. For these four years we have a bargain. Then I'm through pleasing people."

"What's the bargain? Oh, I know. The apartment."

"Yes. I need a place to work. I get the degree, they pay

seventy-five bucks a month towards the apartment. I also get to
hear Meyer Schapiro and the others. It's not a bad deal."

"I don't suppose they know what else they're paying for?"

He grinned. "They only pay half. I'm not responsible for
what goes on in the other rooms."

"They must be rich."

"Not very."

"It's more than my parents could afford."

"Why, what do your parents do?"

"My father sells insurance in Hartford and my mother is a
mother. Very good at it. I have a little sister who's graduating
from high school this spring. Evelyn. She's a bit of a sylph. The
White Rock Girl, you know? I'm the practical one."

"My father is a lawyer. Workmen's compensation, but he's
usually not on the side of the workmen. My mother is a mother
too. She also does good works and takes elevating courses.
Ethical Culture, things like that. She's very, oh, fashionable,
but still I like her a lot. She's more ethical than cultured. I bet
you would like her too. I have an older sister, Lily. She's a
chain-smoker at twenty-four. They didn't make her finish college because she married a urologist. Now they're buying a
house in Westchester, which a year of prostates will pay for, I
suppose. Lily is pregnant—soon I'll be an uncle. How do you
like that? Uncle Victor." He grinned with pleasure.

Each fact seemed to amuse him in a fresh, kindly way. His
face was mobile and expressive—it altered for every sentence,
every nuance. And the nicer he got, the more wary I felt.
"Where did you grow up, Park Avenue?" I asked.

"Will you hold it against me?"

"Probably." I risked a smile.

"I'm never going to use a penny of their money, after college.
I don't believe in inherited wealth." He waved to the waitress
for another beer. His wave, it struck me, would have been
equally at home in a downtown restaurant with waiters in
starched, ruffled shirts and cummerbunds, as it was in this
Upper West Side bar where the waitress wore an aqua uniform
like a hospital orderly. "Besides, it wouldn't be right to use their
money for things they don't believe in. They think it's peculiar
to be a painter. They'd rather someone else's son did it, if it has
to be done. I have it all worked out. I can work in a bar or

something, nights. Would you like a person who worked in a bar better than a person from Park Avenue?" His eyes were teasing.

"That one hit home, I see."

"Well, it was a switch. In the old days girls didn't want to marry men who were poor. Well, would you?"

"What, marry you when you're poor?"

He started to laugh. "Like me better poor. To begin with, anyhow."

"I hardly know you. I'm not sure I would like you under any circumstances."

"You might get to like me. It's been known to happen."

He had a terrific scriptwriter, I thought, smooth, much better than mine. "I guess I shouldn't be so surprised at this. I remember you once said you didn't like the vestiges of courtly love. It figures that you wouldn't bother with any proprieties."

"On the contrary. I imagine this is how the knights did it, more or less. Don't you think? They certainly didn't suggest going to the movies."

"But you said the feelings were all instilled by custom."

"So what? I didn't say I was immune, did I? Anyhow, when you major in anthropology, it gets to you." He poured his beer. "Look, why are you so bristly? I know I'm not very good at this. But am I being so presumptuous?"

"It reminds me of Walter and Griselda. You've chosen me in my humble surroundings. It never occurs to you that I might not care to go along. I might like things as they are."

"That Walter and Griselda idea is baloney and you know it." He said it quite serenely. "But suppose I did pick you out. Someone has to pick someone out, don't they? Is it only that you didn't do the picking? What do you find unacceptable about me?"

"This is absurd!" I put the coffee cup down sharply. Some splashed over the rim and I wiped it up with a napkin—Victor seemed so well-bred. "I mean the way you talk. What is unacceptable about you? Asking that question is what's unacceptable. Your whole approach. You expect me to feel what you feel because you feel it. And on the spot! You're distorting all the ordinary ways of . . . of . . ."

"Only by saying what I mean. And you're enjoying it!" He

tossed his head back in a swift movement, a blend of weariness and delight, a very private gesture. I watched the pulses in his throat. "Confess you're enjoying it. Say something straight, Lydia. You haven't said one straightforward thing since we sat down. Except that your father sells insurance."

"Okay! The novelty and the flattery I enjoy. But against my better judgment."

"Oh, the hell with your better judgment." He leaned over the table towards me. "We're alike, don't you see? We're the same. We could understand without saying a word. We seem unapproachable, but we could approach each other easily."

"I am not in the least unapproachable. . . . Why, do I seem that way?"

"Yes. Proud. Confident."

"Me!" I forgot about sounding well-bred. "You're the one who's proud. *I* am an ordinary nice person." Even I had to laugh at that.

"You are. But you have great potential for pride. Great hidden reserves. I don't mean in the bad sense. Not haughty. I mean you're not afraid to think very well of yourself, what you can do. It's lovely. I love it in you."

"Don't, please. You're embarrassing me terribly. . . . Why didn't you say that in the first place?"

"I don't know. I thought you were more subtle."

"I guess I'm not."

"No. But anyhow, the way you played the 'Trout' was subtle. I don't know what Schubert had in mind, but . . ."

"Tell me. Tell me anything about it, really, good or bad. I'm not sensitive. I just want to do it well."

"I can't tell you how to do it well," he said softly. "I don't know anything about it. But I loved the way you did it." He reached out his hand as if to place it over mine, then drew back. "I loved what you kept back as much as what you put in. I know it was only a run-through and you'll give more when you really do it. Still, the suggestion . . ." When I could look up again his face was transformed, transparent. It was hard to keep my eyes on him, as if I were seeing more nakedness than I should in a stranger. "You made it very poignant," he said.

"Poignant?" That was my word. "Tell me, I'm curious, do you know what poignant literally means?"

"Of course. Piercing."

"Piercing, yes." He was piercing too, for that brief moment. "Well, thank you." I watched him pour more beer. "Your hand is shaking. What's the matter?"

"Do you think this is easy? I mean, to talk to you like this? Do you think I do it every day?"

He shocked me. He didn't raise and lower barriers or play safe. We were not alike in that. "Look, I have so much work to do—I can't. . . . And George."

"I have work to do too. And George will always take care of himself."

"Stop, please. I don't like being pushed. It doesn't feel right. You're . . . Okay, I see you're different from what I thought. But still, this whole talk is your show, your script, isn't it? My lines are very limited. Yes or no is all you leave for me to say. It's not . . . It makes me feel like . . ."

"I should have asked you if you wanted to go to the movies. It would have sounded better. I don't know how to pursue girls, really. I don't have time. Look, next time it can be your show. I'm democratic. I'd like to see what your show would be like, actually."

"I've got to go now. No, hold it. I'll pay for my own coffee, thanks."

"Fine!" said Victor. "Give me—let's see, two coffees—thirty cents. No, make it . . . forty-two and a half, with tip. Pay for the beer too, if you like. Do you want to pay for the beer?"

"Oh, all right, go ahead and pay for it all."

He walked me back to the library, where we said good-bye.

He interfered with the way I saw George. I thought I had no illusions about George, that I understood his charm and his usefulness. But the memory of Victor and his insistence hung over me, and in the silent clarity of late nights, as I practiced the oboe under the small bedside lamp with Melanie curled asleep, I saw that whether I liked him or not, Victor was emblematical of the world, dense and insistent and intractable. George, with all his cavalier sex, his beard, and his years in the army, gave off something dry and academic, like the odor of library stacks. Even the loving he had learned from books.

"What is in there?" I asked him, lying in bed.

"In where?" He was resting his head on my breast.

"In *here*."

"Blood," he said, "and gray matter."

"You know what I mean, George. You seem so apart. What are you thinking?"

"I'm thinking nothing. Can't you just enjoy it?"

"I don't know what it is. I want to be somewhere else. Outside of me, I mean."

"Oh, Lyd," he groaned. "You are so awfully adolescent. And as of last week you're not even a teen-ager any more."

"What do you feel urgent about? There must be something."

"Nag, nag, nag."

I smiled. I was being unfair: my fingers drew designs on his belly as I asked. "Come on, tell me," I teased, "what your real passion is for. You know what I mean . . . there's God, Art, Revolution, Nature."

"If you must know, Cunts," he said.

A week before I was to perform the "Trout" a most unlikely event occurred. On an outing in the New Jersey Palisades with the Mountain Climbing Club, Henrietta Frye tripped and broke her wrist. The call imploring me to substitute in *The Yeomen of the Guard* left me faintly guilty, even though I had not envied Henrietta since the "Trout" auditions. I cut my Friday classes to practice the score. *The Yeomen of the Guard* was my favorite among the operettas because it ends sadly, a last-minute sadness casting into high relief the inanity of the rest. Our production played up the sadness for all it was worth. The purported hero, Colonel Fairfax, played by George, was a stiff, selfish nobleman, a "peacock popinjay," who steals the girl from the true hero, the jester Jack Point, a man of the world. Ray Fielding was our jester, and miraculous: he gave Jack Point the verve and ambiguity of a Shakespearean fool—fey yet earthly, a sprite yet a man, obtuse and barbed in his wit, yet poignant, quite like the "Trout," in his sorrow over lost love. Ray brought tears to my eyes even as I accompanied him, singing of the merryman whose soul was sad and whose glance was glum as he sighed for the love of a lady. George did very well as the peacock popinjay, very natural. He stood suitably pompous and triumphant with the girl nestled under his arm, while the jester, the artist, cast aside, fell to the ground in misery as the curtain came down. I worked up to the final chords wondering which of them was more real; with which would I find myself in the presence of real life? I didn't think about love.

The next weekend I played the "Trout." Backstage the string players looked unfamiliar dressed in their dark suits. They were tense as they wiped their palms and foreheads with big white handkerchiefs. I was excited and curious. I had the feel of every phrase stored in my fingers like gold in a vault; all I had to do was unlock and it would undulate out—I hoped. Everyone was there, Nina, Esther, and Gabrielle, Melanie and Steffie, George, Victor, Ray, and the other clever boys, as well as my parents and Evelyn, down from Hartford for the occasion. I thought of none of them. If I thought of anything at all besides the notes, it was of the lissome, iridescent qualities of skimming fishes. But mostly I listened to the others and let the stored phrases shed from me into the communal sound we made. It felt like molting. I remembered Professor Duffy telling me not to be afraid to come forth and claim my own during the solo parts, and though I was afraid, for there was such a bare lonesomeness about standing forth by myself, I did it. That was more than molting; it was revealing the naked nerves. I did it for the other four—it wouldn't have been fair to hold back.

It was good. I was satisfied in my mind as never before.

We all went out for pizza to celebrate, three big tables pushed together in the smoky back room of the West End Bar. I hadn't seen my parents in several months. I noticed they were beginning to go gray, my father in streaks at the temples, my mother in patches. Their bodies were beginning to soften, yet their eyes were as eager and beneficent as in those long-ago summers at the beach. They were paying special attention to George. I prayed that my father would not say anything to embarrass me, such as, My little Paderewski, which he was quite capable of doing, with all his beneficence.

"And what are you studying?" he asked George.

"Philosophy."

"Philosophy. Well, well. And what do you do with that when you graduate?"

In his charmingly evasive answer, George managed to mention the family of rabbis, which he knew my parents would find impressive. No doubt they assessed him as a sociable, sensible young man despite the philosophy and the beard. I think they would have been surprised and vaguely distressed, though, to know I was sleeping with him. Esther took a fancy to my mother and got herself invited to Hartford for two weeks in June. Gabrielle focused on my father, for whom she summoned up the evanescent French accent. Nina, who was beginning to don glamor like a costume—black silk blouse and gold chains around her neck—was flanked by a few of the hopeful boys. Steffie and Ray were persuaded to do, a cappella, "I Have a Song to Sing, O!" from last week's *Yeomen*, and afterwards Steffie politely excused herself—it was close to midnight and she had an appointment. Ray moved his chair closer to Evelyn's. Evelyn said little but smiled gnomically. She wore her smooth fair hair back in a knot like a ballet dancer's, though she did not dance. She used to fly down the dunes but lately she had grown languid; she took long, slow walks, my parents had told me. She said little, but I knew she was saving every perception for later dialogues with herself, or with flowers, or whomever she was telling her secrets to these days. Evelyn would know what George was right away. Laughing and eating pizza, I experimented; I tried to see him through her uncanny instincts. Yes, I had been right when, taking my bows after the "Trout," exulting in that rare satisfaction of the mind, I decided to finish with him. Even though what George offered measured high on Bentham's Hedonistic Calculus. The only category where it fell short was number six, Purity. The pleasure was not unalloyed—it was mixed with unease and self-doubt. I suspected other pleasures might yield more, and more purely: they were pleasures connected with working at music, with the density and tremulous candor Victor had shown, and with freedom from that dizzy levitation. They were connected, imprecisely, with the quote from Spinoza still tucked in a corner of my mirror, reminding me morning and evening that the effort by which each thing endeavors to persevere in its own being is the actual essence of the thing itself, and causing me discomfort when I returned from my endeavors with George. Those other pleasures had to do, too, with my wish to grasp what abides beneath the daily ephemera; George was part of the ephemera. And also, in a totally impenetrable way, with Thales' waiting, and waiting, to measure the pyramid by the measure of a man and the shadow he casts.

But I had said friends for life and meant to keep my word. I would do without the rest. In the crowd of family and friends, all busy eating and looking each other over, Victor and I gave no hint of our strange talk in the bar on Amsterdam Avenue near the unfinished cathedral. For all I knew, we might never talk again, but he had had his effect. I was feeling a bit sad and cruel about George, stirred by the romance of my own cruelty as the very young can be. Till it struck me, watching him assist Ray in amiably trying to "draw out" Evelyn (hopeless task if she was unwilling), that George would not be devastated. Almost anyone clever and athletic enough would do. I surveyed the table, flushed with my success, and thought, I will give him Nina, cleverer than I, and virginal.

Wedlock

Gabrielle, as a new mother, is bewildered and seeks a way out of her bewilderment through the language she learned at school, a language that sounds out of place in the park among the baby carriages, where we sit in the shade. She says that having been an English major, breathing in stories day and night, encourages the dangerous tendency to think of your own life as a story. No, better still, a novel. Of course, she adds with a meaningful glance at me, the tendency is not limited to English majors. It afflicts people with a certain organizing sensibility, people who expect that the structure of the universe will reflect the structure of the mind.

They used to call God Author of My Being, I say.

Ah, yes! But note, *nota bene* (she smiles at her own pedantry, her eyes momentarily alight behind the tinted aviator glasses, amber to match the copper of her newly cropped hair), how that author is distant and all-powerful. He's got a whole library. I meant each person as the author of her own being.

(*Nota bene*, she uses the feminine pronoun whenever she can, before it was popularly taken up, with the sweetly optimistic notion that a mountain can be removed grain by grain.)

Well, I guess we do act according to a script at times. It can't be helped, I respond lazily, and rock the carriage for her with my foot.

I'm not talking about a script, Lydia. A script is dialogue spoken in a particular setting. And a play moves single-mindedly towards a dénouement. But a novel, the sort of novel one could imagine one's life to be, at any rate, appears to meander, with a ragbag of concerns. Also—as she talks she gazes up at the sky,

shielding her eyes: will the weather stay fine for the baby?
—also a novel has commentary; no matter how absent an author
tries to be, it contains its own interpretation. A novel is an
attempt at interpretation. Your life can't be. That's why the
tendency is dangerous. You try to direct your life along the
route of beginning, middle, and end, but actually life has a
sprinkling of beginnings and middles and ends all the way
through, not in the right order. This—she looks at the carriage
containing Roger—is a beginning but it's also an end of something.
You try to see a cluster of major themes moving along, develop-
ing and elaborating, but actually in many lives the original
themes die out or become sublimated (absently she flexes and
points a foot, the way she used to do when she was training to
be a dancer); new ones arise out of nowhere. Plus we never
escape time, and real time is so dull and even, like a fox-trot. A
novelist can treat it whimsically, make it fly back and forth or
stand still. We never escape flukes, politics, weather. A novelist
makes her own flukes when she needs them, and her own
weather. It's a matter of control, she says wistfully. She peers
into the baby carriage, sprays a few drops of milk from the
bottle onto the back of her hand. If I ever wrote a novel, she
adds, I wouldn't bother trying to hide the fact that I was in
control. And rocks some more. Roger was conceived in foam—
she and Don had volunteered to test a new brand in the interests of science, part of a research project at his hospital.

I am one of those people she meant. I saw myself as a
character, growing and changing as they say characters must in
order to seem real. I would have allowed for inevitable
setbacks—no character evades those—but on the whole it was to
have been a cheerful novel, comedy not tragedy. (Would anyone write herself a tragedy? Perhaps, but not me.) A lifetime of
purposeful effort crowned by fitting rewards. The novel was
imbued with that deepest and most treasured of middle-class
notions: that life should, and would, reward good behavior.

School came to an end. For almost two years I shared an
apartment in the West Nineties with Gabrielle. During most of
the first year Victor was away in Europe looking at paintings—he
had relaxed his rule about not using his parents' money to make
the trip. After he returned he would call me every couple of

months. We would meet for dinner in chummy places where they let us sit for hours. One of our favorites was Simon's, because it had an immense suit of armor in the entryway and in one of the metal hands rested a heap of chocolate-covered mints. Victor pointed out that we chose the same sorts of things to eat, as if that were proof of affinity. What we chose were bloody steaks and shrimp and pasta dishes in winy, garlicky sauces, bitter greens doused in vinegar, pecan pie without the whipped cream. Whipped cream was too insubstantial. We ate greedily and talked about our work. Sometimes he asked to see my hands. He said he was interested in what all that practicing did to hands. I spread them on the table, palms down. "They are changing," he said. He examined the fingers, knuckles. "They look like hands that do something. Know something."

"Let me see yours."

His hands still had flecks of paint around the fingernails, and still looked older than he did. The lines were more pronounced; there were calluses and rough patches, and occasionally a small red diamond where the skin was scraped away and raw flesh exposed. He didn't bother with Band-Aids.

We were not lovers. We played a peculiar game of advance and retreat, with infinitely small, guarded moves. He considered that he had made his major move over two years ago in that bar near the unfinished cathedral: he was still waiting for a straight answer. I hedged, while we both went out with unimportant people whom we never discussed. I had the premonition that our becoming lovers would be an act of closure, that this phase of my life, not a very happy phase but one of curiously suspended potential, would come to a swift end.

He was drawing and painting all day and working in a bar four nights a week, as he had promised or threatened to do, a bar in the East Thirties that served suburban commuters in business suits juicing up for the trip home from Grand Central, and later in the evening, local drinkers. On weekends he went to the galleries, and read, and cooked enormous soups that could last for a week. "And what do you put in the soup?" "Everything I can find. It is an immense, thick, and variegated soup." He didn't accept any more money from his parents. I thought that was foolish. "If my parents were rich and wanted to give me money so I could spend my time learning to paint, I would take it."

"Have your parents offered you any money?"

"Well, yes, a little."

"But you would rather dash around town with four jobs at once, accompany the dance classes and do the children's theatre, et cetera, et cetera. So what's the difference?"

"There is a difference. My parents don't have that much to spare. And accompanying dance classes is not making drinks in a bar. I give them bits of Mozart sonatas. Prokofiev is very good for modern dance. I improvise. I'm a great improviser. So it's not a waste of time."

"I keep my eyes open. It's not a waste of time either. It's the same thing." He poked a fork into the crust of his baklava. Despite the immense and variegated soups he was thinner than he had been in school, almost gaunt, and yet his face was becoming less abstracted. Less secretive too. It was clear now that what I had taken to be critical disdain was simply untiring vision, eyes taking apart the world. The impatience I had sensed around the mouth was simply the wish to see through solid objects into what Matisse, he told me later, called their signs. I enjoyed observing him. I felt close to him now, though still wary. I could imagine us continuing our indulgent dinners every two months, comparing notes on our progress, indefinitely. Although after two glasses of wine I might begin to imagine him leaning close to me, and closer, as in those excruciatingly slow erotic approaches in old movies. But I would stop myself like a child covering her eyes at the scariest, most exciting part. I liked living with Gabrielle and going out on and off with undemanding men I didn't care much about. I told Victor how sometimes Gaby and I sat up at night and talked. He groaned. "Still schoolgirls. Don't you think I can talk too?"

"Well, but I like the idea of the apartment, also. You've seen it. It's nice, isn't it?"

"Very nice," he said mockingly. "Very, very nice."

I was in haste to live, to arrive at life itself instead of preparing. But I needed money. I worked at Schirmer's off Fifth Avenue four afternoons a week. The other clerks were young musicians too; we talked shop and gave each other leads on jobs, and during quiet spells sat in the listening booths with the new recordings. I got the accompanist work through Gabrielle, at the studio where she took classes every evening. Daytime she was a simultaneous translator at the UN, through her father's connections. And I had what Victor called et cetera, et cetera: the Children's Theatre, the Golden Age Club. I even played hymns in a Greenwich Village church Sunday mornings. Weekdays I got up at six and practiced in my nightgown for four hours, agonizing over whether or not to enter competitions as others were doing. I didn't feel myself a soloist; I had never liked being alone in a large space. I was an ensemble player, the kind of musician who comes to fullest life in a group, and I was happiest in the trio I had formed with Greg Parnis and Rosalie: we played at community centers, weddings, fancy parties, for a hundred or so dollars an afternoon. Rosalie was always late and frazzled because of three young children, but when she sat down with her cello it was worth the wait. And Greg was enterprising—he hunted up the jobs.

I was in haste to live, and yet everything I did felt suspended in an ether of tentativity. All impalpable, all potential. I had no patience with process. I envisioned real life as a fixed point of arrival, Evelyn on top of the dune at last, waving her arms triumphantly like a semaphore: Here I am! I was beset by fits of irritation and I read gloomy writers to give my irritation the firm grounding it lacked. In my purse was a depressing little quote from Schopenhauer about endless striving and the impossibility of true satisfaction. When I was feeling most impatient I took it out and read it with a perverse spite. Gabrielle scolded me. She refused to listen to Schopenhauer and sent me out to free concerts. I came home exalted and inspired. Until the doubts began again. What exactly was I preparing for? How to go about it? I looked at middle-aged people with wonder. Completed, their entelechies all unfurled, they had no questions in their lives, only solid answers.

Victor asked me, the second spring after I finished college, to come see his forty-five-dollar-a-month apartment on East Twenty-first Street. I hesitated, which amused him.

"Leery of men's apartments, Lydia? You spent half your junior year in that apartment."

"That was the year I was all mixed up. I've reformed."

"I know what it is. You're afraid you'll have to marry me, now that I'm poor."

"I thought I was supposed to like you better first."

"Oh, you like me well enough. Look, this isn't a come and see my etchings kind of thing. You should know that by now. I really want to show you what I'm doing. I come and hear whenever you play, even if it's *Oklahoma!* in deepest Queens."

He was right. I went. The apartment was in a bleak neighborhood, not slummy but quietly desolate, and the name V. Rowe, neatly printed below the mailbox in the downstairs hall, was shorter and simpler than its neighbors. The large room where he worked was freshly painted white, but the rest of it—kitchen, bedroom, bathroom, and hall—was the color of coffee with a few drops of cream. The kitchen contained one brown folding chair at a square table with a white porcelain top, the kind of table I remembered from my grandmother's house, when I was a child and it was wartime. The linoleum on the floor, supposed to look like red bricks, was pockmarked and curling at the edges. Apart from the minimal amenities, he had done almost nothing in the way of decoration. I would have thought an artist needed more visual thrills. And except for that one large windowed room, the place seemed hung with gloom, a gloom not created by Victor—he was never a gloomy person— but left behind by dozens of cramped, wretched families. Or so it felt to me. He was oblivious to the legacy of gloom; he said the apartment did not depress him in the least. It was more space than he had ever called his own, and he possessed the only key. That was thrill enough.

The small kitchen window faced another small kitchen window some five feet across a dingy airshaft. On that neighboring window was a tan curtain with a knotted fringe, between whose halves I could glimpse a table with a mottled top like the cover of a composition notebook. It held a potted geranium, a jar of Maxwell House instant coffee, a box of Rice Krispies, and a white flowered mug. Victor said an old woman lived there, and at eight sharp every morning she watered her geranium from a jelly glass. The window in the bedroom looked out over a half-empty parking lot, and his living room, or studio, windows faced a narrow concrete park where old Italian men in black jackets were playing a sober but joyful game of bocce. We stood at the open window—it was a warm twilight in April—and watched the balls bump into each other and roll about. Victor said he had figured out the rules of the game from watching so long.

He offered me a beer but I reminded him that I hated beer, so he gave me ginger ale instead and showed me drawings. Dozens. No more abstract blobs pushing each other around. There were drawings of the old woman across the airshaft, frail and angular in a cotton housedress that hung loosely on her bones. Her fine hair was in a knot. He had drawn her watering her geranium, eating her bowl of Rice Krispies, wiping her table with a rag. There were drawings of the Italian men playing bocce. Their bald heads and the bocce balls were akin and offered up lovingly, like Cézanne fruits. There were drawings of the parking lot—empty, with one car, with five, with many, yet always looking faintly bereft. Some cars had dents in their fenders, a couple had flat tires. I understood then that he worked with what was at hand and made much of it. The drawings were respectful of the significance of each thing, not reverent. They were truthful and without pretension, except for one of the old woman wiping her table. That one's sinuous lines seemed to romanticize penury in a way I didn't care for. What I found beautiful was how he treated each object with equal attention. There was no hierarchy of priorities, no background sketched in or merely suggested. The folds of the dish towel hanging from the handle of the old woman's refrigerator were drawn with as much care as the lines on her face. Except for the one, they were calmly celebratory, a triumph of attentiveness. I told him so. I said I liked them infinitely better than the blobs, and he smiled gratefully and kissed me lightly on the lips. I began to have one of my fantasies where we approached each other slowly, slowly, as in those movies, but he said he was starving, let's go out and eat, there was a good Italian place on Eighteenth Street.

After we studied the menu intently he reached out for my hand and this time completed the gesture, clasped it with fingers interlocking. We sat that way for a time. The food was brought but we ignored it for once. I was aware of the entire surface where his hand touched mine—the heel, the warm hollow of the palm, the press of the fingers—and from that clasp, as though it were captured in one of those optical toys that multiply and ramify a segment of space into a world of spaces, I could imagine the whole surface of his body and how it would be. Like finding the other half, as in the myth I loved in the *Symposium*. I didn't want the other half just yet. There was something equally tantalizing about being incomplete.

He looked at me in that piercing way that made me lower my eyes, but I didn't withdraw my hand. "So come back with me. Bring your piano and your toothbrush. It's about time, isn't it?"

"I've got to figure so many things out. I'm in limbo. About work, I mean, what to do next."

"I'm talking about love and you're talking about work. You can work all you want."

"If I just had a firm footing . . . I'd get distracted."

"That's ridiculous. You weren't distracted back when . . . you know."

"That was different. You're different. It would be the end of something, I know."

"Yes, the end of this stupid—" But he disciplined his temper, let go of my hand and smiled. "Do it the hard way, okay."

"I'm afraid of making a mistake."

"*I* would not be a mistake."

Oh, the arrogance of him. I thought love had to shake a person like an earthquake, but I was quite calm. A friend was another self, too easy, too comfortable. Slip right into it.

He gave a raffish tilt of the chin and dug into his saltimbocca. "You've lost all your nerve. It's a pity." Cutting, but I thought he was wrong. I thought it took nerve not to give in.

Lately Gabrielle had a strange, almost indifferent air about her dancing. The head of the company at the studio had told her that in a year or so, if she kept on, she might get to do small bits in performances. I was elated—real life!—but she was cool. She had a distraction. Don was a resident in orthopedics, and on his free weekends he took Gabrielle to dinner and the theatre. Formal dates, I teased. She told me, after the first date, that he had lived in a fraternity house at Amherst. "A frat house! Really, Gaby." She smiled as if I were a child who had missed the point entirely, and murmured that it wasn't important. Don was tall, though not as tall as Victor, and competent-looking; his smooth longish blue-eyed face had an ingenuous charm, glowing as if recently splashed with aftershave. He was nothing like his ingenuous face; he was sharp and even sardonic, though well-meaning. A pragmatist, a man who would go far, operating with brains and efficiency within defined boundaries. Even as a resident he had the assured, paternalistic manner of full-fledged doctors. I had to admit he was attractive, but, "Smooth and ordinary," I said when she asked. I never repeated it because the dates continued week after week.

When she was not quite ready, I, like the mother, made conversation with him in the living room. "And how is your music going, Lydia?" He crossed his impeccably trousered legs and leaned back on the couch, arm stretched across its upper rim, face fresh and expectant. Questions like that made me want to kill—how unlike Victor, who wished to see what was happening to my hands. But for Gabrielle's sake I said it was going well and asked politely how his orthopedics was going, and if he found that facetious I thought it no more than he deserved. When she entered the room he rose to his feet, a graceful unfolding, and radiated adoration.

They were all slipping into it. Esther had married Ralph, purveyor of the ocean, soon after college. Nina was engaged to a fellow graduate student at Princeton. And Evelyn! Towards the end of her junior year abroad, six weeks before she was expected home, came that letter announcing her wedding in June. We must come. René would send us the tickets and we would stay at his house. My mother phoned me from Hartford. My father was not accepting any tickets from a Swiss banker. "What do you think we should do, Lydia?" Since I had finished college she had taken to asking me for advice as if, with the degree, I knew something she didn't.

"We'll go," I said firmly. "But Daddy's right. We'll pay for our own tickets."

And so I spent a swift, baffled week in Alpine greenery, among oak furniture, leatherbound books, and *objets d'art*. Evelyn! My nighttime companion! Would she whisper secrets to him in bed at night? He was in his middle thirties, ruddy, exquisitely dressed and mannered, but I could not picture him appreciating the secrets of a girl like Evelyn.

I was spoiling for a fight and hadn't the heart to fight with Evelyn, who was sublimely inscrutable. In the ladies' room of the airport in Geneva, going home, I said to my mother, "What do you think he has, a gold-studded prick?" I would have been pleased had my mother threatened to wash out my mouth with the soap she was about to squirt into her hand. But she tilted her head sideways, pursed her lips, and shrugged, lifting her free palm eloquently to the ceiling as though I had expressed her thoughts to perfection. It was a new vision of my mother.

On the plane, while my father slept in the window seat, I thought I might try for another. "What do you think of this, Mom? Listen. It's about wanting things." I read her my quote from Schopenhauer. " 'The satisfaction of a wish ends it; yet for one wish that is satisfied there remain at least ten which are denied. Further, the desire lasts long, the demands are infinite; the satisfaction is short and scantily measured out. But even the final satisfaction is itself only apparent; every satisfied wish at once makes room for a new one; both are illusions. . . . No attained object of desire can give lasting satisfaction, but merely a fleeting gratification; it is like alms thrown to the beggar, that keeps him alive today that his misery may be prolonged till the morrow.' "

This time she looked as though she would have liked to wash out my mouth. And then she sighed—she had a wonderful, encompassing sigh for the mystery of it all—and patted my hand. "They have some very nice magazines to read if you're so desperate. All you have to do is ask the stewardess."

Two months later Gabrielle married Don, as I had known she would the minute I said "Smooth and ordinary" and saw her eyes bright blue and green with hurt.

I drank too much champagne at their wedding dinner at a French restaurant in an East Sixties brownstone. It was the sort of restaurant that had no sign outside denoting its existence and no prices on the calligraphic menu, but did have a silver medallion hanging from a heavy chain around the neck of the wine waiter. Gaby seemed very much at home in such surroundings; the more I drank, the more there grew in me a subversive notion that those four years in the dormitory and two years in the apartment, she had been an impostor. Maybe Evelyn was an impostor too.

Victor was not. Back in the empty apartment I phoned him, first at home, then at the bar.

"Hi. This is a surprise. I didn't even know you had the number."

"I know how to use a phone book. What are you doing there on a Saturday night?"

"Filling in for someone whose wife is having a baby. Watching a movie about the *Titanic*."

"I called to ask if you want to come over. If you can desert the ship."

"Is something the matter?"

"Does something have to be the matter for you to come over?"

"Of course not. But for you to invite me. I get off at midnight."

"I'll wait."

I knew I ought to drink coffee or take a cold shower, but I sat on the living room couch in a stupor. In my head blossomed images of the wedding—Esther holding hands with Ralph, Nina and her fiancé from Princeton clinking glasses, Gaby's dress, ivory with seed pearls. The images floated around, divagatory and surreal. Hypnagogic, Esther told me later when she was in social work school, is the word for that lush phantasmal quality of our thoughts on the verge of sleep. I moved in and out, listening for the doorbell.

He was dressed in an old denim shirt and tan chino pants, as he used to dress in college. I stared. The clothes made him younger. The intervening years might never have been. Kids again, and he was flirting with that rare lanky grace, one of a kind.

"Are you planning to ask me in, or don't you recognize me?"

I moved aside. "I'm sorry. Come in." It was so easy.

He put his arm around me. "What's the matter? You're all pale. And you're thinner. We haven't had dinner for a while."

"It's nothing. I'm a little drunk. I'll make some coffee. Is instant okay?"

"Sure." He followed me into the kitchen and watched my very slow and careful movements. "Why are you all dressed up? And you cut your hair. It makes you look like a boy."

I shrugged. I couldn't fix the coffee and converse at the same time. We stood waiting for the water to boil. "Hey, do you know I can play the harmonica? Since I last saw you." He pulled one out of his pocket and played snatches of songs: "Camptown Races." "This Land Is Your Land." "Auld Lang Syne." And the theme I loved from the "Trout."

"That's terrific. All by ear?"

"Yes. I remembered the 'Trout.' Are you touched this time? You're supposed to be."

"Well, I'm surprised."

"Come on, Lydia, after midnight on a breezy August night when you're drunk, you're allowed to be sentimental. I won't tell anyone."

"I am touched." I kissed him lightly. I swayed, and we laughed because it was so clearly not passion making me sway.

"I'd better pour it," he said.

We drank it on the couch. "Listen, I don't mind saying I'm touched. The reason I didn't want to say it is I wanted to say what I had to say first. So you wouldn't think it was because of anything you said. It's on my own. Do you follow me?"

"Barely. Come here and lie down." He pulled me over to him, with my head in his lap. "I think it's time I took advantage of you." He started to unbutton my dress. "What a nice dress. This blue is right for you."

"Wait."

"Wait?" He laughed. "It's the middle of the night, Lydia. You've obviously been out with some guy and got slightly looped and then you felt lonely. So you called me. Now what for, am I supposed to think? Okay, I'm not above that sort of thing."

"That's not the way it was at all. All wrong." I sat up. "Do you still want to marry me?"

"Yes. But less and less as time goes by, frankly."

"Oh God. Do you have to be so frank?"

"It's still a lot."

"All right. I say yes. I do. I mean, I will."

"Just a second. Why all of a sudden?"

"I want to, that's all."

"You just broke up with someone. You got ditched."

I shook my head. "I wouldn't do it like that."

"No? What if you change your mind when you sober up?"

"I won't."

"But you don't love me."

I looked at him. For one instant I felt sober. "I don't know, I might. I will, anyway. I promise."

"Ah, that doesn't sound so hot to me." He got up and walked around the room, running his finger nervously along surfaces.

He might have been checking my housekeeping abilities. "Why should I, that way? I could get over you. I just haven't tried."

"Oh Christ, Victor! You pestered me all this time. Didn't you think I was paying attention? So okay! But first go ahead and—what did you call it?—take advantage of me. I mean, we ought to see if it works, shouldn't we?"

"If it works! Oh, you're too much. Ought to? All of a sudden I ought to?"

"You wanted to a minute ago."

"'Tis a consummation devoutly to be wished, baby. But the way you say it makes me nervous."

"That's two of us, then. Well, go ahead and drag me to the bedroom by my hair."

"But you have no hair left."

I touched my bare neck. "I forgot. By an arm, then."

"What about Gabrielle? Is she going to walk in? Or is she out somewhere with that bone person?"

"Gabrielle?" I pulled him by the hand towards my room. "You are nervous, aren't you? No, she won't walk in. Anyhow, I'll close my door."

Victor looked around the bedroom. He had been over before, but never in my room. I knew how he liked to examine places at length. My room was brightly disorderly, a graduate student sort of room, with madras curtains, a Cézanne landscape, a piano, all my college books still alive with the aura of having been recently read. "Victor, you can study the place later."

"You are in a hurry." He put his arms around me. Every gesture he made was slow and attentive. His touch was less ardent than curious. It was wonderful, far better than I had allowed myself to imagine, but another feeling was even more powerful. He kissed me. "I've never seen you in this sort of hurry before."

"Because I'm going to pass out very soon."

"Lie down, then. What a seductress you turn out to be." He lay down next to me.

"I should tell you something." I could hear my own slow voice drifting peculiarly above my body. "Gabrielle just got married."

"Really? To that doctor? . . . Oh yes, you mentioned something about it last time."

"Yes. That's where I was all evening. That's where I got drunk. It's only fair to tell you."

"Fair?" He sounded puzzled. "Okay. I see." He didn't see yet, but I couldn't explain any more. He unbuttoned the rest of the dress and took it off me. I shivered. "Chilly?"

"Yes. Pull up the sheet. . . . Victor, I'm very sorry. I can't stay awake, even for you."

I thought he might be angry—he certainly had a right to be—but he only smiled. Maybe he was glad of the delay. He folded the dress neatly over a chair, and the last glimpse I had, he was at the bookshelf, looking for something to read.

It was pitch dark when I woke. I sensed someone there and got rigid with terror, then I remembered. "Victor?" I whispered. He touched my face. It was an unknown hour, and in the dark I felt I was seeing him. He was not the composed and bantering man I knew in daylight. I had never made love with someone who loved me. I found something out. I found out how a woman might be content to do nothing but tend her body and her surroundings—an extension of her body with a particular domestic appeal—content to wait in a vague mist of anticipation, for an hour of being made to feel like this. She could become a happy machine, greased and used and satisfied once a day, dormant and amorphous the remaining hours. Of course I couldn't take this seriously. Only a ripple of atavism—but it left a faint wake.

He turned on a lamp. "I want to see you. I could look at your face forever and never get bored."

"It's not so beautiful."

"No, I didn't mean that. I mean all those very distinct lines and planes, all the declivities. It changes from moment to moment—there's always something happening."

"Oh." That was an artist's eye, not a lover's.

"Don't worry. I also like it in the regular way."

I looked at him too, naturally at his body—young women are insatiably curious about men's bodies—but mostly at his face, which I had never seen so transparent since the day we first talked in that bar on Amsterdam Avenue near the unfinished cathedral, and I asked myself, could I face that face and body all the years to come, accept whatever unknown meannesses they hid, whatever seeds of unforeseeable change and drift, circumstance and accident, they might endure or provoke, and despite all, keep welcoming him home and in me? I thought I could. I didn't know, still, if all that added up to love. I had loved the making love, but that was not it. Perhaps the brimming willingness I felt, the admiration, and the desire already returning, with an exponent of time, added up to love. There was no ready-made calculus for this. I was so rapt in thought I missed something he whispered.

"I said, are you happy, Lydia?"

"I have never been this happy."

He wanted to make love again but I said, "There's something else I want to tell you, so my conscience is clear. So you won't think I've played any tricks."

"You're not pregnant?"

"Oh no."

"Don't give me any confessions, then. At least not right now. I don't expect you've been a nun. Neither have I."

"What a cute nun you would make, Victor. No, it's nothing like that. It's that Gaby and Don are going to live in the apartment."

"This apartment?"

"Yes."

"So?"

"Don has a place up near P & S, but it's two tiny rooms. It's really not possible for them. They were going to try it, but this place would be ideal. Except Gaby didn't want to put me out. She's very noble about things like that. But I insisted. Otherwise they'd both have to move, and this is rent-controlled, and she was the one who first found it, and it's so nice. . . ."

He was running a questioning finger back and forth over my lips. Over my words, as they spilled out.

"So Lydia winds up homeless."

"Yes."

"I get it."

It was a while till he spoke. "Lydia, if what you would really like is for me to help you find an apartment and rent a U-Haul and move your stuff in, I'll do that. You don't have to sleep with me for that."

"No. Now I want to live with you."

"Now? As opposed to when? A half hour ago?"

"Victor, I don't know myself any more. Now, that's all."

He rolled over onto his side with his head propped in his hand, and stared at me. I wanted to hide, or weep—there was such distrust in his eyes, but the same longing. I wanted to tell him that Gaby's wedding, the baffled week in Switzerland, all my uncertainty and confusion, my impatience with waiting for life to happen, had nothing, nothing to do with my phoning him at the bar—for they didn't seem to any more, now that I lay next to him. But I wanted also not to tell any lies; he never did.

"You can move in anytime."

"Thank you." I had to turn away. "The truth is, I don't know how to be alone. I need to be part of something."

He took my hands away from my face. "Look at me. When you said before that you'd never been this happy, was that true, or was that also convenient?"

"True."

"I have to take your word. What is your word worth?"

"If I tell you, it's still my word. Please." I pulled him close to me. I was afraid. "Let's not talk about it any more. It's splitting hairs. Don't you see how I feel about you here and now? Can't you trust that?"

"It's not true that you don't want to play tricks. You want to play them and then get credit for winning straight anyhow."

"But you won, Victor. You wanted me." I sat on top of him and moved around till he was inside me. He didn't help, just lay still. I had to say something to make him trust me again. It was crazy that I felt free enough to climb on top of him but not to honor him with the truth. If only I knew it. "That first conversation we had, in the bar. Remember I said it was your show and your script, and you said next time it could be mine? Remember?"

He closed his eyes and nodded.

"Well, so can't we leave it at that?"

It was a perilous moment, so close it was burdensome, so peeled we felt raw. So this was how it might be—we would scratch away each other's surfaces. There wasn't time to wonder if we wanted that, simply because it was impossible to stay still any longer. In the midst of it he stopped and pulled me down close to him. "But if you come to me this way, and I take it, then you must never leave, do you hear?" I nodded.

And then there was a moment when I longed to say, I love you, but I held back. People say things at those moments and aren't judged by them, everyone knows that—things like, You must never leave—but I felt this night could bear no more ambiguity. I would have to wait, for the luxury of saying that truth, till a moment when I was quite cool and he was quite sure of it anyway. That was the price.

The Greek Atomist Leucippus believed that every event in nature is inevitable, a result of the movements of certain groups of atoms in conjunction with other groups of atoms, and could we but be privy to the laws governing those movements we could understand and trace the inevitability of everything. It seems to me now, though, that none of it was inevitable. We engineered it together, this conjunction, over a period of three years. It didn't have to be, he would surely have gotten over me, while I consciously chose to fall in love when it suited me, which is not to say I fell any less; none of what came later had to be, either. We engineered the whole thing: out of an abrasion of wills and desires and affinities, we ourselves set in motion the movement of atoms, and with each of the million not inevitable but careless choices we made we narrowed the path, moved the atoms closer to their point of collision. All this we did in love and ignorance, trying to write our lives as best we could. For I never stopped feeling we were entitled to a good life. Leucippus believed that "Nothing happens at random; whatever comes about is by rational necessity." What necessity? Why? Why did our love necessitate what it finally did?

Esther was divorced after Ralph's breakdown and her miscarriage, her auto accident, and her visit to her senescent mother who asked if, despite all, she was happy. "If you're happy, then I'm happy too." And then in 1975, in the lingering wake of a Vice-President turned out of office and a President forced to resign, when the country was led by a man who had trouble delivering complex sentences extemporaneously, who innocently embodied a triumvirate of confusion, optimism, and righteousness, she remarried. How we marry! Our grandparents were forced to marry for convenience; our parents married for love. In the therapeutic seventies again we married for convenience, psychic convenience, to "satisfy needs"—quite different from love since love, in the long run, is rarely convenient. Her new husband's name was Clyde Powers.

"Clyde Powers?" said Victor when I showed him the invitation that had arrived in that Saturday morning's mail. Victor was not yet forty; those big bones and flat belly stood him in good stead. Even at moments when his intransigence pained me, I could still look at him with a primitive pleasure. "Clyde Powers? That doesn't sound like anyone's real name. Isn't it the name of that fellow in *An American Tragedy*?"

The invitation was a large glossy folded white card with a black-and-white photo of the nuptial pair covering the entire front. The smiles were beatific on faces pressed cheek to cheek and framed by halos of hair—Esther's fair and frizzed, Clyde's dark, long, and lank. Each head was crowned with a ring of daisies. Clyde looked some years younger than Esther, who was thirty-seven. His face was narrow, with small, avid, but unlit eyes. His lips were the only appealing feature—full and beautifully curved like a bow—but square little teeth spoiled the smile, and the wide gap in the upper row gave it a raunchy look. He was bare-chested except for a chain around his neck from which an obscure abstract pendant hung—it resembled the dove of peace but seemed to have excess wings, and it nestled amid copious hair. Esther was bare-chested too. You could see the beginning of the curve of breasts, but there, to my relief, the photograph was cropped. One daisy hovered fetchingly over her right eye. She looked luscious and hypnotized. Clyde's stubby fingers clutched the flesh of her shoulder as if for balance.

Victor opened the card and read aloud. " 'Esther Brickman and Clyde Powers. Holy Matrimony. June 8, 1975. Please come and share our feelings. SAVE Community, RFD No. 2, Pinecrest, New York.' SAVE?" He looked at me across the kitchen table—not the white porcelain table at East Twenty-first Street; we had come uptown to space and bright rooms and colorful streets. "What is SAVE?"

"Turn it over."

" 'SAVE. A self-help community of like-minded sharers united in Selfhood, Awareness and Acceptance, Vital Energies. Derek Holbrook and Clyde Powers, co-leaders.' "

"Let me see that," said Althea, raising her eyes from *A*

Wrinkle in Time. Althea, sophisticated at nearly twelve, liked to pretend she was a third adult in the family, and often sat drinking coffee with us weekend mornings. " 'Selfhood, Awareness, Acceptance, Vital Energies.' That should really be SAAVE. Like an ointment."

"Well, whatever it is," I said to Victor, "we really must go." *"Save* the date," Althea chirped, making us both groan. Victor raised one eyebrow in the droll and skeptical gesture he knew would make me laugh—he looked like Vincent Price haunting a house, especially since he had a beard now, grown during a fit of depression over his work. No one had wanted it and a critic called it derivative. If life was barely worth living, he said, shaving was worthless. After a while he had a show, sold a few paintings, and the feeling passed. The beard remained, for vanity.

We drove out to Pinecrest in Don's green Volkswagen bus which had taken our two families on countless Sunday outings over the years, with cries of When will we be there? erupting from six kids in the back. This time Gabrielle was missing— away for a month in France, showing the children to aging relatives. Nina sat up front with Don, George in back with Victor and me. It was the sort of day believed perfect for a wedding, but our spirits were not balmy. Don steered with an indolent thumb at the bottom of the wheel. "Does anybody know what this person does for a living?"

"Yes, as a matter of fact," Nina said in her lady professor's voice. "Right now his work is running the community, or commune, I guess I should say. He used to be a rock singer with a group called The Ramrods, but apparently there was something wrong with their vibes. Spiritually, not musically. He's also training to go out and run these, uh, self-evaluation gatherings, at which people save the good parts of their pasts and discard the bad parts, in order not to waste their vital energies brooding. That's one reason it's called SAVE, you see. Also, breathing properly is very important." She breathed herself; it was more of a controlled sigh. "He was married before, to a singer too. His wife ran off with another woman, I think."

"How do you know all this?"

She lowered her sunglasses and peered round at us from above them. "I spent a weekend there." The lady professor pose was gone; a sly urbanity replaced it. Nina was protean.

"A weekend? Then maybe you can tell me how to go, because I think we're lost."

"I took a bus. My car was in the shop. Sorry."

"You never even told me," I said. "How was it?"

"It didn't go terribly well. They told me I didn't relate enough. I said I was only there for a weekend, but that didn't seem to matter. Everybody watches everybody—do you remember *Candid Camera?* It's bad to show hostility. No, maybe it's good to show it, I forget, but in any case it's a crucial issue. Also, to be concerned with politics is bad. I was trying to make conversation—I mentioned something about whether Ford could ever get elected on his own steam, and they said if we all worked on ourselves the state would take care of itself. It's a farm. You'll see, they milk cows and make butter and cheese. The cheese is not bad." She took off the large sunglasses and turned to me with her special look of despair well under control. "I would say the cheese was the best part. The women bake bread but it seemed underdone to me. I don't know, though— I've gotten used to ethnic bread in the Village."

"It was nothing like the Pythagorean Brotherhood, I gather?" Zestful spiritual communion. Mathematical studies. Now and then, the music of the spheres.

"Nothing like it. I tried to take a walk in the morning but they asked me to stay and dish out granola."

Victor said, "It's not going to be so funny when she phones in hysterics. I remember the last time."

"It is the easiest thing in the world to mock an experiment," George said. "I think you're all just jealous that this sort of thing came into vogue when you were too old to enjoy it."

"That's not true!" They all laughed at my vehemence. Maybe George was right. I had spent the sixties dealing in diapers and puréed food, listening with passion to the radio accounts of revolution at Columbia, longing to be on the barricades. No matter what the dispute, simply to be in it, to be *with* and together *against.* Those were my buildings being captured and countercaptured, and I was not much older than the rebels. But I had one kid in kindergarten and one in nursery school and a third growing inside. Rocks were flying. I stayed home. "I'm not too old," I snapped at George.

"I for one am not jealous." Don let the bus steer itself for a few seconds while he tried to relight his pipe. "There's no need to throw out the baby with the bath. I managed to run the antiwar program at the med school quite nicely without behaving like a gypsy."

"Modesty, Don, was never your strong point."

"Well, and what of it? I got the job done when no other teacher would risk it. Here." He gave the pipe and matches to Nina. "Would you do this for me, please?"

"Incidentally, Clyde Powers is not his real name," Nina said with the pipe between her teeth. "His real name is Barry, or Barney, maybe, Weingrad."

Victor raised his eyebrow at me in the leering manner. "What did I tell you?"

"Oh, all right. Did you try to talk her out of it?" I asked Nina.

"Of course not. She seemed very happy. I didn't think I had any right to interfere. Aren't we a little old to tell each other whom to marry?" She lit the pipe and gave it to Don.

"In the case of Esther, I don't know. . . . I wonder if she'll change her name too. Remember Esther was the only one of us with the patience to get through *Being and Nothingness*? To go from that to SAVE!"

"It may be because of *Being and Nothingness*, not despite it." Don smiled appreciatively, as he always did at his own jokes.

"Bad faith. Remember how for a whole month she lectured us on bad faith? The forms bad faith may take are infinite. Denial of your own identity. Denial of the motives for your actions. Denial of your true situation in the—"

"Oh shit, Lydia, I just missed what might have been our turnoff." Don pulled over to the side and got out his map of New York State. "We are lost on our way to being saved. Hey, do you know, this must be skiing country. There are pictures of skiers all over the map. I bet in January this road is crammed with buses."

We arrived, eventually. A half-hidden sign led to a winding, branching dirt road, and from there on, the invitation was spiked to trees like blazes along a forest trail. We left the car in a pasture designated as a parking lot and walked through bristly grass towards an adjacent meadow where a group was gathered. George was doubtful about the scattered cows gazing at us with dusky, somnolent eyes, but Nina, who had grown up in farm country, assured him cows were not predatory. "Just leave them alone and watch out underfoot." One black and white cow accompanied us all the way to the wedding.

It was a set from *Oklahoma!* The women wore long skirts and bright, frilled, high-necked blouses—hybrid offspring of pioneers and European peasants. The men were dressed as cowboys, in fringed vests, plaid shirts, and boots, except for one man in a shiny black suit and black string tie, who was carrying a Bible. Victor, ignoring my advice, had perversely chosen to wear one of his two suits, the one that made him look like a stockbroker, even with the beard.

Esther rushed to greet us with hugs and kisses, rosy and aglow in billowy organdy, a wreath of daisies in her hair. She looked wonderful.

"I feel wonderful too. I have all my energies going for me, finally. Do you like the dress? Lillian made it for me, by hand." She pointed to an obese red-haired woman with a naked infant in a sling on her back. "Lillian went to Barnard too, but a few years after us. She was a math major but she wasn't happy with computers. She does all our clothes, so we can avoid the whole consumer trip." Her father would have been pleased: she was not being seduced by the offerings of capitalism. "Wait right here. I want you to meet Clyde." She brought us Clyde, who was exactly like his photo, except that his hair was clean today and tied back in a rubber band. Clyde looked long and steadily at each of us in turn, clasping our hands in both of his. This took a while. The SAVE emblem, that abstract design of a possible bird with a superfluity of wings, was tattooed on his right forearm in blue. "It is a real pleasure to know you," he said in an easy, midwestern accent. "Esther has spoken so much about you." He wore a red cowboy shirt with a small charging bull embroidered on the front pocket, perhaps by Lillian; as his chest rose and fell with conscientious deep breaths before each sentence, the little bull appeared to be charging off the shirt, at us. "I hope you'll all get into our reality while you're here, and allow yourselves to experience the ethos of SAVE, which is something real unique. We try to dig out and bring forth our root feelings of caring and sharing without blocking—"

"Clyde," Esther interrupted, "why don't we introduce them to some of the others."

"That's a good idea, Esther." He led us around to various members of SAVE, who greeted us with pats and strokes. Nina was generally taken to be paired with Victor, which was understandable: she was dressed in a white linen suit and silk scarf, as befitted the consort of a stockbroker. One graying man slipped his arms around their waists and patted their hips. "Have you people attended our SAVE gatherings or are you just friends?"

"These are old friends of mine, Phineas," Esther explained, gently withdrawing his hands. "And you remember Nina Dalton."

"Ah, yes. You were shy about your hostilities. Well, that's all right. Have no anxiety. We'll help you all get in touch with the deeper participation levels."

"Thank you," said Victor. "We're a little thirsty after the trip, actually. . . ."

"Oh, of course. I'm sorry," Esther said. "There's homemade apple cider over there on that table, and some rum punch too."

A man with a very long, wide white beard like Walt Whitman's came up to Nina and took both her hands in his. "I believe I've seen you here before. I am interested in you. I am interested in the kinds of feelings that must be straining to emerge, since you appear so put together. What's your trip?"

"My trip?"

Victor was tugging at me. "Let's go over there. I want a drink." We left George hovering protectively near Nina and the Whitmanesque man. Don, already at the bar, handed us each a glass. Victor examined his suspiciously. "What is this stuff? I want a real drink. Especially if I have to get in touch with myself at the roots."

"It's not too bad."

Victor sniffed it, drank it in one gulp, took another, and placed a hand flat on my breast. "I am interested in you. In the root feelings that are straining, I mean, all those vital saps and so forth. Your deepest participation levels."

I brushed his hand away. "Look, as long as we're here, would you please . . ."

"Well, if you don't want to get in touch with your vital energies, I'm going off to, uh, relate to others who do."

I stayed with Don. I was hearing, as I often did, the soothing voice of Professor Boles. Empedocles, reconciler, doctor as well as mystical poet . . . He too sought the roots—fire, air, water, and earth—from which the earth proliferated like a wondrous plant. He did not need to dig up the roots, though, in order to appreciate the plant in its infinite variety. Poking at the roots destroys the living plant; Mr. Wilson, back in the garden at the brown house, warned Evelyn and me about that.

"Do you think there'll be anything to eat, Lydia?"

Don sounded so plaintive that I laughed. "Of course there will. Do you see those women with the checked aprons, carrying buckets and pots? Their role is to prepare the feast. It will contain lots of homebaked bread, plus there will be sprouts. Every kind of sprout you can think of. Cheese, vegetables, lots of salads. It will be very good, as well as good for you."

"But I feel like oysters. This kind of thing makes me feel like eating oysters."

I nodded, and we stood companionably silent. Don was not an exhilarating person, but he had many placid, Nordic virtues: He could keep his feelings to himself; he would never behave in an embarrassing manner; if any of the Saviors wandered over to talk he would listen politely. I realized I had grown very fond of him over the fourteen years. Maybe Gaby hadn't been mistaken after all.

"It also brings out my worst impulses," he said. "Reminds me of what I did to Mr. Dooley when I was in college."

"What did you do to Mr. Dooley?"

But he had no chance to tell me. "Please assemble, please assemble for the ceremony." The tenor voice of the minister in the black string tie. With the Bible tucked under his arm, he clapped his hands for order like a dancing master. Nina and George and Victor drifted back.

"That guy with the Bible is Derek Holbrook, the other leader," Victor whispered to me, "but that's not his real name. He changed it from Joe Rossino."

"How do you know?"

"He told me. They don't believe in books. The Bible is just for show, because some members aren't emotionally ready to give it up at weddings. It's called a transitional object, like a baby's blanket."

"Come on, you're making this up."

"No art, either. Music is okay, but they prefer to compose

their own. Like in *The Republic*, you remember. Artists from the past inhibit the flow of vital energies. The past does not exist. Dead. Life begins anew each day. If you're hung up on memory it means you're into death, which is of course not good."

Gradually the guests formed a large circle around Derek, Esther, and Clyde.

"Sex is not more than twice a week," he breathed hotly in my ear. "The vital energies, you know. Once is even better, if you can manage it." He put his arm around me. "We could kidnap her. They wouldn't prosecute. Law is repression of individual vital energies. Not that they're anarchists; they just don't relate to government."

The black and white cow that had ambled through the festivities mooed loudly, which silenced the crowd.

"Dearly beloved." The ceremony began.

Derek explained that weddings at SAVE did not follow the traditional format, which had originated in a long-dead age and thus had no relevance to the needs of Clyde and Esther. Weddings at SAVE were a celebration of openness and awareness, which meant going around the circle asking the guests to state their feelings on this occasion. In that way good feelings could be exposed and maximized and bad feelings evacuated, leaving the vital energies to flow creatively from their roots, without hindrance. He would begin with the bride.

Esther must have been prepared. With just the proper degree of warmth and reserve she announced that she was very happy, she loved Clyde very much, she was grateful to all the friends who had come to the wedding, and she hoped she and Clyde would continue for a long time to be good to and for each other.

I turned reflexively to Nina and found her clever, doleful eyes waiting for mine. We exchanged a glance of pride and relief, as when an unruly child performs well in public. Women's colleges do foster a certain adaptability. Esther could also pour tea admirably, which might win her praise in SAVE's kitchen, where she would no doubt be spending a good deal of time. But her composure made me shiver. In college when she read Descartes she vowed to believe only what she had proven for herself. "Nothing on faith!" And we had laughed at her.

It was Clyde's turn. He disengaged his arm from Esther's and rubbed his hands together, the gesture of a man about to dive into a feast. "As I look around me on this wonderful day," he said, looking around him, "I see old faces and new ones, faces from the past and faces from the present. And yet they are all sharing in the one reality that is right now, which is all we have. That and our own energies, our needs and gratifications." Esther's face was beginning to show the signs of heat and weariness. She shifted her weight from one foot to the other and cleared her throat softly. "I want to say that on this occasion of my wedding I feel I am getting in touch with and reaching into a deep part of myself I have never reached before, and which will yield more and more awareness and energy." With each deliberate breath the little bull on Clyde's shirt lurched. "I'm glad to have Esther to share this exciting awareness with me." He grabbed Esther's hand and raised it high above his head like a prizefighter accepting the championship title. People applauded. Behind me George moaned.

A wispy girl of about nineteen with hair like straw said a wedding out in the pastures with the cows made her feel close to nature. A dark man in mirrored sunglasses and overalls said he felt happy for Clyde since Clyde was his friend and he loved him, but at the same time he had to acknowledge he was sexually attracted to Esther and therefore experiencing some envy; he hoped he would be able to overcome those feelings but if not he hoped they could all get together sometime and talk about it. Esther turned pink while Clyde nodded judiciously like someone making a mental note. The next speaker was convinced from his own experience that marriage could be a trap; he advised Esther and Clyde not to become emotionally dependent but always to preserve their own spaces. Esther's face was all earnest attention (perhaps what SAVE called "openness"), so unlike the morning Professor Mansfield asked her to adopt the sensibility of another age and suspend her judgment. "I will never suspend my judgment!" I could still hear the fierceness in her voice.

"We're not getting any sharing from the people in back," said Derek. "How about you, Vic? You were just telling me you needed to learn the language of feeling."

"God, you didn't!" I jabbed him.

He nodded. "You don't get all that information for nothing. I'm afraid I'll have to pass," he said out loud. "I can't learn that fast."

"There's no passing at SAVE. We share whatever is in us."

"Well, then, on this unusual occasion I feel . . ." He paused and his silence felt ominous, especially with all the rum punch he had drunk.

I took his arm. "Please don't. Just wish them good luck or something. As a favor to me."

"I wish you both a long and happy life together," said Victor. "And may your hopes in each other be fulfilled."

I breathed. George volunteered that he felt hunger and thirst and sexual desire and he wished they would move along with the ceremony so he could at least get something to eat. The SAVE members tittered. That propitious *savoir faire* doubtless came from the numerous marathons George had attended, studying experimental therapies.

Derek called on me. I said that Esther was one of my oldest and dearest friends, and since she seemed so happy, I was happy for her. Neat, honest, more or less—I congratulated myself. Then I remembered her mother—"If you're happy, then I'm happy"—and I wanted to die of shame and remorse. Esther did not give any outward sign, though. She went on smiling the same modest, composed smile. Her liberal education served her well.

"I think we've had a pretty full expression of the ongoing feelings here," Derek said. "Is there anyone I missed, before I go on to the mutual vows?"

"Yeah, you missed me." It was a pale, bedraggled young woman in baggy jeans, standing disconsolately on the outskirts of the circle, her arm around another woman. They might have been sisters.

"Why, Floral, certainly. Please go ahead."

"Yeah, well, I'm glad of the chance to say what I feel on this occasion. I'm not sure why Clyde invited me—I never thought I'd see this place again after we split up—but as long as I'm here . . . I sincerely wish Esther luck because you're going to need it, Esther. Clyde is a person who is only into his own need to be told how terrific he is. Anyone who doesn't do that, he gets rid of. Also, he can't take the slightest criticism, like if you say he hung a picture crooked he thinks you're hostile and trying to castrate him." Floral's voice was extremely low and hoarse. I couldn't imagine her as a singer. She coughed as she spoke, a curt, stifled cough that barely interrupted the flow of words. "As far as a wife, forget it. What he really needs is a slave. I know he goes around saying I walked out on him, but it was the other way around. I was the one who wound up in the hospital on lithium, and if it hadn't been for Susan I wouldn't be standing here right now. And believe me, I'm not saying any of this out of jealousy or because I want him back, God forbid, but I wouldn't mind getting back some of my records that he took, especially the Janis Joplin and the—"

"That's enough! Shut the hell up!" Clyde shouted. "You're as crazy as ever and you're not going to mess up—"

"Don't you tell me what I'm going to do! We're not married any more, remember? I'll talk as long as I damn—"

Clyde lunged through the crowd. Floral's friend Susan tried to pull her away toward the parking lot but Floral shook her off and braced herself to receive Clyde. Some of the SAVE members caught him by the arms. He struggled to get free. Everybody was shouting. "Let him get it out!" "No, keep her back!" "Hold him!" "Get the fuck off of me!" "Violence is cathartic if you really get into it!" the man with the Walt Whitman beard roared. There was a bunch holding Floral back too. "Dumb dyke!" Clyde shouted at her. He got one arm free and swung at a man restraining him. Another man swung at Clyde and missed. Factions pushed and shoved; the wedding was a brawl. But it quickly dissipated. Susan pulled the reluctant Floral off in the direction of the parking lot, and the SAVE people broke ranks and smoothed down their cowboy outfits. The next moment their smiles were back in place, and they were patting and stroking each other to maximize the good feelings. I thought again of Empedocles, prophet of Love and Strife. "Now one prevails, now the other, each in its appointed turn, as change goes incessantly on its course. . . . Interpenetrating one another they become men and tribes of beasts." He called his time the Present Age of Strife, "a land without joy, where bloodshed and wrath and agents of doom are active; where plagues and corruption and floods roam in the darkness over the barren fields of Ate." " 'I wept and mourned,' " Gaby had read to us years ago, " 'when I discovered myself in this unfamiliar land.' "

Derek was brief; the incident that had just occurred would be evaluated later, he said, at the evening meeting. As he pronounced Clyde and Esther man and wife the group took up an unmelodic chant whose syllables refused to congeal in my ear as words. It reminded me of the early computer music the professors at Columbia were experimenting with back in 1958. To this wail, Clyde took Esther in his arms for the customary kiss. He kissed her long and with a show of passion, forcing her to arch her back and neck the way Charles Boyer used to do to his heroines in the movies, a position I was sure must be hard on those muscles, delicate since the whiplash she suffered in the auto accident years ago when her first marriage broke up.

Nina was wrong about the bread—it was excellent.

"Do you have to go so soon?" Esther asked.

"Yes, we'd better. It's a long drive. The sitter . . . Come into the city for a weekend. We have more room now."

"I'll see when I can get away. Listen, I'm really glad you all came. I appreciate it. I know it's not your kind of thing but . . . It's really okay. It's going to be fine."

"Of course it will," said George. "Congratulations." And he kissed her sweetly good-bye. I kissed her in bad faith. Nina offered Victor the front seat in the VW bus so he could see the countryside better—it was a soft amber and rose twilight. He and Don took off their jackets and ties and speculated, in a quiet, desultory way, about what kind of deal had been made when Ford pardoned Nixon. In back we were silent. After a while Nina rested her head on George's shoulder and they held hands. So this would be another of their sporadic nights together. To cheer them up, as she once explained. Yet now that I thought of it, those nights were not always on depressing occasions; they were really rites of passage. They made love for weddings, births of children, the time Nina got tenure at NYU, Esther's divorce, George's setting up a private psychotherapeutic practice, the openings of Victor's shows every few years, some of my concerts, a party for Gabrielle when the cast was removed from her broken leg. They prolonged the good feelings, smothered the bad ones. Something like SAVE. I closed my eyes and tried to sleep, but Don was telling Victor the story about Mr. Dooley. It seemed Mr. Dooley was the boss of a messenger service where Don worked with a bunch of kids the summer he was eighteen.

"What an old bastard that guy was! Like something out of

Dickens. We decided to take revenge. He had this big black cane, and when he left it in the office during lunchtime one of us would go in and saw off an eighth of an inch. Only every few days, though, so he wouldn't notice. He had a funny look once in a while, but he never figured it out. It was terrific. He didn't know why the world felt a little more askew each week."

"What a sweet boy you must have been," Victor said.

"No, I was, actually. He just brought out the worst in me."

"So what happened?"

"He fell getting into the elevator and broke his ankle."

Mr. Dooley and his cane became a hypnagogic image, and I slept.

"Lydie." Nina nudged me. "Wake up. We're in the city. We've decided we need a drink."

We were parked in front of a bar in the Village, not far from Nina's apartment. Victor phoned to check on the children, and then we all settled in peacefully, for though we were sleepy and glum we were not yet inclined to part. George, never much of a drinker, which he attributed to his Judaic upbringing, asked the waiter for a glass of seltzer. "Not club soda. Seltzer. Do you have it?" He was in luck.

"Comfort me with seltzer," George said, "for I am sick of love."

"Tell us the seltzer story," Nina urged. "We need it."

"Oh, I've told you a dozen times." He took her hand and kissed it gallantly. "Aren't you tired of it yet?"

"No. Are we?" She looked around.

We were not, so he told us once more how, when he was a small boy in the Bronx, every fourth Wednesday morning at seven-fifteen a seltzer man would ring the bell and he, being up and dressed for school, had the job of letting him in, giving back the box of empties and accepting the box of fulls, while his father and his two uncles puttered around, shaving, dressing, saying their morning prayers with a special mention of the Jews in Germany and Poland, and fixing breakfast. "He was a huge man with a huge belly, and he carried a long wooden box with ten bottles, two rows of five, on his right shoulder, plus two extras in his other hand. I thought it was marvelous, how he kept the box balanced up there with one hand. I thought he must be the strongest man in the world. And the bottles were so beautiful—blue and translucent, with blue bubbles inside, because they had been jiggling around on his shoulder all the way up in the elevator. They had chrome squirt tops. He carried it all the way down the hall to the kitchen, with me following him, and when he set it down on the floor he always let out a great groan and said, 'Well, my lad, how many this time?' It was always twelve, every month, but each time he said, 'How many?' and I said, 'Twelve, please.' My father had told me I must say please. Then he took a deep breath before he lifted the box of empties, and I followed him back down the hall. And then my uncle, the senior rabbi, would come to pay him at the door and make polite conversation—my uncle believed in treating every person he met with equal regard. But he never seemed to grasp that while he was chatting on about the weather, and the war, and the rationing—wasn't it a good thing they didn't ration seltzer?—and so forth, the seltzer man was carrying these ten heavy bottles in the wooden box on his shoulder, plus the two in his other hand. The seltzer man was very polite too, an Irishman, I think, and as soon as he could get a word in he would say, 'Righto, well, I'd best be on my way.' At supper they would always let me squirt the seltzer into the glasses, and when they asked me what I wanted to be when I grew up, I said a seltzer man. Even now, I must say, I still have these fantasies. . . ."

The waiter brought the drinks and George drank his seltzer with zest. Don downed his martini very quickly. "Tell me something," he said to George. "What is the difference between those people in Pinecrest and what you do? No offense, of course."

"Of course." George, master of tolerance, smiled, the way Charlie Chaplin might smile at William Buckley. "The difference is that I don't attempt to evade the human condition. Freud was right, you know. There is no remedy, there is only alleviation. The remedy is death."

"I didn't know you were a Freudian," I said.

"Well, not in all the particulars, no. But fundamentally . . . Look, nowadays there are the saviors, and then there are the repairmen. Freud would have hung in with the repairmen, I'm sure. That way you keep some self-respect, professionally. I'm like the guy you call in to fix your washing machine. You know it's going to break down eventually, but meanwhile you want to keep it running as best you can for as long as you can, get the worst kinks out so it can do its job. Saviors scare me. There are enough built-in dangers around."

"Excuse me." Nina got up. "I'm going to stroll home. It's been a long day, and I am still not saved."

"I'll walk you. It's dark." George got up too. I always found this absurd pretense of discretion very touching. "Good night, good night." Kisses and handshakes. Still full of energy, he took her firmly by the arm and led her away.

"Off to consummate the marriage," said Victor morosely. "That's nice."

"It's funny what weddings do to people," Don said. "I mean even good weddings. I had a patient once, a young woman with a case of hysterical paralysis. She couldn't move her legs, but there wasn't anything organically wrong. It started a couple of days after her wedding. All she could tell me was that she had danced and danced till she was ready to drop. At first she thought it must be a charley horse."

"So what did you do?"

"I sent her to a shrink."

"And?"

"Oh, eventually she walked. Everything worked out all right. She even became pregnant."

"Remember when Gaby broke her leg? That was pretty soon after you were married too."

Don looked at me keenly. "Gaby was thrown off a horse."

"I remember. But still. She had ridden all her life. It was only a few months before she was supposed to join the company."

"The horse was galloping, Lydia. It took the fence all wrong. It sometimes happens."

"Yes. But dancers break things all the time and then they go right back to dancing. You of all people know that; it's half your practice."

"She had to stay off her feet a lot. She got pregnant." He smiled with appreciation.

"It's not a laughing matter." Foam, good Lord. But I held my tongue.

"You know, Lydia, you wanted her to be a dancer more than she wanted it herself."

"Maybe. Maybe." But he hadn't known her in college. All

those nights, all that flexing, pointing, arching, dreaming, the passion in it. Did she widen the space between her thighs to a hundred eighty degrees just to take him in? Sure, things changed, lives changed, and we all needed our children, if only to affirm the roots, seeds, growth, and flowering of the universe. But beneath that were supposed to abide earth, water, air, and fire, unchanging. Most especially fire, the wanting and the striving. What happened to douse hers?

Don ordered his third martini; Victor and I got coffee. I suddenly felt obnoxious, spoiling for a fight as I had in the airport in Geneva after Evelyn retired to the mountains at twenty. "Why do you guys think they used to bind the feet of Chinese women?"

"Wasn't it supposed to make them more attractive?"

"Discipline," said Victor. "So they'd take small steps, literally and figuratively."

"Ah, Victor, you're so poetic, my love, it's beautiful. Did you learn that in CC? No, I'm sorry, you really are. All right, but in practical terms, they bound their feet so they wouldn't run away. Ask any girl—she doesn't have to be educated to know that. Ask Althea. You ask Cynthia, Don. Your patient was well-trained, that one who got paralyzed. These days we bind our own feet." I got up and stalked to the bathroom. I glimpsed them looking after me, bewildered—poor guys: what did we do this time?

When I came back they were laughing and horsing around, Don with the defiance of a man who has been unjustly scolded and is getting good and drunk in return.

"Sick as hell anemia," he was saying. "You wouldn't believe what people report that they have. Fireballs in the uterus. Jesus."

"*What* in the uterus?"

"Just true medical tales again, Lydia," said Victor. "Forget it, you wouldn't approve."

Don put his head in his hands. He had stopped laughing. "Smiles of Gentle Jesus."

"What?"

"Spinal meningitis. In Appalachia, when I was an intern. The mother said he had Smiles of Gentle Jesus." He looked up; his face was drained of color. "I had to watch that kid die. I still remember his face from seventeen years ago." He took another gulp of his drink and shuddered.

"Don't have any more, come on. This is no good. Have some coffee." Victor pushed his cup over to Don, squeezed my leg under the table, then took my hand.

"What a day. God, I wish Gabrielle would come home. I'm a mess alone. I can't even match my socks. Well, no, of course I can. I mean, I just miss her. I haven't seen my kids in three weeks either. I miss those sullen adolescent faces."

"Enough. It's time to take you home in your little green bus," Victor said. "I'll drive. We'll get a cab from there."

"I'll drive," I said. "I'm sober and I've never driven a bus."

"Oh," sighed Don, drinking some more. "Poor Esther. The crazy reasons we get married."

"You seemed quite sane, as I remember. You went about it very methodically, bringing her flowers, taking her to the theatre, all dressed up."

"It was lousy, being a resident then. Besides all the people crippled and dying, we had to work round the clock. We didn't know enough to organize for better conditions. You remember what it was like. No one thought of protesting. They have it much easier now." He swallowed the last of the martini. "We, on the other hand, longed for a little comfort. And she was oh so comfortable." He winked lewdly.

"In all these years we've never seen him like this," I said to Victor. We laughed, holding hands and gazing at Don.

He set down his empty glass sharply. "How did you two happen to get together?"

"Us?" Victor turned to me with that raised eyebrow again. He was really overdoing it. "Oh, we got married because you and Gaby got married. Isn't that right, Lyd?"

Superstition

When Althea was born, in 1963, my mother and Victor's mother came over nearly every day to help, because I was sick and weak, my mind torpid from anesthesia. In the hospital a realization had crept up on me insidiously like a mouse in the dark, a mouse whose presence you suspect, yet who you hope will never appear. I was responsible for the survival of this creature. It was paralyzing. Who the creature was in relation to me, my body, was a riddle: no longer part of my flesh, yet if I accidentally pricked her with a pin my nerves jumped in harmony with hers. I had headaches and inexplicable spells of fever, and my stitches were infected. The infection was painful and lingering. I took it as symbolic—I had been torn and would never heal.

My mother and Edith, who behaved in a saintly way, were in what they only half-jokingly called the prime of life, their middle fifties. My father had been promoted and transferred to the New York office of his insurance firm, and my mother loved the change. She became chummy with Edith. Afternoons, they went to matinees and movies, occasionally to lectures or panel discussions at worthy institutions. Victor said a peripheral benefit of our marriage was the bringing together of two such compatible women.

My mother took on an elegance but I knew it was detachable, like a zip-out lining. I remembered her before she had had the leisure for elegance, before the prime of her life. I remembered her with metal clips in her hair, a frumpy apron tied round her waist, her hands sunk to the knuckles in raw chopped meat. I had seen her scale fish for dinner (the man in the store did not meet her standards), with newspaper spread on the kitchen table and scales spattering like hail from the quick strokes of her knife. I had seen her rub lemon juice on her hands to get rid of the fish smell, then patiently hook up the long-line bra that disciplined the flab around her middle. My mother's newfound elegance was a triumph of pride against a backdrop of labor. But I had never seen Edith other than flawlessly mannered, dressed, coiffed, and accessorized, and so I was embarrassed by the shabby chaos Victor and I lived in. I needn't have been. Edith wished to be neither intimate nor critical, simply useful. She ignored the paint rags and canvases, the piles of music and cartons of records in our living room, the only room large enough for storage. When I halfheartedly apologized, she hushed me gently; she understood we were young people and busy working. But if ever we wanted her cleaning lady for a day . . .

The first two weeks I was home from the hospital their visits often coincided. Together they would change into slacks carried in smart tote bags, tie scarves around their lightly lacquered hair, and vie courteously for the privilege of carting dirty laundry to the laundromat around the corner or peeling potatoes for our dinner. No more snacks grabbed at odd hours: they insisted we eat regular dinners, especially since I was nursing Althea. Together they lugged bags of healthy food from the supermarket on Twenty-third Street. And they sat amid the living room debris, on our Salvation Army overstuffed chairs, drinking coffee and reliving their own ordeals of childbirth, while I lay nearby on a mattress on the floor, reading and eavesdropping. I had been told to get as much rest as I could—besides the fevers and the stitches and the atrophy, I was slightly anemic. I was reading Trollope. Gaby, who knew about childbirth and had unerring taste, had brought me three novels in the hospital. "These should get you through two weeks," she said, "and then you'll be fine. If you need any more, he wrote about four dozen others, all very long." I had a pile of things I ought to have been looking at—Brahms scores for our trio, a new biography of Haydn, the first act of an operetta one of my students at the Golden Age Club was composing. But only Trollope would do. The once-bright paisley cover on the mattress was stained and stiff in places, from love-making; I hoped the mothers could not infer that by looking. I wished they would take it to the laundromat along with the baby clothes, but hesitated to ask. I could not imagine ever flopping down on that mattress with Victor again, throwing our clothes blithely around the room, any more than I could imagine telling my own story of childbirth years from now, interspersed with chuckles. I was busy suppressing it.

When they left, chatting their way down the dusty stairs, I leaned against the doorframe in my bathrobe, straining my ears for the last notes of their voices and feeling the panic approach. I kept it at bay by carefully mapping out the hours until their return, like a child left alone in a strange place. I could feed her and dress her well enough. If only nothing unexpected happened . . . Once I confessed this panic to my mother. She stroked my hair and squeezed my chilly hands. "Don't *worry*," she said firmly. "Every day you get stronger." I burst into tears. I could cry at a touch. The tears were so ready and eager to spring; it disgusted me.

Now and then I would stare at the piano and play a melody with one hand, barely pressing the keys, like a timid student. A few times I sat down, longing for the music, but with a perverse urge to fail. At the first infelicity I would cry, bitter, spiteful tears: I told you so. I knew the effort it would take to get rid of those infelicities, and how unequal I was to any effort. So I would crash my palms on the keys, which woke Althea. I picked her up and we cried together, flesh to flesh, each of us seeking comfort in the source of the tears.

I tried to play records, but I was used to playing them very loud, to hear every detail, and this too woke Althea. I was furious and wanted to leave her crying in the wicker bassinet, but she might choke, burst her larynx, develop asthma, require psychoanalysis in later life. Always an extremist, and proud, I wouldn't turn it down to capitulate to an infant. I turned it off instead. I picked her up angrily and let her suck me dry.

Greg, the violinist in our trio, phoned one afternoon as I lay on the sex-stained paisley-covered mattress. My mother was sitting nearby with the baby in her arms. Greg said he had persuaded the community relations people to have us play at the fair.

"What fair?"

"You remember, Lydia. The fair at All Angels, in three

weeks. They're raising money for their nursery school, or sports program, I forget what. I told you and Rosalie about it weeks ago."

"I didn't even think they had a piano. They probably think you're a string quartet."

"They have a string quartet, for downstairs. Jeffrey Rice is doing that, with Emily and those other two from Juilliard. We're going to be in the main part. They'll bring in a piano. It'll be terrific, Lyd. It's a great place, and we can play anything we like for four hours. The Mendelssohn, if you want. The 'Dumky.' We can take breaks one at a time and do duets. We'll do the 'Spring' Sonata, everyone likes that. You'll be great, you're a closet romantic. It's a hundred fifty bucks, maybe more, depending on what they take in. And the exposure."

"No."

"What do you mean, no?"

"I can't. I don't feel well."

"It's in three weeks! Are you nuts? In three weeks you'll be fine. My wife's been through it twice; believe me, I know. You'll be dying to get out."

"No. I have to go now."

"Lydia, what's the matter with you? We've been doing this for three and a half years and we're just getting somewhere. In the spring we might play at Hunter—Rosalie met the guy who does the programming. Anyhow, where are we supposed to find someone at the last minute?"

"It's not the last minute. There are a million pianists around. I went to school with this girl Henrietta Frye. She's better than I am, actually. I'll give you her number."

After I hung up I handed my mother a slip of paper. "I'm going to take a nap. Could you do me a favor, please? Call this number and ask for Mrs. Rodriguez and tell her I can't come in next week and . . . I can't come in at all any more."

"What is this all about?"

"Look, would you just call, please?"

"No, I won't just call when I don't know who I'm talking to and what I'm talking about. I don't want to sound like an idiot."

I sighed. "All right. It's the Golden Age Club at a community center uptown. I go there one day a week. They have a chorus that I conduct. There's a group that learns sight singing. A couple of them take piano lessons. This and that. I said I'd be back next week but I can't."

"Lydie." She shook her head sadly. "You're making a mistake."

"Ma," I wailed. "I can't sit. My crotch is killing me. I can't play. I can't do anything."

"For heaven's sake, you have a mild infection. It'll be gone in a few days. With all your education, didn't you ever learn that things can change? You're not always going to feel the way you do right this minute. In two weeks you'll feel like a different person."

"I already feel like a different person. Will you call for me, please? I'm too tired." And you never told me it would be like this.

From the bedroom I could hear her deliver my message, not quite as I had given it. I would be out for a couple of weeks. Yes, the baby was adorable, and doing fine. "She'll be in touch with you just as soon as she feels better. . . . Thank you. I'll be sure to tell her." I shook my head in the dim room with the shades drawn. I would be in touch with nobody, nothing. I was too tired to persevere in my being. I thought of Esther's mother, and for the first time I had an inkling of why she might have chosen to spend her life lying alone in a dim bedroom, seeing no one, doing nothing. As I was falling asleep the phone rang.

"Someone called Rosalie," my mother reported. "Is she the one I heard you with that time at City College?"

Oh, Greg had worked fast. "Yes. Can't you tell her I'm sleeping?"

"No. She said it's important. Get up and talk to her. By the way, Mrs. Rodriguez says the senior citizens send their love and miss you. Mrs. Kirchner learned the Brahms waltzes for four hands and is waiting for you to do them with her."

"Thanks." I slogged over to the phone.

"Lydia? What's this I hear? It doesn't sound like you at all. You can't leave us in the lurch." I moved the receiver a couple of inches away. When Rosalie got excited that deep vibrant voice seemed to be delivering the recitative between arias, on the verge of breaking into passionate song. "You have a responsibility, you know. We weren't just fooling around till you became a mother."

"I'm sorry, Rosalie. I'm no good any more."

"Nonsense. The whole world has children. It doesn't mean you have to retire from life. Sit on a pillow and practice. Take codeine, it works wonders. For every day you wait it will take three to get back. I'm speaking from experience, Lydia."

"Henrietta Frye is really good."

"I've played with her. I know she's good. That's not the point. I thought you were serious. Is this how fast you give up?"

"Rosalie . . ." If I stayed on the phone any longer I would cry, and I was so sick of those tears, beyond all control. "I'm sorry. I can't explain. I have to hang up now."

The next day, as I was changing Althea's diaper in the tiny room we had made bright and colorful the week before her birth, I noticed a thin red ribbon tied low around a leg of the bassinet that had been my sister-in-law Lily's, and later Victor's. My mother came in from washing the lunch dishes to view the baby.

"What's that?" I pointed to the ribbon.

"Oh my!" She looked startled, then gave an uneasy laugh. "That's an old Jewish custom, to ward off the evil eye."

"Mother, really."

"Don't look at me!" she exclaimed, looking me straight in the eye. "Since when do I go in for such things?" She nodded with significance; her lips shaped an ironic smile. "Edith must have done it."

"Edith!" I never thought of Victor's mother as being Jewish. She was one of those gracious East Side ladies who seem unmarked by any history, unrooted, adrift in a self-styled bubble of charm. For her to have married Paul Rowe, son of an Episcopalian minister, was a bold and undiplomatic act in 1932. The horror of her Russian-born parents was intense, but luckily brief. Her boldness spent, Edith had been docile ever since, attending Christmas dinners and Passover Seders with equal grace and lack of interest. Or so I had thought. Suddenly she became a romantic, haunted figure, her Lord & Taylor disguise concealing a dark tangle of atavistic loyalties, a female Daniel Deronda.

Later, after my mother left to meet a friend at a matinee, Edith arrived, glowing from shopping and hairdresser. She was

newly frosted, with a pale Chanel suit to match. It wasn't a look
I wanted, and yet it made me feel somehow undone in jeans and
sweatshirt. She found me changing Althea's diaper in the little
room.

"I brought you a sweater, darling," she said, setting down her
parcels. "I couldn't resist, it was so perfect for you. Deep blue,
with a scoop neck. Finish up and I'll show you."

"Thanks. I think I've forgotten how to get dressed, though."

"No one forgets that. The sun is shining. I'll stay with her
while you go out and get some color in your cheeks. Why don't
you call a friend?"

"What is that, Edith?" I pointed to the red ribbon on the
bassinet leg.

She turned, following my finger. "Oh, my goodness!" And
she smiled innocently. "Look at that! That must be to ward off
the evil spirits. My grandmother once told me, ages ago. But
I've never seen it done before. Isn't that sweet! Where did it
come from?"

I shrugged my ignorance.

Edith beamed. "Your mother must have done it." She shook
her head in mellow amusement, tickled Althea's foot, and began
making cooing, grandmotherly sounds at her.

"*My* mother?"

"Of course. Who else?"

In the evening Victor came home and found me in the little
room, changing Althea's diaper. He was still working in the bar
in the East Thirties, but from noon to seven now. He would get
up at dawn to paint all morning, then walk the twelve blocks
uptown. Before I left my job at Schirmer's a month ago, three
or four days a week of bartending had been enough to keep us.
Now it was five or six days. He fell into bed early and hung on
to me all night like the survivor of a shipwreck with a floating
plank. He still had his stubborn will to make it on his own. We
both had it, I should say. There was a ferocity about our
independence and our austere refusals, and until the baby there
had been a certain zing of glamor in watching the week's money
run out, counting pennies and planning cheap treats. Once or
twice we had gone to bed slightly hungry, and there was even a
sporting glamor in that. Not too hungry to make love. We knew
they would never let us starve.

He kissed me and Althea, then fidgeted about the baby things with a bemused gaze that would take months to fade, touching the mobile, the piles of clean diapers, the rag doll his mother had brought.

"What's this?" He squatted down at his former bassinet to get a closer look.

"That's to ward off the evil eye, I'm told. It's an old Jewish custom."

He rose, came over, and embraced me from behind as I was pinning on the new diaper. "You're funny," he whispered, nuzzling against my hair. "You are funny."

"Me! I didn't do it! It's one of our mothers."

"Oh, come on. They're not the type. It's okay, I'm not laughing at you. I think it's very nice." He moved his hands around on my ribs, moved them up to my breasts. It was irksome, while I was trying to get Althea's feet back into the terry-cloth stretch suit. I felt like shaking him off like a hovering fly, but I didn't. I reminded myself that all this was happening because we loved each other. "Hey, baby," he murmured, "when do you think you'll be back in business?"

Remember, I told myself, you love him. He hasn't had a baby, his crotch is not stinging, he has no cause to wish that nothing will happen in that region ever again, no traffic or convulsion of any sort.

"Soon. A week or so. Victor, I really didn't do it. You can take it off if you want. I don't care."

"I have no desire to take it off." He let go of me and laughed. "You take it off if you feel like it."

"It doesn't seem right to take it off. Somebody cared enough to put it there."

"Somebody, yes." Victor grinned, taking the powdered, sweet-smelling baby from me. "Somebody, somebody, somebody," he cooed moronically, rubbing his forehead against hers.

Within about five months Althea could gurgle, laugh, and roll over; she attained a size and specific gravity that made her stop seeming prey to the least passing breeze. I finally took the ribbon off and threw it away. When Phil was born, less than two years later, Edith was in the hospital undergoing tests for mysterious symptoms (not for some time would they be diagnosed as bone cancer), and my mother was in Switzerland with

Evelyn, who had had a difficult miscarriage. When Alan was born, nearly four years after that, my mother had a broken arm from falling off a ladder, trying to hang kitchen curtains—she couldn't have tied a ribbon even if she had wanted to—and Paul had taken Edith on a trip around the world lest she suspect that she had cancer. And by the time Vivian was born, two years later, my father was dead of a sudden heart attack. My mother was spending a year in Arizona with her sister, to recuperate from the shock and grief. Edith was in the hospital. Out of all these mutations there came no more red ribbons. Althea was the only one of the four who had the evil eye warded off. At odd moments I would remember that—after exhilarating rehearsals, when I played the way I did in my dreams, or listening to a student of rare gifts do the Bach Preludes and Fugues (for I did regain my sanity and resume my life; they had all been right, Greg, Rosalie, my mother)—and I would worry for the other three. But never very long or very seriously—it was so silly.

The Philosophy Study Group

"Body of land."
    Esther chose continent. "Asia, in particular. It sprawls and the boundaries aren't clear."

"Peninsula," I said.

"Prairie. No, I guess that's not . . . Forest?" said Gabrielle. "Anything landlocked. Nina?"

"Island."

"Island?" That bothered Gaby. "Well, let it go. Pick a gem."

"Emerald," said Nina.

"Why emerald?"

"Because it's cool on the outside and hot on the inside."

Laughter.

"Ruby," said Esther. "Hot on the outside and hot on the inside."

On the outside, December snow is falling on the playground, etching swings and seesaws in the dark, making the sandbox into a snowbox, and softening the lines of tall slivers of buildings. Inside we are folded in warmth, our toes digging into the shag rug. No longer girls playing games in a college dormitory, but women edging towards thirty in a world spinning towards 1967, and still playing games. We are in Nina's apartment in a Greenwich Village high-rise near New York University, where she is an assistant professor of chemistry. Nina's apartment is sensuous; it suggests the harem. The dominant color is purple. (But in our game she said she was black. Gabrielle: "Rust." Esther: "Green.") Purple and gold. Gold in the lush, mosaiclike

Gustav Klimt prints on the walls, of lovers, flora, and rainbows.
Gold threads in the purple curtains. Gold, or really mustardy,
pillows on the purple couch and on the floor. In the bathroom,
purple towels, and in the kitchen, purple ceramic dishes, purple
mugs, with the rest austerely white, smooth and glistening like
her mind. Like a laboratory, I sometimes think, but are labora-
tories in fact so pristine? Near the refrigerator hangs a bulletin
board with notices of meetings, phone numbers, events she
plans to attend, the edges of every little rectangle of paper
parallel to the edges of the bulletin board. A five-by-eight card,
printed in Nina's narrow, swift block letters, contains a quota-
tion from *The Golden Sayings of Epictetus*, which she says she
sometimes reads to put her to sleep: "Everything has two handles,
one by which it may be borne, the other by which it may not.
If your brother sin against you, lay not hold of it by the handle
of his injustice, for by that it may not be borne; but rather by
this, that he is your brother, the comrade of your youth; and
thus you will lay hold on it so that it may be borne." The long
wall in the living room, where we gather, is lined with
bookshelves. The center, most accessible, shelves hold her thick
science books. Below, books of philosophy, politics, sociology.
Above, novels (Nina is an insomniac; Epictetus doesn't always
work) and poetry: Frost, Marianne Moore, William Carlos
Williams—she enjoys the sanctification of the ordinary. And on
the top shelf, barely reachable, the books she used in college.

By day Nina appears still ladylike, and fashionable; on her
tall, understated body, clothes seem modeled; her oval face,
with dark hair tethered by pins or combs, is assertive yet
reserved about what it asserts; she has a model's look of unlim-
ited possibilities held in check. At home she transforms. She
releases the hair, longer and thicker than it seems when drawn
back, and strides through the apartment in harem clothes—filmy,
rustling shirts, rope belts with bells and tassels, gold slippers.
Once in a while she pulls on a pair of jeans and a mannish shirt
to dash to the corner in the middle of the night for cigarettes or
orange juice, when sleep eludes her, or to drive to Rockaway in
her white Triumph convertible, to walk along the boardwalk
and look at the ocean, which she did not see till she was over
twenty. To an outsider Nina and her apartment with its velvet-
covered pillows and Tiffany lamps would appear exotic. To me

they are an image chosen deliberately out of a range of possible self-images, not an organic growth but like an adopted child no less genuine, no less lovable, and in time, fitting and necessary.

The Philosophy Study Group was Nina's idea, conceived when she returned to New York after five years of acquiring advanced degrees at Princeton. Her engagement to the fellow student was over; he left to work in Colorado, where she did not wish to follow him. She said she missed us. When she visited we were strained and distracted by husbands and babies. The best times we ever had together, she reminded us, were those late nights in her room the year we studied philosophy and took it seriously—before we abandoned the search for truth as sophomoric. Everything had turned around in the few short years since our college days. Hadn't we noticed? Or had we been too busy perpetuating the life cycle? The country was heaving with war, drugs, sex, revolt, throwing up a lava that muddied the mind. Everything they had taught us was in question. What did we intend to do about it? Our plans? "Physical survival," I replied. I had two babies but difficulty believing I was a mother. For Nina survival was not enough. She wanted to uncover the nerves that connected daily life to the metaphysical. She had a theory that the flower-bearing middle-class rebels taking over the public parks were descendants of the Greek Sophists, those slippery relativists, *bêtes noires* of Plato, who spent dozens of glittering pages mocking their claim that man is the measure of all things. She was drawn to that easeful vision too, but suspicious. She went to all the antiwar protests, mingling, signing, getting high, and accepting the handouts of every special interest group, but she couldn't stand their ragged clothes and their hair. A scientist, as well as a sexual rebel herself, she was withholding judgment till all the evidence was in. Meanwhile she wanted to give them the dignity of a history they themselves scorned.

The unexamined life was not worth living. We must come to her apartment, where there were no husbands and babies. I agreed for nostalgia's sake; my prolonged postpartum anomie, boring as a pornographic home movie, had just peaked and seemed to be relinquishing its hold; Nina's exigence would help. She suggested books of philosophy we should read (William James, another Sophist, American-style), but as it turned out, the Philosophy Study Group did not always, or often, discuss philosophy. No. The name was a bit of a joke. Our lives did not encourage abstract thought. Phil was almost two, Althea almost four. What will and stamina I had, I saved for practicing, recovering the lost ground with scales and arpeggios, Beethoven and Bach in slow motion. Like a child who avoids the homework but brings in something cute for show and tell, I came to Nina's purple apartment with tales of Thales, or talies of Thales, as Esther put it, to make it rhyme. I had found them while browsing in the library, with Althea at Story Hour and Phil slung on my back.

"Okay, I'm sure you all remember how Thales measured the height of the pyramid. Well, he also figured out how to measure the distance of ships at sea. He built a tower right at the shore and projected a line drawn from the top of the tower to a far-off ship. He measured the angle formed by the line and the tower, and then, keeping that same angle, rotated the line around the axis of the tower so that it extended in the other direction, inland. The point where the line hits the ground, to the tower, is the distance. How do you like that?"

Applause. Refilling of glasses. Encore!

"One night, as his servant was leading him across the fields so he could observe the stars, Thales stumbled into a ditch. The woman asked him how he could even hope to know the heavens if he didn't know what was right under his feet."

"I was like that."

"You were very good on your feet, Gaby, as I recall."

"You know what I mean."

"We were all like that." Esther laced her fingers in curious designs, like a cat's cradle. She had stopped smoking.

"When asked why he had no children of his own, Thales said it was because he loved children."

Nina said, "I love children too. But I would like to have them anyway."

"I don't, in general," said Esther. "But I would like to too."

"When his mother pestered him to get married, Thales said the right time had not yet come. Years later, when she brought it up again, he said the right time had passed."

"There must be a right time to divorce too," said Esther. "If I can't do it soon, the right time will pass and then it won't matter any more. I'll accept this as my fate. We'll get like those horrible middle-aged couples you see on buses, who stare straight ahead and look catatonic—you don't even realize they're together until they get off at the same stop. He nudges her or she pokes him. You know the ones I mean. You sit there trying to figure out what peculiar nasty things they must do to each other when they're alone."

"My parents were like those couples on the bus," said Nina, "except they would never nudge or poke each other. I'll tell you what they do alone. They never quarrel out loud. But they have long spells of silence. A week. Three weeks. Even a month. The house is filled with that silence—and ours was a very small house, two floors with just the two bedrooms upstairs, so it really was filled—the way a house can be filled with a cooking smell. Cabbage, liver, something oppressive." Nina reached over to get a small black lacquered box from a cabinet. She opened it and rolled herself a joint, which the rest of us declined, Esther with a shudder. Since Ralph had tried everything on the street, Esther loathed drugs; she knew the down side of each high as well as any emergency room orderly. Nina no longer smoked her one cigarette a week. She indulged every appetite, but with a careful, measured indulgence, as she must have measured out her chemicals in the lab, as Thales must have measured. Right now she was intrigued by the biochemical factors in neurological diseases that produce spells of wildness, like epilepsy or Tourette's syndrome.

"The silence in that house was so dense I used to imagine reaching out and grabbing a fistful. It would be like taffy and stick to everything it touched, and if you tried to pull it off it would keep on stretching." It had taken her till now to outgrow the habit of silence. To us, Nina's past was like a burnt book; this was a charred page snatched from the fire, and we listened as raptly as the three-year-olds at Story Hour.

"Only on Sundays, for church, did they put on a show of togetherness. He would wear his best suit, navy pin stripe, and she would wear a fancy print dress, always print. There was one with green birds, I remember, that I especially hated; the birds had their beaks open and I could practically hear them squawking. She would walk into the church on his arm, with me trailing behind in a starched dress. I knew the minister was

fooled, but I used to wonder whether God was fooled also.
That was his house, they told us, where he dwelt, and I
thought if he dwelt only there he would never know. But if he
came into our house too . . . It bothered me that God might be
fooled. They slept in twin beds. I assumed all couples slept in
twin beds, till I saw my friend Kate's parents' bedroom. I was
shocked. My imagination was shocked, I mean." She paused for
a moment and stared blankly. Seeing the beds, I thought, and
the vast space between them.

"I used to hear low whispers sometimes, from across the hall.
I was born very late to them, you know. They were close to
forty. I think after that my mother didn't want to sleep with
him any more. Maybe she never had wanted to—they never
joked about how they met or how they came to marry, that sort
of thing. I don't know to this day. I have these fantasies—that
she objected to . . . some of his, uh, requests. She had a rather
legalistic mind, in fact she'd been a legal secretary for a while. I
know how her mind worked. She would have wondered exactly
how far conjugal rights extended." I had to smile. Nina, whose
appeal for me lay in contradiction, spoke of sex like a vestal
virgin. "I'll never know the truth. I imagine her as very dry,
though. A very dry woman. Never even sweated. I mean,
perspired. She would perspire, if at all."

She was finishing her joint, looking high and dreamy, starting to chuckle. She played with a fringe on her shirt, and her
eyes were very large and ironic. "She had no bodily fluids, you
see, just dust, or something powdery inside, seeping through
her where the rest of us have liquid. You know how they say
some babies just slip out, and you imagine all that slithery stuff
they're sliding through? It's a nice thought, isn't it, sliding out
into the world, something like those twisty slides they have in
motel swimming pools, that the kids pour water on to keep
them wet. But I imagine myself being born by friction. Inching
my way down those tight dry walls. Abrasive. Like peeling a
tight dress up over your head. Actually I did peel her off. I was
a breech baby." She laughed. "They used to tell me I was lucky
to come from such a good home, where I had everything I
needed. And I did, more or less. It all depends on what you
think you need. If that's all you see around you, how do you
know things could be otherwise?"

"How did you ever bear it?" Esther asked.

"Well, you see I didn't. I'm here."

"I guess I mean how do you bear it. Now."

Nina's face took on the shielded, daytime look. She gave a chilly smile. "Just an old Stoic, I guess. 'Everything has two handles, one by which it may be borne, the other—' "

"I know, I know," groaned Esther. "I've been in your kitchen. But some things don't seem to have any handles at all. The best thing to do is let them drop."

Esther did leave Ralph, less than two months later. In the skirmish she lost the baby she had been carrying unawares, when she remarked that she didn't love children in general but still she wanted to have them. Worn out, she went home to Chicago ("Are you happy?" asked her mother, senile or wicked or both. "Because if you're happy, then I'm happy too"), and on her return, got religion. She read the Old Testament, and in envelopes from the shelter for disturbed children where she was working, sent me double-edged missives from Ecclesiastes. Pushing the stroller home from the supermarket with Althea toddling alongside, the groceries tucked under Phil's feet and behind his back, I would arrive and find in the mailbox: "All go unto one place; all are of the dust, and all turn to dust again. . . . Wherefore I perceive that there is nothing better than that a man should rejoice in his own works; for that is his portion: for who shall bring him to see what shall be after him?" Tears still came to me too easily—a vestige of my sickness—but I smiled as well. By works Esther did not mean grocery shopping. She had hated my giving up when Althea was born. I stuffed the envelope in my jeans pocket and for the hundredth time tried to figure out the best way to get children, stroller, and groceries up to the fourth floor without leaving any two items alone either upstairs or down, like the ferryman who has to carry a fox, a rooster, and a bag of corn across a river, the kind of riddle I had always found exasperating. Nina's sort of riddle, Nina's delight, and had I brought it up in the Philosophy Study Group she might have solved it for me. But it never occurred to me there, happily sipping wine.

Upstairs, while Phil napped and Althea colored pictures of fairy-tale characters, I forced myself to work on Mozart trios, dreaming of the time, not too far off, when I might call Rosalie and say I was ready to come back. If they would have me. The next week there would arrive in Esther's chubby handwriting: "Whatsoever thy hand findeth to do, do it with thy might; for there is no work, nor device, nor knowledge, nor wisdom, in the grave, whither thou goest." It made me study my hands, and with some pleasure—they were once again looking like hands that possessed a skill. The grave reminded me of the Golden Age Club. Mrs. Kirchner and the Brahms waltzes for four hands. Was she still waiting? No, surely they had found someone else. Most likely I was too late for any of it, and besides, whatever I earned would go straight to a babysitter. Why bother? Much easier to rot. But the next week's envelope scolded: "He that observeth the wind shall not sow; and he that regardeth the clouds shall not reap." So I pulled together my strength and late at night, while the children slept, I studied scores and drummed my fingers on the kitchen table.

Esther's religion did not get past the Philosophy Study Group unscrutinized. Nina wanted to hear the evidence for her sudden belief.

"There is no evidence for any belief," she replied. "Or else there's evidence for all—it comes to the same thing. We believe what appeals to us, what we can use, whatever satisfies our fears of the unknown. Afterwards we worry about the evidence." With religion and leaving Ralph, she had acquired a stillness of the body that made her seem demure, nearly cherubic, even though her once-rosy face was wan with anguish overcome. She spoke quietly, without the old urgency, and stroked the book resting on her lap. "William James says so. You ought to know—you've read everything. He says a set of beliefs is an emotional response to the world, not an intellectual one. That, let me see, truth exists insofar as we feel it to exist, insofar as it works for us."

"Works, did you say?" asked Gabrielle.

"Works, yes. Don't you remember all that from school? If you act according to a certain belief and your actions yield the desired results, the belief is valid."

"It's so amoral, though. So very American." Gabrielle, knitting a powder-blue afghan to lure Cynthia from crib to bed, yanked more wool from the skein and aimed the needle like a spear. "I can think of a lot of beliefs that worked just fine. How about Hitler's idea of the master race? That was useful to a lot of people; it satisfied their fears; and it worked, Esther. Very efficiently."

"Only for a short time. They lost the war."

"Lost the war? That's a moot point. But anyway, how many people were gassed before the belief stopped working?" Gabrielle dug the knife blade into the cheese. She was angry, an anger that could hook itself to anything. She had put on weight, her beautiful hair had no shine, Don was doctoring for absurdly long hours yet rarely missed a night in bed—sometimes they couldn't get to talk for days, she told me, but he was not too worn out for that. Oh no. He needed his fix so he could go on. She was helping to heal the sick, indirectly. The voracious love left her vacant, her energy tamped down. She was looking for part-time work, but though she could quote pages of Chaucer, the only thing the publishers wanted her to do was type.

"Look," Esther said softly, "I'm not going to persecute anybody. I'm just trying to live. I need the belief, the idea." She gave in, took one of Nina's cigarettes, and struck a match. "The idea is like a prophecy. James says the strength of your belief, the will to have the world be a certain way, can actually make things happen." She had forgotten the match. I watched the flame creep closer to her fingers. "Take Schopenhauer. Say you accept that. Okay, so you think the world is basically—" Her hand jumped, she shook out the match and dropped it, and sucked her fingers. "Basically evil, all it has in store is misery, life is some kind of grotesque mistake."

"Lydia!" For a moment Gabrielle's face was girlish again with the old light. "Remember when you carried around that horrible quote from Schopenhauer in your purse?"

I closed my eyes. That was when we shared the apartment and knew the contents of each other's purses. "Oh yes. Nothing gives lasting satisfaction. The desire is long, the demands are infinite, the satisfaction is short and scanty. It sounds like an adolescent boy jerking off, doesn't it?"

"You have just proven my point." Esther grinned. "You don't feel like believing that any more. Thank God. I remember you after Althea was born, and when you got pregnant again. Ugh, what a mess. But anyway, supposing you did, so completely that you finally committed suicide. Or you might just sit in a room staring at the walls like my mother, which is the coward's form of suicide. You've made Schopenhauer come true, you see? On the other hand, say you accept the idea of a moral universe with a more or less benevolent God, and you live in a decent and optimistic way. Which is what you all do anyway. Chances are you'll find the world will bear out the truth of that belief. The wish is father to the fact."

"Whose chances?" asked Gaby. "Blacks in South Africa? Jews in Germany? Or maybe Vietnamese?"

"We'll end this war in time," said Esther. "You'll see. There'll be a moral victory, coming from the streets."

"A moral victory, sure, over how many bodies piled on the TV screen?" Gaby tossed aside her knitting and went to the bedroom to phone her babysitter.

"So." Nina stretched out languidly, the tiny mirrors on her shirt glinting. "Tell us what he's like, this God of yours. Is he like the devil who visited Ivan Karamazov? Suit and tie? Or noble and sexy like the one on the Sistine ceiling? I'm assuming you haven't seen any burning bushes."

"No. At least not yet," Esther said sweetly, refusing the bait. She flicked her eyes over Nina. "He's not elegant or well-dressed. Or she. I don't know about sexy. More kind of . . . erratic. Like me." She smiled, testing James's theory on us. Would her world respond in kind to kindness, with charity for charity? She opened her book to a turned-down page and read: " 'In this real world of sweat and dirt, it seems to me that when a view of things is "noble," that ought to count as a presumption against its truth, and as a philosophic disqualification. The prince of darkness may be a gentleman, as we are told he is, but whatever the God of earth and heaven is, he can surely be no gentleman. His menial services are needed in the dust of our human trials, even more than his dignity is needed in the empyrean.' "

A cleaning woman! What I needed so badly but couldn't afford. But I said nothing. For the force of her good will did indeed claim, engender, and elicit good will in turn, and we hectored her no more. Only when Esther went to the bathroom, Nina whispered, "Lo, we have witnessed the creation of God, *ex nihilo*."

"*Ex* need, you mean."

*   *   *

The next fall, 1967, Esther went off to pick fruit on a kibbutz in Israel. She was barely gone when the cease-fire was violated once more. The news reports carried tales of weapon caches, sporadic shootings, disrupted settlements.

"What kind of lunatic would go to Israel at a time like this? We don't even know what part of the country she's in," Gabrielle brooded in the Philosophy Study Group. "We ought to look it up on a map—she could have been killed. How would we ever find out?"

"I looked. It doesn't seem to be near the fighting. But it's hard to tell. It's such a small country."

On Nina's lap was Peter Abelard's *Ethics*, her latest enthusiasm, a book about sin. Escape reading, I teased her. I had no time for obscure tracts. I was studying at Juilliard again, and working for Mrs. Rodriguez at the Golden Age Club, where my replacement was taking time off to have a baby. The aged faces, alas, were new; Mrs. Kirchner had not been able, after all, to wait for me to play the Brahms waltzes for four hands, and I suffered remorse.

"Well, I managed to read it," Gaby said, "waiting my turn at job interviews. Abelard says the Lord only tests the strong. Is Esther the strong?"

"He was referring to temptation," Nina corrected. "Tests with temptation, not outside danger. One of us is sure to get a letter any day."

Gabrielle frowned. "I must not be the strong. He never tests me." She was pale, in a nondescript dress. She had brought along four pairs of Roger's corduroy pants, and while Nina explained sin, for my benefit, Gaby hemmed, sipped wine, and hemmed.

"There are two components needed for real sinning: will and consent. If you have the will but don't consent to do the act, you haven't sinned; that's simply the human condition—we all have the will. And if you consent to the act without having the will, like committing murder in self-defense, that's not sin either. Also—this part is rather nice—if you have neither the will nor the consent, there's no particular virtue accruing. Because with no temptation there's no moral strength."

"You know, I still get a funny feeling about Henrietta Frye.

That time she broke her wrist hiking and I got to play for *The Yeomen of the Guard*. Remember? I wished it on her."

"But you wouldn't have broken it for her, would you, sneaking into her room at night with a hammer?"

"Certainly not. . . . I might have gotten caught."

Nina laughed. "I think you're safe from hellfire, Lydia."

"She's moving to California in November, so I'll get my place back in the trio. It was perfect timing. And this time I didn't wish it, I swear. I had something else lined up, with a group of woodwinds."

They congratulated me. Gabrielle etched a cross in the air with her needle. "Go, child, and sin no more. But surely that's not the worst secret wish on your conscience?"

"Not the worst, no." Gaby waited, needle poised over the pants. "I sometimes used to wish I didn't have any children. So I could play more, and go on tour—it's so important. If you can't travel, you're nowhere." I waited in vain for the bolt of lightning from the ungentlemanly cleaning woman. No one showed any horror. Gabrielle began to sew again, Nina popped an olive into her mouth. "I don't wish it any more. Consciously, anyway."

Nina said, "That doesn't count. It's not a real wish, just a passing fancy. Sorry, Lyd."

"I have wished much worse, because I really meant it. I have wished that at one of his many conferences Don would meet some beautiful woman doctor and become infatuated, so that I could be relieved of that endless devotion. Temporarily. It's like a straitjacket, you know. But then, beautiful women doctors are relatively rare." She didn't stop sewing and didn't look at us. "When someone loves you so unconditionally they don't see you any more. It's like you've ceased to exist—as a person changing in time, I mean. Who I am now is invisible. I only needed to exist at the very beginning, to start it."

"Esther's little bureaucrat of a God is so terribly inefficient. That is exactly what I would like," said Nina. "To be loved unconditionally."

"Yes, I can see that. Well, it's a stupid thing to complain about, really. People are being killed in those jungles. . . ."

Gabrielle rubbed an eye beneath her glasses and bit off a piece of thread, then turned to me and said curtly, "You don't suffer from the same problem, I gather?"

What could I say? No, he didn't love me *too* much? I couldn't tell it to anybody; I guarded it as Evelyn had guarded her secret life, confiding only in the sunflower. Since I had recovered and was working, Victor and I again sat up late at night in bed whispering in the dark, hypnagogic murmurs on the fine line of consciousness; we felt born from the same soil, our cells interchangeable, and our love had the heady tinge of incest. Even to say I love you was a semantic error, too great a separation.

"Well, not quite."

" 'To sin is to hold the Creator in contempt,' " Nina announced. " 'That is, to do by no means on his account what we believe we ought to do for him, or not to forsake on his account what we believe we ought to forsake.' "

"Oh, honestly!" Gaby said. "He's such a bore, so vain and petty, always fretting over whether he's getting the proper respect. You'd think someone omnipotent would be above all that."

"No, that's how you stay omnipotent. But in any case he's really talking about self-respect. It's internalized."

Ah. Now I knew why she had chosen sin and Abelard, like herself libertine and ascetic. A new lover, no doubt, maybe even less suitable than the Cuban TV repairman, the Canadian soccer player, the tap dancer attempting to stamp out his homosexuality. There were times I suspected she chose them only to shock her parents, but if so it was a Pyrrhic victory: she wouldn't have dreamed of telling them.

It was a student, she said. Not one of hers, thank God. Not even graduate. Undergraduate, and for Nina that distinction—that he was twenty-one rather than twenty-four—made it more lusciously sinful. Bright but not brilliant, she confessed ruefully, as though brilliance too might have been a mitigating factor. From Jamaica. "Jah-mai-cah," with a musical lilt she had picked up to perfection. He visited late at night and left before dawn. She had a penchant for such arrangements. In the halls they were discreet. Oh yes, I could well imagine. She was incorrigible, and incorrigibly guilty. Guilty of what exactly? I always asked.

If you like them, where's the great harm? Self-betrayal, she said. Bad faith.

"Abelard understands perfectly. He's cleverer than God. God's attitudes are awfully naive, if you think about it. Honor thy father and mother. Thou shalt not covet thy neighbor's wife. They're impossible to obey—they command emotions. At best, all we can do is behave ourselves. Covet thy neighbor's wife if you must, but don't sleep with her, would make more sense. Behave honorably to your father and mother, and take care of your resentments in private. Those are fine distinctions and his language blurs them. While Abelard says, 'There are people who are wholly ashamed to be drawn into consent to lust or into a bad will and are forced out of the weakness of the flesh to want what they by no means want to want.' "

"*That's* bad faith." Again Gaby didn't look up from her sewing. "You want what you want to want."

"Oh no. There's a crucial difference. I want to be a decent, straightforward Bosc pear like Lydia, but I find myself making the choices of a plum. That is, I *wish* I could want to be a pear, but I must want—Wait a minute. This is getting . . . What did I say?"

"Philosophy!" Gabrielle smiled for the first time all evening. "*Ce n'est guère la philosophie*, girls."

"Jejune! Jejune!" Nina and I chorused. In a flash, it conjured up Esther. Continent (Asia), geyser, ruby, peach, poppy, pumpkin. All the identities she had chosen in all our games. Gaby laid down her needle and clicked her tongue, and we brooded, growing cold with apprehension.

Finally she folded the corduroy pants. We stood up and put on our shoes and began clearing away glasses. Will without consent, I thought. Henrietta Frye. Will with consent (the winner). George? Ah no, that was too superficial to be really sinful. No will but consent. Two babies. Those neat boxes nudged something in a corner of my mind. Yes! Win, Place, and Show. "Nina! It's time for another one of our sinful outings. Before it gets too chilly. How is this Saturday?"

"Saturday is fine. Gaby?"

She shook her head. "I've told you before, I'm no gambler. I'd rather ride them."

*   *   *

Wickedness made me merry, leaving husband and two children and work for a day at the races. I had fifteen dollars tucked
in the back pocket of my jeans, play money. It was clear and
hot, more like June than early October, and Nina came around
noon to fetch me in the white Triumph, top down. "I had a
letter from Esther," was her greeting. "She's fine. The kibbutz
isn't anywhere near where the fighting was. She's still picking
fruit." We sped off with eased minds.

Nina had been introduced to the track by her Cuban TV
repairman. The Spanish names of the jockeys slid familiarly off
her tongue. When she dismissed the repairman she recruited
me, wooing me with intricate analyses of odds, lineage, and
track records. But I bet on the names and the bodies. When the
horses trotted around the paddock beforehand to display flesh,
stance, and gait, a wonderful tang of sexual exhibition spiced
the air. I giggled like a teen-ager. Who cared about odds or past
performances? I wanted to run my hands over those glossy
bodies.

The place was constructed in levels, like an allegory, from the
bright green turf up through sections of varicolored bleachers
ascending heavenward. Across the turf, huge boards flashed the
odds, green numbers that changed endlessly (by whim? necessity?), a Heraclitan vision of the abstract concept of change.
Inside, behind glass windows, bespectacled men registered bets
with comic sobriety, and out of their toy-like machines came
tickets to chance, little cardboard tokens of risk. Everywhere
were round-shouldered, unshaven, preoccupied men dressed in
loose gabardine pants and light shirts with wide fluttery sleeves,
and they gnawed their fingernails, scratched their bellies, and
counted their money. Bills flashed—what a tempting display of
hard cash!—but few pockets would be picked. The money was
only the material sign of far more important business at hand.
These men were committed to risk: romantics, existentialists,
they would not stoop to cheating the game of its outcome. Nine
times a day, for three minutes, their drabness got charged with
life, as they were propelled through the stations of emotion like
souls awaiting their fates on the Day of Judgment, voices ragged
from imploring. And in the instant before the end, life's longest
moment, there was still time for a last-minute change, for
irretrievable loss, or redemption. Then the great god Chance

gave his verdict, to cheers and groans. The happy saved all streamed in one direction, tickets in hand, to claim their reward with the careless, cruel, glowing avidity of winners, while the others, downcast, glumly crushed their tickets underfoot, in no hurry at all. I had expected something fairly disreputable, and instead it was a Bosch painting, a human comedy.

"There's no rhyme or reason to this," I said the first day she brought me. "It's pure chance."

"They've found scientifically that nothing is really pure chance. Nature is sightly skewed, on a bias. Circles are not perfectly round. Lines are not perfectly straight."

"But how do you figure out where the bias is?"

"Here? Well, you can't, really. Not with the data at hand."

"So then it amounts to the same thing. Random."

"Theoretically," she persisted, "if you had all the relevant facts you could work out a winning system. Like the Greek Atomists: if you understood where every atom was going and why, you could foresee everything. But then there wouldn't be horse races. On the other hand there's Heisenberg's Principle of Uncertainty. I guess that would have to enter into it." She paused. "This is all lost on you, isn't it?"

I nodded cheerfully. But now I was an old hand. I bet on a ginger-colored horse named Fantaisie-Impromptu, whose parents were Chopin and Music of the Spheres; the jockey's outfit was a flamingo color, with black triangles on the sleeves and black hoops on the trousers. The odds had risen to fifteen to one. Nina studied the racing form.

"I don't know, Lydia. What they say about Fantaisie-Impromptu is not inspiring. 'Needs proof.' 'Has been idle.' 'Recently dull.' " She bet on an unimpressive brown horse called Nobly Built, won fourteen dollars, and brought me back a frankfurter for consolation. I bet on Princess Althea (how could I resist?), while with pencil in hand Nina pondered for fifteen minutes, bet on Captain Marvel, collected seventeen dollars and forty-eight cents, and returned carrying two strawberry ice-cream cones.

"I'm hot," she said. "Sometimes you just know that you're hot. It comes in spurts. Then again you can get cold and stay cold for a long time. You might lose a lot trying, because no one likes to admit they've gone cold. It's like saying the gods have withdrawn their favor." I listened respectfully. She licked her cone as she worked out her bets on the next three races, then leaned back, stretching her legs to the empty seat in front and turning her face up to the summery sun. She sighed contentedly, as after an arduous task.

"If you're hot, why do you have to do all that work?"

"It's like insurance. You can't afford to get overconfident when you're hot. The gods don't like that."

"You mean you've got to be cool in order to stay hot?"

"Sort of."

"Speaking of hot, how are things with your Jamaican student?"

"It's running the usual course. Oh, sorry." She laughed. "I didn't mean the awful pun." She raised her large sunglasses to her forehead and looked at me wistfully. "Do you know what the usual course is?"

"Nope."

"First there's the sexual excitement part, which is like a colored cloud, a very loud color—cerise or fuchsia—surrounding the two of you so that you're not aware of anything else. Very, very nice. Lethe. But that starts to fade, because it's only a cloud, after all. It dissipates slowly, and you begin looking for other qualities—there's some space to fill once the cloud is a little smaller, a little less opaque. You start to talk to the person more seriously, and inevitably you find the limitations, little fenced-off areas you can't talk in, subjects you can't pursue because the person simply has no interest there. Or is afraid to enter, for some reason. I assume he's finding the same in me, too—I don't mean to sound superior. After a while you find so many fenced-off, impossible areas that there's only a very small space left for you to talk in. Too small. You talk around and around in this space like a prisoner pacing the courtyard of the jail—you know, so many steps this way, so many steps that way, till you reach the familiar stone wall. But at the same time you've gotten to like the person; you feel comfortable, affectionate, he's a decent sort. You don't quite want to get rid of him; that would be unkind. You feel a kind of . . . attachment, but not truly a friendship. What you've attached is your body. It's odd. The person knows your body without knowing you. Of course in that first rush, in the cloud, you thought that the body was a . . . a stand-in for the whole self, and that in revealing your body and its ways, you were revealing who you are. But that's an illusion. The body is only the body. So then slowly, from being someone who brought the essential into your life, moments, really, of . . . oh, what can I call it? I guess glory is not too strong a word although I must say it's embarrassing. . . . Anyway, the person becomes a bit of a bore, sort of like an old relative you found intriguing as a child but not any more, somebody you're still fond of and feel you ought to visit every so often, yet you're not eager to. It feels like time taken away from your real pursuits. You're ill at ease. If you stop there, though, it's all right. You can still have good memories. But you don't stop there, usually. You go on till the person becomes truly a bore, and even while you're making love you're faintly bored, bored and excited at the same time, if you can imagine that, Lydia, bored by your own excitement, which is so predictable and so inevitable. And naturally he begins to notice and to ask. You can lie or you can tell the truth—it doesn't matter, because either way it deteriorates, until at the moments you're feeling most excited you feel most disgusted with yourself. And even that can generate its own kind of excitement, a rather perverse excitement. But that kind is thin, and brief, and really not very pleasant, and in the end you're worn out. It hardly seems worth the effort. You start to break dates, and then there is one time that's the last time. It doesn't have to be spoken, you both feel it. You have used the person up, and he has used you up. And you feel when he goes out the door that he's taking away a big chunk of you and leaving nothing in return, and the sad part is that he probably feels the same way."

She lowered her sunglasses. We both leaned forward to watch the horseflesh being paraded along the track.

"It doesn't sound like love, in my experience."

"It's not love. It's more like a shadow of love. Seen from the cave."

"God, you make it sound awful."

"No. It's interesting, or why would I do it? Lots of people do. Of course it has its price. It's a bit eroding."

"I never understood why you didn't marry that one in Princeton. You seemed happy with him."

"Yes, well, he was set on Colorado. I suppose I could have

lived in Colorado if I tried. I think, really, that the right time had not yet come."

We laughed. "And if I ask you in ten years, you'll say the right time has passed?"

"Probably."

Post time was announced. She took off the glasses and got out her binoculars. As they rounded the bend we rose with the crowd. All around us men cheered and shouted. I was jumping up and down to spur my horse, Mood Indigo, who had started out ahead but soon slipped behind. Nina alone was still, more like a spectator at a ballet than at a horse race, chastely in white, blue scarf rippling on the breeze, lips slightly parted, nothing betraying excitement except a quivering muscle near her jaw. Mood Indigo ended in third place, but I had bet to win. Nina's two horses, Social Butterfly and Prince Hal, trailed also. We sat down. She tore up her tickets, extended her hand with the exaggerated gesture of a lady offering it to be kissed, and let the pieces drift to the ground. "That was twenty bucks, dammit. This is no more scientific than a horse race. Ah, well. Do you remember what Gaby was saying about being in a straitjacket from being loved too much?"

"Yes."

"To me nothing could be too much. It's never enough to let me rest content. I'm not talking about sex, you know that."

"I know."

"With the ones who really loved me, two maybe, I always found fault. I start measuring, to see how much. Never with the others. It's a ridiculous kind of . . . Ah!" She waved her hand in resignation. "They fall short, of course—they have to."

"Short of what? What's the standard?"

"What indeed? In Sunday school, when I was a kid, we'd have lessons on stories from the Bible. Lots of miracles. My favorites were the parts where Jesus healed the sick or made the lepers' sores disappear. I once told that to the minister, and he smiled and said maybe I would like to be a nurse. That could be my way of following Jesus. I had no interest in being a nurse. He didn't understand at all. I liked the idea of its being a miracle."

"Ah, a faith healer."

"Exactly." She laughed. "I would have liked that—transform

with a touch. Anyway, at the end of the lesson, after we sang a couple of hymns, we would all file out, and the teacher, who was skinny and his hair was so oiled your fingers felt greasy just looking at it, would say good-bye to each of us in turn. He patted each of us on the head and said, 'Remember, Jesus loves you. Jesus loves you, Nancy Dalton.' Oh, at first it made me feel wonderful, bathed in that vast love. But after a while it wasn't any good. It was too vast and abstract—I couldn't get my hands on it. It didn't help in little daily things, to remember that love. There was a painting of Jesus on the wall, just the face. He was supposed to be smiling down on us. But if you took a good look at the smile, it wasn't connected to us at all. It was very self-absorbed, as if he was amused by a private joke and we were excluded. It irritated me, and so did the teacher, because he said the same thing to every child. There were about twenty of us. I knew that in every town in the world some oily teacher must be saying that to some kid, and I thought, How can he love so many? He couldn't even remember all the names. That wasn't love, or it was love so diluted there was no kick left. You know I always drink everything straight. I didn't want to be loved as part of a category. I wanted him to love me in particular. It's terribly self-centered, I know. I want to be the world, for somebody. I know I'm not a world. But I want someone to find the world in me and never want to leave."

"You would get bored even faster. Look at Gabrielle."

"Possibly. Still, it's the truth. Not a truth I'm especially proud of. It's certainly not what I want to want."

"Nancy?"

"I changed it when I came East to college. Nancy is so . . . oh, simpering. I wanted to leave home that kid who curtsied and behaved herself in Sunday school and never let a boy put his hand under her blouse. Who wasn't even used to being touched." She gave me a wry smile. "That was a good idea you had that summer, to hand me George. He did a lot for me."

"Hah! I can imagine."

"More than that. He was the finishing touch. His mind was so unfettered."

"Yes, that's the trouble."

"No, unfettered is fine. The trouble is something not there."

"Passion," I said. Nina laughed and I blushed, a decade after the fact. "Well, that kind he has. I mean passion about life. Passion makes the fetters."

"He suffered a lot as a kid," she said.

"So did you. That's no excuse."

"You're hard on him, Lydia. For you the past is always present, isn't it? And yet he did you no harm." She was silent for a while. "I think the only time my mother touched me was to do my braids. She brushed them out morning and night and did them right up again, as if it was perilous to leave the hair unbraided. She brushed so hard, it was like a punishment. Yes, I'm sure it *was* a punishment." She laughed again and tossed a stray lock off her forehead. "She made those braids so tight my scalp ached. That's why I finally cut it off, my freshman year. It was a great moment, when I realized it was my hair and I could do what I liked with it. It was gradually dawning on me that the rest of me was mine too. Now I brush it with such affection, Lydia, you would laugh if you saw. I had a man once, who brushed my hair. He did it so well. He used to . . . Ah, this is all very silly. I don't know why I'm telling you all this."

"No, go on. You always stop at the best parts."

"Yes. Well, I suppose Nancy hasn't changed all that much. Still pure in word if not in deed. Nina was the name of someone in a novel, the kind I couldn't bring into the house. I had to read it in the lending library, in snatches. She was a *femme fatale*. She had flaming red hair and breasts that were forever quivering."

I smiled. "In all these years you never even told me your name. Or that you were a *femme fatale*."

"Hardly. I'm just a repressed academic." I must have looked doubtful. "What I mean is that I've repressed the cravings for the ordinary. I did it backwards. The ninth race is coming up, Lyd. We can do a triple."

We both bet on Slalom and Stately Minute for Win and Place, and I picked Dapper Dan for Show, a ruinous choice, Nina pointed out, since in the opinion of the handicappers, Dapper Dan was "hardly the one." But the three jockeys wore purple, gold, and green—how glorious they could look together at the finish line. At the last minute Dapper Dan did zoom up from behind, but only to fourth place. Luckily for me, Nina

was not a gloater. Suddenly, strange green patterns flashed on
the boards, and the crowd held its breath. Chance was a foxy
god: the horse in third place—Nina's Old Curmudgeon—was
disqualified for some breach of equine etiquette, and Dapper
Dan was moved up. Forty-six dollars! I could buy Victor the
print he wanted from his friend Tom's show down in a Village
loft.

"You're the one who's hot now. I've transferred my heat.
What on earth made you pick Dapper Dan?"

"That's my father's name. And he's dapper, too. Pin-striped
suits, folded handkerchief in the jacket pocket. When I was a
kid it made an impression. Also, when he and Evelyn and I
watched prizefights on television Friday nights, he taught us
always to root for the underdog. Nina, what are those people
doing?"

All around us, the sallow, unshaven men in baggy pants were
bent over, swishing their hands through the racing tickets that
papered the floor.

"Looking for a winning ticket thrown away by mistake."

"Hey! Come on, we might pick up a few bucks."

"Oh Lydia, stop it. Get up! Really!"

"Aha! That's Nancy speaking. Okay, okay, I'll be a lady.
Even at the track."

We got back into the Triumph I so loved to ride in; when she
speeded I tasted adventure on the wind, and an impossible
freedom.

Out on the highway she glanced over and read my mind.
"Maybe I'll run away someday. Would you care to come? We'll
take the car, and find two men who like to eat and drink and
swim, and we'll drive around stopping off in motels with pools,
like in *Lolita*. We can follow the sun and the horses, and shoplift
caviar from supermarkets, and chill our champagne in rivers.
Just you and me and two fly-by-night men, if such exist."

"It's a deal. Just give me a couple of days' notice." I didn't
want to spoil her mood or her fantasy; I found her delectable
and tingling as lime ices, as well as gallant in her solitude. Why
tell her I had never been further from running away? I was hot
and running back into my life. Back to Victor, to my work, and
to the children, whose infancy I had known only through a
mist. What I wanted now was the adventure of being happy in

the ordinary way. But I felt shy about telling her. Compared to what she had to tell, it sounded banal.

It was not the moment, either, to tell her I was pregnant. No accident. I was stronger now, and I yearned for another chance, to prove I could do things right, like everyone else. A question of pride. Victor had been easily persuaded. He loved children, and as the embryonic Alan was later to do, loved landmark and ritualistic events in his life. He was beginning to sell paintings, teaching at Parsons, and tending bar rarely. I was earning some money by teaching too. We had moved uptown to a solid apartment building with an elevator that could hold groceries, stroller, and a whole troop of children. Things were so much easier; possibly I missed the eerie thrill of living on the edge.

Through the fall and winter, as my belly grew, I sat at the piano and practiced. Rosalie kept watch like a warden and I was a model prisoner. I never missed a lesson or a rehearsal, and I did two concerts at Saint John the Divine, the unfinished cathedral, wrapped in her voluminous gypsy dresses. I kept on till the last moment, which came at the end of March. My mother, her broken arm in a sling, was summoned to stay with Althea and Phil. She turned on the TV to hear the President, while Victor hunted for the car keys. Victor's ambivalence over so middle-class a concession as a used car took the form of misplacing the keys.

"Lydie, did you hear that?" my mother gasped.

"What?" I was in the hall, tossing the old Trollope novels into the overnight case.

"He said he's not going to run again."

In a moment we were all in front of the television. "Shush," Victor told Phil, and picked him up.

It was true. He would not seek another term because of the public outcry against his waging of the war. Althea, on my mother's lap, wanted to switch to *Sesame Street*. "Shh, darling, there's no *Sesame Street* at night."

"They should be in bed, Mom."

"You should be in the hospital. Why are you both standing here?"

"Shh, wait a minute," said Victor.

Johnson's face had become human again. Those deep grooves were where our marching feet had tracked. He had felt it. We stood for five more minutes, mesmerized. I had another contraction and grabbed hold of a chair. "Victor, the keys!"

"I never would have thought it." He put Phil down and went to continue the search.

The phone rang. It was Gabrielle. "Did you hear him?"

"Yes! Isn't it incredible?"

"Maybe Esther was right about the moral victory. . . . What did she say, the wish was father to the fact?"

"Yes, her William James phase."

"Lydia," Victor called from the kitchen. "This is no time for one of those girlish chats."

"I have to go. I'm having the baby."

"I want to see the baby!" Phil whined.

"Oh! Good luck!" said Gabrielle. "Or should I say break a leg?"

"I'd much rather, believe me." I hung up.

Victor dashed in, jangling the keys. "Who put them on top of the refrigerator?"

"Not me," said Althea. "I can't even reach."

He pulled on his coat. "Did he say anything about ending it?"

"No. Would you two go already? The war will wait, I assure you."

"Okay, come, Lydie. Come along. Are you timing them? Keep track." He nudged me out the door. "Good-bye, Althea. Good-bye, Flip. Good-bye, Francie, I'll call you. Move, sweetheart. You don't have all day."

And lo it came to pass, as Ecclesiastes might have put it, that Alan slid out like a child going down a wet slide, and I actually laughed, lying on the table, when the doctor held him up high like a coveted football in her large and gifted hands, shook her gray curls, and said, "If there's another you might not make it to the hospital." After the infected stitches I had found her, a painstaking lady, a woman who would take pains.

The first day home I wheeled the white wicker bassinet (unberibboned) over to the piano and played Brahms and Rachmaninoff so he would get used to sleeping through the loudest, most urgent of sounds. Rosalie told me that trick and it worked. I did it for my survival, but I did it too for those little missives of Esther's. I wanted to be worthy of that chubby, loving handwriting.

It was a Pyrrhic victory for the moral force. The wish was not father to the fact, or not yet. The gestation was endless; four days after Johnson's speech Martin Luther King was killed in Memphis, and the other, anonymous, bodies kept piling up on the TV screen.

By 1971 Esther had been back from Israel for a year. The kibbutz was "fantastic," but, well, she had had it with communal living. Now she "had" social work school, and was having psychotherapy, with a woman who was a Gestalt therapist, an anarchist, and a feminist. Her father's daughter, Esther felt cozy in the company of people whose views could be encompassed by "ist" words. Ralph had been a Marxist as well as an addict.

We all "had" something new. At the monthly magazine where three years ago, to her chagrin, she had begun as a typist, Gabrielle was an associate editor. They had recognized her brains and her durability. We were acquiring our lives, like the consumers Esther's father scorned. Choosy shoppers, though, we paid dearly for our goods and we treated them well. Collectively we acquired children, skills, work, lovers, trips, experience—and we thought that these things constituted ourselves, and that without them we would no longer be who we were. As if they were barnacles lodged to the bottoms of ships. Or as if they were swallowed and assimilated. Or better still, implanted.

Nina had been promoted to associate professor, and she had a new lover. Freed from that unhappy pattern at last, she told me: he was much more appropriate. A lawyer. Civil rights. A Jewish lawyer, no less, a dozen years older than she, and married. "Appropriate? I can't see what's so appropriate." "Lydia, you're being parochial. You know what I mean. He's someone I can talk to, for one thing." "You wanted to be the world for somebody. How much of the world do you suppose you can be for him if he already has a wife?" "His wife is not my business. That's his problem. I've got to think about me." "I am thinking about you, Nina." But she was in the fuchsia cloud, from which neither common sense nor the stringencies of Abelard could extricate her. Did she receive him at midnight in the harem outfits, Epictetus at her bedside and bangles on her wrists? I knew several Jewish lawyers in their mid-forties, politically liberal and sexy. Such men would love the harem outfits and the brainy, lapsed Sunday school student in them. But would not find the world there, nor bring it.

It was 1971, the war was still going on, and the promise of the sixties was turning like aging milk. Disheartened, Nina said we must go back to the beginning, where the crucial questions were first and best articulated. Plato, Aristotle, Marcus Aurelius, Epictetus. But how could we? The Philosophy Study Group was meeting more sporadically than ever. Gabrielle and I zipped from home to work like frantic mechanical toys, Nina herself was deep in a study of the biochemical roots of schizophrenia, and Esther refused to come: it might interfere with her therapy. "Considering the depth of our inquiries," Gaby commented, "I think her alarm is excessive." But Esther was firm. Her therapist was teaching her, among other things, to say no.

"Therapists are the sophists of the age," Gabrielle said testily as we fell onto the purple pillows.

Nina handed us gin and tonics in tall glasses. "Four ice cubes, Lydia." She knew I loved ice.

Outside, a heat wave was stifling the city. From the huge windows, in the seeping dusk, we could see young mothers in shorts and halters, their backs shiny with sweat, slowly pushing strollers one last time around the playground to calm the fretful babies. Someone had opened a fire hydrant, and little kids splashed in their underwear. Passers-by walked through the spray with peaked smiles. It was a New York August. Inside, Nina had the air-conditioner on full force. We pinned up our hair and sat with our loose summer dresses pulled high on our thighs.

"Therapists"—Gaby spoke the word with contempt—"are the real sophists of the age. They travel around and give lectures—those marathons—just like Protagoras. They also take money for their teachings. In Greece the real philosophers didn't condescend to take money."

"But they don't claim to be philosophers." I was thinking of George, who was really quite humble.

"Don't they? They teach skills for getting by, as Protagoras did. Only back then they called what they taught wisdom and virtue; we don't even bother. Just a certain efficiency. Self-help.

How-to. Truth is whatever works for you. The only difference
I can see is that in Greece they manipulated words and emotions to succeed in politics, and here the action is all in the
private arena. You know, 'relationships.' Being with people is a
technique."

I remembered her great tirade in the dorm, when she raged
through the room in her blue leotard, splendid in her indignation against philosophic bad faith. She no longer raged. It was
too hot, for one thing, and she had grown subdued, earthbound.
More out of sorts, it seemed, than truly indignant. Maybe she
was getting her period. I scolded myself for such retrogressive
thinking.

She was smoking again too, French cigarettes. She tossed a
still-burning match into an ashtray a foot away, as Esther used
to do. It landed on the purple rug. Nina, once so quick to
restore safety, sat unmoved while Gaby absently retrieved it
and rubbed at the dark spot on the rug. "Look," she went on,
"Esther will always be Esther. She'll always fumble around,
and not because she doesn't understand her own motives. I give
her more credit than that. She understands fine. What she
doesn't understand is the world, what's happening around her
and to her. Protagoras says you can give the same food to a
healthy man—well, let's say woman—to a healthy woman or a
sick woman. The healthy woman will say it's good, the sick
woman, bitter. Does that mean the sick woman is mistaken? Oh
no, perceptions never lie. Only it's better to be healthy, of
course. So the job is to change the sick woman into a healthy
woman, so that she can find the food good. How? By words.
Now isn't that exactly what a therapist does? But—the food is
what happens to you in your life. And the point is, the food *is*
good or rotten in itself. Everyone's forgotten that. Let the world
fall to ruins, we'll just refine our coping techniques."

"Good grief, you've become an absolutist," said Nina.

"Why should you care if she goes to a therapist? If it helps?"

"No, you haven't mastered the proper vocabulary, Lydia.
You're supposed to ask, why does it make me feel threatened."

I felt a chill in the Philosophy Study Group, beyond air-
conditioning and ice cubes. I got up and walked around the
room. Gabrielle stubbed out the cigarette and crossed her legs
Indian fashion. Then, as if to show she could still do it, she

arranged her legs and bare feet in the lotus position. She looked at us with a peculiar, needless defiance, her eyes blue and green, flamed by discontent.

"Not just an absolutist. A Stoic." Nina laughed as she rose and took our glasses. "I can see it in the way you sit." She went into the small kitchen, and through the connecting window, as she fixed the drinks, peered out at us. "Bear and forbear," she said with a jaunty tilt of her head. "Those *Golden Sayings of Epictetus*. Death, disaster, loss, all wonderful opportunities to prove your mettle. Bear whatever comes, and forbear from evil. Bear the pain and forbear from the pleasure. Charming, isn't it?" Ice cubes crackled out of a tray, and in a moment she was back.

I took the frosty glass. "It's not all so priggish. Marcus Aurelius has that lovely part about the emeralds. Although he too— Gaby, don't, what is it?" I reached over, but she shook her head.

She was crying with her face in her hands. She waved us away, and in a moment was composed again. Not menstrual pangs. A man in her office. It was driving her mad. She had never felt this way before—with eyes averted. She hadn't known it could be so bad. It. Her face darkened. She thought about him all the time. *All* the time. She banged a fist on her knee, still captive in the lotus position.

"Well, what are you doing about it?" Nina asked. "You've got the will. What about the consent?"

"I'm doing nothing. What can I do? Wait it out. It's no good, but it'll pass. The hard part is . . . I have to see him every day. It's funny—I lie awake at night and think that with a few well-aimed words I could have him transferred. He's in the Art Department. He could do the same thing for another magazine in the group. It would be a relief. But of course I would never do that. It's wrong. I'd rather leave myself."

"After all the effort you've put in! You said in a couple of years you could be the arts editor."

"No, I'm not planning to leave. That wouldn't be right either."

"Your vocabulary," Nina remarked, "is somewhat limited. Right. Wrong. Good. Bad."

She smiled. "Unthreatening, I guess. Look, I know I could

push words around to make it all right. I mean, all right to have the affair, or all right not to. With words you can do anything. But they don't change the truth of what's happening."

"Yes," said Nina. "It's like that story about the student who wouldn't pay Protagoras his fee."

"What story?"

"Oh, you don't want to hear a story at a moment like this. Go ahead, indulge yourself. Tell us all about him."

"No, no. Tell it. It'll distract me."

"Okay. Protagoras taught the student how to be successful at argument, and they agreed that the student would pay his fee only if he won the first case he pleaded in court. Well, he kept delaying his first case, till Protagoras threatened to sue him; he pointed out that the student didn't stand a chance: if Protagoras won, the student would have to pay by the judgment of the court, and if the student won he would have to pay according to the terms of their agreement. But the student—he must have been a pretty clever student—pointed out that Protagoras didn't have a chance: if he, the student, won, he was freed of all debt by the court's decree, and if Protagoras won, he was free and clear according to the terms of the agreement. There's your typical sophist argument. You choose what you like and find words to justify it."

I was never good at riddles. I sat puzzling, while Gabrielle made an effort to smile. The next minute she was in tears again.

"Oh, it's really too hot to cry, Gaby," Nina said. "It's too hot even to talk. Let's go to the beach, just for a look. The car's right outside."

I was up and ready. Gabrielle looked at her watch. "I don't know. . . . Don . . . the kids . . ."

"Is it right? Is it wrong?" Nina mocked. "Shall we bear the heat, forbear from going to the beach? Or maybe we should forbear from denying ourselves the beach. Let's sit and analyze it."

"Okay, okay." She wiped her eyes and turned to me. "What was the part about the emeralds?"

"I'll tell you another time. Come on, up! It'll do you good."

Nina put on real clothes, and we trooped downstairs to the aging but still plucky white Triumph. We sped over the bridge, with the Watchtower, home of the Jehovah's Witnesses, glaring

at us severely, warning of imminent apocalypse, then through
the broad, stolid avenues of Brooklyn, past old people in sturdy
white laced shoes, taking the night air on plastic chairs set on
narrow stretches of grass. Very soon the smell of ocean sea-
soned the air. On the boardwalk were other seekers after a
breeze and a glimpse of infinity. We took off our shoes and
went down to the sand, cool on the soles of our feet. The beach
itself was nearly empty. Wire trash baskets loomed like animals
in the night; here and there a bulbous lump shifted on the sand,
couples rolling in blankets. We didn't dance or frolic as we
used to, but walked sedately to the water's edge and stepped in
almost up to our knees. The surf knocked against our legs. Far
off, a yellow light from a ship at sea (how far, Thales?) cast a
ray on the water like a mistaken sun, out of season. The water
was warmish, having been heated all day, all week, all month; it
was comforting to think that even the sea, under a planetary
sway, was subject, like us, to small fluctuations of temperature.
A few gulls swooped overhead, plummeted, skimmed the surface and shot upwards into a black sky full of stars promising
more heat when the dark lifted. We walked along the water's
edge about a quarter of a mile, stopped as one and turned back,
not speaking. We were cooled. The heat and the day and the
facts of our lives drained from us, and we were creatures
unspecified, abstracted from ourselves, poised at the rim of the
sea.

We sat down on the sand, not close together but together. I
saw a shooting star. It went by so fast I had no time to tell the
others. No, I wanted it all for myself, because it brought back
to me the night Vivian was conceived, thirteen months ago,
when there was also a shooting star.

"Did you see it?" Victor had said. It was a weekend camping,
our first weekend away alone in years. "Yes, I saw it. Ah, come
here, Mr. Watson, I need you." Our words came so slowly and
lazily, everything else so fast. "First put the damn thing in,
Lyd. Come on, baby," he drawled, and I drawled back, "I can't
reach it, and I can't get up. It's too chilly out there. Look at all
those cold stars. So cold. Yes, oh that." "Lydie, I don't want
. . . Let's just—" "One time out of so many. It can't happen.
Oh Victor. Love." "Baby, move over, yes. Oh Jesus. It's always . . . I could die in you. It would be all right." "Stay still

for just a minute. Can you? Oh that's good." "Listen, I'd better not. It's too risky." "Oh Victor, don't, don't. It doesn't feel nice. Stay, please. Don't go 'way."

Vivian was what we had. We thought of an abortion and we remembered that moment on the damp earth, when I had pleaded and he had been unable to leave me, and we couldn't bring ourselves to deny the fire that was her source. It was as if we knew it would be Vivian, child of air and water, conceived lakeside, child of the elements, magical, careless, with glistening shy black lake eyes; as if we knew in advance her delights and would not miss having her for the world. The world well lost. We would manage somehow. Four of them! There was something seductive, wonderfully outrageous about it. A game, like playing poor. People thought us stupid, but were too discreet to say. Had they heard how it happened, they would have thought us stupider still.

Gabrielle waited but the feeling did not pass. It wore her down like a disease; she got thin from it, and her blue eye and green eye both faded to gray. Yet she would do nothing but abide with it, speaking of it rarely, bearing it like a disease, not progressive and not terminal. In Don's spiffy green Volkswagen bus we drove out to the country for picnics on warm Sunday afternoons, children bouncing around in the back, clamoring, How much longer? Sometimes she invited us for dinner and cooked fancy French food. There seemed little change between them. As ever, she was the gracious wife, receptive to his affection, but quieter. A weary kind of stillness settled on her movements. She glided around the table carrying dishes with almost no sound, deft, light, and self-absorbed, while he continued to dote, never letting on if he knew anything.

Holding me in bed, Victor whispered, "What is the matter? Is she not well?" "She's well." "What is it, then? Something between them?" "No, I think they're all right." "Someone else," he said. It was terribly difficult not to respond; this murmuring was the core of our life. He nudged me. "Lyd? You up?" "I'm up." "You can't tell me?" I shook my head against him in the dark. He could feel it. "But Don. She still loves him. Doesn't she?" "Oh yes," I said. "Otherwise . . ." "What if that should happen to us?" "She's good," I said. "I wouldn't be such a good

girl." "No," he said, "I don't imagine you would." "I don't see
it happening. I don't have the time. Move your elbow, Victor.
My arm's asleep." He did, and began to caress me. "Come here
again," he whispered, and moved to pull me on him. "I'm tired.
Can't we just lie here and talk?" He stopped and simply held
me. "I could not love anyone else," he said. "Of course you
could." "Maybe. That Jasper, Lyd. Jasper looks at you . . .
Greg never looked at you that way." I moved off a bit. "Jesus,
what is this, 'The Kreutzer Sonata'? First of all, Jasper is
homosexual, Victor. If he looks at me it has to do with what
we're playing. There's an intimate current in a chamber group.
You have to keep checking out the others. You can sense what's
going on in them. Musically. It may be analogous to sex but it
is not sex. Besides, Jasper is better than Greg. Maybe that's
why he looks more." "Then why is Greg the one who got the
job in the Philharmonic? And incidentally, Jasper is bisexual,
not homosexual. Didn't you ever notice?" "You know, Victor,
with all your perception, sometimes you seem very ignorant."
"I suppose when I want to make love I get ignorant." I moved
back to him. "In that case you should insist." "Ah, I don't like
to insist. All right. I insist. No, I'll urge. Like this." I laughed.
"Not bad. You're funny, Victor." "That's why you married
me, right? For laughs." "It's after two, though. They'll be up in
a few hours." "Quick, then. We'll make it very quick this time.
No fooling around. You can even count. You tell me how
many, uh, thrusts you require, and I'll deliver, like George's
seltzer man. You can be asleep in five minutes if you concentrate.
Ready, Lydia? One." "Stop horsing around. I couldn't count
past two." "Two," he said. "Shh." He stopped and stroked my
face. "Don't ever fall in love with anyone else. Please." "I
won't, I won't . . . Oh!" I clasped him tighter, and when we
parted I burrowed into his shoulder, almost asleep. "I'm glad
you urged. Good night." Hypnagogic pictures began, with
music to match. I was almost gone. "Twelve," he said in my
ear. "Victor, how could you? How could I love someone who
could do that?" "I'm just kidding. I made it up." "Hah! I
wonder."

Gabrielle saved her good grace for Don and their kids; with
her friends she was moody. Unexpectedly, Esther turned up
one evening, strengthened and impervious to whatever damage

latitudinarianism could do. She said that the Gestalt wizard had transformed her, or rather, enabled her to transform herself.

"She doesn't operate on a Freudian model. She thinks the process is more like a Socratic dialogue." Esther's face was ruddy and radiant again, and her voice clear, not raspy—she had stopped smoking for the third time. Her hems were not hanging, she wore a bra, her hair had been recently washed. "It all has to do with figure and ground, the boundary where the organism meets the environment. That's a dynamic relation. You'd be surprised—your boundaries are more fluid than you think. You operate in a field, and you keep changing according to how things in the field move in and out of you."

Nina brought us a bowl of grapes and Gaby, as she clutched a handful, said, "That's all very well. But a women's group might do more for people our age."

Esther gave a newly ironic smile. "Couldn't you call us a women's group?"

"No. If we were we'd do something practical. Instead of sitting here we could be learning to use a speculum, for example. Why shouldn't a woman know what's inside her?"

"I'd rather know what's inside my head," Esther said, quite without irony this time, twining her fingers, feeling for the absent cigarette.

"We don't accomplish anything. We have a friendly feeling, that is all. Warmth does not get you unstuck."

"Gaby," I said, "you want a women's group, go find a women's group. I *like* what you contemptuously call a friendly feeling. And a speculum—are you kidding? After four pregnancies I'm not looking for any gratuitous probing. Thanks anyway."

"That's pure ignorance speaking! You of all people should want to know—"

"Ignorance! I know it so well I could be a midwife! Oh, sleep with the man already, will you? Enough of this saintly shit. It's pure self-indulgence. Give your consent. Do you think a women's group would tell you any different?"

"What man?" Esther glanced warily around the room as if he might materialize, an intruder come through a window. Then she looked at each of us. "Oh, I see. I've really been out of touch." Silence. "Silence makes me anxious. . . . I recently learned that."

"I'm sorry, Esther, go on," said Gaby. "You were telling us about the Gestalt person."

"Oh, never mind. Frankly, I don't see any point in a false purity. . . . He's on your mind so you might as well . . ." Clearly Esther was not of the school of Abelard. Still siding with God: lust in the eye is as good as done.

"Yes? And then what? Have a secret life? Or give up everything? I don't want to. I'm too entrenched. I can see it all. Notes in the office; surreptitious phone calls; I'd arrange to meet him when Don was away, or else I'd make up excuses, say I was here or there, with one of you, maybe—I'd have to drag my friends in. You'd lie for me, you'd feel contempt, he'd be humiliated. I've been through it a million times in my head. I don't want that kind of life."

What a talented projector. She could map the movements of Leucippus' atoms to their inevitable destiny; life could be over, in abstraction, before it was even lived.

"But when you were with him," Nina said. "That's the part you're leaving out. That part might give you . . . oh . . ." Glory was the word she had used, with embarrassment, at the race track.

"No one seems to remember that I once made a promise. But let's drop the subject. It's my private life."

"You didn't promise to suffer," said Esther. "Your first obligation is to take care of yourself. If Don doesn't satisfy all your needs—"

"Oh, please!" Gabrielle cried. "Don't give me that cant about needs! This is not a matter of need but of greed. He satisfies what you call my 'needs.' He gets it up, all too well. That is what you mean, isn't it? Oh, if only it were that simple! Who knows what needs are? Needs conform to the available satisfactions."

I often recalled that little epigram of Gaby's, aimed at the narcissism of the age and as out of step as a Jesuit at a disco party. Three years later, in 1975, after a visit to India in the entourage of a swami, Esther married Clyde Powers of the SAVE community, child of rampant sophistry, nephew of Richard Nixon's Doublespeak, and fifteenth cousin of Freud, though surely the master would have turned from him in disgust, as Shakespeare from Caliban. Clyde was available and Esther was in need.

Nina and I told Gaby about the wedding, soon after her return from France. Again it was late summer, again hot, again we saw the open fire hydrant through Nina's wide second-story window, and the perennial young mothers pushing fretful babies one last time around the playground. And for us, again the comfort of family without its blood resentments. Nina was the one who actually told, in her most arch manner. "In touch with himself, he boasted. But if all you touch is a void . . ." I sat and drank. With my skirt pulled up for the cool air, I examined my legs for red and blue streaks of aging. I was thirty-seven, a good but not great pianist, locally known but unable to travel as frequently as I should. When the trio or my woodwind pals had a gig of more than a couple of days, they got someone to fill in, while I ground my teeth at night and muttered, like a prayer to rout frustration, Althea, Phil, Alan, Vivian, the world well lost. It worked, most of the time. But I had too much to do and was showing inevitable signs of wear—intimate little occurrences all over my body that I wished Victor could not see. Having studied me so long, drawn me and painted me as well as loved me, he could not help but see, though he was far too chivalrous to mention them out loud. A foolish worry, I was aware, but it sufficed in black moments—and Esther's wedding had gotten me down.

"What's the matter, Lyd?" Gaby said with the old gentleness. Her passion, and the bile it oozed, had finally passed, as she had trusted it would. "You haven't spoken a word since we got here, except to ask for ice."

"It seems such a waste. Our going to school together, our talking. And she goes and does that with her life. Even India—at least it was India. There is really nothing to discuss. Nothing ever changes. I have no more taste for argument for its own sake."

"We never did engage in argument for its own sake. It was for our sake. Except maybe in school."

"Yes, what a falling off was there. From the cosmic to the personal. Gossip."

"Esther will pass through this like everything else," Gaby said. "She'll be the same, but the way she'll be the same will change, and who knows, the next way may be better."

I wasn't sure I believed her, but her serenity was a pleasure to watch. She possessed the grace that comes with ripeness, with having become what one was meant to become and has accepted as fitting. In college she had been an arty American girl, member of a genus. With age she looked more European, or perhaps it was the month in France that had given her eyes their allusiveness and tinge of history, her wide mouth its ambiguous curve. She did not look young for her years as Nina and I did: her various renunciations, and the unlovely virtue with which she had sustained them, had toughened her skin and left narrow ravines of strain around the eyes. But she had followed her anachronistic lights, and the stubbornness of that journey showed in the earned repose of her face and the lines of her body. She no longer kept the taut readiness of a dancer. She looked smooth, almost sleek, and satisfied. At the magazine, where she was arts editor now, she had a reputation for being tough and shrewd. She played no favorites, was afraid of no one, and never grumbled about compromises with commercialism—that was part of the job and she knew it. The mobilities of her face were carefully monitored, and hinted at vast inner rooms of privacy, a secret life. The secret life was not erotic but verbal. She wrote mysteries under a pseudonym. They were cool and caustic and elegantly plotted; the characters who toed the line were rewarded in the end, Nina and I noted, while those who followed aberrant paths were punished. In real life she was tolerant and forbearing. Having denied herself, she could allow others their divergences. Smugness, maybe, but she never flaunted it. Her auburn hair was cut razor straight, reaching not quite to her shoulders, and had streaks of gray that made it more beautiful. Her two children not only were bilingual but had excellent manners in both tongues, more than I could say for mine. With Don she was the same, gracious and receptive at a slight distance, which was perhaps where he wanted her. He touched her a lot in public, on the arm, the shoulder, neutral places emblematic of the others. I don't imagine she liked that but she gave no sign. I imagine she liked it all well enough in private. I think that after her love affair, her non-love affair, she was drawn to

Don again, as sometimes happens, with a passion of her own, not merely a reactive one. I think she took the longings she had felt for the man, in their most elemental form, the hollowness and quickenings in the cavities of the body, and brought them to Don to have them allayed, and she knew exactly what she was doing and forgave herself. The forgiveness was what saved her, and gave her mouth and eyes that humane ambiguity. I think.

"It's true, our interest has never been disinterested," I said. "Maybe that's why it didn't do anything for Esther. We discussed everything for how we could use it. We foraged. We picked the prettiest flowers and out of them we made our soups."

"Lydia has grown so facetious in her advancing age," Nina said. "I don't think you're a kindly Bosc pear any more, Lyd. You'll have to be something a little odd, like a fig, or endive."

"Endive is good. A fig is too exotic. For that matter, Esther's not much of a peach any more, either. More of a . . . watermelon. She can still be a ruby, though. What about you, Gaby?"

"Topaz," she replied instantaneously, and with perfect accuracy.

Nina said, "Emerald," and we all laughed. Hot on the inside and cool on the outside.

"Emerald . . . emerald. You were going to tell us something about emerald once, Lyd."

I shook my head. "I don't remember."

"Well, what are you?"

"Something blue. I can't think of what it's called."

"Sapphire?"

"No, sapphire is too gaudy."

Nina got up and fetched her huge Webster's dictionary. She opened to the array of gems, a shiny thick page amid the dry definitions. We huddled around it. Each color was discrete and luminous.

"How wonderful. I've never seen this page. This is the one." I pointed. "Lapis lazuli."

"You would pick a rare one. Well, enough of childish things. I've got to go. I promised to pick up Cynthia by ten-thirty. She's making posters to protest cooking classes. It appears the girls are going to strike."

"But school's out."

"They're getting their strategy set—it's only a few weeks off. I think she eavesdrops when the women's group meets at my place."

"Oh, I meant to ask, did you ever learn to use a speculum?"

"Yes. We had someone come in to teach us."

"And?"

"Interesting." She smiled gnomically, a bit like Evelyn. I could see I had forfeited the right to details. "Want to share a cab, Lydia, or are you staying?"

"No, I'll get one later. The air is too good to leave." I remembered the many nights when a cab would have been out of the question, and with that sense of time and change came a premonition that the Philosophy Study Group was over. Friends forever, very likely, but no more half-purposeful fooling with ideas. We would never be true believers. Things had fallen off too far—fruits, gems. Not ideas, but the intangibles of identity.

At the door Gaby said, "Wait." Perhaps she had the same intimation of closure. "It was from Epictetus. We were talking about bear and forbear. When I was . . . you know."

"Oh yes! That was years ago. It was Marcus Aurelius, but I can't remember what any more."

Nina went and knelt before a low shelf, stretched her arm directly to the book she wanted. What an efficient retrieval system! Perhaps her whole life was coded that way—given the topic and the year, could she lay her hands on anything? "Here. Find it."

I found it. It made me suddenly very happy—one of those moments when the shards of life fit together like a prehistoric bowl, and the mind is flooded with contentment. " 'Whatever anyone does or says, I must be good, just as if the gold, or the emerald, or the purple, were always saying this, Whatever anyone does or says, I must be emerald and keep my color.' "

Gaby laughed, a laugh of concealment, not candor. "I've kept my color, all right." Then she kissed us good night and was gone. We sat back on the pillows again. After a while I said, "So, Nina? How is it going with you?"

She leaned over, took the lacquered black box from the cabinet, and rolled a joint. She undid her hair and let it tumble down her back, smooth and thick. I thought of the man who

used to brush it. She smiled slowly—it was almost seductive—
and shook her head. "I don't want to talk about love. I'm sick of
love. He's very much there, that's all. And his wife is there too,
and her diabetic comas. Let's not talk about anything." She
passed me the joint. "What would you like to hear?"

"Wanda Landowska. Do you have any Scarlatti?"

She reached a hand out and found it immediately. We sat and
smoked. The pungent smell was good accompaniment for the
relentless, supple sound of the harpsichord. I could listen better
than look. I studied Nina, wishing for Victor's eyes. After all
the years of the Philosophy Study Group I still wasn't sure I
understood how she saw the world. A scientist first, that I
knew—her mind open to experiment, but her allegiance given
only to evidence and proof. She had changed the least since
college, except to become more talkative. The enormous change,
the metamorphosis of Nancy into Nina, had taken place in
school, right before my eyes, but I had been too inexperienced
to know what I was seeing. I envisioned it now as a huge
reconstruction project, where sometimes the shell of the old
becomes the skeleton of the new; the dirty work is surrounded
and hidden by makeshift wooden boards with tiny windows cut
out to satisfy curious passers-by, but often the windows are too
remote for the eyes of youngsters. Then it is unveiled, a suave
modern building with a glassy facade, beautiful in its way but a
trifle forbidding. She was wearing a loose and shiny black shirt
with a gold chain given her by Sam, the civil rights lawyer. A
noose. To his credit, though civil rights were no longer a
glamorous or fashionable issue for whites, Sam persisted. For
glamor, he had her. She sat with her knees drawn up. Listening?
Or maybe working out some formula in her head. She narrowed her eyes, played with a bracelet, drew in the smoke so
deeply I could see the muscles around her collarbone twitch.
She had been home on three occasions in the sixteen years since
college, and returned the first time looking frayed, and picked
up a stranger in a bar. The only time, she told me. "I thought
he might kill me and I didn't even care. He was all right,
though. I was lucky." She didn't go to see them again, but
telephoned regularly, honoring her father and mother long-
distance, sending money for a cataract operation, a new roof.
The other two occasions were the funerals.

The music stopped and we looked at each other and smiled. "It's peaceful here," I said. "I could sit here all night, listening." She shrugged. "Stay if you like. I don't sleep much anyway." "No." There was a silence.

"It's always been Victor, hasn't it?" Her voice was low; it made the very air heavy.

"Yes."

Then she smiled again, and I was grateful for this fine agility of hers. "Do you know, I still sometimes ask myself those Pythagorean questions at the end of the day. Can you believe it? A way of life and a salvation, Professor Boles said. In what have I failed? What good have I done? What have I not done that I ought to have done? A lot!" She laughed, head tossed back, eyes half closed. "The answers are interesting, but I don't really care. I mean I can't feel guilty about much any more."

"I can just see you kneeling at your bedside, the way you used to say your prayers with your mother standing by."

"Yes."

I was high. My thoughts were swirling lazily, like the smoke. I saw our lives fulfilled and, in a way, over. We had arrived at who we were, emerald, lapis lazuli, and the rest would be simply acting out the roles of ourselves, creating scenes in which our natures and talents could unfurl, the way a playwright writes a part for a specific actress. There would be no more great changes, I thought. I saw myself continuing to play, with new groups forming and dissolving, and perhaps in a few years going on tour. I saw myself continuing to love Victor and to raise our four children, subject to their delights as well as their selfishness. It was a vision pleasantly boring. Perhaps my greatest problem would be boredom. Not surface boredom or dullness—not with four children—but the kind of profound and temperate boredom you can feel in the midst of activity, a placidity that comes with the relief of growing up and believing that nothing wonderful or terrible will ever happen to you again. Or rather, that things will happen, but you will be so ripe with experience as to be unable to feel wonder or terror, knowing that anything is possible and everything finally subsides.

That was what I thought, high and ignorant, in Nina's purple apartment.

"I'd better go," I said, "before I start staggering."

"Yes, go." There was a touch of approaching middle age in the slow way she stood up: she used to spring from the floor like a beanstalk. She rested her hand on my shoulder. "Who knows what exotic adventures might befall you, Lydia."

"Thanks for everything."

"Shall we go to the races soon? About two weeks? I'm hot, I can feel it."

"Two weeks is fine."

We kissed, hugged, and parted. She felt light and soft, for an instant sinking in my embrace. That must be the feeling men loved. I must ask, some night in bed.

II

THE END

Snow, 1981

"Some say the world will end in fire, some say in ice." For us it was both.

Cremation is in. It shows ecological awareness. A sophisticated approach to the nature of flesh and spirit. All values Victor and I subscribe to, in the abstract. But when it came right down to it, we couldn't.

"Oh God, no," I said, I forget to whom. Maybe Victor's sister Lily. Our living room was so crowded with sagging bodies, and all of them, even Nina, seemed to be wearing bleak and ugly clothes. From the kitchen there came a minor racket—Gabrielle being useful but dropping things in her confusion.

"Burn me! Let them burn me!" Victor roared. He charged through space waving his arms, jostling people, knocking down a lamp and one of his own paintings, a small still life with seashells. The men had to quiet him. Don gave him a pill. He put it in his mouth obediently, but then he pursed his lips and spit it halfway across the room. Finally I took him out to the park. I told him to run to the Soldiers and Sailors Monument and back a few times—I would wait on a bench. He ran like the wind. He is not particularly athletic—I hoped he wouldn't have a heart attack.

When we returned the scene was unchanged. Nina was still sitting on the couch with her arm around Althea, stiff and chalk-faced, and Phil was huddled alone on the floor against the wall, crying sullenly, with horrid wet croupy noises. I went to sit alone in the kitchen for a few minutes. George arrived, for once not the customary portrait of *savoir faire:* beard unkempt, fly half-open, eyes filmed with terror. He was carrying three bottles of seltzer, those beautiful blue bottles with the chrome squirt tops that he had described so many times, and as he put them in the refrigerator he glanced at me sheepishly. "They're not for you. I know you don't like it. I thought maybe you could use it for the others."

"Mm-hm." I nodded.

He pulled a chair opposite mine so we were knee to knee like children about to play pat-a-cake; he took my hands as though he were about to say something formally condoling. Then he dropped his head onto my knees and began to cry. "I'm sorry," he said. "I should be taking care of you."

"Well, you will, later." I sat very still, stroking his head on my knees. "It's all right. I'm sure you will."

When he stopped we went inside where neighbors, mostly old people, a few young gay couples, walked in and out carrying casseroles, bags of fruit and cookies. Patricia and Sam, the very young pair across the hall, came in one at a time, the other staying home with the new infant—embarrassed to appear with the infant. The old people came over to Victor and me and in Middle European accents said things like, "What can I say to you?" Victor sprawled in a chair, still breathing heavily. And all the while I had the mysterious throbbing in my left ankle—I couldn't remember from what.

It is not true, of course, that my children are dead. Other people's children now and then die, and how sorry we feel, we may even shed a tear. Not mine and Victor's. We are among the fortunate people and we have worked strenuously for our good fortune. We have known hardship and overcome it; have been poor, cold, sick, and frustrated. We have seen our parents sicken and die much too soon. Oh, we have not exhausted the possibilities by far, but have endured our fair share without complaint. Is this the reward? This is America, too, remember. Our grandparents ran from atrocities to these benevolent shores, and fulfilled their part of the bargain. For our sakes, they came, for our safety. (Were we insufficiently grateful? We were born here—it never occurred to us to be grateful.) No, no bus carrying our children home in the dark from a long-awaited school ski trip, in the early stages of a snowstorm, would dare skid off the road to career into a clump of bushes and fall fifteen feet with a crash of thudding metal and cracking glass, outside a town called Pinecrest where a few years ago we attended an absurd wedding. Even if they died instantly. Even if their bodies were barely licked by the flames of the exploded engine. Even if "they were not the only ones," as the curly-haired policeman told me, and oh yes, I remember, that's how I hurt my ankle—I fell when he told me, onto Alan's skateboard, which fled down the hall away from the news. Even if some of the others were burned past all recognition, with nothing left except maybe a heart like the heart that remained of the steadfast tin soldier, which I had to read to Vivian every night for a month when she was eight, a heart that outlasted flames. Of all the possibilities for their young lives, this one possibility is out of the question. What is unthinkable is untrue. Some philosopher offered that little conundrum and we puzzled in the dorm, uncomprehending. Now I comprehend. This is unthinkable and I will not think it. God moves in mysterious ways—we know he leans toward the theatrical. Remember what he pulled on Abraham? Well, he demands that we stage this melodrama and we obey. But before long a stranger in a dapper pin-striped suit will appear—the angel—and announce that it was only a test. Wake up your kids and take them home. Amen.

Meanwhile we do have to stage it. Victor, with all his taste for ritual, was in no mood for piety, nor was I. Our conventional parents wouldn't care: three dead, one senile, and for the first time I was glad—they could miss this. And envious. We confessed to each other, though, that we wanted to hear something reverberant, something with pretensions to cosmic meaning, intoned over the bodies of our children. We wanted to hear a voice ordained for the purpose say in ripe, firm cadences, "The Lord is my shepherd; I shall not want. . . . He leadeth me beside the still waters. He restoreth my soul . . . I will fear no evil . . ." Well, of course fear no evil. What nonsense! What have they to fear now? Skidding buses? The dead can be fearless, and with good reason. Still, we wanted it.

"That would be good, if they said that."

"Yes. Yes," Victor answers. "That would be good." This is hours later, two in the morning: we sit at the kitchen table drinking tepid water out of coffee mugs Gabrielle left out to drain. We can't put anything else in our mouths. We told Althea and Phil they must try to sleep, and finally they went.

But they never turned off their lights. In the dark hall, light slid from the cracks below their doors, and soon we heard Phil come out to knock on Althea's door, and enter, and stay. I hope she let her younger brother curl up on her bed and held him in her arms while he cried. She always tells us she is a woman and we smile indulgently. I hope she is woman enough to do that. Victor, at the kitchen table, is still wearing his painting clothes— dabs of rich color on denim—but above the neck he is gray. His features look diminished and sunk in an expanse of skin with the sickly hue of dusty pewter. His hair, the sand color edging towards gray, is matted as though he has just risen from sleep. He looks defeated and homeless, a bum needing a shave. No beard any more—it was a passing thing. His voice is different, thick and hoarse, like an old man with phlegm. He wore it out shouting, the first twenty minutes. But when we find we are still so well suited, that we both harbor a desire so specific and so irrational, so futile—that is a slightly better moment. He closes his hand over mine on the kitchen table.

Don't take on so, love. We're only pretending. They'll be back. That view—a thousand hours ago?—was not our last. Not possible. I cry only because I am supposed to, as the mother, and because even the pretense is enough to bring tears. Those bodies we saw and identified (three of us—Phil insisted on coming, there was no restraining him; Althea did as she was told, spared herself), those soft unmangled bodies (and who dared to touch my babies, take off their clothes, pull those coarse white sheets to their necks! They don't even sleep that way! They like to sleep on their stomachs), bodies not too badly burned, only a little bit smudged (in a Heraclitan, generative fire, sowing a new world for fifty-seven parents), were not them at all. Pure artifice. Oh, they do these things so cleverly nowadays, but I was not fooled. Years of school mornings, all I had to do was stand over their still bodies and they woke. "If you just stare at a person who's sleeping for long enough, they'll wake up," Vivie noticed.

We must go to bed now too. But as soon as we turn out the light I get waves of nausea and panic; the ceiling lowers, the walls approach, my throat closes, and so we lie for the few hours with a bedside light on. Eventually Victor falls asleep and I watch, as if by watching I might partake of his forgetfulness.

His head is far back like someone proffering a throat to be slit. His mouth is open, the breath stale. The hairs on his chest are turning gray. His fine hands are dirty. His eyeballs are still, no dreams, and his brow is furrowed in pain; no, even asleep, he has not forgotten. Was it for this that he fell in love? My own body, which drew him and bore them, has been an instrument of ruin. I light a match and hold it close to my wrist, very close, just to know how it feels, but at the first real twinge of pain I shake it out. Coward. Children have known it. I wish this night would last forever. Bad as it is, it is better than what will come.

In the morning Nina calls—her tone soothing and low, perfect, only it does not soothe—to say she has spoken to a Reform rabbi who will conduct a brief and not very religious service including the Twenty-third Psalm. Nina has a wide acquaintance. How she persuaded him to alter the routine I will never find out. "Fine and dandy, just like sugar candy," Nina's parents made her say, with a curtsy, when grownups asked how she was. A woman who could survive that upbringing with her lifeblood still thickly warm can accomplish a great deal, even with a rabbi. Did she approach him in the harem outfits, the bangles? Surely not. Perish the thought. She approached him as a college professor and woman of impeccable and adaptable manners. She will take care of everything.

We considered having a few poems read. I remembered one I had liked in school: Ben Jonson on the death of a small child. The required survey of English literature, first half—I sat next to Steffie Baum, bright-eyed and bathed in a sexual afterglow. And so later in the morning, Phil saw me climbing on a chair to reach the top bookshelf where I kept old college books.

"What are you doing up there?" he asked, but without any surprise. Nothing would surprise him for some time. He was sitting on the floor against the wall, drinking a can of Schlitz, exactly his pose of yesterday, as if there had been no intervening night. Except his crying was silent. Crying into his beer.

"I'm getting down a book."

He took another swig. Since when does he drink beer? Should a boy of fifteen drink beer at all? Maybe he will develop a drinking problem. Teen-aged alcoholic: drowns his sorrows in beer first, then on to stronger stuff. Well at least he is not sneaky about it. At least he does it in his own home, in full view of his mother. Alan used to do a wicked imitation of a drunk flopping and flailing, not that he had ever seen one. He got it from movies and TV.

I climbed down with the book, careful not to rest any weight on the left ankle, and went over and knelt beside Phil. I smoothed his hair, wiped his cheeks with a crumpled tissue—liberties I would not usually take. "Let me make you something to eat. If you drink without eating you'll get sick. How about a grilled cheese sandwich?"

He shook his head and guzzled expertly from the can. His Adam's apple jiggled like a car riding over a bump. "I'm not hungry."

I eyed his crumpled, sour-smelling clothes. He must have slept in them. "Why don't you go and . . . fix yourself up a bit. Take a shower. You'll feel better."

"No I won't."

"All right." I sighed and started towards the bedroom with my book. An eerie part of my mind was clicking away in a vacuum: how unusually still it was; awfully late for Vivie and Alan to be sleeping; maybe go in and see if they were all right? The phone rang.

A man identified himself as someone from the funeral place. "I'm extremely sorry to interrupt you at this difficult moment, Mrs. Rowe, but it has come to our attention that you are a well-known musician in our area, and we wondered whether you had any special preferences in regard to music. . . . During the service tomorrow?"

I heard the words clearly—he enunciated with great clarity—but I couldn't seem to grasp the meaning. "What?"

"It has come to our attention . . ." He said it all again.

"What?"

"Mom!" Phil sprang up. Suddenly his eyes were dry, he didn't stagger like a drunk—he leaped to my side like a grown man. "What is it? Who is it?"

"It's . . . Hold on," I said into the phone. I was without words. It was like a dream where you forget your native language.

Phil took the phone. "Hello . . . Yes . . . Yes, this is her son. . . . I see." He waved me from the room and I went, as though he were the parent. "Let me think it over," I heard him say, "and discuss it with my family, and I'll get back to you soon."

This could only be a dream. That could not be Phil talking, who from the pits of adolescence found it too arduous to greet neighbors civilly but instead mumbled, not meeting their eyes. Who detested telephone formalities, who garbled messages, who wouldn't even call to ask the time of a movie unless there was a recording.

A little while later Althea knocked twice on our bedroom door and immediately entered. Victor, feeling sick, was stretched out on his stomach on our new king-sized bed ("I can ravish you at any angle," he said last Wednesday with glee, after the delivery men left). I sat near him cross-legged, leafing through pages.

"Mother, Nina is here again, with Gabrielle and Don. Aunt Lily and Uncle Lew are on their way up. Rosalie called and said she's coming. What do you want me to do with all of them?"

"Oh, give them lunch or something. See if there's any food."

"Gabrielle brought a lot of food. She's unpacking it."

"Good, they can eat that."

"I don't see why so much eating is involved. Mother, are you actually reading?"

"I'm looking for a poem."

Althea came closer. Unlike Phil, she smelled sweet and looked fresh. I had heard the shower early in the morning. She takes lengthy, epic showers. Victor and I have speculated on what she finds to do for so long under the spray: dance, act out fantasies, wash every square inch seven times in a circular motion while reciting a mantra? Her face was scrubbed shiny. She was wearing a navy corduroy jumper with a white blouse, and her blond hair, drawn back with a band, was still damp. So clean and so small, so staunch, she seemed younger than her years, a heroic child lacerated within but determined to behave well. A look Nina might have had as a child. I could hardly bear to see it. She would have been better off as Nina's daughter, not have had to go through this. If I had known Nina was never to have children of her own maybe I could have given her one?—I had so many. Did I need that many? And what for? What am I thinking. There was not one I could have parted with. Like Lear's entourage, reason not the need.

"You look flushed, Mom. Are you sure you're all right?" She

put her cool palm on my forehead to test for fever, as if I were the child.

I gave her a small smile of approval. Big girl. Just like Mommy. They never stop needing it. "I'm all right."

"But what do you want a poem for? For the funeral?"

However capable and kind, she is relentless in her pursuit of lucidity, clinging to sequence and causality. Very like me, in so many ways. Not in appearance—she is fair and delicate like Evelyn. But inside. Our minds work alike. She speaks the things that I think; she is too hasty to speak, too crammed with ready opinion, but so was I at her age.

"Uh-huh."

"I don't like when they read poems at funerals. It's so affected. Like those people who write their own wedding ceremonies."

Yes, like Esther's in Pinecrest, now a scorched field. Fire, Heraclitus said, lives in the death of earth, and Esther didn't like that notion of one element's flourishing by the other's demise.

"How would you know? How many funerals have you been to?"

"A lot." She listed them for me. They were a remarkable number for a girl just seventeen. Besides her grandmothers, there was the father of a close friend, a favorite English teacher, and a classmate who died of knife wounds from a mugging in the subway; the whole student body turned out. At the last three funerals poems were read, Althea said, and they made her uncomfortable, especially "Do Not Go Gentle into That Good Night" (the English teacher). She didn't want to hear that again.

"I wasn't thinking of that one," I said. "That's for an older person."

Victor moaned loudly, coughed, and shifted around on the bed, clawing at the pillowcase. His complaint was vast, inclusive: not only the accident and the decimation of his family, but this conversation he was forced to endure.

"Althea, before we decide anything we'll talk to you about it, okay? Please go and take care of the people now. You're very good at that. Be nice to Lily and Lew, no matter what they say. I'll be out soon."

"Do you think she's right?" I asked Victor when she left. "Victor, I know you're not sleeping. Please."

He rolled over. On his face were lines I had never seen before, running from the corners of his eyes down the outer edges of his cheekbones, and from mouth to chin. A muscle low in his neck twitched with an irregular pulse—the skin puckered, relaxed, and puckered. His eyes were the color of slate, and his hands, sculpted by labor, lay across his stomach limp as empty gloves. "I don't know. Maybe. She has good sense."

He went into the bathroom, leaving the door open, and vomited, while I sat staring at the poems by Ben Jonson. Not merely one but three on the subject. His First Daughter (infant mortality), his First Sonne (at seven), and a child actor (scarse thirteene). "Here lyes to each her parents ruth, MARY, the daughter of their youth." Well, not exactly. I was thirty at the time of Alan, Victor nearly thirty-two, and Vivian was two years later. I heard Victor brushing his teeth. He came back greenish and unsteady on his feet, wiping his mouth on his sleeve.

"Do you feel any better now?"

"I went to bed with this woman last week. Oh Lydia! It was not even the first time. It was the second. Lord! On a white shag rug." He gagged, pressed his hand to his mouth and swallowed his gall. I didn't speak for a long time, though he stood above me waiting for a reaction.

"Uh . . . not now, Victor, all right? Don't tell me that now. Don't tell me at all. Forget it."

"That's why."

Men like to overestimate their personal impact on the universe. In the book on my lap it said, "Farewell, thou child of my right hand, and joy; My sinne was too much hope of thee, lov'd boy."

"That's crazy. Be quiet," I said.

"It's a punishment."

"Stop it! Don't fall apart on me. Please."

"It just happened. I didn't think . . . It didn't mean—"

"Will you shut up? Do you think the whole world revolves around where you put your prick? That that could cause anything!"

Victor sat down with his face in his hands.

"I don't care anyway, I don't care, I don't care." The words came out of me like a chant, over and over; the sound was horrible and wouldn't stop. He pinned me down on the bed and lay on top of me like a blanket, his hand over my mouth stopping the sound.

It was too nice, that being covered and flattened by all his weight spread over me, and that warm palm on my lips. I didn't want comfort or any soft feeling. I didn't want any part of his superstition or repentance. The cause? I knew all about causes. I had not sat up nights memorizing Aristotle for nothing. Material cause, Victor: heavy snow, obscuring vision; slicked asphalt; a vehicle traveling at fifty miles an hour with a fallible driver. Formal cause, sweetheart: the laws of physics (the nature of the universe), decreeing that such a vehicle at such a speed, at such a bend in the road, in such weather, risks certain odds of going askew, wild but inescapable as the odds at a horse race. Efficient cause, baby: the tired driver lost consciousness for an instant, slipping into hypnagogic thought, or lost control, remembering a rankling injury done him by a loved one, or saw a light ahead and misjudged its position. Maybe even a deer in the glare of headlights, or an imagined deer. Final cause. Aha. The abstract purpose for which the event took place? That, my dear, I can't . . . discern. To demonstrate something? What? And to us in particular? No. No Greek can make me believe this was some necessary alteration of the universe.

"All right." I nudged him off and got up. "Let's go inside. They've come to see us. We have to." I combed my hair.

He got up and combed his hair too. So we had no poem at the funeral. We never got around to discussing it, never resolved the question of the good or bad taste of poetry read at funerals. (But "cover lightly, gentle earth"—how could anyone object to that?)

The funeral escaped me anyway, or I escaped it. There was a tall broad man in a charcoal gray suit standing in the front corner of the chapel, near a door. Not the angel; an employee, I suppose, maybe the man who telephoned. In the upper left-hand pocket of his suit jacket was a triangle of white handkerchief in the style of former days, and this handkerchief tucked so neatly in its pocket drew me into a trance. Those innumerable pockets. So much to hold, to hide. No, not innumerable, for once, the night before we set out for the brown house, I enumerated, gazing at my father's navy blue suit on its hanger while he stood in his underwear holding the tiny scissors he used to clip his mustache. Upper left hand, he told me: handkerchief, folded in triangle. Upper right hand: pens, sharpened pencils, cigars. Inner breast pockets, best of all because so hidden: business cards, letters, more pencils, gum. To have business cards! To be a grownup and possess so many worldly things! What a superb gesture of power, that reaching in like Napoleon and pulling something out, like a magician. And that strange little square pocket near the belt. Watch pocket, he said. Watch? Watch what? For a watch, silly Lydia, rumpling my hair. Rumpling my hair! God, how many ages ago! Never again to be a child. Always and always to be this grown-up woman now, with this past, these worldly possessions. To have a man, with a suit full of pockets.

The trance weakened for a moment; I heard a snatch about shepherds and pastures, rod and staff, all that bucolic rot. Better stick with suits. Something came creeping into my head and I pursued it like a bug. Yes. The spies in Alan's spy-story-in-progress, which he used to read to me in segments while I cooked dinner. The spies wore three-piece suits. Chapter One mentioned the master spy unbuttoning his vest. Last week while I was listening to the latest episode and making chili, there was something important I meant to tell him, but by the time he finished, the chili was ready, everyone came in, and I forgot. The master spy and his Russian counterpart, both double agents and both in three-piece suits, were meeting in Central Park where, concealed by bushes, they wrote notes to each other lest the bushes were bugged. And to avoid leaving scraps of paper that might be found and pieced together, they wrote on a Magic Slate, which could be erased. What I meant to tell him was that a Magic Slate, too, could be stolen and interpreted by experts, since the magic pencil leaves impressions on the cardboard beneath. I hadn't meant to spoil his idea; I was merely going to suggest that they destroy the Magic Slate after each meeting and buy a new one—the security would be well worth the expense. Suddenly I had the most urgent need to tell him this, and I glanced around in panic, searching in the crowd. . . .

There were hundreds of things left unsaid (and undone: those new sneakers he wanted so badly), but for some reason this about the Magic Slate was supreme, and the fact that his story would remain flawed, the spies would remain in grave danger

and I would never see him again to tell him how to protect
them, was absolutely, physically intolerable. I felt faint and
lowered my head to my knees. Victor's hand stroked my back.

When I could sit up again the rabbi's voice had stopped. I
couldn't see well—nothing was in focus—but things seemed
about over. Some shuffling, a clicking noise, and—surprise:
music. Music I had heard a thousand and one nights coming
from his room. A song by John Lennon, the late: "Golden
slumbers fill your eyes, Smiles awake you when you rise,
Sleep, pretty darling, do not cry, And I will sing a lullaby."
Paul McCartney's voice is hoarse, cracked, and tragic, as if he is
announcing, with an irony bitter as gall, Lennon's imminent,
premature death. The kids went to the memorial service in
Central Park three months ago, all except Althea, who dislikes
crowds and public demonstrations. They returned shaken and
subdued, with banners: John Lennon Lives. Well, let it be. Let
golden slumbers fill his eyes too. This is Phil's doing. Where is
he? Beside me, I forgot. I turn to him and pat his hand. "Good.
You did good." "Carry that weight," all four of them sing.
"Boy, you're gonna carry that weight a long time." There is a
long, intense, and complex drum riff. Then, after a few more
clicks, comes *Appalachian Spring*. Oh, very different, exultant.
The life force, la-di-dah. Not from the beginning, rather from
the point where the melody of "Simple Gifts" enters. My son
the taciturn adolescent turns out to be a genius impresario. He
must even have marked the place on the record for them. He
has behaved like a man, indeed is wearing a suit. I think maybe
he has done a little too well, like God with the Egyptians.
Dayenu, enough, because I am hearing her high, true voice in
the shower: "When true simplicity is gained, to bow and to
bend we will not be ashamed. To turn and to turn will be our
delight, Till by turning, turning, we come round right." All my
arts of numbness have been to no avail. I try to turn to Phil,
again to tell him, "Good," but I cannot move my head. Dissolved.
She was not to be thought of, Vivian, too hazardous. She is
unthinkable but I am thinking her till she fills me, her body
occupying mine, not like an embryo but arms inside my arms,
legs in legs, heart inside my heart.

Instead of taking the limousine home we ride in Don's and
Gabrielle's Volkswagen bus. With them in the front seat is a

stunned Cynthia, acne fading, body thinning—soon she will be a lithe but less subtle version of her mother. Well-bred Roger, away at Amherst, phoned us yesterday to speak his piece with a somber grace, and I bet with no prodding from his parents. Althea sits with Victor and me, and in the back, Phil with his old friend Henry, who sniffles for the whole trip, I don't know whether from emotion or the icy weather. Henry also suffers from allergies but it is February, a chill parody of all our Sunday afternoon picnics, pleasure-bound via this old bus, six children boisterous in the back. Today no one is asking how much longer, no one even speaks. Today so many warm live bodies capsuled against the cold are no match for the Long Island fields so richly sown with corpses, richer now.

George rode with Nina, so she would not be alone. She told me, later, that in the evening, after leaving us, they went to his apartment and made love, to feel better. She had not made love with him in so long, since Esther's wedding, perhaps? She wasn't quite sure. Oh no, there was that time after our Seder of last year. George had mellowed, she said. Well, naturally. I would have loved to hear exactly how, every blow-by-blow detail, but of course she didn't go into all that. She did mention that afterwards he wept and said he had loved me best of all the women he had known, and should have married me when he had the chance; then this terrible tragedy would not have happened to me. He can be so obtuse. And tactless. It was not even true. He hadn't loved me best and he hadn't had the chance.

Since Don's muffler had broken on the way out, making that awful clanking noise, he couldn't take the highways but drove through a succession of drowsy towns, past small half-timbered neo-Tudor houses with rooftops trimmed in snow and shrouded front lawns—the same snow that had coated the windshield of the chartered bus and slicked the macadam beneath its skidding tires. There had been a while, early in the morning, when the sky was flat, the color of dusty pewter, like Victor's face, but soon the sun came out. And now the snow glistened innocently in the crisp Northeast winter light. Every line on the horizon was drawn with a knife edge. Not a soul was out in the pretty towns; maybe they were all in church: Sunday morning. In this stillness and beauty, this probably specious serenity, I spied out the window an incredible thing.

Victor had his arm around me; on the other side he held
Althea's hand. All morning Victor had held me up, his hand on
my shoulder or pressing at my waist, nudging his limping
sleepwalker in the right direction. Always the touch of him, so I
never felt alone. His shouting and moaning were over. Now it
was he who took care. Chivalrous, to break the heart. He had
turned on the water in the shower and handed me the soap. He
zipped up my skirt as I stood before the mirror, arms hanging
useless with amnesia; he knotted the woolen scarf around my
neck. When he found me standing in front of the wide-open
window gazing up at the sky, he gently drew me away and shut
it. Maybe he thought I was going to jump. I had no thought of
jumping; I was entranced by the flight pattern of a great flock of
birds against the pewter sky, and thinking, Evelyn, Evelyn. No
plane fast enough? Tomorrow, you wired. But I wanted you
yesterday. Too vague, Evelyn, unattached, light, fey. Vivie
was magic like you yet she would have made it on time. She
had more guts. The birds kept circling, first in a shapeless
mass, then they formed a dense triangle, then a slender V.
They beat their wings hard in unison and abruptly coasted in
unison, as if their patch of sky had uphills and downhills. I
tried to count them as they circled: nineteen, seventeen, nineteen again, no, twenty—hopeless. I tried to see whether the
same one was always the leader and another one always the last,
but that was hopeless too; their swoops were quicker than my
eye, and dizzying. I tracked one who kept falling out of forma-
tion and lagging behind, then made frantic efforts to catch up, a
spastic agitation of the wings. Sometimes he succeeded, but
more often he lagged so far that the circling group would catch
up with him instead, and for a while he would travel in the
front ranks, till some weakness or perversity made him slip back
again, and again batten his wings desperately to rejoin. They
circled the same patch of gray sky so many times—were they as
hypnotized as I? Did they have the illusion of progress or was it
their recreation, their rehearsal for migrating south? Strange
that they hadn't already gone. Victor drew me from the window and closed it. He told me to put on a little make-up, for
my own sake—I would be glad of it, later on. He forgot
nothing, even that my pride would survive my children, and
perhaps my grief.

Assembled by Victor, and held by him, watching the towns pass by from the window of the Volkswagen, I see the thing. Incredible, yet I do see it.

Most of the pretty half-timbered houses trimmed in snow are fronted by broad lawns sloping down towards the road. At the edge of one snow lawn, near the sidewalk, is a clump of metal garbage cans; and lying in the snow, partly hidden by the cans, is a woman's body in gentle repose, curved on one hip. Only the lower half is visible. She is wearing something pink and light, a nightgown or slip (a smok?) that ends halfway down her thighs. Her legs are slender, fair-skinned, and bent slightly at the knee. It might have been a painting by Victor: it had that reverence for detail, that cool accuracy and sinuosity of line. Odalisque. She does not move.

I swivel my head to keep her in view, but in a moment she is blocked by a stand of trees. Then gone. But not from the inner eye. A white woman half-draped in pink, embedded in snow. A woman who has stumbled and fallen while taking out the garbage and will instantly pick herself up? A discarded doll, a heap of garbage artfully arranged to resemble a female form? I don't think so. A half-clothed woman, lying out in the cold. By choice? Or by design, accident, circumstance, necessity?

I may be dreaming. But there are the commonplace houses, the diurnal sun, the raw sounds of the broken muffler and Henry's sniffling. There is Victor's hand on my right arm, the heads of our friends in the front seat, Althea's profile on my left, sharp as a cameo. The woman was as real as any of this.

After a while it occurs to me that we are fellow creatures also in the most ordinary sense. "Don, we have to turn back. I saw a body in the snow."

Tactful disbelief. They think shock has brought delusion. But in the end they humor me. Don turns around and the morning rewinds on the spool of road. "Say when, Lydia." I manage to locate the house, the lawn, and the garbage cans, but the body is gone. Their troubled concern is not for the woman but for me; to ease them I say very little, making sure to sound controlled and sane.

Once out of the town I whisper to Victor, "There was. I swear it."

"I believe you," he whispers back.

Where did she go and what will happen to her? During the long trip home a cold curiosity spins bizarre possibilities. They unwind to infinity like broad white ribbons, rippling strips of snow, snow ribbons wrapping up the world till the world is a covered ball, all done up in satin snow, sealed and ready to be given over. Surrendered.

Mother

I discovered, taped to the side of Alan's desk that faces the closet, a picture postcard of some white stone structures in the Mesa Verde, in Colorado. The card showed a tall ladder connecting two levels of the Indian settlement nestled in an enormous cliff against an azure sky. Alan had drawn a circle around the ladder in red Magic Marker, then drawn an arrow going across the card and the light maple of the desk to another circle, where he wrote, "7/13/76." More than once I had told him that he could write on his desk in pencil, but please not with Magic Markers, which is why he did it on the hidden side.

Millennia ago, perhaps while Thales across the sea was pondering how to measure the pyramids, the Mesa Verde was the site of a thriving, self-sufficient Pueblo Indian community, eventually conquered and abandoned. Early in this century, two men on horseback happened upon its remains. Imagine their surprise, to round a bend and find extant, in those vast copper-and-ochre-colored cliffs, white buildings tucked in the cavernous hollows dug by wind and rain. The cliffs themselves are separated by deep ravines, creating a three-dimensional jigsaw puzzle split apart. The stone dwellings, in their linear, geometrical groupings, foreshadowing Euclid, are lucid and harsh, with rock for floor and rock for ceiling. Above on the mesa, their roof, the Indians cultivated crops, scaling the cliff by an obscure path of carefully bored finger- and toeholds, a path indecipherable to outside marauders.

We climbed that perilous ladder, 7/13/76—Victor and I and the little ones, off on a three-week jaunt while Althea and Phil were back East in camp. Below us was a bottomless chasm.

"Don't look down," the forest ranger warned. "Keep looking straight ahead, at the person directly in front of you." Directly in front of Vivian was a retarded boy of about fourteen who moved clumsily, and I feared he would make a false move and topple us all. I saw us hurtling through the cubist landscape like falling rocks. Earlier, the boy had tossed a rock down and we never heard it come to earth. He lumbered up one step at a time like a young child, unwilling or unable to go on till he felt each rung of the ladder firm beneath both feet. With every step the ladder trembled. But he didn't make a false move. He managed as well as anyone else, and up on the grassy mesa at last, I felt like falling to my knees and thanking him, as you might thank an indifferent god who has spared your loved ones out of pure caprice.

In the pottery and artifacts of the Pueblo Indians recurs the motif of a serrated line. After much study, said the forest ranger, archaeologists have concluded that the motif represents teeth. Because of their particular diet (and with no dentists, she added coyly), the Pueblo Indians must have suffered greatly from decaying teeth. So the image for their intractable pain finds its way repeatedly into their art.

I suppose the Magic Marker could be scrubbed off as in the past, but really, what would be the point? What is the point of so many minor restrictions? Most of them are concerned with the setting of precedent and habit, presupposing long life. I should have let him draw all over his room, if he chose. Drink milk straight from the half-gallon container. Live on pizza. Crawl into our bed in the middle of the night way past the age of four. For his whole life, if he liked. I also should have let him do things related not to setting precedents but to my own discomforts: keep a pet mouse, ride his bike alone through Central Park, see *Star Wars* for the fourth time. Refine his tastes? For what? And I should have gotten him the Adidas sneakers he craved, immediately, not put it off till the snow melted because I was busy, not said they were vastly overpriced and wouldn't Keds do as well.

One wall of his small room is painted midnight blue and dotted with all the stars in the heavens, each constellation clearly labeled in his slender, neat letters. He writes like a draftsman, Victor used to say. Several weeks have passed and

the Beatles records still lie scattered on the bed like huge coins.
I select one at random to play while I limp around. When he
first played *Abbey Road* for me, he pointed out how the songs
ran into each other; despite their different moods, they were
connected musically, thematically, like a suite. He didn't use
those words, naturally, but that was what he meant. I was
impressed and pretended I hadn't noticed. Vivian remarked that
the songs on one side of the *White Album* were connected too:
they were about animals. "Animals?" said Alan. "Sure. 'Blackbird.' 'Piggies.' 'Rocky Raccoon.' " Alan looked closely at the
record label. "Three out of nine." "Well, still," said Vivie. I
stuck up for her. I thought she had a point. Tenuous, but a
point. "Why Don't We Do It in the Road?" was certainly
animallike, though I didn't suggest that aloud. "Blackbird" is
playing right now—it has a feathery, airy grace. "Blackbird
singing in the dead of night, Take these broken wings and learn
to fly. All your life, you were only waiting for this moment to
arise. You were only waiting . . ."

The spy story is on his desk, the spies in their three-piece
suits scribbling notes on the Magic Slate in the bushes of
Central Park oblivious, forever now, to the danger they risk.
But so is the danger, forever now, forestalled. Also on his desk
is the report he was writing about Egypt. "Religious Beliefs" is
the heading. "The ancient Egyptians believed that when a person dies and goes to their Day of Judgment, their life is put in a
balance scale and in the other side is a feather called The
Feather of Truth, and if the person's life tips the scale even a
little bit then he does not go to heaven." A winsome notion of
truth, compressed into a feather, far from the Truth we were
led to envision: solid, unbudgeable, forbidding, and quite lacking in charm. Evidently for the Egyptians it was the lies that
were heavy.

The old *Ranger Ricks* can go to the school library. The base-
ball cards should really be given to his friends—they are valuable,
I understand—but since I don't want to see his friends I drop
them in the metal wastebasket, where they make a hollow,
accusing thud.

There on a shelf is that stupid wooden pig. Flat, barely an
inch in depth, only the vaguest outline of a pig, it is a small
bank designed by one of New York's less prescient shop teachers.

Its legs—front two and back two merged—can hardly support it. If you move the shelf the slightest bit, it tips over. I move the shelf. The slit on top is too narrow for nickels and pennies: a dimes-only bank. But there is no provision for getting the dimes out, no secret cloacal exit, only that one thin slit on top. And being so flat, the bank fills quickly. Like doing penance, you need to turn the pig over and shake out the dimes one by one, which requires a certain strength of character. I would occasionally shake out a few for bus fare. Alan could empty the whole bank. Every child in the seventh-grade woodworking shop made the same pig and brought it home this past Thanksgiving, which means that in thirty-three families dispersed through District 3, someone shakes out the dimes, humming or cursing, depending on temperament.

Through my years of experience as a mother, it has in fact come to my attention, as the funeral director would say, that the New York City schools are obsessed with turning out small household articles. For girls it begins with potholders, which Althea wove out of colored loops on an eight-by-eight metal loom that she brought home at the end of the year. One potholder even had my initial woven into it; a week later, so as not to appear sexist in outlook, Althea made one with a V, much more tricky. The potholders were useful and pretty but deteriorated rapidly, while Althea moved on to woodworking. Luckily Vivian took over and kept me well supplied; I have not bought a potholder in years, but soon I shall have to. I cannot ask Althea, at seventeen, to weave potholders on a baby loom. Besides potholders, we have half a dozen clay bowls, a dull-tipped letter opener, sand sculptures in applesauce jars, and a lamp made out of a Chianti bottle. We have a bulbous green vase that came home wrapped in newspaper like the Maltese falcon. We have ceramic ashtrays and ashtrays of mosaic tiles, although till lately only I smoked, and not very much. Now, unfortunately, Althea smokes an occasional cigarette. We have boxes made out of popsticks and boxes made out of toothpicks, boxes that hold seashells, playing cards, matchbooks, painted pine cones, stubby candles. All these things we welcomed with fulsome praise.

During his last weeks, Alan gave us periodic reports on a certain crumb pan he was making in the seventh-grade metal shop, successor to woodworking. He first mentioned it in his tongue-in-cheek way, like his father but more pronounced, with a toss of the head so his longish, tawny hair rippled then settled like a sleek cap. I was stumped. Was it something to put underneath a toaster, or maybe under a pie plate? "A crumb pan," he explained soberly, "is like a dustpan, only smaller. You use it to sweep up crumbs." "Oh, I see." I wasn't sure whether to laugh. "Do you make a little brush also?" "No, Mom, I'm afraid you'll have to supply your own little brush." Ah, so it was all right. "Well, good. It's what I've always wanted, actually." "I thought so," said Alan. "I sensed there was something vital missing from your life." "Yes, an unful- filled need, as George would put it," I said. Phil said, "We'll have to leave more crumbs around, though. I think we may be too neat for a crumb pan." "Yes, all you kids better start leaving crumbs." We asked him at odd moments about his crumb pan—its dimensions (four by six) and its progress. "So, how's the crumb pan coming?" It was taking what seemed an inordi- nate time. It was not the process that took time, Alan explained, but waiting to use the machine that bent the metal, of which there was only one, because of city budget cuts. He was unfail- ingly good-humored and deadpan, even when Althea said she could think of nothing in the cosmos with less *raison d'être*. He explained carefully how it was made. First you do a stretch-out on cardboard, then you scratch the outline on a sheet of metal, then you cut it out of the metal with tin snips. . . . Victor was the only one who saw some merit in this project; he had nostalgic memories of metal shop. "Did you make a crumb pan for your mother too?" I asked him. "No, I can't remember what I made. Oh, a belt buckle, I think. Maybe a napkin holder." "Well, we already have a napkin holder," said Alan. "That's why you're getting a crumb pan." "Yes, I know. Phil made the napkin holder." "No I didn't," said Phil. "Alan made that too." "Oh, really? I could have sworn you made it." "*I* made a napkin holder," said Althea resentfully, "but you never use it." "Is that true? I'm sorry." "Your napkin holder only held seven napkins," Phil reminded her. "So what? It's the principle. It's not my fault they make napkins so thick." "I use your little blue ce- ramic pot for thumbtacks," I said to Althea consolingly. "That's not hers, that's mine," said Phil. "Is it? I'm sorry. I'm sorry,

children." It was true, there were so many of them and so many
artifacts, as though our apartment would someday be studied
by archaeologists for clues to our joys and pains, like the Pueblo
Indians' dwellings, that I couldn't keep things straight. But I
would have remembered that the crumb pan was Alan's. None
of them but Alan could have described with such aplomb in the
face of the ridiculous how it was cut and bent into shape. I can
hear his voice lingering over the words "tin snips," with a soft
merriment at the sound. Now that I can never have my crumb
pan I feel an absurd longing simply to see it. I could call the
metal-shop teacher and ask if I might pick it up, in whatever its
stage of development. Or I might just go in to look at it, after
which the teacher could throw it out or, given the state of the
budget, unbend the metal and reuse it, if feasible.

Of course there is not the remotest chance that I will pursue
the crumb pan. I would never go mad in quite that way. My
curiosity will have to remain unslaked, that's all, along with my
curiosity about how tall they would grow, how their features
would sharpen, what surprises their talents would lead them to,
what kinds of lovers they would choose, how they would take
the world and its vicissitudes—would he really become a Quaker?
would she always prefer sleep to spiritual communion?—and
what they would be and mean to us, grown. "Will you still
need me, will you still feed me, when I'm sixty-four?" Last
night, lying alongside of Victor in the dark—guarded, stiff,
tense as stretched wires yet for all that companionable, an
impossible, agonizing mix—I said, "Oh Victor! That crumb
pan." "Jesus, I forgot all about it. The crumb pan." And for a
teetering instant we didn't know whether we would cry or
laugh. But nothing happened. The moment settled in balance
between us and we lay silent, breathing slowly.

I'm shaking and shaking this damned bank, but it's too full
for any dimes to escape. What a waste, to lose so many dimes.
How often, in the early years of our marriage, fifty or sixty
dimes would have made a difference. They would not have kept
Con Edison from turning off the gas and electricity in the bleak
old apartment so that I had to warm Phil's bottles under the
tap, raging, till Edith came, took a look around, and for the one
time in her life, maybe, lost her temper and told Victor his
pride was insane, and drawing in a deep breath for courage,

turned to me and said I was no better, then snatched the bill from the kitchen table, slamming the door on her way out. But the dimes would have reheeled shoes, bought a steak, or two tickets to a movie. Our pride was insane. But no longer.

I fetch a hammer and screwdriver, and sitting on the floor of Alan's room, assault the piggy bank. The screwdriver is less violent but also less effective; I have to use the hammer, and mercilessly. The wood cracks and splinters, soft wood that, once split, I can even rip with my bare hands. I take care not to hurt them—I am not planning retirement again, oh no. Never that again. Dimes spill out on the floor, a small fortune in dimes. A legacy.

Finally I sit down on the wide windowsill, rubbing my ankle. I have come to savor that other, duller pain and would miss it if it left. On a nearby roof across the back alley is a young black woman with an Afro, a bright golden dress, and Frye boots, hanging baby clothes on a line. Even though it is warmish for early March, the sky is overcast, portending snow or rain. An optimist. I shake my head at her innocence, slowly, like an old lady.

Why did I lose my children? That's what I want to know. But the question is loaded, no good because it's not phrased right. It embodies some fallacy or other I learned about in school, an egotistical warp. As warped as asking why did Victor lose his children. A better question would be, Why did these particular children die? To that there are reasonable answers having to do with chance and the law of averages. Also, cosmically: everyone dies. Locally: whatever that official doctor said was the cause of death. I forget the Latinate phrase.

Marcus Aurelius, the Stoic and prig we used to mock, counsels that we be content with whatever happens to us: "Because it was done for you and prescribed for you, and in a manner had reference to you, originally from the most ancient causes spun with your destiny."

But *why* did I lose my children? Precisely that loaded question is what I want to ask, whose obvious, built-in answer is that I didn't deserve to have them. That's crazy, be quiet, I scolded Victor for thinking that way. Do you think the whole world revolves around where you put your prick? No matter. Why didn't I deserve to have them?

For the answer, months, years of my life that I repressed for my own ease come flooding back, now that I neither have nor seek any ease. They were not truly repressed, in the sense that psychiatrists use the term, but suppressed, as truth is suppressed but not forgotten under authoritarian rule and floods back with an upheaval. The dam breaks in one crucial place, we might as well let go the others. I need no longer pretend that I have always been this cheery, competent creature, my life a rational passage from sturdy rung to rung. Under interrogation, stripped and spotlighted, my body becomes an open book.

There is an essential and profound strangeness about being a mother that is rarely spoken of, and yet religion does make much of loving others better than one's self, which suggests it does not come naturally. Maternity, though, is considered in the nature of things: that mothers gladly endure pain so that their children may thrive is a useful, sustaining myth. Also something of a cultural joke: the mother as sucker. And between saint and sucker, two sides of one thin coin, is little room to maneuver.

In childbirth we tunnel through a dark passage to the new and strange place, to find there that the myth about mothers is true and so is the joke, the corrosive humor. At one in the morning in a room barely lit, two nurses from Trinidad sat at either side of the bed where I sweated in panic my first time, and in between discussing young men they had known in Port of Spain—Desmond, a big spender, Hugo, a terrific dancer, and Patrice, out for what he could get—they peered up my legs. There was going to be a party on Saturday night. "And do you think William be there?" the plump one asked. The thinner one sounded irritated. "I don't know if William be there, but if he be there he better not be looking for nothing from me. Or that brother of his either. No, mon, I finish with William and William whole family." The plumper one giggled. "Not if he treat you right I bet. Offer you with sugar coating." I groaned in pain, and she took another look. "Nothing doing yet, lady. You got a long time yet." Panic locked like a shackle. This was another country entirely; I had no preparation, no passport. "I wept and mourned when I discovered myself in this unfamiliar land," Gaby had read aloud in the dorm. She had a baby now, yet neither she nor any book had ever told me it meant this. I asked for the doctor. I only wanted a familiar voice and face. "Don't put me to sleep. I told you I want to be . . ." But he jabbed me, stopped the world. I went out with the luscious West Indian rhythms vibrating in my ears—their voices were lilting and trilling and hard, like a xylophone.

The drug was sodium pentothal, also called a truth drug, also used on criminals. You wake as though from heavy blank sleep, but in truth you have been awake all the time (telling the truth), living in scenes that live only once, never to be retrieved by memory and granted their proper place in your life. Sensations and all their possible harvest vanish without the supreme gift of the echo that graces them with humanity. For everything that promises our lives the resonance of a third dimension must recur. Even hearing music for the first time is not truly hearing it, only the prerequisite for hearing. The next time, and the next, we hear with the fullness of anticipation and foreknowledge, having had the pertinent nerve paths cleared for the feelings that will travel them, strewn like seeds. Everything destined to be real and permanent happens to us over again, in the act of remembering. What abides, along with Empedocles' elements, fire and earth, water and air, is the past. We possess nothing securely but the past and that simple gift of turning and turning, to recreate it, to come round right. Nina was wise when she took those early morning solitary walks in college, trying to reconstruct the events of the previous day in their proper order, after the edict of the Pythagorean Brotherhood, "that there is nothing more important for science, and for experience and wisdom, than the ability to remember." And for salvation, they might have added. This I know from my own life.

So that what happens only once, like Althea's birth, never to recur in the life of the spirit, didn't happen at all in any subjective sense. It happened like the tree falling in the forest: I not there to hear it, and yet all the while there for strangers, telling them the truth. What truths? Universal? Hardly. The most secret and incriminating, probably, the ones I would never have told a soul. That after Victor and I decided to marry I called George, one last fling for old times' sake? And did I say what a good fling it was? Exactly how, and how many climaxes? That while in college I shoplifted a bra from Macy's by wearing two out of the store, to see what it felt like? I had been reading Gide; I wanted to perform an *acte gratuit*. Or that earlier, much much earlier, against my mother's express injunction I opened the locked drawer in my father's bureau and found pulp magazines with stories set in Paris and pictures of girls in black stockings and garter belts kneeling with men's penises in their mouths? What a peculiar thing to be doing. It didn't seem quite sanitary. I was sure my mother wouldn't approve. The doctor who heard my true confessions, the sloppy stitcher, is dead now, which gives me satisfaction. The nurses wouldn't remember: they must hear volumes of it; they must watch that feather of truth rise on the balance scale every day, mortifying even us milder liars. But I, I remember all about Patrice and Hugo and Desmond and William!

When I awoke, alone in a bare room, my stomach was flat. Hours later they brought me a creature swaddled in a pink and white checked blanket, and I was expected to assume that she and the lump absent from my stomach were the same. I did as commanded: civilly, I offered her a breast. Not till the next day did I undo the blanket, count her fingers and toes, look at her eyes, her ears, up her nose and in her mouth, and at the rotting black knot of flesh at her navel. Mark of Eve. In sorrow, meaning travail and pain, shall you bring forth children, but I had had little travail or pain. I had fallen in the forest; all unfelt. I had plenty of pain now—the stitches stung and ached—but even I knew that infected stitches from an episiotomy were not the pain God was referring to.

Lying idle, I was able to sort out the pervasive din of the hospital into distinct sounds, like sorting out sections of the orchestra: wheels large and small, voices, footsteps (rubber-soled staff and clicking visitors), ringing telephones, buzzers, pagings of doctors for God knows what calamities, moans, baby cries, and an occasional shriek from the labor rooms across the courtyard. Time jerked by in green and white flurries—aides depositing trays or snatching them away, nurses with orders: get up, walk, urinate ("or else we'll catheterize you!"), take a shower, attend a meeting. A meeting? I looked up, puzzled, from my Trollope novel of parliamentary intrigue. Yes, dear.

Meetings for breast-feeders. Meetings on bathing the baby. The nurses reported to Victor that I was uncooperative. I refused to go to meetings and I refused to urinate. "Do them a favor," he said to me, "and piss at least."

I woke from a nightmare to find a large man at my bedside; in the dim he resembled a Samurai warrior. "Give me your arm, please." I didn't remember the dream but knew it had been violent—it still wrapped me round in its terror. "Your arm." He had come to chop it off—I looked for the sword and cringed in the bed. He reached for my arm. "Blood pressure," he said. I have always thought the dreams I cannot remember are dreams of Althea's birth, those buried few hours fighting to take their rightful place in my life, so I might understand where I had been. I gave him my arm. "What time is it?" "Early. You can go back to sleep." "Goddammit, can't anyone give a straight answer around here?" "Five-thirty." I came to anticipate his footsteps and thrust out my arm at the sound. The fourth and last morning I raised my head and spoke. "Tell me something. Isn't there any other time of day you could do this?" He smiled and said, "Sorry."

There was one moment of peace. Althea lay asleep in my arms after nursing. No one came to fetch her and since I didn't know what else to do with her, I held her. I lay back and placed her in the crook of my arm with her head on my shoulder, as you hold a lover after love. It was startlingly quiet—a lull in the usual din—and gradually, in the quiet, my terrors fell away like ugly old rags, leaving a brand-new skin, a layer of peace exposed to light for the first time. "We won't let them get us, will we?" I heard myself whisper. "You and me, we'll take care of each other, like now. Just quiet." We were not in a hospital but on some blessed island, and I heard Debussy's L'Île joyeuse. There was nothing I needed to do for her that would not come instinctively; tears of relief streamed down my cheeks. We had escaped into a state of grace, out of this world, isolated and safe, one flesh.

After they took her away—"Anything wrong, dear?" the nurse asked keenly. "Anything wrong with Baby?"—I dried my tears and feared I was mad to be so frightened, living in madness like a place, a last resort.

I felt the tug of the weird twilight sleep for many months. I wished I could sleep all the time, that same terrible Lethean sleep, being there and not there, and wake years later to find her ready for school. I couldn't move fast. My legs dragged as if they pulled weights. I couldn't read anything serious. I could barely think—my mind was milky fog. When I listened to music I heard only the surfaces of the sounds. While I nursed Althea I played endless rock and roll on the radio. The Four Seasons sang "Walk Like a Man"; I could barely stand straight. When she sucked at my breasts she was drawing the life out of me, and when she was done I swayed on my feet; sap gone, I was a brittle tree, liable to blow over in a breeze. I was cut off from the subtleties of common language, and like a non-native speaker, stopped short by idioms, arbitrary usages. My breasts ached with more milk than she wanted; when I asked the doctor how to give up nursing and he said, "Cold turkey," I held the phone, dumb. What magic in chilled turkey could dry up my milk?

A pamphlet suggested I would feel better if I expressed the milk. "Express the milk" sounded like something to do with a train. Oh. *The Milk Train Doesn't Stop Here Any More*, baby? But I figured it out, picking apart the syllables like a foreigner. I opened my old red terrycloth robe, bent forward so my breasts hung over the bathroom sink, and squeezed out the milk. I was a machine or an animal, one side or the other of human. Dark blood oozed below, milk dripped above, my body was beyond control, churning out its liquids. Like a machine or an animal, I felt no modesty or desire for privacy. I didn't bother to close the bathroom door. Edith, come to help, civilized Edith with her lightly sprayed fair hair and her sweet manners, passed by. Curiosity conquering discretion for once, she paused. "Lydia, what *are* you doing?" Edith had never nursed. "Getting rid of the milk," I said ferociously. My face was contorted with concentration like a scowling animal's. Edith drifted away. If she thought I was offended at her intrusion she was mistaken. I was bitter at being no longer human while she still was. See, Edith, I've become an animal! Grrr . . . grrr! The milk spurted out like semen, only thinner and not sticky, and swirled down the drain. Guilt! Think of the starving children in Europe! I didn't care to taste it. Victor did. I imagine lots of men do, though at the time we thought it a highly original and slightly perverted thing to do. He tasted it in bed, in a boyishly salacious way, and we laughed. I could still laugh. Laughter was on the surface; my panic was deep, deep.

"Well, how is it?" "Not bad. Try it. I'll give you some on my finger." "No, thanks." He sucked some more. "Sweet. Aren't you even curious?" "Not particularly. I'll suck you, if you want, though. Do you want me to?" He looked up, startled. "Well . . ." "I thought maybe you could use something. I mean, those stitches, and all." "You make it sound like . . . you'd be, you know, doing a service. It doesn't feel right." So scrupulous, so evenhanded, ah, he always was. Only it never occurred to either of us, back then, that I too might work in a bar and bring home the money and thus feel justified spending my mornings practicing. "Well, I'm offering. Take it or leave it." "Lydia." "What?" "Don't . . . don't talk that way. You never used to." "I can't help it. I've become an animal." He laughed. He thought I was joking. "All right, let me see what it feels like with an animal." I did it not with any particular allure, but in a service-able way, just as I would willingly have spoon-fed him had he broken both arms. He didn't seem to enjoy it very much—men with broken arms must not enjoy being spoon-fed either—and I didn't offer again.

There was another moment of peace, when the ugly rags of terror fell away. Althea was about two and a half weeks old. Amid the debris of jars and brushes and half-finished paintings, we sat side by side on the couch on a snowy afternoon, she in her infant seat, I with my legs cautiously crossed (the stitches refused to heal, itched and stung). Out the window was the small concrete park where in fine weather the Italian men played bocce; now it was patched with graying snow, deserted except for a lone boy in a plaid jacket, throwing snowballs at the iron fence posts. My mind was quiet and empty. I watched the boy scoop the snow in both hands, cup it, and pat it into balls. The time since she was born felt like time not marked by passages of darkness and light but one long span of wetness—diapers, laundry, nursing, bleeding. Life is a fountain, all right, and I smiled in spite of myself. It struck me that this was the first time in Althea's life that she had been awake for twenty minutes neither hungry nor crying, neither being fed nor being changed, not needing anything, merely sitting on the couch and gazing at her surroundings, like any other person. I had a vision of such grandeur and beauty that I wept. It was only a vision of Althea growing into a real person, with longer and longer periods of just such commonplace peace, and myself someday not needing to devote every moment to her survival but sitting calmly beside her, living.

The season began to change. The sun climbed higher each day. I didn't need a hat and scarf and gloves any more when I took Althea out; she didn't need sweaters under her snowsuit. Mornings, I scanned the sky like a farmer with his mind on crops. Beyond that I ignored the offerings of weather. I carried around my own weather, graceless January. I awoke from the twilight sleep: I could move quickly, I could read. But I did not pick up my life. A spiteful element in my nature took over, like an extremist political party that seizes power when moderate ones default. Compromise demands subtlety and inventiveness. All or nothing was my spiteful slogan. I had a baby? Then I would damn well be a mother. I took good care of Althea, much better care than anyone would have expected, those first foggy weeks.

My mother helped, but she could not take my bitterness very seriously. And why should she? This was no crisis—this was the life of an ordinary woman. Everyone had to learn it sometime. She was not unkind; she had a certain perspective. "You'll see. Right now you can't wait to get a little time alone, but later on you'll wish for company. Children get to be thirteen, fourteen, they come home from school and shut themselves up in their rooms—you'll wish someone would come and pester you."

Did Evelyn and I, Ma? Sorry about that. Anyway, you were more correct than you ever dreamed. I wish for their company. Any of them, the living, the dead. The stillness of the house, and its neatness, are oppressive. No music is ample enough for its abandoned spaces. Things stay where they are put. The closet swells with clean towels, while the refrigerator is impoverished. Althea, who once trailed after me, seeking my company, my conversation, ferreting out our likenesses so that she could proceed to deny them, is occupied elsewhere these days; she returns with a flock of friends to cram the void in her twin-bedded bedroom. Their hellos are enthusiastic. They like

me. I wear jeans and can speak their language, and they sense I
like them too. I have always liked teen-agers, their amorphous,
spurting, ribald personalities. But chatty greetings soon subside,
and the bedroom door clinches their withdrawal. Six months
more and she will be away somewhere at college. Phil does not
have so many friends. He comes home alone late in the day and
is too big for me to demand an accounting, too sealed for a
friendly inquiry. I twitch at the sound of the key in the lock,
step forward gingerly to say hello. The emptied apartment is
suddenly warmer, habitable. My son, home. Snare him with
offerings—brownies, an egg cream with George's seltzer? No,
thanks, he had something on the way. Stopped off for a beer?
Or is he stoned? What are the signs again? Do his eyelids
droop, his words sound remotely mumbled? Yes, but not from
drugs. School okay? He humors me with a few scraps of unclas-
sified data, goes into his room, and shuts the door. All those
years I trained them not to disturb me while I was working!
Too well-trained! It's all right, I implore the closed door. Disturb me! Please!

After the first birth many women swear they will never go
through that again, but they do, soon enough. When Althea
was ten months old we decided we might as well have the other
one, the boy, while we were still awash in infancy and had nine
hundred dollars in the bank. For Victor had been in his first
group show and sold two paintings, miraculous in the age of op,
pop. Representational was generally too multisyllabic a word,
its visions too multifaceted, for the ruling simplemindedness.
Paintings depicting the real world were called derivative, which
was true enough. The thrill of the show was keen but brief, just
enough to make his return to obscurity a letdown. Pregnant and
dull, I would wander over to where he stood working in the
living room and make encouraging remarks, wifely, ignorant,
and I don't think very helpful.

Phil was born. I was no longer undone by the liquidities of
the body, but when I found a roach in my hair I wailed and
ranted, thrust my head into the kitchen sink and turned on the
hot water full force. Anywhere else, I could slaughter them in
cold blood. But my hair! And what if it had laid its eggs? I was
a nesting place for vermin! In the midst of my wails I remembered that the effort by which each thing endeavors to persevere

in its own being is nothing but the actual essence of the thing itself, from Spinoza, and I was disgusted. The person I had planned to become did not wail but was resourceful and stoical in the face of adversity. With a huge scissors I chopped at my hair in front of the bathroom mirror till I looked as ugly as I felt, and I vowed to be bitter in silence: I had some pride left.

The hair grew back, in time. I was not very successful at silence. Victor came home from the bar one evening as I was shouting at Althea, "Why do you have to be so selfish about it? Can't you share things?" Phil sat on the floor banging a spoon on a pot.

"It's my book!" Althea yelled back. "My book!"

"I was trying to help you!"

He came into the kitchen where I loomed over her, a tiny three-year-old blond thing stamping her foot and waving a coloring book. When he sat down heavily, a screw fell out of the chair. He picked it up and spun it on the table like a dreydl. "What is all this screeching about?"

"She—" Althea stabbed a menacing finger at me. "She colored in my book!"

"Oh for Chrissake." I took the spoon from Phil's hand and gave him a cracker instead. "I only did one page, Althea. I did a very good job, too."

Althea thrust the coloring book at Victor. "See! *She* did it! *She* did a whole page. It's all done."

Victor accepted the book and glanced at me in a tired way, his head cocked to one side, his eyes squinting. He sucked his lower lip warily. There were artists we knew who had vehement objections to coloring books on all sorts of grounds— aesthetic, philosophical, even political—but Victor was not one of them. "You don't have to color in her book, Lydia. If you need to color why don't you get a book of your own?" He smiled ever so slightly, timorously, as if a wrong move might tilt the room off balance. But it was a sly smile too, the smile of an adder. I grabbed the book from his hands and threw it on the floor.

"Great! Great! If that's how you feel you can buy me one." Phil snatched up the book and prepared to rip it. I snatched it back. "If that's how you feel you can at least admire my work." I opened it to my page and tossed it onto the table, in front of

Victor. Phil whined and scrambled to get it back, but Victor held it out of reach. Althea was astonished into silence.

It was a coloring book of nursery rhyme characters, and the picture I had done was the Old Woman Who Lived in a Shoe. The profile of an enormous shoe dominated the page, a worn shoe with a firm square heel and high ankle, like a work boot. I had colored it black. The laces, which I had colored pink, were half-undone and the tongue hung out limply. The shoe had a little door and window with curtains I had colored pink to match the laces. Out of the top of the shoe tumbled children of all sizes. Some scampered down the front; a few rolled on the ground nearby. They were chubby and frolicsome, not like children whose mother habitually whipped them all soundly and sent them to bed. I had colored their play clothes in bright hues, carefully adding contemporary touches—patches, peace symbols, tie-dyed effects. Also, by coloring their skins I had made them interracial—there were black children in various shades, a few I hoped looked Oriental, and one I had attempted, without much luck, to give the brick-like tone of an American Indian. The old woman was not in the picture.

Victor studied it. "This is pretty good for a first effort, Lydia. You definitely have possibilities. You need to work on your skin tones, though." He let the book drop and leaned back, hands clasped behind his head. "God, I am so exhausted. There was a bunch celebrating something this afternoon. I thought we'd have to float them out on a raft."

Althea, made pensive by Victor's comments, looked at the picture again. "It's nice. But it's my book."

"I'm sorry. I should have asked first. I had an uncontrollable urge."

Victor pounded his fist three times on the table. "Okay! Enough of this! Where's my dinner? I want a groaning board! Someone go and unsaddle my horse!"

The children burst out laughing. Phil, sitting at Victor's feet, pounded his fist three times on the linoleum. "My dinner!"

I laughed too, though I didn't want to. To my surprise, Victor's face relaxed; his eyes lightened with relief. I hadn't grasped how I had unnerved him. It was a kind of power.

"Did you children do your spinning today? Did you churn the butter? Shear the sheep?"

"Oh yes, sire," said Althea. "We did everything you commanded."

"And you, milady? Have you had the plumber to fix the moat?"

"Oh, I don't want to play," I said sullenly. "You're such a good bartender, why don't you fix me a drink."

"Are you really going to buy Mommy a coloring book?" asked Althea.

"Why, do you think I should?"

"Yes!"

The next day Victor brought home a coloring book. He placed it on the kitchen table along with a small brown paper bag. He came to the stove where I was sautéeing onions for a stew, and bent to kiss me; I tilted my head so he could reach my cheek. From the living room came the voice of Mister Rogers, demystifying for a rapt audience the parts and uses of a toilet. The TV was turned up loud so I could hear it in the kitchen. I liked Mister Rogers; I liked his flat lulling tones, his enchanting dullness. From his supernatural calm I suspected he was strung out on some very high-quality grass, even better than Nina's, and I fantasized writing to him: Dear Mister Rogers, I wonder if you could put me in touch with the person who supplies you . . . "The seat can go up and down," he was saying. "We try not to drop it because it makes a very loud noise. Would you like to hear the noise, just once?" Not especially; I heard it every day. "Now that didn't sound very pleasant, did it?" "Not pleasant at all," murmured Victor, his arm around my waist, stroking my hip. "Give me some of that onion, Lyd. Oh, it's good. How are things?" Grease popped and spattered our foreheads.

I opened his gift at the kitchen table several hours later, after we had cleaned up the remains of dinner, gotten the kids bathed and in bed, mopped up the bathroom floor, picked up the scattered toys, and folded a batch of diapers. I had declined Victor's invitation to make love. "Too tired to move." You don't have to move—I could feel it on the tip of his tongue. I was asking for it. I wanted to hear him say it. But he refrained. No animal, but forever well-bred—Edith's doing. Score a point.

The theme of this coloring book was fairy tale characters. I chose the Little Mermaid, sitting on a rock combing the tresses that concealed her breasts, while a few fish gamboled at the surface of the water. In the brown paper bag I found a box of sixty-four Crayolas. How thoughtful. I did the entire Little Mermaid page, including her hair, in marine colors, shades of green and blue; except that in the fish tail beginning below her navel, exempting her from carnal knowledge, I added flecks of yellow for an iridescent cast. I admired the results and turned to Puss in Boots. Gold and maroon would do nicely for the boots. Victor came in from painting, took a beer out of the refrigerator, and peered over my shoulder.

"I didn't think you'd really do it, you know. It was just a joke."

I kept silent. He said in his calm way, but not as thoroughly calm as Mister Rogers, "You don't have to stay in the lines."

"I know, but I prefer to."

He sat down opposite me at the kitchen table and drank from the can. "Do you want anything? Coffee?" I shook my head. "So, are you happy with that, Lydia?"

I looked up to see him grin. Exquisite, that grin, and at this moment enraging, a blend of dismay, irony, and acceptance. His whole appeal was locked into that grin: as dense and seductive as the very first time I talked to him, in the Lion's Den with a gang of kids from the Chaucer class, when he perceived me, he later revealed, as similar to him. I thought then that he would be supercilious, shrinking from anything common or distasteful, but I was wrong. He was altogether too tolerant if he could tolerate me and my coloring.

"Quite happy, yes, thank you. It was very thoughtful of you. Crayons, too."

"It doesn't take much to make you happy."

"Mm-hm."

"Look you could practice in the evening," he said.

"I'm too tired."

"You could at least look at the scores or listen to some records. You used to do that."

"I said I'm tired."

"Too tired to listen to a record? I don't understand."

"For the way I would have to listen, I'm too tired." I bent over my coloring.

"You're not too tired to go meet your friends over at Nina's place. Is listening to a record any more demanding?"

"That's different. It's not work, it's relaxation."

"You're doing this for spite. Whenever I try to talk about it you clam up. You know you could find some women with babies to change off with, and have a few hours to yourself during the day. What about Gabrielle?"

"I do use her. When I have to take one of them to the doctor, or shop, things like that."

"You could do it on a regular basis."

"Victor, I don't want to talk about it. You don't understand anything about it. What's the use of working on something three hours a week? That's a hobby. Would you like to paint three hours a week?"

"I would if I had to."

But he didn't have to. "Well, this is different. It's a technique. I mean, there's a physical skill involved." I looked at my hands, smudged with crayon. For an instant they ached, the way the body can ache to touch and be touched. "Go paint, and leave me to my coloring."

"How many hours a day would you need?"

"What is this, *Let's Pretend*?"

"How many hours?"

I shrugged. "Six."

"Okay, let me talk to my parents. They'll loan us the money. Get someone to take care of the kids six hours a day. You can go back to Juilliard."

"I don't want your parents to support my studies. Aren't I a little old for that? And anyway, they're *your* parents. We've been through this before."

"I know. But this time we'll do it. Because before you said you'd manage on your own, and you're not."

"No! I know you hate the idea. So do I. Just forget the whole thing."

"So I hate the idea. So what? If it's a matter of your survival we'll do it and we'll hate it. People do a lot of things they don't like, to survive."

"Oh, survival. Don't exaggerate. I'll survive. And if not, well, what's the big deal?"

He stood up and yelled, "I can't stand when you talk like that! Stop it!"

"All right, all right. I'm sorry. You'll wake them."

He quieted down. "Listen, I love you. Maybe it slipped your mind. I care about what's happening to you."

"You care more than I do. I'm hardly worth it."

"You make me sick." He squashed the empty beer can in his hand, held it tight for a second as if preparing to hurl it, and then tossed it gracefully into the bag of garbage under the sink.

"You love me, I make you sick. I can't, uh, assimilate all that at once. Please leave me alone. It's been a long day."

I did "assimilate" every word he said, though, even if I pretended not to. Two nights later I sat down at the piano. Victor said, "Mommy has to work now," as he carried the children off for baths. I played a simple sonata by Haydn, who has charms to soothe the savage breast. Like me, he prefers to stay within the lines, and like my coloring, within the lines his music vaults through broad arcs of possibility: rich, ornamental, exalting, and safe, like a cathedral. A pianist can get lost in Haydn, not in any grand emotion but lured into the cunning recesses of the music, and into the trimmings, the trills, the turns, the cadenzas, the sheer gratuitous delight of it. A delight similar to what Victor finds in Matisse, where what begins as decoration pervades and becomes the essential, altering our notions of necessary and contingent. It is possible to be faintly dismissive about Haydn, with all due respect. Program opener, I have heard a few musicians say. Gets the audience in the mood. Formalist. But programs do have to be opened, and forms set, and those who perfect them, decorate them and gild them, are scarcely less original than those who break them, only more serene perhaps.

I was afraid of what I might hear, but the sound was not too bad. There was a remnant of me. More than a remnant. My fingers still knew what they knew; it was the control I would have to work on, the isolating concentration. At the start of the Andante, Althea appeared, naked.

"Can I play too?"

"No, not now."

"Play 'Skip to My Lou.' "

"Not now."

" 'I've Got Sixpence'?"

"Althea, please, just be quiet. This is a different kind of song."

She sat down on the floor, sending up potent waves of injury. A moment later she decided to accompany me on her toy xylophone.

"Althea, please!"

Her eyes brimmed with tears.

"Althea, your turn. Come on," Victor called from the bathroom. She ran off. I was halfway through the third movement when Phil darted in. Soaking wet and naked, he banged a soppy fist on the bass notes. I screamed at him and he fled, howling. I wiped the keys with my shirt and began again, but I could hear him howling, and Victor quieting him, and then the howling once more. I dashed to the bathroom ready to kill; he stood shivering and crying amid wet towels and rubber toys strewn on the floor, while the bathwater, filmed with pinkish bubbles, slowly gurgled its way down. As I threw a dry towel over him, Victor appeared in the hall, holding Althea, one half of her hair combed, the other half a wet tangle.

"What happened? . . . I'm sorry, he got away while I was doing her. I told you both," he said sternly, "Mommy was working and not to bother her."

"She wasn't working, she was playing," said Althea.

I sat on the edge of the tub and cried.

"Look, Lydia, everything is hard at the beginning. You have to persist. We'll set up a routine and they'll get used to—"

"Get out! Get out! It's not worth it! Just leave me alone!" I slammed the door on them all and locked it. It was a simple hook and eye lock I had screwed in myself, to keep the children out. "I've had enough!" I shouted. "Let me get it all over with!"

Victor pounded on the door. I wouldn't open, but I opened the medicine cabinet. He would hear the click and the squeak. The bathroom door began to shake. He was heaving his body against it. I watched my hook and eye lock quiver. It rattled. Both parts started to give. All at once I was seized with curiosity, to see which part would surrender first. I bet on the hook, but it was the smaller, eye part that sprang from the frame with a groaning of the wood as Victor burst in, flushed and sweating, and grabbed me by the arm. I was humiliated. I had done nothing, no aspirins, no razor blade: I had made a fool of him, and I felt cheap.

"Let me go!"

"Get the hell out of here!" He shook me hard. "Go to bed! Go put your head under the covers. I'll take care of everything."

Later he muttered that he was going out for a walk, and left. I didn't hear him return but he was there, asleep, when I woke in the morning. The dishes were washed, the toys and the towels picked up, the children dressed in pajamas suitable for the season, which was early spring. Except that tucked in a corner of the armchair was a half-drunk bottle of Phil's. I felt a vicious glee when I found it and scrubbed away the white ring circling the inside. He had not taken care of absolutely everything. I was a mother; I would have found the bottle. It was that minute lapse of attention that left his will the freedom to live and to paint. I had no will left over, and I was wretchedly victorious, as though we were competitors in martyrdom. We were not competitors, though. He had never entered the race. I was running against myself.

All but the most tenacious depressions can yield to circumstance, and to instinct. Mine was not truly rooted; I knew I didn't really want to die at all, even figuratively. I looked at my hands and recalled how the Haydn had sounded those fifteen minutes, and how Victor had heaved against the bathroom door. Out of shame as much as desire, I tried. I set up a routine, the children got used to it. It took an incalculable expense of will, but only at the beginning; after that, life carried me. Esther sent me her portentous notes from Ecclesiastes about the work of the hands, and I practiced till I could get my job back at the Golden Age Club. I used the money to study at Juilliard. Eros wins over Thanatos, as George, another optimist, likes to say. Self-destruction yields to instincts, and I had good instincts, he remarked years and years later.

"Good instincts! I have horrible instincts. You don't know the half of it, George. I couldn't even cope with a baby. How's that for instinct?" I paused, suppressing. Couldn't even enjoy nursing a baby. Nursed fantasies of ancient infanticides: exposure, suffocation in a crowded bed. "I'm only grateful Victor didn't strangle me. He had sufficient provocation. For him, it must have been Eros over Thanatos, though God knows I was hardly erotic." And I laughed. I was working, and happy, full of banter.

"No, you don't understand. You were waiting to die in a more fitting way. That kind of downer just wasn't . . . significant enough to destroy you. After all, you're not just a little trout in the stream who's too dumb to put up a fight. Remember that? We know you have character, don't we? Uh, do you mind if I make myself an egg cream?"

We went to the kitchen, where Vivian sat poring over the illustrations in *Now We Are Six*. "Do you mean to say I'm waiting for something more worthy?"

"Do you want an egg cream too, Vivian? Yes? Ah, that's my girl." He busied himself with the milk and chocolate syrup. "Didn't I tell you once before what Freud said about the instinct of self-preservation? Its function might be not so much to keep you alive as to see that you return to an inanimate state in some natural way, a natural death suited to your organism, that is—that you're not stopped midstream by some extraneous force, a brick falling on your head and such. 'The organism wishes to die only in its own fashion.' " He squirted his beloved seltzer into the two glasses and gave one to Vivian. "Here you go, sweetheart. That was simply not your fashion, Lyd."

"And what is?"

"Well, how would I know?" He drank his egg cream. "Ah! You don't know what you're missing. Purist."

"I don't like a lot of bubbles. It's a pretty grim hypothesis. It doesn't sound like Eros struggling against Thanatos at all. Just between the right kind of death and the wrong. Or maybe between premature death and timely death."

"Aha!"

"Come on, George. You don't really think that's what the whole struggle is all about?"

"I think maybe it's a case of semantics. The will to live, the will not to die . . . So how is that, Vivian?"

She nodded beatifically, immersed in her book.

"Did you like your trip out West?" he persisted.

"Yes," she said. "I'm reading."

"I beg your pardon, ma'am. By the way, Lydia, I must tell you about this terrific woman I just met. She's into child abuse.

You know what I mean . . . she doesn't do it, she works with people who do."

Perhaps I had good instincts, but I had good circumstances too. It would have taken someone more perverse than I to resist them. A few months after that terrible night, Victor found a teaching job; we moved uptown, overlooking trees and river, and closer to Juilliard. To our devoutly middle-class parents it was still a slum, with its flamboyant street life, its shabby and chic patches side by side like a homemade quilt, but to us the place was Eden. It had an elevator. Space. Light. Air. The best things in life were rent-controlled. The mothers in our new neighborhood were tireless activists; we found an array of cooperative nursery schools and play groups. I stepped out into the world to see what was happening. Everything! Amid assassinations and bouts of public grieving, city people were fleeing to fantasy communes in the hinterlands, suburban children abandoning home for the city streets. Everyone was getting high and everyone was in wondrous costume. The world was a rough carnival, where cops and kids exchanged rocks instead of flowers, while in the wings, in the jungle beyond, war raged. And all the time this had been fermenting I had been . . . I didn't know what to call it. Was I too old to put on a costume and join the parade? When I saw women my age marching with babies slung on their backs I was ashamed of how I had spent nearly four years. "You've no cause for shame," said Gabrielle. "You were . . . sick. It comes from the situation." She spelled out the ideology for me. "Weak," I corrected. "All right, weak. Weak is a kind of sick." Is it? But I would never be weak again. "That's absurd," Gaby said. "It's like vowing never to be sick again. You'd be better off vowing to resist the dynamics of the nuclear family." "Words, words." I laughed at her. "I will never be sick again." She shook her head and laughed back at me.

I rejoined the trio when Henrietta Frye moved to California. Rosalie introduced me to musicians; the phone began to ring. I flitted from group to group—like our President, I would go anywhere and do anything, only he didn't. Humble second beginnings, and late, but this time I felt I was constructing something. "Your career," my mother called it, and she stayed with the children, cooked a week's worth of dinners and froze them, while I was out rehearsing. As the war ground on, we flourished. Victor was happy. I no longer made him sick, nor was I too tired to move. Quite the contrary.

The preceding years, with their wretchedness, became a blur, as though they had passed in some drugged twilight sleep; I suppressed the details. But I knew their texture and color, stony and dun, and I puzzled over how I could have managed motherhood so badly, been so strangely helpless. Why on earth hadn't I practiced in the evenings, or at least studied scores or listened to records? Too tired to listen to a record? I didn't understand. Why hadn't I found some women to exchange babies with a few afternoons a week, in order to work? Crazy! Ah, if only I had it to do over again! How much better I could do now! My permanent record card need not show an abject failure. I would repeat the course and pass with flying colors, have that shameful F blotted out.

"Have you lost your mind completely?" Victor's tone made other diners turn and stare. Out to dinner! Something unthinkable a year and a half ago. It was Simon's, the local pub near the university with the suit of armor in the entryway, where we used to meet before we were married, for those orgies of food and mutual evasion. He gave his wily, amorous smile of then, but confident now. He had me. "You're a most irrational woman. You actually *like* to court disaster. We finally have a fairly normal life and you want to start that whole mess all over again?" Not a statement, *nota bene*, but a question, open-ended. In his rising inflection was a quaver of interest. Victor was a child-lover, and a lover of happenings.

"I'm sure it wouldn't be that way again. I'm different now. You weren't so terrific yourself either. Buying coloring books! Anyway, now we could really enjoy it. All those things that passed me by. I can't even remember. You know, first word, first step, like in those baby books."

"You do have a short memory! Have you forgotten the time you locked yourself in the bathroom to slit your wrists? I don't want to see you do—"

The waitress arrived, in her rimless glasses, leather miniskirt, and beads made out of dried lentils.

"The steak, please," said Victor.

"And how would you like it?"

"Dripping blood."

"Dripping blood. Very good." She made a note on her pad and turned to me.

"I'll have the same."

"Also dripping blood?" Her suave, narrow mouth began to curve, unwillingly. A student, no doubt, maybe at Barnard.

"Dripping blood, yes."

"Would you like anything with it?"

"All the perfumes of Arabia," said Victor, and the girl began to giggle. Like Nina in college. So proper, so ripe to lay aside propriety.

"I was not going to slit my wrists," I said as soon as she left. "I just wanted to be alone. It was the only room in that apartment that had a lock on the door."

"You were so. I remember your words distinctly. You said you'd had enough. You wanted to get it all over with."

The couple at the next table had ceased their conversation and were frankly hanging on our words. I felt like turning aside to them with an explanation, as in a Brecht play. "Talk is cheap. I didn't mean that. I'm not the type. I wanted to scare you."

"Well, you did. It was unforgettable."

"I'm sorry. I won't do it any more."

"Oh Lydia." He put his hand over mine and tapped several times. "This is pretty dumb, you know."

Althea and Phil were cranky babies (small wonder), but Alan was the jolly kind a father could bounce around in the air or sit on the back of a bicycle and display to friends in the park. A showpiece. He took lengthy naps, during which I practiced. Our dovetailed schedules, Victor's and mine, were masterpieces of cooperation, whether from fear or feminism or some mingling of the two hardly mattered. Victor worked on with his calm persistence though the public rewards were typically meager: a few weeks in a gallery, a few reviews, a few sold, then back to solitary labor. But I saw his paintings forever ramifying, complex and convoluted now, like his life. They showed city crowds, the trees and river and ships seen from our windows, skaters and ballplayers in the park, and the children and me, over and over, all with the early respect for the inner signs, and the sinuosity. He was growing in vision, I in proficiency. Way in the distance I spied the limits beyond which I would not pass. I

would be excellent, not great. Not entirely because it was too
late, or because half my mind was on children. Because my gift
itself was not infinitely expandable, as a precious few are. I
accepted it. I was happy and the limits still far off. I was willing
to keep getting better, knowing I would never get best. What I
could do was play with delicacy and make fine discriminations
of tone and texture, and with so much practice those skills
seeped through me. It would have been indelicate indeed to
pine for genius, while simple gifts abounded; I understood why
people loved babies—first word, first step. Only domestically
did I learn to be lax and inefficient. So lax that under the cold
stars Vivian was conceived. Get rid of it? Ah, we couldn't. We
gloried in it. Four! Piquant, original. We could handle anything
now.

Just as the carnival cavorted with war in the wings, our
sprightly family comedy, too, was performed in the shadow of
death. First my father, shocking us by keeling over at his desk
in 1969, he who could never be rushed into anything, who had
to be the last man on the beach at the close of day, and then
Edith. But she was going slowly, slowly. Bone cancer was her
license to relax, maybe what she had waited for all her life:
finally she said what she thought. Her mannerly evasiveness,
her patina of refinement, were cauterized away by the searing
pain, exposing unsuspected qualities, strata of rock beneath the
surface vegetation: fortitude, penetration, a pragmatism of the
emotions. Long-secreted nuggets of her self—her Jewish upbringing, for one thing—wound their way up to split the surface and greet the light. Her face was transformed, hollowed to
the bone. The charming, pampered, obedient face gave way to
a stark, shrewd old Russian Jew, incarnation of her forebears.
So that watching Edith die, her bones settle into sand, was not
only wrenching but inspiriting, like watching a birth or a
resurrection.

Phenomenal, but it was also taking forever. "Why so long?"
Edith griped. "Can't you . . . uh . . ." She flicked her head
sharply towards her husband and made a swift, beckoning,
peasant's gesture with her fingers. "Grease the doctor's palm a
little, eh?" Paul gasped. He had never heard her talk that way.
"Do everyone a favor, Paulie?" He couldn't. "How long can this
drag on?" Victor whispered in bed. "It'll be over soon, dear."

"Oh sure, soon. And then what? Two more to go?" He was so bitter and angry. "No, no," I whispered, "they can't all be as bad." Still, we knew it was in the course of things, the grief we were born for, unlike . . .

"Be good," this new, toughened, skin-and-bone Edith said to Victor from her hospital bed. His mouth fell open, he was so startled. "Stay good, I mean." Later, close to the end, drugged and barely awake, she said something to him in Yiddish. This too was very simple. *"Zeit gezunt, mein kind,"* I repeated for him at home, when he asked. "Be well, my child. No, more like stay well." The most common phrase, I told him. People said it every day—they didn't have to be dying. I must have heard it a thousand times from my grandparents. But for Victor, in that language, and from her, it was the first time. He wept, and Vivian, who was almost two, climbed up onto his knees.

Edith had always liked to soothe, to smooth. She left us money to soothe her leaving, money we might have had earlier but for our insane pride. We moved into a bigger apartment in the same patchwork neighborhood. Victor rented a studio in Soho and his paintings grew larger. I hired men to do the housework, young actors and singers, mostly, who whistled as they worked and were charming to the kids. I felt a barbaric, utterly shameless thrill watching men scrubbing bathroom tiles or prancing around with a feather duster. Oh, there was no denying now that we were in the cozy middle class. No more playing poor. Hadn't we earned the comfort, though? Not only by labor but by suffering? And suffering right. Everyone suffers; the important thing, the experts say, is knowing how to "handle" suffering. (". . . two handles, one by which it may be borne . . .") Except in their unnaturally hushed offices they call it pain. Suffering is too tactile a word for them to bandy about—you can feel what it means when you say it. Eventually you might learn to handle it so well that there would be no pain too devastating for you to overcome. So it seemed.

I did do better the second time around, with the second pair, as I promised. And even now, God almighty, after everything, I still feel a twinge of childish pride. I told you so. Okay, Lydie, clutching your exemplary report card to your milked-out breasts, you did do better, you did fine, no one can dispute it. But you lost them.

I lost my children because I was unworthy of them.

Oh Jesus, Lydia, what kind of primitive horseshit are you throwing around?

No, no, just listen! You don't understand. I don't mean because I was working day and night; that part is okay. Acquitted. And not because I let them go on the bus. Acquitted. But with those first two . . . I was a sadistic, self-pitying bitch.

But you know all about—

No, no, never mind the reasons or the justifications. I've heard it all from my friends; their logic is unassailable; I bow down to it; I stand explained. Nevertheless, that is what I was.

Okay, smartass, then why weren't the first two taken?

Aha! God moves in mysterious ways. His wonders to perform. "Because it was done for you and prescribed for you, and in a manner had reference to you, originally from the most ancient causes spun with your destiny."

I also hear the dying voice of Edith croaking to me, an Edith not as she was or even became, but beyond herself, pushed still further back into her ancestral past; an old Jewish lady with a heavy accent and Yiddish intonation, but she still retains a certain Upper East Side savvy. Croaks: So this, Lydia, after all your hemming and hawing, this is the conclusion you come to? What are you, *meshugah?* This is your life, all your nice accomplishments and you're drowning in guilt? *Vey is mir!* Plus with up there someone spinning threads like a fairy tale! You, on purpose, they picked out? What's the matter, you don't believe in accidents? You think you can be the boss of this life? All right, so maybe once in a while you thought it would be nice to be free. Since when is that a sin? Even your smart friend, what's his name, you know, the psychiatrist, psychologist, what's the difference, the one whom I never liked the way he looked at you, a married woman and to my son, even him and his modern ideas didn't teach you anything?

No, Edith. I think I was not meant to be a mother. I trespassed into the wrong myth.

Oh dear, she says, resuming her usual voice and diction. Oh dear, oh dear.

Zeit gezunt, mein kind, she whispers, and sinks back into her grave.

I lost my children because . . . Ah, at last it comes! Because I did not want them in the first place. Not for themselves. For me. To prove a point. Because they, those two, were an experiment in pride. And you mustn't experiment with human lives! Everyone knows that! Mustn't, mustn't! Stand up against the wall so I can smack your face. Back and forth and back and forth with a flick of the hand, the gifted, experienced hand. Mustn't play games, Lydia!

Still, the experiment was a success. The operation was a success, but the patients . . .

One of the most beloved and talented girls in our class in college died eight years after graduation, trying to save her child. I read about it in *The New York Times*. I lay on a blanket at Jones Beach reading the paper while Victor splashed around in the surf with Althea and Phil. It happened in a house in Cambridge, Massachusetts: the four-year-old boy had found a cigarette lighter upstairs. Before the firemen arrived she had run up the flaming staircase to roll him in a bedspread and toss him out a window. The child was saved, but she died of burns and asphyxiation. Steffie had done well after college. Done good, that is. She was a lawyer of some repute. Deep in the South, Birmingham, Selma, she accompanied voters to the polls, talked protesters out of jail, defended activists. Even in college, we had known she would serve good causes and serve them well.

"Look at this," I said to Victor when he came back to the blanket. As he read, I dried the children, squealing and jumping (alive!) under the towels.

"How awful. But which one was she? I don't remember any Stephanie Rosenberg."

"Of course you do. Steffie Baum, then. She was the small, very pretty one who wore her hair a different way every day and had a lot of boyfriends? She used to sneak out at night. We thought she was very daring. She sang in Gilbert and Sullivan— Patience, in a blue gingham dress, don't you remember?" I was starting to cry, rubbing my eyes with sandy hands.

"Oh! Of course. She was almost the valedictorian but someone else got it in the end."

"Yes, that's right. That's her. She went out with your friend Ray Fielding for a while. She wrote an article about the slums around the college and that we should pay attention, and she got the Service Award. She also loved Mallomars. And she never slept with George, either. She had to really like them."

"This is terrible," said Victor, and he sat down on the blanket. "Wasn't she the one who got all those Patient Griselda poems printed in the paper?"

"Yes . . ." I looked around. "Where are they? Oh Lord, they're in the water again." We leaped up.

When we got home I called Nina and Gabrielle, and George, who had sung but not slept with her. They had seen the article too, two and a half inches on the obituary page. I talked on the phone all evening, about Steffie Baum, now Steffie Rosenberg that was. And about that awful child. Careless, disobedient wretch, to kill his mother.

Steffie, how I envy your fate. Why wasn't I given a chance to be a hero and save them? I would have, just like you. Even though I wasn't as useful or as large-spirited as you, still, I swear I would have done it too. And not for pride, either. For real. For it *was* real. It became real. I became it. I too would have gone through the fire to pull them out, dammit. But then, you were always a step ahead.

Bed

Victor and I no longer make love. We lie side by side chastely in the new king-sized bed. Like brother and sister, yet brother and sister side by side each night might not be so chaste as we. I don't like the new bed—too large, ostentatiously large. It was Victor's idea. He is not ostentatious, he simply wants to sprawl. He would like to make love sprawled at an angle, feeling an expanse of usable space around him. Only when we were discussing a new bed two months ago did he reveal these yearnings. "Do you mean to tell me you felt cramped for over nineteen years and never said so?" He became mock-pensive. "No, I wouldn't put it like that—cramped for over nineteen years. That would be overstating it. But as long as we have a big enough room now . . . Wouldn't you like to feel space around you?" "I don't care about space at those moments. Why don't you go ahead and pick whatever sort of bed you like, love, and I'll lie in it."

The bed is really two beds hooked together. One sheet, but I can feel the crack clearly dividing the territories—his, hers.

We lie awake together, sometimes clasping hands, flat on our backs like the flat figures carved on sarcophagi, shadows of the substance entombed beneath. I've always liked his hands, warm, dry, and rough, the fingertips especially rough, from working. I rub my fingertips against his, a sensuous, asexual exploration. We lie for hours, mostly silent, now and then speaking into the dark.

"I can't stop wondering what it was like," he says.

"Quick, I'm sure. They hardly knew."

"Do you think they might have been asleep?"

"I doubt it. It was only six o'clock."

"But maybe they were tired out from the skiing."

"Maybe."

We lie still for another half hour.

"The fire," says Victor.

"I don't think they felt much. It was very quick." Quick and erratic. The phases of fire, Heraclitus said, are craving and satiety. It throws apart and then brings together again; it advances and retires. Also cruel: "Fire in its advance will catch all things by surprise and judge them."

"But their clothes were charred."

"They were? How do you . . .?"

"The down jackets. I mean just the . . . the backs. The man took me aside and showed me, in a bag. He said we could have it but I left it."

Again. He has become a spring. Victor, who wept only five times before in my presence. When his mother was dying, then died. Once in despair that he would never sell another painting, and once when the first two were babies and things were so bad between us we thought of parting. Last when on the platform at a disarmament rally a paraplegic Vietnam veteran strained to rise out of his wheelchair and throw his arms around the speaker from Japan, most of whose family had been wiped out in Hiroshima but whose two daughters lived on diseased. Death-in-life, the wrinkled, elegant Japanese man called it. And now so readily. I, who wept vicariously for movies and books, weddings and assassinations, massacres in Cambodia and bombings in Israel, am dry.

He is crossing over from his side to mine to be soothed. I take his head on my breast and stroke his hair, but say nothing. He would probably like it if I spoke, crooned something, but I feel ungiving. I have nothing to croon, and I don't like this new bed he chose. After a while he moves back to his side, switches on a lamp and picks up the book which for a week or so has been lying open, face down, on the nighttable, one side gradually fattening, the other shrinking: a work of Malinowski that he read long ago in college—*Magic, Science and Religion*. A book filled with myths.

Less often it is I who speak into the dark.

"Maybe they should have had seat belts."

"There are no seat belts on buses, Lydia."

"Maybe there should be."

"Then they would have been trapped. It would have been worse."

Worse? What is worse? "Do you think they were sitting together?"

"I don't know. Did they usually, on those school trips?"

"I don't think so. They must have been sitting with their friends."

"Which one was her best friend now? I lost track."

"Monica." I pause. "She was that redheaded girl, Monica."

Victor clears his throat, a recognition of the fate of Monica. "I guess Alan was sitting with Joel."

Vivie was fickle, but Alan had the same best friend for years. Joel escaped; concussion, burns up and down the left side of his body.

"They must have been hungry. It was six o'clock." I had packed lunches, but lunch was a long way back. Alan couldn't stand mustard. He made me put margarine on all his sandwiches, even salami. Salami with margarine is outrageous, I tried to explain, but he didn't understand. Did they buy a snack for the trip home? They started out with three dollars each in their pockets, two bills and four quarters. Vivian might have dropped some on the slopes. Well, so they were hungry. So? If they had stopped on the way back for a snack. If some kid had complained that he was starving and couldn't they please stop. If this same kid had then eaten too much or too fast and implored the teacher to make the driver stop again so he could get out and throw up. Then the driver could have stepped outside for a moment too, to clear his head. Any of this might have saved them. Usually there is that sort of kid on school trips. Why not this time?

"What did they have for lunch?" Victor asks.

"I don't remember." I do remember, but I will not say. That is going too far, going overboard.

We lie silent awhile longer, with the crack between us, till we fall asleep. Who knows, maybe we fall asleep at the same moment, like a simultaneous orgasm, a voguish goal in our youth, vestige of the era of togetherness. Something one mastered, like a soufflé. We wake early on far sides of the bed and roll closer together; he studies my face. My face: he could look at it forever and not get bored, he said when we first made love, but I sensed he meant it as a painter, not as a lover, and was disappointed. Later on, older and less romantic, I grasped it was far better that he should mean it as a painter. Right now I'm not sure how he's looking at it. Eyes alert in a sleepy, craggy face, he studies, maybe touches, and we get up. We go into the bathroom together; he showers, I pee and brush my teeth. He shaves, I shower. Such proximity implies that we are very close. In fact we are very estranged. For once, not at all similar. We are going about this process very differently. "Handling it," as George would say. But some things are too hot to handle.

And yet our nights are not without diversion. We peruse the TV listings for late movies.

"Oh, the one about the *Titanic*! I must see that. Rosalie always used to tell me about it." In the distant past, she told me about the musicians who keep on playing while the ship goes down. The best part, she said.

"I saw it years ago at the bar, before we were married, but not the whole thing."

"That night, that's what you said you were watching."

"What night?"

"When you came over to my place. The night Gaby and Don got married. You brought your harmonica and played part of the 'Trout.' "

"Ah." He smiles. "How could I forget? You were so touched that you, uh, proposed."

"I accepted, you mean."

"Well, why quibble now? Okay, let's give it a whirl."

We pile up pillows, and sitting side by side, hand in hand, Victor sipping Jack Daniel's, we enjoy the sinking of the *Titanic*. The musicians, playing aslant and wet as the great ship lists, as families split, chaos threatens, and people's true natures are ruthlessly bared by disaster, are inspiring indeed. I can see why Rosalie held them up as an example, joking yet earnest, when my children were small and I had to struggle to get to rehearsals, against the lure of weariness and inertia. They play till the very end, serenading death and mocking it. Not to keep up morale, nor to shield their spirits from the inevitable. They play be-

cause it is the best way to spend their final moments; they play
to prove that something of them abides to the last breath.

Once upon a time a movie like this one might have made me
weep: women and children setting out in lifeboats, fathers left
behind to drown. I sit and smoke; Victor yawns. During the
last quarter of an hour or so he plays absently with my hand,
places it on his leg, spreads the fingers, draws designs on the
back, traces the outlines of the fingernails, rides the bumps of
the knuckles. Very estranged. Afterwards we agree it was a
terrific movie. An emotional workout. "Good show," says Victor,
and kisses my hand, rubs it along his lips. He flicks off the set
and dims the lights so we lie in near-darkness.

"Lydia? Do you think Althea sleeps with any of those boys
who come over?"

"I don't think so. I think I could tell. But then who knows
what they do these days? Maybe she used to with Darryl."

"With Darryl? She was barely sixteen then. You think so?"
There is a prurient tinge in his voice.

"They must have done something together."

"I wonder what it's like when you're so young. I wasn't
that young when I first started." He pauses. "They—" *They*,
in that tone, is a code term. "They never got to feel any of
that."

"No." Alan had reached the stage of pushing and poking girls
he liked. Vivie found the idea of romantic love laughable. But
Victor, I can tell, doesn't want to talk about them tonight.
Victor wants to talk about sex. Why just now is curious: the
sinking of the *Titanic* was scarcely an aphrodisiac.

"Haven't you any feelings left?" he says into the dark.

"Apparently not."

"You're not going to bed with anyone?"

"Who would I be going to bed with? I'm right here, aren't I?"
This is a diversionary tactic. He wants to tell me about the
woman on the shag rug. Well, there's plenty of time. Take your
time, Victor. The nights are long.

"I thought maybe George. You see him a lot."

"Yes, I'm very fond of him. I find him entertaining. However,
I don't sleep with him."

"I thought maybe you did."

"You thought wrong. If ever I have a lover, I'll let you know, if it's so important to you. I'll tell you all about it, blow by blow. But it seems unlikely at the moment."

Victor sighs. "Don't be so bitchy."

"Well, it's irritating when you ask like that."

We lie there another half hour, holding hands. I could turn on the radio; they play chamber music all night on WNYC. *While the City Sleeps*, it's called.

"What was it like, with George?"

This is an interesting question. Funny he has never asked before. But before, in our innocence, we were principled and discreet. I wouldn't mind talking about it either. Maybe we could work ourselves up in the dark, Victor and I, like dizzied adolescents reporting back to their pals. Like Esther, on her trip to Coney Island with Ralph: He put his hand on my knee. He moved his hand up my leg. He put his tongue in my ear. He rubbed his, you know, thing against my stomach. And for such dazzling originality she went and married him.

I sit up in bed. Victor turns towards me, head propped on his hand. It is like telling a bedtime story in the dark. "I was very young and inexperienced, as you know. There was that boy in high school but . . . He managed to find his way but that was about all. And George—well, you know George. *'Purchè porti la gonnella.'* Anything in a skirt, that means. They sing it about Don Giovanni. So I was very impressed."

"Yes?" he encourages.

"He was . . . oh, how can I put it? Quite . . . lively. He bounced around a lot." Victor chuckles. He is beginning to enjoy himself. "He was all over the place. Oh yes, and he suggested I read the Marquis de Sade. Not that he had such bizarre tastes; I wouldn't say he did anything especially weird, but I think he wanted me to get an idea of the range of possibilities." I'm really playing to my public. Catering, Rosalie calls it. And this is only the opening. The exposition. "I did read it, in parts. But it was boring. Also, I could never figure out how many people were present or keep their positions straight—there were so many at once and they kept moving around from one to another. And then when they came, it was very peculiar—they got strangely articulate. Poetic. They would say things like, Oh, I'm coming, it's like this, it's like that . . . very sort of rhapsodic imagery. Maybe it made more sense in French." Victor is a fine audience, listening intently in the dark. Is he getting an erection, maybe? Can I do that with banal words? "But George was too serious. I don't mean there was no humor. I mean . . . purposeful. Oh, he was okay, but there was something basically wrong. For me, anyway." Ah, I'm starting to fade, losing the concentration, diffusing into abstraction. I'm no pornographer.

"What do you mean, wrong? Did he come too fast?"

Men show such a lack of imagination. There are only two things they can readily think of that could be wrong with a man. Of course with a woman all sorts of things could be wrong. George was curious to know, vaginal or clitoral. I found it hard to make the distinction. He would look at me as if I were half-witted. Had it been ten years later he might have said I wasn't in touch with my feelings.

I groan with sarcasm. "No. Well, sometimes. But that wasn't it. You all do that sometimes." From what vast experience do I sound so knowledgeable, I who have been such a faithful wife? Hearsay. "Anyhow, being George, he was glad to do it again if that happened. Or at least lend a hand. That wasn't a major problem."

"So what was?"

"His soul was not in it."

"His soul?" Victor is astonished. "Is that what you said?"

"Yes, his soul. It was as if he had read too many manuals. He was too accomplished. It was like a showcase production."

Victor clears his throat. I know what is coming. "Is my soul in it?"

"Absolutely."

"Well, that's a relief. But I'm not sure I can . . . put my finger on what you're referring to."

"It doesn't matter. You don't need to put your finger on it."

"Where would you say his soul was, then?"

"I would say . . . his soul was extracted like juice from an orange. The juicer was his Freudian psychiatrist. George has been distilled. He has only a self left. Pulp. That is what makes him interesting. He is highly evolved and self-aware, but lacks a spiritual dimension." This is the development section, swirling off with the theme.

"How about getting back to the facts, sweetheart?"

"Ah, men. Okay. When I came he used to watch me. My

face, that is. It was embarrassing. He didn't watch as part of the
pleasure of it, you see. I wouldn't have minded that. He seemed
to be watching acutely because he was proud of what he had
achieved. It made me feel like something you wind up with a
key and then you watch it go."

He reaches over the crack between us and puts a warm hand
on my leg. "Lydia . . ."

"Please. I can't."

He removes his hand. How easily deterred. He is not the
man he was. The death of his children has taken the iron out of
his spine. I can play with him like putty. I don't like him this
way. In the silence he hears it.

"If you don't like me any more, you could do it with someone
else. Do it, if you need to."

Don't tell me what I need, you fucker. I know what I need.
But I say, "And whom would you suggest?"

"Jasper. Didn't you ever sleep with Jasper?"

"God almighty, I never slept with anyone, Victor. Especially
not Jasper. You know who I would like to sleep with? Marlon
Brando. Harry Reasoner. John Lindsay. Julian Bond. Jon Voight.
Ralph Nader. Humphrey Bogart. Rudolf Serkin. You see I'm
not just a sucker for a pretty face. All of these people have—"

"Oh, cut it out, Lydia, will you?"

"Well, those are your rivals. You wanted to know. But they're
all unattainable. Particularly Humphrey Bogart. He is without
a doubt unattainable. Those are the people you need to worry
about. Not Jasper. Jasper should be the least of your worries."

"You have turned into a real bitch," Victor says quietly.
"There is simply no way of reaching you."

It is five and a half weeks that they are dead. He wants me to
make love. He feels I have been . . . what do they call it in the
women's magazines? Withholding sex. (How the phrase would
make Rosalie screech, as she does at all moronic infelicities of
language, "I love it! I love it!") But I haven't really refused until
a moment ago; he has not suggested it, explicitly, at any rate.
Waiting for me to volunteer to caress his guilt. Now that he has
tired of waiting, I am supposed to be the string that quivers at
the approach of the bow.

"Do you want to tell me about the one with the shag rug
now?" I ask politely.

Victor switches up his bedside lamp, reaches into a drawer of the nighttable, and on a tissue spread on the blanket, rolls a joint. Then he dims the lamp. Lots of drinking and pot smoking for a man your age, Victor. I can't say I approve. The sweet rough smell rises around us.

"I met her in a bank."

"In a bank!" I laugh.

"If you laugh at me I'll kill you." He sounds as if he means it.

"Okay, I won't laugh."

In the dark the lighted orange tip comes towards me. He is offering me the joint. I accept, take a couple of drags, and give it back. The smoke is in my eyes, my throat, my hair. Is this what burning hair smells like, perhaps? Hair that easily ignites?

"She's the director of a Montessori nursery school near the studio. I used to see her in the bank a lot. Finally one day we spoke. I don't remember how, we were on line together or something. It turned out she knew Tom's latest wife. Tom's wife's kid goes to her school." Tom shares Victor's studio. His custom is to marry women with young children—he has never had any of his own. "We had coffee, she seemed interested in paintings, so I asked her up to see them, Tom's too. She came, not that day but another."

"What does she look like? Is she very attractive?"

"Not as attractive as you." This line is delivered straight. No more sense of humor, kid? "She's shorter, and a bit overweight." I smirk secretly in the dark. "She dresses in a rather conservative way. Skirts and blouses, not jeans or anything too colorful or offbeat. You know the way I mean. Pre-sixties." I stifle giggles, taking another drag, and another. I'm not used to smoking much grass—everything about this woman is turning out to be hugely funny. "She has an apartment in the East Sixties."

With a white shag rug. "The East Sixties! Hm!" I pass him back his joint.

"Ordinary people live there too."

"I thought mostly expensive call girls lived there."

Victor keeps silent. He could burn me with the cigarette, but instead he passes me the shrunken butt and I inhale deeply. "I suppose she's very young."

"I think you're getting the wrong impression. She's fifty-one."

"Fifty-one!" I can contain myself no longer. I burst out laughing, wild, rollicking laughter, and Victor grabs the butt from my fingers and punches my shoulder. I punch him back and we tussle for a moment, but halfheartedly; he is restraining himself, ever the gentleman, not even hurting me. Ah, this man is really shot to hell.

"An older woman."

"Nine years older than you, Lydia. That's not so old."

"But this woman is a mother! Don't you see it? You've gone to a mother, Victor."

"No, I don't think that's it. . . . Maybe. Actually she isn't a mother. I mean she has no children. She was widowed very young and never remarried."

"Ah, she must love it, then. Does she love it? Tell me how she loves it."

He puts his hand on my throat, the source of the words. "Shut up and listen! The first two times, I did it . . . the way men do these things. That was before. It didn't mean much. I don't know why, maybe to prove something, see what it would be like. Because I never—I was so goddamn attached to you. Somehow it . . . And I liked her. Look, I did it, all right? For whatever reasons."

He removes his hand and I breathe. "Only you should never have told me."

"I know. And I wouldn't have, except for . . . It would have been over by now. I would have felt whatever regrets I had to feel on my own. But after that day, when you got like this . . ." The silhouette of his upper body looms, a dark shadow in the dark. "You're not the same person," he hisses at me. "I can't tolerate the way you are. All during the days, it's as if nothing happened, as if that snow never fell and the bus never crashed and your life wasn't split open. You go around exactly the same as before, only at night you're like this. You're like a witch in a fairy tale. A woman by day and a witch by night. You do your work, you go to rehearsals and teach, you even go to concerts—"

"For God's sake, I went to hear Rosalie at Lincoln Center, dammit. It was a great thing for her."

"I don't mean you shouldn't have gone. Jesus, what do you think I am! I'm glad you went. I mean you have it to spare for Rosalie, but— What I mean is, you shop and run things, you're

so fucking efficient about everything! Where's it all coming
from? You've even got their closets almost all cleaned out and
the stuff out of the house. Like they were never here. I liked
seeing that stuff around. Why'd you have to get rid of it so fast,
for Chrissake!"

"I'm sorry."

"It doesn't matter, that's not the point. You look terrific. You
fix up your face every morning so no one can tell you've barely
slept in over a month. Only I know it. You even bought new
clothes, I noticed. Oh, you look fine. No one even comes near
you, and they haven't lost their children. You don't cry, you
don't scream, you don't need anyone, do you? You sent your
friends away when they wanted to help you. You don't need to
touch me or anyone else. What are you doing, setting some kind
of example? For whom? Pretending you don't care? Just a minor
change? Oh God, even the kids are smarter than you are. They
cry themselves to sleep. No, listen!" He pulls my hands from
my ears. "They do! But you're so damn perfect! So self-sufficient,
it's horrible. How do I live with someone so perfect, Lydia?
Tell me. What could you possibly need me for?"

"When you wanted to marry me you thought I was perfect.
For you, I mean. I thought you liked perfection."

"That was different. This is no time to be perfect. I liked it
better when you threatened to slit your wrists and didn't comb
your hair because you couldn't cope with two babies. At least
that was the truth."

Oh, so you'd like to see that again, buddy? Sorry, no go. I'm
playing to the last breath. The message of the *Titanic* was not
lost on me. Never that again.

"You can cope with anything now, can't you, Lyd? You just
can't fuck. That's the only little problem you have. Otherwise
you're adjusting fine. But no one has to know about that, right?
The world will never know. The world will see only the
perfect—"

"Stop it!" This time I smack him hard, and he takes it. "All
right, you've made your point. You're right, you've justified
yourself. Go to her. Tell me something, though. Don't you
work also? You go to the studio every day."

"No. I don't do any work. I look at the old paintings. But
that's all right. I'll get back to it in time."

Besides that, unlike me, he looks awful. The Greeks believed that land where blood has been spilled by violence suffers blight, from seepage. He is a land struck by blight. His face is hollowed and sallow, his hair grayer, lifeless. His clothes hang on him. He clears his throat a lot. He drinks. Once in a while, in the evening, he is a little vague from drinking, and the children, especially Phil, look at him with censure. He is kind to them, though, kind to everyone, considerate of feelings even as he trips over things and forgets things—to bring home milk, change a bulb, return phone calls, pay bills. Sometimes at dinner he will stop eating and stare, and his eyes will fill with tears. Phil leaves the table. Althea starts a bright conversation. After dinner he lies down on the livingroom floor on his stomach with *The New York Times* spread out before him, open to the same page for an hour. He rarely answers the telephone, and only after four rings. With the overweight nursery school teacher, maybe he comes to life.

"I thought you were doing some work. Please try."

"Lydia." He takes my hand and speaks softly. "Why are you being so perfect?"

"I don't know what else to do. I learned how and now I can't stop. I'm afraid if I stop I'll . . ." I am endeavoring to persevere in my own being.

He takes me in his arms. "You have no more babies. You can cry, it's allowed."

No. But how good it feels to be held. By him. This good feeling is what destroyed us. It set the atoms in motion, bopping along to their inevitable end. We could have escaped by denying love, saved our children by not having any. I could have found another apartment when Gaby got married, could have not proposed and not accepted, sent him home with his harmonica, maybe slept with him from time to time as Nina does with George. We could have tricked the atoms by aborting their course.

I whisper, "How can you do it with her? How can you forget?"

"For a little while, I almost forget. Afterwards I remember and I feel shitty. But for that little while."

"Does she have a nice body?" I whisper.

"Well, large. Lush."

"Lush. I'm not lush."

"No, you're different," he murmurs. "You're—" But he doesn't say what. He takes my hand and puts it on his penis. He is all ready.

"All right," I say. No preliminaries—neither of us is up to that. That would be too purely for delight. We are reduced to essentials. He slips it in, except slips is not the word; it's not so easy. I'm cooperative but I cannot will lubrication. Once he's worked his way in it takes him a long time. I hope he's not gallantly waiting for me, because I feel nothing but the friction. Finally he clutches tighter, shudders, moans. Over. He stays awhile, then slips out and lies back on his side of the bed, and very soon in the dark I hear him quietly weeping, so I reach out a hand.

"Vic."

"You make me feel I'm not a man."

"You're a man, believe me. It's not your fault."

This has been a longer night than usual. He drinks some Jack Daniel's—he has taken to keeping a bottle in the bedroom closet. Dawn creeps in around the curtains.

"The fire," he says.

"It was very quick. Try to sleep now."

I should never have laughed at her age. How far I am from perfect. Worse than stupid, it was a strategic error. It's not true that I don't need him. I must keep him here in this bed at all costs, a last wrap against the snow. Yet what I need more is them. Without them the world is dead, the field is blighted. Victor is feeling and alive, and left his sap in me. A live disturbance in a dead field.

A week later, side by side with the crack between us, we watch the one o'clock movie, *Casablanca*. Two-thirds of the way through, we turn off the sound since we know the dialogue by heart and it's fun to read their lips. "We'll always have Paris," etc. As Ingrid Bergman points the gun, Humphrey Bogart moves closer as if to embrace the barrel with his heart. She might obliterate him, in the fervor of her need for the letters of transit. But we know she can never obliterate her memory of him. We also know she can't shoot—her pointing the gun is more of a sexual assault. The small space between them is weighted with erotic tension: inches apart, they quiver attractively, and we learn that the invulnerable Humphrey Bogart can be overcome by a woman, if by nothing else. But all their erotic tension leaves me cold; the character I would like to be overcome by is the obese proprietor of the Blue Parrot café, pitiless Sydney Greenstreet, gross and dapper in his white suit, sinister in his fez and phlegmy accents; greedy, sensual, and oily. I imagine him as hairless. His fingers would be smooth and unctuous, his fat smothering. Yes, something about that sleek white corpulence slowly lowered onto me is alluring, exciting. I would levitate into it while he fell into me, and rest forever suspended, wrapped in his flesh.

But Sydney Greenstreet disappears from the plot, and my flicker of excitement along with him. In the end Humphrey Bogart relinquishes Ingrid Bergman (surprised and not entirely pleased) to her husband: she must board the waiting plane with that moral hero of the Resistance, himself appealing in the noble style, but with whom sex evidently yields less in the way of fireworks. No doubt she will ever after feel a pining for Humphrey Bogart between her legs, but such is life. Fighting the Nazis is undeniably of greater moment than a woman's secretions. We sigh ruefully.

Victor goes to switch off the set, pours himself half a glass of bourbon, adds a little water from the bathroom sink, and returns, leaving the bedside light on. He hands me the glass. I take a sip, but it's too strong and too warm for me.

"Tomorrow," he says, "is the night I had those three tickets to the hockey game."

"You could have Phil bring a friend. Maybe Henry would like to go."

"Henry is going. It's all arranged. Another boy is going too, Christopher. There's no point in my going along with Phil and Henry. I'm not the hockey fan—he was." *He* is Alan, of course.

"So you'll be home tomorrow night?"

"Yes, probably. Why?"

"Althea is sleeping over at Diane's, and I'll be at Rosalie's, rehearsing. You know we have the Donnell again next week. Also there's that Stravinsky festival at Purchase we have to get ready for. Do you want to come and listen? We're in pretty good shape—it'll be practically like a performance."

"I can't tag along with you, Lydia. It's all right. I can be left alone."

He'll drink, with *The New York Times* spread out on the floor. Or if he can't stand the emptiness and he's not feeling too guilty, he'll go to her. I'd almost prefer that.

He lies in bed naked. I watch his chest and belly rise and fall with his deep breaths. He picks up *Magic, Science and Religion*, reads for about ten minutes, and puts it back on the nighttable, open, face down. "I can't concentrate—I keep hearing them sing the 'Marseillaise.' " He smiles, then the smile is pained. "I was in there this morning. I noticed she was reading *Green Mansions*. That's not an easy book," he says with pride. "She had the page turned down at the part where Rima the bird girl first appears, with that mess of hair."

"I'm so tired, Victor. Let's not, tonight."

"Do you want to go to sleep? I'll turn out the light."

"No."

"What shall we do, then? Play cards? Battleships?" He turns to me quizzically and smiles anew. "I know. I have an activity to suggest." He puts a hand on my breast and circles the palm against the nipple. My eyes cloud over. He kisses me. "You're going to do it. You're going to like it, too," he says gently. Victor is starting to find his strength once more. I do not think I will be any match for him. Blighted, at least he is real.

"Do you really want to?" I ask. "I have the feeling you're just looking for something to do."

He finishes his bourbon, pours another quarter of an inch, and drinks that up. Then he glances over at me again. Very sexy, though he's not even trying. "I'll want to, after a while. I'll get there." The smile edges into that intimate, ironic, accepting grin. "Why don't you take off your nightgown? I'll look at you and be fired with passion."

I have to smile too, despite myself. I have no more resistance. I take off the nightgown while he gets up and locks the door.

He looks at me, and his eyes, the way they meander, are like hands. Yes, he is more himself, but I must try not to . . . I must feel nothing. Fight it if I have to, for I know exactly what will happen otherwise.

He strokes my cheek with the backs of his fingers. "Do you remember," he says softly, "after you had Althea, those stitches, that first time? You pushed because you said there had to be a first time. You said it would only hurt once. You were right. I didn't like hurting you but you said go ahead, it's the best thing for it. Remember?"

"That was different. That was birth. I was all sore."

"Well, this . . . You're sore again."

"I wish you wouldn't do me any favors, Victor. Do it for yourself, please. It's fine, I don't mind."

"You don't mind? A woman who doesn't mind? I don't need that. That's not you. You'll see in a minute who you are. I'll show you."

He moves down to get his face between my thighs, and he licks. Slowly. The sure-fire tactic. When in doubt, gentlemen . . .

Well. I am only human. I have a long, reflexive history with this man. He pushes my legs further apart. After so long it feels very new, yet very familiar. It also feels like fire. The phases: craving and satiety. It throws apart and brings together again; advances and retires and advances till we reach the edge where, researchers have discovered, orgasm is inevitable. A subtle boundary, and really rather clever of them to have pin-pointed it. It is inevitable, and sure I need it, I can't deny that. Except the more inevitable it grows, the more clearly the jumbled images come into focus, exactly what I expected and dreaded. I knew, I knew I shouldn't do this. Flames lick at the down jackets and the damp heavy corduroy pants. The burning books slide from their laps. Smashing noises, a shattering of glass, and we hurtle through the snowy air, hurtling torches past white-branched trees. We are stunned, falling, breathless, terrified, and I scream, "Stop! Stop! For God's sake, stop it!"

I have said stop before. A game: at that peak, pleasure slides easily across the border to pain and back again. The sensation can be played with to the point of mock danger, to the point where I nearly dissolve in a puddle like the Witch of the West. Victor has heard me say stop before. He likes it, why not? It makes him feel powerful, and when he stops—relents—he is a sultan showing mercy. But this . . . he doesn't see . . . this is no lovers' game with its moans for mercy, its teetering boundaries. I can't bear the fire any more! Her hair is aglow. Hair that easily ignites. Fine dark hair like mine. My baby, all alight.

He has to stop because there comes a pounding at the door.

Althea, banging and yelling, "Mama! Mama! What is it? Open the door!" She hasn't called me Mama in fifteen years. Mother.

Victor looks up, gray with shock. And he thought he was doing so well. I raise myself to my elbows, still on fire.

"It's all right, it's all right," I call out to her.

"Open the door! Who's in there?"

Thank God he locked it. Did he know?

"No one, just me and Daddy."

She pounds. "Open the door!"

I get up and throw on a robe. Victor covers himself. I unlock the door and show myself intact.

Althea looks very small and suddenly still, standing at our doorway in a pink flowered granny nightgown that reaches to her ankles. Her taut neck rises, pale, from a white ruffled collar. Her face is pale and sharp, each feature as purely and delicately traced as in a Botticelli. Her pale hair is pulled back; her gray eyes are pale too. Caught short and frightened, the face looks about twelve years old. I gaze down at the rest of her: five feet two, narrow-waisted, full-breasted, slender wrists, small hands and feet. When I reach out to touch her shoulder she shrinks slightly from my touch.

"It's all right, dear. I'm sorry I woke you."

She is not twelve, she is seventeen, and as she stares at my flushed face and rumpled hair, my hand clutching the front of the robe together, my pupils probably large and ablaze, she is busy figuring, figuring, trying to work it all out in her head.

Down the hall, rubbing his eyes and stumbling around the doorframe, Phil appears. "Phil, it's okay, go back to bed. I had a dream." Phil shuffles to the bathroom, half asleep.

Althea stands as if frozen, her lips closed tight. I see she has not slept with Darryl or with anyone else.

"I'm sorry I woke you," I repeat softly, keeping my hand on her shoulder. She peers past me into the bedroom, but from that angle all she can see is the edge of the bed. As she steps back her eyes darken accusingly. A look of cunning comes into her face.

"It's not what you're thinking, Althea. It's not like that. Really, everything's all right." But what is she thinking? Love is not like that, I want to tell her. Do not catch by surprise and judge, like fire. But I cannot. Because love is—she has seen and heard for herself. At last she turns to go, tossing her ponytail, a pert aloofness in her walk. Still I'm throbbing. All the time I have faced her and talked to her I have never stopped feeling it, advancing and retiring, craving satiety.

I shut the door, lock it, and throw off the robe.

"Oh God," Victor says, clapping his hand to his head, as I switch the central light on so the room is bright. Blazing. "Does she think I—or we—"

I shrug and raise my eyebrows and fall onto the bed. Slowly, wickedly, we start to laugh, quiet hard laughs. For they are only our children; what do we care for children now? So easily lost, easy come, easy go. *This* is important. This is revenge.

"Well, finish up," I say in a hard low voice. "Do you mind finishing what you started? It wasn't quite finished."

He gets back to work. "Yeah, but listen, baby, not so loud this time." He has become Humphrey Bogart, lisping nasally out of the side of his mouth, to make us laugh. This time I keep my eyes as well as legs wide open and my heart closed—I keep a hand flat on my chest, holding it down—so there is no fire and no shattering glass and no hurtling through the snowy night, only wet furious pangs, nothing but biochemistry going about its business. I'm quiet, too. I'm experienced—four kids, always a sleeping baby in the house—I know how to keep quiet. I also know these bodies very well; if we stop at a certain instant and he gets inside me fast I can prolong it, make it seem endless. Oh, I know this system like a machine. So does Victor. At the right moment we bustle around efficiently. It works. But I'm not finished with him yet. The nights are long, I'll milk him dry. After a while there is a slight scuffle—he wants me on top now, but I decline the honor. We are a living contradiction to the sexual politics of our age: here nobody wants to be on top; here each one wants to be smothered. He wins, naturally, with a fifty-pound advantage—a gracious, grinning winner, gasping, "You'll have your way another time, kiddo." Finally he falls back exhausted, spreading his arms like a crucifixion. "Lydia, enough already. I'm a middle-aged man."

Yes, and you're screwing another woman besides. You have to husband your resources. We both have a drink of bourbon, straight, and he tells me he sees what I mean about doing it without the soul. My soul, in particular, was not in it. He says it uncritically, simply as an observation.

"So what? You got what you wanted, didn't you? You wanted to see me let go. You wanted to see me need you. Use you."

"Yes," he says. "Plus I saw the fire too. I know all about it. But I didn't stop."

"Oh. Is that the lesson? To walk right through the fire? No, thanks." To rescue them, yes, like Steffie. But now, what for?

Our bodies are coated with sweat and sticky patches. We lie in a close embrace on his side, sticking together, and tonight we will sleep well.

This land of ours, coarsened by blight, cannot endure. It's only a matter of time.

A Day in the Life,
or Taking It

The people in my building are afraid to look me in the face. They murmur hello, uncertain whether to smile any more; their diffident half-smiles wobble on and off like failing light bulbs. Should they talk as usual about the mailman's erratic hours, the recent rash of burglaries on our block, the state of the plumbing? Is someone in my position still concerned with such things? They needn't be afraid. There is no danger that my face will crumple. I wear make-up, the expensive kind that looks like young skin; my face is masked as in a Greek play, and I do the usual—say hello in the lobby, hold the elevator door open for my elders and for mothers with strollers. I am "taking it"; to the point that Victor's frustration has spilled over the dam of his endurance.

Not all of them. An ancient Greek woman lives on the floor below mine, her face a brown web of wrinkles pierced by sparkly blue eyes. She speaks only Greek but manages to keep up with local events nonetheless. When we meet in the elevator she mutters strange syllables, shaking her head from side to side, the bright eyes moist. Can she be muttering wisdom from her ancestors, the great philosophers—"Bear and forbear"? Once she caught my hand and squeezed it for the eight-floor descent. My hand, greedy. Was she trying to recall to me Epictetus' story about greedy hands? "See children thrusting their hands into a narrow-necked jar, and striving to pull out the nuts and figs it contains: if they fill the hand, they cannot pull it out again, and then they fall to tears.—'Let go a few of them, and then you can draw out the rest!'—You, too, let your desire go! covet not many things, and you will obtain." At last she released the hand; I held the door open for her, and outside, walked in the opposite direction.

And three floors down lives a large and splendid minister who became famous opposing the Vietnam war and now runs a disarmament program at his large and splendid church. Victor used to stop and talk to him on the street, and we attended his rallies. I am afraid, when I meet this imposing man whose energy radiates to fill the elevator so that I want to cower in a corner—I am afraid he may say something infinitely wise from Ecclesiastes or Job, and I stand aloof. But he has never said a consoling or a wise word. He alone greets me as before; looks me in the face; mentions the weather, the noisy punk rock party that kept us all up half the night; holds the elevator door not with pity but with old-fashioned chivalry.

Thursday morning, mid-May, going out after practicing for three hours, I find my neighbor from across the hall at the elevator. "Patricia! I haven't seen you in ages. Where've you been?"

"Hi, Lydia." She looks past me, embarrassment compounded by her baby carriage. She wishes she could tuck it in a pocket, make it disappear. Oh Lord, she is thinking, it's so damn *obvious*—the enormous shiny black kind with high wheels and a canvas hood, from which a row of colored plastic rings hangs to amuse the baby, Bobby, whose head lolls on a blue satin pillow with an eyelet ruffle. Patricia's disapproving parents bought the carriage. They also help pay for the apartment she lives in with Sam, her husband, a lifeguard at a midtown health club. The sweet-natured Patricia is twenty years old and five feet tall, with long smooth light brown hair and placid eyes, a capable girl whose stance toward life is sanguine and accepting. She wears drab old army pants, a green army jacket, old sneakers. She met Sam in high school and at sixteen was pregnant. The baby was Samantha, now in the nursery school Vivian and Alan went to. Patricia helps out there two mornings a week, as I once did. She never got to finish high school and before long was pregnant again—not handy with birth control, she mumbled to me, and residually Catholic besides. I used to feel sorry for her, but soon realized she likes having the children, she is happy with Sam, happy to have her own apartment and no longer live cramped in her parents' furnished basement in Port Washington. When she first moved in two years ago she called me Mrs. Rowe, but I told her I was not as old as all that, she could call me Lydia. Sam could never stop calling me Mrs. Rowe. Occasionally Althea would babysit, but since the accident Patricia has not asked. The new baby is about five months old.

"How's he doing?"

She arranges the blankets as if to conceal him. "He's fine," in a thin voice. She fusses in her canvas bag, finds a tissue, wipes Bobby's nose.

We enter the elevator together. "Come on, Patricia, you can't avoid me forever."

"It's only—I don't know what to say."

"Don't say anything. Just talk like before."

She sniffs and blows her nose with the same tissue she used on Bobby. "How are Althea and Phil?"

"All right."

"And Mr. Rowe?"

Victor. I haven't seen Victor in several days.

"Fine. Listen, you can still drop him off if you need to. Really. He was never any trouble."

During our freezing, snowy winter, Patricia now and then parked the infant with me while she "dashed out" to pick up Samantha or run errands. He could sleep while music played: while the repatriated Henrietta Frye and I worked on a four-handed Debussy suite; through the Beethoven G major trio with my old woodwind friends, a flute and a penetrating bassoon; with Rosalie and Jasper and me stopping and starting our way through the "Archduke." Such a remarkable sleeper—I worried that he might be deaf or brain-damaged. "Nonsense," said Rosalie. "He's just a placid baby." While Jasper tuned we would stare into the carriage nostalgically, Rosalie and I, wishing we could pick him up just for the feel of it. But we knew from experience you never wake a sleeping baby.

"I didn't think I should leave him," says Patricia, maneuvering the carriage out of the elevator. "It didn't seem right. But if you really mean it."

"Sure, I know what it's like." The doorman bows his head in

awe as I approach, and hands me the mail with a sorry, balletic extension of the arm. "Thanks, Carlos. I'll see you around, Patricia. I've got to rush to a lesson."

The first of two students, a brand-new one of about twenty, talented but sloppily trained, wants to talk at length about the Chopin Ballade I have him working on: the emotions—melancholy, passionate, nostalgic, etc. I interrupt and tell him to forget all that until he has gotten every detail of the timing and phrasing and dynamics with perfect accuracy. Then he can talk to me about emotion, if it is still necessary. He stares as though I am something monstrous, but he will come round in time, when he hears the results. The other is a prodigy of twelve who plays her Beethoven Rondo with astonishing technical skill. She sounds like a music box. She has to be reminded that music is more than timing and phrasing and dynamics executed with perfect accuracy. When I mention a sense of narrative, the unfolding of a passage from here to there like a journey, she blinks in bewilderment. She too will come round, but it will take longer.

On my way out I hear mistimed snatches of a Schubert sonata mingled with shouting, and as I move closer the voice is unmistakable: Irving Bloch again, martinet of the strings, in the East European accent which grows thicker when he loses his temper. Passing the room, I cannot resist peering in the back door.

"Ah, Lydia!" he shouts. "You appear like a miracle! Mrs. Rowe will show you how to do this together," he says to the quaking pianist and violinist. "Together! Come, come, Lydia, come here to me."

I smile at the two students and frown at Irving, but he insists—"Come!"—points to the place in the music, and raises the violin to his grizzly chin. The girl hurriedly gets up from the bench. Irving and I play the sixteen bars, *allegro vivace*. My hands seem yards away, my arms long ribbons from a wooden spool. But it sounds fine, not merely correct but rich with vivacity. The vivacity comes from the hands alone; they were well-educated, and they continue to transmit life and feeling, just as hair and fingernails grow for a while on a corpse. I imagine my hands could be lopped off and continue this way indefinitely, like the Red Shoes.

"There!" he shouts triumphantly to the pianist. "You see it can be done together! And hear the exuberance, the *joie de vivre!* That is how it should sound."

While he rants on I show the girl the sixteenth notes she is playing as eighth notes and the two rests she is misreading. "And don't mind Dr. Bloch. He's that way with everyone except the strings. Count. Don't be afraid to move your lips."

"Thank you," she whispers.

"Irving." I take his arm and drag him to the door. Outside he is transformed, warm and paternal.

"So how is it going, my sweetheart? Everything all right?"

"Fine. Look, Irving, I know I shouldn't interfere, but you can't keep on doing this. It's no way to teach. You don't help them, you paralyze them."

No one scolds Irving to his face. He has been here twenty-three years to my eight and has an unchallengeable manner. Moreover, his temper has been shorter since his wife died last year—but how long must we indulge him? He squints in surprise and ponders for a moment. "Yes, patience, patience. I do try, believe me, but the ear hurts, you know? I feel it like a pain—I cry out. You look a little pale, *mein kind.* You're sure you're all right?"

Again I shake my head at him. "*Joie de vivre!* At this stage, Irving? Really!"

"Ach, I'm sorry for that."

"Not *me!* It's them you should be apologizing to. Give them a little time. As it is, when I get them it'll be days before their hands stop shaking."

Chastised and shocked, he kisses me good-bye on the forehead.

"Oh, I'm still planning on that evening chamber group, starting next month. Are you going to do it with me?"

"A diplomat you're not. First you yell at me, then you ask a favor? I said I'd do it, didn't I? But maybe you want someone sweeter?" He grins flirtatiously. He knows he is the best.

"I want you. Let's talk about it tomorrow, okay?" I am a little shocked too. Protocol no longer seems to matter; restraint doesn't matter today.

Under massing clouds I limp down Broadway to the supermarket, where I consult my list like an ordinary woman. I used to shop at eccentric hours and save this precious solitary time for work. But I've decided on a day of self-indulgence. Anyhow, I have all the solitude I need. I buy butter and rice and saffron powder and a four-pound chicken, a chicken possibly not as good as the one I could get at the butcher's, but I have been avoiding my butcher. We have a long and intimate relationship. Anybody privy to one's choice of dinners for nine years becomes an intimate of sorts. Together we have been through the death of his father-in-law, his son's acceptance at medical school, his daughter's marriage, miscarriage, and more adherent pregnancy—she should be due any day now. When Althea became a vegetarian two years ago I told the butcher. He did not take it personally. "Well, children, what're you going to do?" He shrugged. That is his sentence for all regrettable turns of events. It's I who cannot look him in the face. The last time I did, nine weeks ago, he said how grieved he had been to hear the news. His white apron was spattered with blood and his hands looked raw. He is a slender, balding man with a long nose, a curving mobile mouth, and thick glasses. He told me feelingly that he remembered how many long years I had been a customer of his, how I used to come in holding them by the hand and they would play with the striped cat amidst the sawdust on the floor, and how he would give them each a slice of bologna. "You too, sometimes. You would take a slice, I remember. Maybe you'd like a slice now?"

"Thank you. Very good."

"You were always a nice family. Well, what're you going to do? Things happen. So, what can I give you today?"

I asked for three pounds of chuck for stew. At the time I was wondering also, well, what am I going to do? But I'll go back someday soon. I don't want to hurt his feelings. I don't want him to think I've deserted him after so long for no good reason, or that I no longer appreciate his excellent meats. And I want to find out what kind of baby his daughter had.

In the Koreans' fruit and vegetable store I buy garlic, mushrooms, lemons, the fixings for a salad including some very cheap and very bitter lettuce I have recently discovered and taken a fancy to, whose name I do not know and the Koreans cannot tell me since they speak hardly any English (they are learning Spanish first), as well as three huge, thick-skinned, costly oranges, the kind I have been eating since I was a child, whose tart rinds I munched slowly in the college dormitory to the benign indifference of Melanie, who piled up banana peels. Picking out my oranges, I notice, and not for the first time either, the son of the Korean couple who run the market. He is arranging lettuce. When he sees me looking he nods and lowers his intelligent eyes. Not from fear—the family is new here and doesn't yet follow neighborhood gossip—but from shyness. A tall, lean, muscular boy of about nineteen, he wears tight jeans and a black turtle-neck jersey through which I can watch his back and shoulder muscles straining to lift the crates of lettuce. He moves lightly, almost stealthily, in his silent Adidas sneakers, the kind Alan craved. He has large boyish hands and fine wrists. He has wonderful coarse black hair, perfect for the flowing styles of today; it hangs, clean and thick, over his forehead. I wonder if he blows it dry, if he is vain. His cheekbones are high and set wide apart, his eyes dark and magnificently soft, his lips large and soft too, his teeth perfect. What a beautiful boy. I tuck him away in the back of my mind.

I'm in the Koreans' place rather than the Cubans' grocery not merely because the fruits and vegetables here are better and cheaper, but also because I resolved a while ago no longer to subject myself to the political views of the Cuban store's Jewish fruit man. The fruit man lost his entire family in a concentration camp in Poland. He barely escaped, clawing his way through the forests of Poland with the Germans at his heels. From his descriptions I envision Poland as a heavily wooded country. As he dropped McIntosh apples into a paper bag, he would tell me of his journey with a numbed but unyielding wrath, in a flat sneering voice that was a personal accusation and a threat. His face would go as gray as his smock. Imagine, forty years later—and here his voice would shrink to a whisper—he has to listen all day long to the anti-Semitic remarks of his Hispanic and black co-workers. They hate him but he pretends not to hear, what does he care? If I chatted with the black and Spanish clerks his eyes would brood over me, mocking and resentful. "So, what do you think about what happened to us now?" was a frequent greeting. "Us" means Israel. A raid on a kibbutz, children killed. Terrible, I groan. "Animals," he sneers. "Why do you think they call them gorillas?" Yes, terrible. But that would not suffice. No other nation in the world has any moral probity. "We are the best people in the world." "We" never hurt anyone, just mind our business, unlike local muggers. He waits for me to agree. My response is judged halfhearted; he says I understand nothing, nothing. Ever since the Republicans were turned out of office in 1976, he informs me, the Jews have had nothing but trouble. Is that true? Hastily I would try to recall recent history, but before I can get anywhere: Do I know—he shakes a finger while he weighs my bananas—who would be the best President for Israel? No, who? Nixon. Nixon? Oh, come on, Mr. Zeitlowitz. Sure! What would be so terrible? Doesn't everyone cheat a little? Ah, they made such a fuss over that business. But when he was President things were good for Israel. But . . . but—I try not to splutter—but what about *us*? How about what would be good for *us*? (How about not even arguing with him?) If anything happens to that little country out there, he threatens, shaking the finger in my face, where would those poor people go? I retreat from the finger. "I don't want anything to happen to them. Did I say that? I wish them all the best." "You just don't have the feeling I do," he accuses with a weak smile. I can't deny that. Guilty! I did not claw my way through the forests of Poland. "So!" He spreads out his arms, a paper bag of fruit dangling from each hand. "We disagree! That's that!" He gives me a sardonic, condescending smile: how stupid she is. Actually I should be flattered: it is the kind of smile reserved for intimates, *landsmann*, whose loyalty can be taken for granted. He thinks he sees through me, and perhaps he does. "Okay, then, that's that." I too smile familiarly, and reach for the bags of fruit. "But if anything happens to Israel," he snarls, shoving the bags at me with contempt, "it will be here just like in Nazi Germany." He nods his head up and down ominously, twice. "You'll see!"

I would slink away reminding myself that above all I must remember and respect his sufferings and not hold him to account, and therefore when the Koreans' store opened with its beautifully superior fruits and vegetables and the fruit man's customers deserted him, I remained. I suppose I wanted to demonstrate something to him, more out of pride, I see now, than humility: did I imagine my loyalty could nullify the Second World War? But the tirades became unbearable. Loudly, he cursed his defecting customers. "They'll see! They'll see! It's garbage they're buying over there. Horse manure! What do they know from fruit! You think I care? Listen, I been through worse. I been through plenty troubles." And lowering his voice, he would recount once again clawing his way through the forests of Poland with the Russians at his heels. "The Russians?" "Sure, you think the Russians were any better than the Germans? Ah, a baby—what do you know? They're all the same, every one of them."

I raised the dilemma one night at dinner. I told the children about the fruit man's sad past, the loss of his family, and about the better fruit in the Korean market. The economics of *laissez-faire* was heartless; how far must I compensate? Where should we shop? Althea's opinion was prompt as usual. "You say the fruit in the Koreans' place is better and cheaper?" "Yes." "And besides that, you don't like him?" "Yes. I mean, no. It's hard to say, really." She gave a disdainful shrug. "It seems to me there's nothing to discuss." Phil didn't care where we got our fruit. He wanted to be excused; he had to call someone about the trigonometry homework. As he left he took an apple from the refrigerator. Alan and Vivian agreed that I should keep going to Mr. Zeitlowitz. "His fruit was good enough before, wasn't it?" said Alan. "So make believe the other place never opened. Then you won't have a problem." "And whatever he says," Vivian added, "you can just smile sweetly and keep your thoughts to yourself." Ah yes, I knew that strategy from growing up with Evelyn, but I doubted if I could carry it off.

Althea said, "You people amaze me. I mean, we didn't persecute him. From what I gather, he persecutes you."

"Yes, I serve a purpose for him. I think in a way he needs me."

Althea laughed, and then we all laughed.

Victor suggested that we buy some fruit from Mr. Zeitlowitz and some in the Korean store, which surprised me—I had expected him to react as Althea did. But that was impractical and time-consuming, I replied, besides which it was embarrassing to walk into one fruit store carrying a bag from another. That might inflame Mr. Zeitlowitz further. By this time Althea was laughing uncontrollably.

"You don't need to be a human sacrifice, Lydie," said Victor. "You go to the Koreans and I'll go to him, for your conscience. He never bothers me."

"Yes, and why not? That's an interesting point. Have you ever thought about that? No, it wouldn't be the same if you went."

I took an apple from the refrigerator. It had a large soft brown spot. I examined another. Every apple in the refrigerator had at least one large and spreading soft brown spot. This is truly absurd, I thought. Althea is right.

So I started going to the Korean fruit market, where the air is hushed and smells of crisp wet greens. The proprietors do not burden me with their psychopolitical woes but nod with consummate reticence. Today as always I nod in return at mother, father, and son, and arms laden, limp on towards Woolworth's. The sober mien of people hunting down the essential trivia is pleasantly contagious, and I too grow intent as I choose: Scotch tape, a note pad, shampoo, a measuring cup. Rounding a bend, I pass a rack of coloring books. It was both for charity and for spite that he bought me one when I was disintegrating in the walk-up flat on East Twenty-first Street, panicked that I had no identity. Now, with my identity so fixed and compulsory, that state seems enviable. On display are *Star Wars* coloring books, *Superman* coloring books, *Sesame Street*, *Flintstones*. None of those would suit me. Half hidden behind *The Partridge Family* is a *Medieval Times* coloring book: knights on horseback jousting in tournaments; monks and prioresses; cathedrals (the possibilities for stained glass!); lusty peasants gathering at the town well; ladies-in-waiting in luscious low-bosomed gowns. It reminds me of Chaucer. Griselda in all her pomp, before she was stripped down to her smok. I buy it. I buy a box of sixty-four Crayolas and head home, clawing my way through the forests of Broadway, only no one is at my heels. No one will even look at me. They avoid me the way I avoid the fruit man. I may yet come to resemble the fruit man.

Back home I listen to the recording of Schubert's "Trout" Quintet with Hephzibah Menuhin playing the piano part. Rosalie wants to do the "Trout" at an important concert at Lincoln Center this fall and I have promised to think it over. Rosalie is excited at the prospect: she has a violist and a bass player lined up, and waits on my decision. I should be playing it rather than listening, but not today. Today I indulge. Let her wait.

Hephzibah's suave playing begins like a controlled ripple. She launches with vigor into her first solo, and I curl up in the soft wing chair and leaf through the pages of my *Medieval Times* coloring book. The ladies-in-waiting, perhaps? When the doorbell rings I hide the book and the unopened box of Crayolas under the cushion. Patricia with the baby carriage. "I wonder, Lydia. . . . It's starting to sort of rain and I've got to—"

"Of course, bring him on in."

"Fifteen minutes is all."

She races to the elevator to show her good intentions. Bobby sleeps serene on his blue satin pillow; his cheeks are puffed out from sucking; his long brown lashes flutter a jot with each deep breath. Hephzibah eases into a lyrical passage with wit and finesse. She is dead, died some five months ago, early January, at age sixty, and *The New York Times* headed her obituary, "Hephzibah Menuhin, Sister of Violinist." Once more in my chair, I cannot choose from an embarrassment of riches—the potentially gorgeous dresses of the ladies, or the cathedral at Amiens, which I could do like Monet. Derivative. I hesitate; to color anything would be crossing to a place from which it might be hard to return. And yet it is so seductive, staying in the lines. This time the phone rings.

"Hello. Is this Mrs. Rowe? This is Miss Fosdick, from New York Telephone." What a musical, ingratiating voice. In those few words she has tripped through almost an octave. She announces that our telephone number is going to be changed. We will be given our new number within the month.

"Hold on a minute, will you?" I turn down the "Trout" at a *crescendo* in the second movement. "Now, what's this all about?"

Certain of the numbers in this neighborhood must be changed for technical reasons. Miss Fosdick is extremely sorry for the inconvenience this may cause, and will be glad to supply me and my family with fifty postcards for notifying our friends and associates. From the voice I can see Miss Fosdick, ruddy-cheeked, hailing from someplace wholesome like Nebraska, with pert, pointy breasts and short athletic legs; she was lately graduated from the state university with honors and came to the big city to pursue a career. She was picked for Customer Relations because of her faultless diction and the cordial, ingenuous smile in her voice. I, on the other hand, seem all at once to be shouting.

"You can't do that! That number is mine! You can't just . . . take it away like that! Who do you think you are? You big corporations think you can push people around however you like. Well, I've been paying for that number for nine years and I intend to keep it. You can take your new number and you know what you can do with it."

"I'm terribly sorry, Mrs. Rowe," says Miss Fosdick ever so gently. "We're aware that it will be a disruption, especially for people who've had their number for a long time and have paid the bills promptly as you've always done. Unfortunately, technical problems require that we—"

"Technical problems! What are technical problems anyway?"

They turn out to be much too boring to listen to. They also sound inexorable. "Fifty postcards!" I interrupt. "How far do you think I can get with fifty postcards!" I don't really believe this hysterical sound is my own. Some harpy is lodged in my throat. "We would need at least two hundred! I work out of my home. I have students, colleagues. And my husband . . . We have a very large family, they all have friends!"

"In that case we'll be glad to let you have a hundred postcards, Mrs. Rowe. No problem."

I sink to the floor, exhausted, and say weakly, "But we're all very attached to that number. After so long it becomes a part . . ."

"I understand," Miss Fosdick says very softly. Like a psychiatric nurse, trained for any eventuality or maniac. "But you'll get attached to your new one too, I'm sure. You'll be surprised at how quickly it happens." We are like adversaries in a Greek tragedy, Miss Fosdick and I, where the hero learns to yield to Necessity—in this case corporate necessity—represented by some mean-spirited goddess.

When I hang up it is perfectly quiet. The record has stopped and Bobby is asleep. Sitting on the floor, still for the first time today, I feel the fact that Victor has gone like an intermittent thorny migraine; it intrudes whenever it can; it may be assuaged, blunted, or ignored, but not expunged. He left Monday morning with a suitcase. He would be staying at his studio for a while, he said, till . . . "Till I don't know, Lyd, till things work themselves out. This is no good for either of us. It makes it more painful. It isn't livable." I think he went to the Montessori teacher rather than the studio, though it hardly matters which. I pictured him not on the subway headed for West Houston Street but on the Broadway bus, requesting a transfer for the eastbound crosstown at Sixty-fifth. Or maybe he walked across the park—it was a balmy May day and the suitcase was small. If she gave him a key perhaps he stretched out on the white shag rug in all his glory and waited for her to return from school.

It was not a question of loving or not loving, he said, as if he had passed beyond such banalities. No; to be quite fair to him, he meant his love was not in question. It was irreversible (Heraclitus, I thought: the way up and the way down, reversible, ceaseless). He loved me, except he couldn't live with me this way. This was late Sunday night, sitting at the kitchen table with only the dim light over the oven lit. It was labor enough to get himself moving every morning; he couldn't face the way I was taking it besides. Anything else—if I screamed or went wild or didn't speak at all. But my "sleekness," he said. We were drinking tea and eating gorp and his mouth was full: Althea's gorp, heavy on the figs. "Was that slick or sleek?" I asked. "Sleek," he said carefully. "I can't even approach."

We appear unapproachable but we could approach each other easily, he said more than twenty years ago in the bar near the unfinished cathedral. "Don't you remember?"

"Of course I remember. It's my life too, you know. It was true then. It isn't any more. When you're young you think those truths are going to last forever." He really meant it. His voice was even, his eyes steady. Still strong but older: he had lost his look of temperate eagerness.

"You don't know me at all, then. I'll never forgive this."

"Forgive? How does forgiveness come in? You want to be alone with it. It's clear. You've done everything to get that except show me to the door. Forgive, Lyd?"

"You don't want to coexist?"

"No. I want you. Or not at all."

We had the bowl of gorp between us. He was picking out two or three pieces at a time and meditatively bringing them to his mouth, while I dug out handfuls, bent my head back and tossed them in. Me, sleek? "Do you love her too? Your friend?"

"Oh, at moments. Not really." He sighed. "But I don't pretend to."

This was not Victor. These were two other people, strangers to us both. We were decent, I always thought. Not the sort who would split in a crisis, but the sort who would abide. The stranger I had become found this impossible to say. "Do you realize what a brute you sound like, Victor?"

"I would say you're the one being brutal. But let's not turn it into a competition. You remember Highet. He was so right."

Together at Columbia we had attended the famous lectures on classical tragedy. Gilbert Highet in natty gray flannels and lustrous black shoes was thrillingly debonair, a triumph of civilized Western manhood, striding back and forth across the platform, fluent on the brutalities of Hecuba. In the world of Euripides, he said, the victims become as bad as or worse than their persecutors. Earnest yet forever debonair, he reminded us time and again that suffering is not ennobling but brutalizing.

I wrote a term paper about Euripides' *Suppliant Women*—Victor read it. Mothers of the seven heroes who died attacking Thebes, they supplicate for the return of their sons' bodies so they can render the proper burial rites. They lament so incessantly that they lose all personal identity but that of grievers. Emblems of grief, they grieve therefore they are. Maybe that's what I'm afraid of. "What need had I of children?" is their bitter cry. "Would that in death I might forget these griefs!" Well, of course. But what would Victor say if I went about the house swathed in black, intoning, "Alas, alas! Where is the labor spent on my children? Where the reward of childbirth . . ."? Nothing. He would take it, and be relieved, and hold me in his arms. That is precisely what he wants.

So why not give him what he wants? Our neighborhood shelters many ex-mental patients who walk the streets raving to invisible companions. In the park they perform strange and solitary antics. Last week a woman sitting on a bench slowly unwound an entire roll of paper towels, tearing off two sheets at a time. When she was done she made a fat pillow of them, put her face in it, and cried. Is it any wonder I'm afraid? The sound I would make is beyond imagining. The Greeks had their formal modes, their Necessity, their Destiny, their ritual responses. I have no speeches, no suit to plead, only this shape-

less blob the size of the universe and choking as mud; it is all I
can do to slog through it, coated in it; it does not wash off; it
muddies the eyes; I cannot see Victor through it; I cannot make
great poetry of it; I cannot make art of it as the Hopi Indians
made of their toothache. It is formless and useless. "What need
had I of children?" I used to think that when Althea and Phil
were babies and wore me down to the bare nerves, in ignorant
bitterness when I couldn't tell griefs from simple gifts.

"Well, what about the kids? When are you planning to tell
them?"

"I'll call tomorrow night. Or the next night. As soon as I feel
up to it. And I'll be back on the weekend to see them. I'm
twenty-five minutes away, Lydia. It's not as if I'm deserting my
children."

As soon as he feels up to it! Why not as soon as he feels ready
to "deal with" it? And he dared to be contemptuous at Esther's
wedding six years ago! He dared to say the fray reminded him
of a Bosch painting. He whose patience stopped short at the
fatuous, the trendy, the emotionally shoddy. Purist, who once
wept tears of rage when a critic said his work was derivative.
Listen to him now!

"I'm going to bed." I got up to put the garbage out the back
door.

"I'll do that."

"Oh, don't be gallant, please, Victor. It's my turn."

"Have it your way."

Out in the hall I bumped into his sister Lily's TV as usual,
and cursed. It never did work, even after he had it repaired last
year for forty dollars. The fault of the twin towers, he said.
Any other neighborhood. We tried to give it away, but everyone seeing the parallel lines and the snow said no, thanks. So
there it has sat for over a year now, jammed in with the garbage
cans and bikes and sleds, and whoever puts out the garbage
bumps into it and curses. Vivian liked to say it tripped us
because it resented its fate, back there with the garbage. I
returned and said, "Maybe you'd like to take that damned TV
with you?"

"What for?"

"I don't know. You don't have one in the studio. It would be
nice to get rid of it."

"No, someone will want it someday. Leave it."

The next night after dinner, I told the children he had gone. Initially I had lied—"Working late"—and then over coffee I changed my mind. Didn't they deserve better than to be lied to? I watched Althea pour coffee and thought of how we had done for them, how we should do for them. Maybe it was a mistake even to let them drink coffee so young. But then we had often permitted things other parents didn't: staying up very late, painting their rooms in outlandish ways, reading dirty books. . . . Someday we'll go too far, I used to worry; something will happen. . . . The formative years are over, Victor said last summer when Althea blew her babysitting savings on a Berlitz course in Swedish, having seen five Ingmar Bergman movies; we must let them live their own way. Very well, and one of us must tell them the truth. Promptly.

"It may be just for a little while, maybe longer, I don't know. It was too hard here. He has to pull himself together on his own. Don't blame him, it's as much my fault. He'll call you later to tell you, and you'll see him whenever you want to."

Althea had a million questions. Like a Socratic dialogue, ever bifurcating and ramifying the issue. What do you mean, maybe a little while? Either he's left or he hasn't left. If he's left, it's either permanent or temporary. If it's permanent . . . She could not have known she was employing an ancient method called a tree of Porphyry—Professor Boles once diagrammed it for us. Phil grunted and got up to leave the table.

"Wait." I grabbed his arm. "I know you're shocked. But please, will you please not just grunt and leave, okay? It gets me very upset."

"I have a lot of homework. I have a chemistry test tomorrow." He turned away, tilting his jaw like Victor. In the adamant profile was a retraction of all the evenings they had spent talking together behind his closed door, one voice aggrieved, the other tempered with limitless, loving patience.

"Phil!"

"I could get a job or something after school. Can you manage by yourself?"

"It's not like that! He's not deserting you. Just sit down awhile, all right? Finish your coffee."

"I'm finished." He left the room.

"I always thought you two had a fairly good relationship," Althea said. "I realize there's been a lot of stress. But still, it would seem to me that at this point he'd want to keep the stable elements in his life." She lit a cigarette, bending her head over the flame on the stove. Your hair! Watch the hair that easily ignites!

"I wish you wouldn't smoke, Althea. This is the third night this week I've seen you smoking. Do you want to ruin your lungs?"

"I don't have an addictive personality. I can smoke when I choose and not smoke when I choose. Don't you do the same? Anyhow, this seems to me very illogical on his part. It's probably related to a mid-life crisis, in addition to everything else— he's at that age. But I would think that being so committed to his work, he wouldn't feel the same lack of . . ."

On and on, like a TV documentary. The unexamined life is not worth living, Victor believed, and yet he needn't have toiled. Teen-aged children are only too glad to examine it for you. Finally I said, "I might as well tell you, since you say I should talk to you like a woman, you smoke and every-thing. . . . He has a . . . a lady friend."

She started coughing, not a very proficient smoker. "You mean like a younger woman?"

"As a matter of fact, no. An older woman. Slightly older."

A long pause. "A mother figure," Althea said.

"Oh, come on. She's not old enough to be his mother. I don't know if he'll mention that, but . . . well, you're not a baby any more."

The hands of the self-possessed Althea began to shake. She prowled around the kitchen, puffing. "I don't . . . uh . . . maybe I shouldn't go away to college. I don't want to leave you all alone." For two years she had dreamed of going to Middlebury to study languages, an excellent choice—she has a verbal soul.

"Oh no! You're going no matter what. Besides, he's not exactly out of my life, you know. It doesn't happen like that. And Phil is here."

"Phil! What use is he? He hardly even speaks. Living with him you might just as well be alone."

"He is not here for my use, and I don't like hearing you talk that way about him. It's not right."

"It's true, though."

"It seems true on the surface. It's not really true. But even if it were, does the truth, what you think is the truth, need to be blurted out all the time?"

"Yes." We have discussed this before. She believes that any truth justifies its own utterance. Moreover, she claims it is her nature to speak the truth, like Cassandra. Woe to any who heed not. If I urge diplomacy in the exercise of her powers I am trying to stifle or change her personality, which is a crime. She will never change, she says proudly. She will be this way for life.

"You of all people should understand. You're close to his age. You know the kinds of things he's going through. Besides—" My eyes measured the large empty kitchen.

"It's precisely because I do know. Why does he have to repress it all? He should learn to express his needs—then he might get some of them satisfied." She grinned but quickly composed her face. "He also might be a little more sensitive to the needs of those around him."

"Oh, stop sounding like a social worker. What he needs is a little patience from those around him."

"He's just acting out, Mother."

"Acting out?" I smiled. "Who isn't? Look at your father."

"*I* am not." She stubbed out the cigarette righteously. "I'm a reasonable person. I try to be governed by reason. I don't see why other people can't do the same."

"I wish you luck. Now would you help me clear the table?"

"Sure." Always willing and able. An oldest daughter, she sees responsibilities everywhere. And a true communal spirit, too—not one shirking cell in Althea. So when she speaks so ungenerously, I remind myself she is the most generous nature of them all, though she might not wish that particular distinction. Someday she may even allow herself some tolerance for human frailty, and then what an excellent person she will be.

"Will you look at that!" The sharp voice, the cutting consonants. "He left his plate, his glass, his dirty napkin, everything. Does he think we're servants, to clean up after him? If I were you I would call him back and make him clean that up."

"Oh, Althea, one plate more, what's the difference? I'll do it."

"It's the principle. No, get away from the sink. I'll do the dishes."

"Don't you have homework?"

"It's all right," she said with impatience. "I'll do them. You've done them the past two nights. Go on, go on, out. Practice. Read. Do something," she ordered, so I obediently turned to go.

"Mom? Will he still come to my graduation?"

Should I go and put my arms around her or leave her dignity be? Leave her. "Of course he'll come. What are you thinking of? We'll come together." I did go over after all. "Althea . . ."

She shook her head, scrubbed the dish hard, and shuddered me off. "It's all right. Go."

Victor phoned every evening except that first, but Phil would not go to the phone. In two days, Saturday, when Victor comes over to see them, Phil is planning to be out, as I am. If he ever marries this Montessori teacher I shall appear at the wedding like the bad fairy, like Clyde's ex-wife Floral, and when they ask if anyone knows any reason why this pair should not be joined in holy matrimony I will stand up and shout, Yes, yes, because he walked out on his two remaining children, grieving children, and waited thirty-six hours to explain. Never mind me—I would have left me too, believe me I wish I could have, I was intolerable—but those children, whose eyes have never been the same . . . The formative years, I shall tell the assembled well-wishers, are never over.

I get up from the floor and replace the telephone (which I still imagine to contain the voice of Miss Fosdick, like those toy phones that speak when you lift the receiver), turn over the "Trout" recording, and curl back in my chair with the coloring book and Crayolas. I think I'll do the knights gathering for their tournament. I can give the six horses all the glossy horsey colors I recall from my race-track days with Nina. As I hold Burnished Gold poised above the page, the delectable fourth movement of the "Trout" begins, the theme and variations using the melody from that silly song about the fish: the ascending fourth, then third; the descending third, then fourth—the way up and the way down, syncopated and then even, making audible the idea of the teasingly indecisive, the reversible, the ambiguous.

The crooked and the straight in dialogue, and finally in truce. The late Hephzibah, here immortalized, enters with supreme self-possession, with a controlled sweetness that never droops into sentimentality but instead has lightness and subtlety. One instrument after the other plays in turn with this delicious theme. What was first stated so simply they twist and invert, embellish, tickle, unravel and ravel again; they virtually torture that single sweet and faintly melancholy theme. They are so dazzling that I am drawn in, lifted away, and unraveled myself; unknotted, allowing the variations to be played in me and through me. It is almost like before. I almost forget. Something demonic still wants me to color the horses. Become a dribbling idiot, let's see how far into idiocy you can go. But I won't. I strain to hang on to the theme. For the truth is, I'm not so young any more, I can't afford to play games with coloring books. And I'm not ready to go yet, to forget these griefs in death; this organism insists on dying in its own time and in its own way, not when some chance angler throws down a trap. Which is to say, it insists on living. In any old way.

For the first time in my apartment, Bobby starts to cry. Those small half-whimpers to begin with, then bigger gasps, rattling breaths, till he has worked up to the standard infant howl. I can't see him from my chair but can well imagine the red face and round open toothless mouth, the fists battering air. Alone with a howling infant, to the brash, assertive last movement of the "Trout," I grow cold. So cold I shiver. Outside, the raining sky is the color of dusty pewter. Across the room the carriage shakes eerily. I go over. He rolls his head back and forth, catches sight of me and pauses for half a second, then resumes howling. I get very hot. I don't feel sorry for him, a mere red blot on the pillow, but I need that terrible noise, that noise as much a part of me as my own name, to stop! How? My past has been scraped off me with a knife; I can't summon up how. I jiggle the plastic toy dangling from the hood of the carriage. Not the way. His howls keep filling my empty house like clouds of smoke. I reach down and touch his cheek with a finger. Spit slides out the corners of his mouth. I open my hand and slowly lower it like a wrecking ball, till it rests lightly on his face, then spread the hand wide so the sound comes through the lattice of fingers. The hand is large, veined and articulated, the fingers stretched beyond their natural potential, a hand with a use. The fingers rest on his forehead and temples, the heel of the hand at his chin, and I imagine pressing down, hard. For an instant it seems I will do it. Then I race back to my chair to huddle deep, hugging my knees to my chest, squeezing and punishing the murderous wet right hand.

A key in the door. Hide the coloring book and crayons under the cushion and huddle up again.

"Hi." Phil tosses his book bag onto the floor. "What's wrong with him?"

I frown.

"Shouldn't you pick him up or something?" Pushing six feet, he stands slumped, yet his boy's body is tight under the corduroy pants and baggy sweatshirt. His hair is damp. His hands seem tense and chapped. "Are you okay?" he asks.

"Mm-hm." What with the final jubilant bars of the "Trout" and the howls, my silence and Phil's tangled presence, the room is oppressive, crammed to bursting. Phil casts me an odd, reproachful look, takes off his sweatshirt, and reaches into the carriage with his long gangly arms. He holds Bobby on his shoulder in the correct position, and as he paces, gently patting the baby's back, the howls diminish. Phil pauses to stare out the wide front windows at the park and the river. In a moment the record stops, all is quiet. He looks at the baby with a kind, amused gaze I haven't seen on his face in months. He touches Bobby's chin and cheeks, pinches his plump feet, and makes shy cooing noises at him. Then Phil looks at me and grins. He actually smiles! When the doorbell rings I jump up. "I'll get it."

"I'm sorry it took longer than I thought," Patricia says. "There was such a crowd at the butcher's. I should have asked you if you wanted any meat. Did you?"

"No, I shopped before."

Phil brings the baby out into the hall. Bobby is happy to see his mother—he smiles and vaults his body into her arms. I guess he is not brain-damaged after all.

"How was school?" I ask when they've gone. His smile is gone too.

"Okay."

I follow him, limping, to the kitchen, where he opens the

refrigerator and regards its contents with the obscurely dissatisfied air he has perfected.

"We have some good apples. Also banana bread. Or would
you like some hot chocolate? It's raining so hard—you must be
chilly."

"I'm not hungry." He lets the door swing shut and takes a
glass of water. He is once more armored, and the scene painted
on his armor is resentment of the world. For the moment I
represent the world. It is quite some time since I have heard his
natural tone of voice, which was rich and combative. He is
withholding his voice, himself, all but his body, from this
house. As I watch him drink the water, with head back and
eyes half-shut, I grow angry. I feel exactly as Althea does:
living with him I might as well be alone. "Phil," I say sharply. "I
think you might speak to me when you come home. Just a few
civil words would do. We're still a family. And to Althea when
you see her. And—" I stop to soften my tone. "I'd like you to
speak to your father when he calls."

"But if I have nothing to say to him . . ."

"Yes you do. You can tell him you're furious with him."

"He must have figured that out for himself."

"Come on now. Not speaking is so silly."

"Can I go to Boston in two weeks with Henry for the weekend?
There's a Bruce Springsteen concert. His father got tickets and
is driving us there and back and we'll sleep in his uncle's
basement."

I see the future—Cassandra! More and more time away, and
soon he won't feel he needs to ask. Two weeks: that will leave
Althea and me. "I guess so." I must arrange something to fill
the space, though. The best one for this job is Esther. Tomorrow I will call her in Washington and request my semiannual
visit, long overdue.

Phil retires to his bedroom and I to mine, with one of the
thick-skinned expensive oranges I bought at the Korean store
earlier, plucking as I go a paper napkin from the blue napkin
holder made two years ago by, I think, Alan. It is five-thirty. I
change into old clothes, and for a most indulgent treat, turn on
the TV to *The Electric Company*, but not too loud, so Phil won't
hear. I've missed it. They had all outgrown it except Vivian,
who happily shared certain of my regressive tastes. This last

December, her last December, she was shut in with a cold and bored. I came home to find her stretched out on our old bed, her fine hair in braids and decorated with a tiara of Woolworth's pearls. Wearing my blue velours robe with high-heeled shoes, as well as lipstick, iridescent eye shadow, and several ropes of beads, she raptly watched Jennifer of the jungle swing from tree to tree in a leopard-skin costume while below an entourage sang, "Who looks so fine hanging on any vine? Jennifer of the Jungle. Who brings a smile to every Nile crocodile . . ." I stretched out beside her, tucking her under my arm like a baby. She smelled sweet and chocolaty and was warm with fever. When Jennifer was over I tapped her lightly on the chin and teased, "I think you may be getting too old for this." "So are you," she replied.

Well, just for old times' sake—I wonder, do they still do Jennifer of the Jungle? Fargo North, Decoder? Your Rich Uncle Died and Left You All His . . .? Starts with an M. Marshmallows? Yes indeed they do. And here comes Vivian's and my favorite: "Punctuation." Rita Moreno sings in a heavy Spanish accent, "Now a period is just a little dot, But it occupies a very special spot," and Victor Borge intersperses popping and slurping mouth noises to illustrate the period, the question mark, the comma, and his *pièce de résistance*, the exclamation point. How on earth does he do that, she used to marvel.

When I'm done eating the quartered orange I start on the rinds, a slow process with small bites, since the rinds are so acidic. To Althea this habit verges on the disgusting; to Althea many innocuous things verge on the disgusting—they need only be things she has no inclination to do. "That's no great accomplishment," she once said in irritation. "Watch this." She cut a lemon in quarters and sucked one quarter dry without wincing, though tears rolled down her cheeks. "Very good, Althea. That is an accomplishment. But I happen to like the orange peels. I was eating them long before you were born. I'm not trying to prove anything." Vivian would stick up for me. Like Voltaire, she did not share my taste for orange peels but would defend to the death my right to eat them, and did.

After "Punctuation," the Electric Company kids sing "Hard, Hard, Hard," to demonstrate the "ar" sound, as I start on another stinging peel. "Oh yes, it's hard, hard, hard, Nothing's easy in this life, you see." The song has barely begun when the

telephone at my bedside rings. Rosalie, her hello as exuberant
and breathy as if she has won a race. Who would ever suspect
she is at her best in the plangent, exalted Andantes of Beethoven and Brahms?

"So, have you made up your mind?"

"Not yet. I listened to Hephzibah Menuhin do it this
afternoon."

"And?"

"Well, it's a big job."

"Yes, that's what we need. Enough of this futzing around."

"Mozart is futzing around?"

"You know what I mean. We need something with a broader
line. For this concert anyway—we need to show some range.
Maybe one of the Brahms. Fauré. We have to work it out with
Jasper very soon."

"I'd rather do something by Telemann."

"Playing it safe, aren't you? Listen, I understand about the
Romantics, but really, Lydia—"

"All right, all right." She knows me too well. That music
demands something different. Not simply emotion, as my floun-
dering student would call it, but a consciousness of its infinite
span. A certain expectant, welcoming embrace extended to
emotion, in all its possible variations and modulations. To perform them with willing hands.

"Anyhow, you've done the 'Trout' before, you told me.
Haven't you?"

"Years ago."

"Well, then it should be easy. What is that awful noise?"

("Oh yes, it's hard, hard, hard, If it's good then you can bet it
isn't free"—they sound like a hard rock group, something Rosalie loathes.)

"Nothing. The TV. Hold on, I'll turn it down. . . . Rosalie,
did you know they're using the fourth movement of the 'Trout'
in wine commercials? I heard it on WNCN yesterday."

"So what?"

"Maybe it's becoming trite."

"What do we care about wine commercials? You know very
well it's not trite. For a pianist you can't do much better. It has
everything."

"I know, but . . . I had this strange time listening to it. I

could hear all the separate parts but they wouldn't come together in my ear. I couldn't get the mix right."

"Don't listen to it. Just do it."

"Did you see Hephzibah's obituary in the *Times* this winter?"

"Yes! I certainly did!" Indignation. I can see her smacking
her knee, tossing her black hair. " 'Sister of Violinist'! But what
can you expect from the *Times*? Look, Lydia, I have another
idea. I've told Jasper and he likes it. I want to try some ragtime.
Joplin."

"I think that revival is about over. In one ear and out the
other."

"That's exactly why. Now it can be done seriously. It's a
tremendous sound, and they have some arranged for string
quartets. I could get Carla and someone else. I have this new
friend, a kid at WBAI. He's always looking for something
slightly bizarre. You'll play the original and we'll do the
arrangements. Then he'll interview us, we'll talk about its great
classical qualities, the problems of adapting for a quartet, et
cetera, et cetera. And they record."

"I don't think I'm in the mood for ragtime."

"Oh, mood, schmood. We'll even do something from *Treemoni-
sha.*"

"Where are you going to dig up an arrangement of that?"

"I'll do the arrangements."

"Rosalie, that's so much work."

"So? I have time. I have no babies pulling at my skirts. Oh,
by the way, I saw Karl again last night." The husband she had
her fill of a year and a half ago and has been unable to stop
talking about since. "We had another—you should pardon the
expression—date."

"No kidding? What did you do on your date?"

"We had dinner at a Chinese restaurant, then we went back
to his apartment."

"Ah! A very thorough date this time, sounds like. So, do you
think he's someone you'll want to see again?"

"He seems to have recovered from that spell of premature
ejaculation, for one thing."

"Jeepers. To what do you attribute this miracle?"

"Other women. I suppose he figured out if he could do it for
strangers he could do it for me. He says it's because his hostility

has decreased, but of course he has to say something like that. Frankly, Lydia, the whole evening was . . . not bad. Not bad at all. I always did like the guy, you know."

Rosalie! After your hours of recrimination! He called your mode of living acting out! The neurotic artistic temperament! And then his insane working hours. Psychiatry his mistress. Preoccupied: you didn't know whether you felt more alone with him or without him. Controlling: opened your mail. Occasionally forgot his children's names. Once a raised kitchen knife. Lesser-grade evils: Cigars in bed. Couldn't cut the nails on his right hand. Congenitally incapable of refilling an ice-cube tray. I know this man so well I could have been married to him myself. The brief times I met him he seemed pleasant enough.

"I know exactly what you're thinking. But after all, twenty-seven years. You become attached. Three children."

"They're all off on their own. Remember?"

"Well, we'll see. I'm not rushing into anything. It was nice to be with someone who didn't ask questions about what I like, for a change. I hate this new business of utilitarian discussions in bed, having to verbalize every little whim. How is Victor, speaking of . . .?"

"Oh, all right, I guess."

"And the kids?"

"Phil's okay. Althea's away in Princeton till tomorrow. There's some conference about Romance languages. She got special permission to go because of Middlebury."

"She's impressive, your little Althea."

"Expressive, anyway. She does get around."

"That reminds me. We are going north sometime in November, you and Jasper and I, maybe a few others, I'm not sure. New Haven, Boston, some of the college towns around there."

"What are you talking about?"

"We've been asked by some arts council. For two weeks. I'll tell you the details tomorrow when we rehearse—they're in my briefcase. Lyd, are you still there?"

"I can go, I guess."

"Yes." The dynamo stops for a moment. "Yes," she says quietly, "you can easily go."

"It is strange, isn't it, how things turn out?" I can feel her listening. She does everything so intensely. "All I do is pack up and go. The kids can manage now. I can't think of a single excuse."

"Well, good. You'll travel a lot, then. It's what you always needed anyway. It's why you didn't—"

"Oh, it's too late for rich and famous, Rosalie. I don't need that."

"You never know. Look, before I go there's one more little thing."

"You're so full of little things today. I gather this is supposed to be a therapeutic conversation?" She's quiet again, and wounded. "I'm sorry, really. Don't mind me. What is it?"

"Actually it's something I need from you. A favor. You know this all-day Bach thing I'm putting on at the Calliope Center? Well, Sandy Schuster had to leave town for a sick mother. So we are sort of without a harpsichordist. We have someone to do her thing in the evening, but there's a three o'clock bit. . . ."

"Rosalie, I'm not a—"

"Wait a second before you say no. It's a Handel violin sonata, you don't have a lot to do there, and a Brandenburg. The sixth."

"I'm not a harpsichordist."

"I've heard you plenty of times. At the school, at that church in the Village. You were fine."

"That wasn't serious. Look, there must be a dozen decent harpsichordists around. Even one of the students."

"I've *been* looking, Lydia. The good ones are all busy or out of town or want more money, and the others . . . well. I need someone who can at least stay together."

"I won't be able to do much more than that."

"I'll bring the music tomorrow. You have a week."

"A week. Oh, terrific. I'll have to practice there. I'm not taking any chances with the instrument."

"Fine. I'll arrange everything. If you want to go at night I'll even get you a key. And thanks. So listen, make up your mind about the 'Trout,' bring it along tomorrow, and also the Brahms and the Mendelssohn, and I'll see you at two."

"I'm worn out just talking to you."

"Get a good night's sleep, then. Say hello to Victor." She whirls off; her voice hangs in the air another moment like the last descending dust of a tornado.

The Electric Company is over. I carry the remaining bits of peel into the kitchen and pour Scotch over ice, then turn on the "Trout" again, to accompany my cooking. For my shopping spree is about to achieve Aristotelian entelechy—its potential becoming actualized. I no longer feel the obscure yet keen longing that in the morning made me plan this elaborate dinner . . . but I might as well. As I set out my purchases, the kitchen table takes on the cheery demeanor of a photo from *Woman's Day*—fresh ripe this, plump succulent that. Where to begin? *The Raw and the Cooked* was a book Victor read and admired a few years ago, but I couldn't get past the introduction. Surely this is not the way real cooks begin, a dozen colorful items waiting, mute and attentive, on the kitchen table? How did I ever manage to cook for six? Using sense memory, a redemptive faculty that lets me play pieces I haven't done in years but whose patterns are stored in my fingers as in a data bank, I prepare the chicken and arrange it in a Pyrex pan. Cloves of garlic, pats of butter, wedges of lemon, sprigs of parsley. Vivian once recited to me the wealth of terms for animals in groups: flock of sheep, gaggle of geese, pack of wolves, pride of lions . . . She loved peculiar usages, also puns, anagrams, palindromes. (Onion. Onion? Why not onion? And how do you weigh air, anyhow?) Into the oven it goes; one sure thing on this changeable earth is that an hour and a quarter from now, at seven thirty-eight on a Thursday evening in mid-May, Lydia, eleven and a half weeks from the demise of her younger children, will have baked a lemon-butter chicken, Amen. Well done, Lydia. Turn the record over and have another drink.

While I make saffron rice and a salad with the cheap bitter lettuce, I pay close attention to the "Trout." Yes, I could do that again. Not perhaps with the seemingly effortless buoyancy of Hephzibah Menuhin, but respectably. If I work at it, and shun the temptations of coloring books and educational TV. If Victor keeps his telephone voice out of my life. Tomorrow. Meanwhile, drink up. Tomorrow I'll tell Rosalie that yes, I'll do ragtime on WBAI, the gig in New England, even the harpsichord, though the last is definitely an error in professional judgment. Rosalie is trying too hard, but what the hell? Life is not all bad. Everyone's got troubles. And Scotch is a fantastic thing—what it can do for you, that is. I set the table for two.

At seven-fifteen, shortly before the feast is ready, Phil appears, wearing the same old corduroys but a spiffy plaid shirt. "I'm going to Burger King. I forgot to tell you. I'm meeting this girl—Ilana? The one who calls about the trig." Like the neighbors, he avoids my eyes.

Fortunately for him I am well into my third Scotch. "Uh, that's very nice. You might have said something, though. I cooked this whole meal."

"Well, I wasn't really sure. I mean, I just called. . . . I'll eat it tomorrow, okay? I've got to go."

He is not here for my use, I so nobly told Althea. Very well. "Have a good time. Take your keys, I might be sleeping."

"I've got them. 'Bye."

Going out with a girl! The first time, as far as I know. Well, that is a fine thing for solitary Phil—I'm not too mad to be pleased. Only what shall I do with this dinner? Were I a reader of *Cosmopolitan* I would know how to invite a friend to drop over for an unexpected treat. Any angle! But I don't have those kinds of friends, alas. I could call George or Nina, Rosalie, even Irving Bloch, thinner since his wife died. The splendid minister, to minister? Patricia and Sam, who don't get out much—but no doubt they've eaten; they keep baby hours. How about Victor and the Montessori teacher? We could try being ultra-civilized.

In truth there's not a living soul I'd care to see right now except maybe Evelyn, but she is in Switzerland; most impractical. She was so fluid and calm and captivating, my sister, so like Vivian, the sort of person whose presence, for no evident reason, is a treasure like grace. I might entice her as I did when I was thirteen and she was ten and our parents went to the movies, leaving me money for an excursion to the corner store. "Evelyn." I'd knock on her closed door. "I've got chocolate chip mint ice cream. I've got Yankee Doodles." And she would come out and listen wide-eyed and serene to my chronicles of junior-high life. How we loved to eat and to laugh! I could call long-distance, all the way to the Alps: "Evelyn. I've got lemon chicken. Saffron rice. Bitter herbs." I can see her seated at my table, smiling and quietly vibrant, listening absorbed and radiant. It would be like having Vivie back.

I eat it myself, listening, with the score spread out on the living room floor. And then I take the score to bed. I can hear it better without the music; the ensemble does not splinter apart quite so badly that way. Yet it's hard to concentrate, all alone in the house at night. I'm not used to it. A skill you develop with practice, Nina once said of being alone. He bought this huge bed to make love with a sense of space. Ravish me at any angle. Far across the space, over on his nighttable, is the book he left half-read, open, face down: Malinowski's *Magic, Science and Religion*, the book of myths. Why was he rereading that? He knew it—he studied anthropology in college. And why didn't he take it with him—did he expect his evenings would be too sizzling for serious reading?

All alone and still; something in the back of my mind stirs, shoves its way forward, and bursts out full-blown like Athena from the head of Zeus, a fantasy: the Korean boy stands beside the bed with that shock of coarse black hair, those lowered dark eyes, wide cheekbones, perfect teeth. The big bony hands used to hauling crates of fruit, their fingers stretched from piling pyramids of honeydews, hang idly by his sides. He wears the coveted Adidas sneakers. He stands gawky and puzzled though he must be nineteen at least. Can he be so innocent? I beckon.

He doesn't seem to know even where to begin. Is he frightened, bashful, repelled?—I'm an older woman, old enough to be his mother. Will he cooperate? Ah, clay under my hands: I will shape him into a slavish lover. Do this. Do that. Do whatever pleases me. See how I move in mysterious ways. Let me ravish you at any angle. The boy awakens, begins to seek after his own desire. I am his Frankenstein and his landscape both. I found what made him work and he found his desire. No speech, only brute grunts. His face has become brutish too—the heavy lips hanging open and wet, the luminous eyes dulled, the hair in disarray. That fine intelligence has fled from his face, leaving a generic male. I have created a brute. So it was done to me; I pass it along. Our arms and legs coil and entwine. We paw and scrape at each other's want like dogs at the site of a buried bone, and when we find it we gnaw till the marrow is all sucked out. And then he sleeps, flat on his back on Victor's side, and his human identity returns: the lips soft and sensitive once more, smiling faintly. The fine intelligence too. Beneath his lids is rapid eye movement: he dreams, not of me. No urgency in his body now, no trace of it except for the slick wetness. Pleasure has made him weak as a worm, and as shiny too. Now he is at my mercy. But the myth of the castrating female is all wrong—an asinine projection. That's not the place that's done me harm. Let him keep his useful worm. Esther was so naive when she made Griselda do that to Walter. I would make the slice and draw the blood across the throat, and watch the face that can change so swiftly from human to brute to deceiver change its last, and bloody Victor's pillow.

He shrinks and vanishes unharmed, once more a small furrow in the back of my mind. What puny revenge. I get up and catch a glimpse of myself in the mirror, in Phil's gray corduroy pants and Althea's green T-shirt. Even through this nondescript outfit the body shows itself trim and youngish—miracle, after all those pregnancies. But from the neck up, oh dear. Not at all sleek. Tomorrow will be different—such indulgence as today's is killing. I put away the leftover dinner and take the garbage out to the back hall, where Lily's TV trips me, resenting its fate, and I curse it as usual. In the shower I study my body clinically as Victor might have done—an object with bumps and planes and hollows. Clay, like the woman Evelyn and Mother and I shaped on the beach, where the waves rushed at her. The gentler ones merely eroded her, the most violent one tore off chunks, till at last I kicked at her remains with exultation, for she was only clay and had no feelings, and anyway, what use was half a woman?

The next morning as I practiced the "Trout" in my small studio off the bedroom, a substantial shadow passed over the corner of my right eye. For two bars I ignored it, and then I went to look. A boy stood in the center of the bedroom. No product of my imagination, this one, but a real, short boy with a slight frame and a wan, wary face in which the eyes bulged unhealthily. We stared at each other for I don't know how long. My knees didn't turn to water. Concrete: a game of statues. His dark hair was greased back, and he wore a well-ironed red cotton shirt tucked neatly into his jeans and open halfway down an unimpressive chest; the short sleeves were rolled up, showing puerile biceps. The fire escape window was locked, but the other one, three feet away, was wide open. Stretching over from the ledge of the fire escape, he could have fallen into the rear alley. He fell instead into my life, and seemed even more stunned there than I. I breathed first. "What do you want?"

I was bigger than he was, possibly stronger. He made no move to speak, but with rabbit twitches glanced to right and left: there was only the stillness of an empty apartment.

"You really think it's worth it, risking your life to steal something? Nine floors!" And how your mother would have grieved! Look how beautifully she ironed your shirt! Unless he didn't have a mother, like George, or had one who didn't give a damn.

At last he ventured to look straight at me—crazy lady!—for an instant. His bulgy eyes grew larger with confusion. He was a year or two older than Phil, seventeen, maybe, and like Phil had a volatile, uncommitted sulkiness around the mouth: I will not let you find me out. He took a breath and finally moved; reached in his back pocket and brought out a knife. The blade shot forth like a snake's tongue.

I folded my arms across my chest. "Oh for Chrissake, will you put that thing away? What could I do to you? And you don't even look like you could use it." He switched the blade back in but kept the knife in his fist.

"Anyone else climb in with you?" He shook his head. "You can't be all alone. This is not your line. They're waiting down in back, right? Sent you up to see if you could get anything?"

He nodded once, stiff as a doll. His face was gleaming with sweat and his red shirt was darkening under the arms.

"Your first time, I bet. What'd you do, take gymnastics at school or something?"

His shoulders jerked as he took a quick step back. Yes, kid, there's not much I don't know about you kids, I made a career of it. He was in a nightmare; I was his tormentor. Nothing anyone had taught him had prepared him for this. I knew precisely how he felt. He glanced over his shoulder at the open window, and when he turned to me again his eyes were filmed with panic.

"No, you better not try getting out that way. Don't push your luck. You'll walk out the door. Listen, I have just the thing for you. Come along. I mean it. I'll give you something your hot-shot friends will like." I had him precede me through the hall to the kitchen and out to the rear landing where the garbage cans, bikes, sleds, and TV were piled. "Take this." He stared, then his eyes darted as if I had some trick up my sleeve. "I'm not kidding. You'd be doing me a favor."

He put his knife away and lifted the TV tentatively. "No shit?" he asked.

"I said take it. Yes, that's right." I led him back through the kitchen and to the front door. "Take the elevator to the basement, make a left, go past the boiler room to a blue door, and make sure to slam it shut behind you. If you meet anyone you can say the lady on the ninth floor gave it to you."

He coughed and rested the TV against the doorframe. He was breathing hard. Victor had carried it with no trouble. Maybe this kid had a rheumatic heart, or a slight murmur like Vivian's but not innocent. I pointed to the elevator and he pressed the button and waited, his forehead dripping, his shirt not quite so fresh. Only the greased-down hair still lay unperturbed. He tried to avoid my gaze but I wasn't ready to release him yet. I noticed his blue Adidas sneakers. Good Lord, every kid around had them! Why did I have to tell him to wait till the snow melted?

"What do you do with it now, take it to a fence?" Safe in the hall, he sneered at the crazy lady. "Tell him it'll work fine anywhere but in this neighborhood. Around here it needs to be hooked up to the cable." With his face screwed up and his body curved under the weight of the TV, he was a squirrel hugging an enormous nut. "Get away fast and don't come back, because the next burglary on this block, I'll go straight to the police and tell them exactly what you look like, sneakers and all. You get it? Tell your friends too. And try some other line of work!" I called as he struggled to open the elevator door. "You don't want to get yourself killed!"

For Phil and Althea I would have to invent something: a new student who was glad to take it off our hands. For Victor? It would be a long time before he noticed, if ever. Elsewhere, what a story this could make! How I could regale cocktail parties! But unfortunately it is a story that cannot be told, at least by me. I am so tired of curious oblique looks, solicitude, sorrowful head-shaking, friends being "supportive." It embarrasses me. They make me feel that by losing my children I have done something shameful, profoundly antisocial, but never mind,

I will be magnanimously forgiven. Meanwhile I am on probation; my behavior is watched closely for deviance.

Come to think of it, there is someone I might safely tell: my coiffured sister-in-law Lily in Westchester, who has always judged me slightly wacky anyway, who lives and thinks like the Russian landed aristocracy in a Chekhov play. Linked together by cozy mutual disapproval, we have always gotten along rather well. Our dialogue might go something like this:

Oh Lily, remember that old TV you gave us for Vivian and Alan to use? You'll never guess what happened to it.

I hope it didn't break down or anything. It was a good little set, if you're not too spoiled for black-and-white.

It never worked in our apartment. We get terrible reception because we're due north of the twin towers. We need the cable to get anything halfway decent. A boy broke in one morning so I gave it to him. Ha ha ha.

Lily turns ashen beneath her make-up, and slams down her vodka martini, which nearly sloshes over the rim of the glass. What do you mean, gave it to him? Broke in when? What are you talking about?

It's nothing personal, Lily. It's just that frankly, it was a lousy set to begin with, and with almost everyone gone—you know Althea will be away at college soon too—there was really no point. . . . I mean, to each according to his needs (I throw this in to irritate her), and Phil and I are not big watchers. So I figured, here is this desperate kid, here is this TV taking up space—they're made for each other.

You're not serious!

I'm perfectly serious. Why would I lie to you?

But are you okay? Did he do anything to you?

Not a thing. Didn't even say thank you.

This city is more like a jungle every day! She shakes her head and makes clicking noises with her tongue. And you! To each according to his needs! You're too much. It's a miracle you're still alive.

Yes, that's what I'm thinking too. Not about the boy, though. I mean that when the things you thought you possessed, what you thought were necessities, the things that made you who you were, even your goddamn phone number, start to go and yet you remain—it's kind of a riddle, Lily. Don't you see?

There you stand stripped, the same person, more or less. But what are you now? What is left? Something does abide but it's only a certain feeling of continuity . . . I don't know what.

Lily sighs. Everyone knows all that, Lydia. (Do they really?) She lights a cigarette with some discomfort at my speaking the unspeakably banal. Listen, sweetie—her hoarse, smoky voice sincerely attempting to be kind—it's natural to be confused. But remember, people have lost a lot more—she pauses for a sense of the sweep of history, of which my losses are clearly not a part—and they all go on. And on.

Oh Lily, don't tell me about the ones who clawed their way through the forests of Poland, our distant relations. I know about them. It's a miracle they're still alive. Please believe that I'm not trying to compete, only to clear a path also.

And to be satisfied to possess simply this voice in my head which speaks and remembers back to when, the same voice that spoke then and dreamed ahead to now. And the child who dashed in the waves on the beach, whom they cannot take until they take me with her. She is the only child I will ever keep.

Reunion

Grief, Aristotle wrote in his chapter on friendship, "is lightened when friends sorrow with us"—I looked it up before Esther arrived. He ponders, then, why this should be so: do they help shoulder our burden, or does the pleasure of their company simply lessen it? Well, this is too academic a point even for Aristotle; he quickly moves on to undercut the reassurance he first offered: "People of a manly nature guard against making their friends grieve with them . . . but women and womanly men enjoy sympathizers in their grief, and love them as friends and companions in sorrow. But in all things one obviously ought to imitate the better type of person."

Smooth, soft, and colorful, settled on a large pillow on the floor with her peasant skirt spread around her, Esther suggested a floral arrangement. A large bouquet just past its prime, at the edge of blowsiness. She was munching from a handful of cherries and blowing the pits into her palm. Every so often her voice wavered—she had been telling sad tales of mistreatment at the hands of men—and from living so long in Washington among black Southerners she had the tinge of a drawl.

"Enough masochism," Nina said. "Two hours is enough. I have discovered just the thing in the personals column. It's for me and Lydie, though. You're too earnest. And Gaby, well, you of course . . ." Nina was flat on her back on my couch, all in black—black pants, black sweatshirt, black beads—and pale from a recent bout with the flu. With time she had grown far-sighted: the *New York Review of Books* wafted high above her head.

"Oh, those. They're awful. Althea used to read them aloud to me and Victor every week."

"This one has class. 'Wanted: Two ladies who would like a summer jaunt in a VW convertible. Must be sweet, loving, able to read a racing form and drink their fair share.' There's a New York phone number, then it says, 'Ask for Steve or Cal at any hour.' What do you think, Lydia?"

"It's a gem, all right. Except are we sweet and loving?"

"We could be, given the right conditions. Do you want Steve or Cal?"

"Hm. Steve, I think, if it's all the same to you."

"Fine. I wanted Cal anyway." Nina sat up nimbly, tossed aside the review, and withdrew behind her *New York Times*, folding the pages vertically, half over half, with the skill of a business executive on a crowded subway. All afternoon she had slipped in and out of attendance. I sensed a vague halo of anticipation, and was willing to bet that posed Indian fashion behind the stock exchange listings, she was off in some fantasy. Not with Steve or Cal. With Sam, the civil rights lawyer. Scattered evenings and weekends over the years, lifted out of his quotidian regularity of wife, kids, and job, enhanced by infrequency. I thought Nina deserved better, but it was what she had chosen, or been chosen by.

"I knew a Cal. I bumped into him on the bus one afternoon a few months ago, a friend of Clyde's," said Esther, undaunted. "He wasn't one of those SAVE types; he did something with computers. I never knew him well—he used to come over to play chess with Clyde. I couldn't figure out how such a straight guy came to be a friend of Clyde's."

"Clyde played chess?" Nina lowered the paper momentarily.

"Yes. He wasn't stupid. Misguided, maybe, but far from stupid. Anyway, I hadn't seen this Cal in almost four years, since we were divorced. We said hello, how do you come to be in Washington, and all that. I swear I did not say a thing that might be construed as encouragement, but the next thing you know he's telling me about his wife's various uterine problems and asking if I might care to stop in the Holiday Inn for an hour or so. I mean, really!"

"So what did you say?"

She jerked her head towards me. "I said no and got off the bus, Lydia. What'd you think I would say?" She turned to Gabrielle, who was active in several women's protest groups, for support, but Gabrielle just sipped her wine and continued to tear the edges of a paper napkin, making a neat half-inch fringe along the perimeter.

Gaby was withholding herself out of righteous anger. " 'A friend is another self,' " she had quoted weeks ago, looking wise, her glossy hair streaked with gray. "You wrote it on the philosophy final, Lydia. Don't you remember we drank to it and then danced up Broadway together? So why can't she manage to get herself up to see you for one weekend?"

"You can't hold people to things they felt twenty-five years ago. That's silly." I was not offended. Esther was working in a ghetto with clients she insisted on calling old, not senior citizens, and her weekends, she wrote in voluminous letters, were claimed by crisis: Mr. Green's food stamps mistakenly discontinued, Mrs. Brown's apartment cleaned out by junkies (fortunately she was not home at the time), Mrs. Gomez's grandson needing fast help with English to pass his driver's test and take that hospital aide job in Virginia. It appeared she had reverted to the school of William James, trusting her good actions would elicit the universe's better latent meanings. Her letters had postscripts: " 'Say not thou, what is the cause that the former days were better than these? for thou dost not enquire wisely concerning this.' " And in one that complained of my silence: " 'The fool foldeth his hands together, and eateth his own flesh.' " I didn't have to look them up; I recognized the equivocal voice of Ecclesiastes.

Besides, I had had ample companionship in sorrow. Nina and Gabrielle were no Job's comforters, either. No rationalizing or justifying or holding any hypersensitive power accountable. No dissecting my virtues and vices, my pride or humility, nor exhorting me to mend my ways. All they told me, at the beginning, was to get up, wash, dress, and see that Victor did the same. Gabrielle brought roasted chickens and vegetable casseroles and commanded that we eat. After our first week of utter sloth, she phoned every morning to make sure the children were going to school. When she appeared one day after work with a shopping bag from some East Side gourmet shop I felt the old suspicion conceived at her wedding stir again: friends with me, she was slumming, an impostor. Now a rich doctor's wife as well. "Gaby, pâté! For heaven's sake!" Long silver earrings danced along her jaw as she flicked her head up from unpacking the bag. "Would you prefer ashes?" Gaby was so rarely sarcastic that Victor and I blanched with surprise and dutifully ate the pâté. Nina came every few days and went about serenely emptying ashtrays and sorting laundry. She took off rings and jangly bracelets and dipped her lacquer-tipped fingers into steamy suds. Evenings she sat on the floor with Althea and Phil, going over the chemistry and physics they had missed. And the two of them nagged at me till I brought my puffy ankle to Don's office to be X-rayed. After two and a half weeks I told them to stop, we could manage now. The house had never been so orderly.

"Another time I was on a bus," Esther went on, "and got to talking to this young guy next to me. It started over something trivial—my library books dropped, he helped pick them up and said they felt like heavy reading."

The young man was polite and soulful, Esther said, and when they got off at the same stop he invited her for a cup of coffee. In the coffee shop a faraway look came into his eyes. He declared she was his fantasy woman come true, what he had been dreaming of for months. Maybe years—she couldn't recall his exact words. But for that very reason they could never meet again—he wanted his fantasy to remain intact and unsullied by the inevitable disappointments of reality. Esther didn't know how to respond. She drank her creamy cappuccino while he sipped a muddy espresso. He mentioned Proust and Stendhal and the psychology of love; she wondered if he might have taken CC at Columbia. Then he had to leave, but would remember her forever. She found herself sitting alone at the wobbly wrought-iron table. He paid the check on his way out, she had to grant him that much, but she left the tip.

"I dreamed about him for a couple of nights. I couldn't help it. You can't control what you dream. He wasn't my fantasy but he seemed rather nice, at first anyway. I might have risked a little reality with him."

"Maybe your problem is spending too much time on buses," I said. "Why don't you try driving?"

"I haven't driven since that accident when I had my teeth knocked out and almost my eye. I observe the world through the windows of buses."

Gabrielle frowned. "Aren't you being a bit melodramatic?"

"What do you know about it?" Patches of color studded Esther's cheeks. "You've never been mortified or treated like some kind of less than human."

"Esther, do you think there's any one of us who doesn't know what it's like"—Gaby paused as if she were sorry she had begun—"what it's like to lie awake half the night wanting someone? Do you? That is not politics."

"Well, whatever it is, it's too rough for me. I must have a way of picking them. I think I'll try women and see if they're any better. I'll come out of the closet."

"But, Esther, you've never been in the closet," I reminded her.

She spit a pit into her hand. "I'll go in, so I can come out. I'm glad to see you're all so amused at my expense. Well, it's better than silence. Silence makes me anxious."

"Still?" I asked.

"In school there was hardly ever silence," she said. "We had so many thoughts and theories about everything."

"Yes, we were so determined to understand." Nina's hair tumbled down her back and she swiftly coiled it up again, pins between her teeth. "We really expected that what was in all those books would have some bearing on how to live."

Nina rose and went to stare out the window, fingering the leaf of a plant. She still walked and looked like a lady, even in her sweatshirt. Through the radicalism of the sixties, the flaccid confusion of the seventies, she had moved and spoken like a lady. Like a lady she had marched, like a lady lectured at teach-ins on the effects of chemical warfare, and perhaps even made love like a lady, if that is possible. Now that gracious ladyhood was back in fashion she was not caught unprepared, like some. She had kept pace yet relinquished nothing. For all her escapades, her glittering jewelry and despairing eyes, there was a virginal, *noli me tangere* quality about her. Not girlish. More like a mature nun. She turned round and smiled. "We're not so bent on understanding the world any more, are we?"

"No," Gabrielle agreed. "Now we're content just to live in it, without understanding."

"Well, I understand plenty and I am not content." Esther scrambled up and pushed frizzed curls off her forehead. She announced, "I've got to be off. I'll just go wash my face and pee," at which Gabrielle winced.

"You've barely arrived. At least stay and have dinner. I thought you'd spend the night—there's room."

"I wish I could, Lyd. But I've got to get back tonight. I promised to be in church early in the morning."

"Church?"

"One of my clients is the lead singer in the choir in a Baptist church. She's been asking me to come hear her for weeks now. I promised. I've always wanted to go to one of those rousing black churches where everyone gets all excited, but you can't go as a spectator—it wouldn't feel right. I finally got an invitation. Maybe I'll have a religious experience, you never know." She flounced off to the bathroom and returned with the scrubbed look of a child. Still pink-and-white-skinned, in her light ruffled clothes she might have been an illustration in a toddler's book of nursery rhymes; she lacked only the broad straw hat with streamers. But the page was a trifle faded, a trifle smudged from being left out in damp weather. She had not combed her hair, either. Maybe her hairdo was the kind that couldn't be combed: wild floppy curls. Maybe she just toweled it dry every morning and let it settle at random. For all its breeziness, it did not strike me as hair that would easily ignite. She twisted her skirt around till the zipper returned to the left side, then said her good-byes. Kisses and hugs. "If any of you are ever down in Washington . . ."

At the door with me, alone, her face relaxed. "You don't look so bad, Lydia, considering. How is Victor? I'm sorry I missed him."

"He's all right. Look, I'm sorry too, that this didn't work out. I thought it would be a good idea, but I see I should have arranged for us to be alone. We still can, if you want to stay. Victor is—he'll be out late."

"I can't. It's true, about church and Mrs. Barker. Lydia, did I ever really thank you for the time you and Victor rescued me from Ralph and I slept on that mattress with all the baby toys around?"

"That was so long ago. You must have. What does it matter now?"

"I didn't. I was so wrapped up in myself. Anyhow, thanks."

"You're welcome. Forget it."

"Why are you limping?"

"I tripped over a skateboard and sprained my ankle."

Esther clicked her tongue. "How'd you manage that?"

"When the police came to tell me, I fell. There was a skateboard in the hall."

"Ah." She nodded, as if this were an everyday occurrence.

"Yes. Well, thanks for all your letters."

"You didn't mind those little . . .?"

"No, I've always liked them."

"Well, Lydia." She sighed and hoisted her small overnight bag onto her shoulder. "Things happen. What're you going to do?"

The words of my butcher! I had returned to my butcher yesterday, in fact, after three months. A man of elegant manners, unlike the fruit man, he had no questions, no recriminations. No nostalgic slices of bologna, either. A cordial greeting, a "What can I give you today?" His daughter had given birth to an eight-pound boy.

"Okay, if you're going, go. You'll miss your train and church and all."

She smiled shyly. " 'Where shall wisdom be found? And where is the place of understanding?' "

"Ecclesiastes?"

"Job."

"Job! So, where?"

"Well, it doesn't say explicitly. Then it wouldn't be a great book."

"How come you know all of that by heart?"

"Hah! I'll tell you—all the time I was in SAVE, they had no books around except pamphlets on organic gardening and righteous cookbooks. They didn't want to be inhibited by established thinking. Each person was supposed to reinvent the wheel, more or less. There was a Bible, though. I guess that wasn't considered dangerous. After a while I got desperate for something to read, so I read it."

"Nearly two years, Esther. How could you?"

"What're you going to do?" she repeated. "I did it. It's done. I can quote a lot of the Bible, though. I'll see you, Lyd."

"Thanks for coming." I went back to the living room. I wanted a crowd of people there. I should have invited everyone

I knew; a growing crowd, not a shrinking one. Gaby was telling Nina the plot of her next mystery; it involved a woman diplomat from an imaginary South Pacific republic, caught up in a whirl of crime and intrigue at the United Nations. I stood a bit apart, half-listening to this woman's existential but also fairly droll bewilderment, so far from the land of her birth, the grass skirts, the sea, the tropical fruits. . . .

"Lydia, the phone? Don't you hear it?"

"Oh!" I dashed to the kitchen. Althea, itinerant student. What a wonderful day ambling through Greenwich Village! A Fleetwood Mac record on sale for three dollars! A fantastic guitar player in Washington Square! Jugglers, acrobats! She'd even had a second hole pierced in each ear; Diane held her hand. The ear-piercing place was called The Primitive Urge. "How apt. Perhaps you can have your nose done next time." "Oh Mother." "I told you how I felt about two holes, Althea." "I know. But remember, you also told me it was my body and I had to use my own judgment about what I did with it." "You know very well I wasn't referring to your ears." She giggled. She wasn't calling to discuss her ears, though. Would I mind if she slept over at Diane's house on Roosevelt Island? An impromptu party. Everyone was meeting at the cable car, to swoop over together. I didn't mind. What had I been doing all day? My friends were over. Oh good, Mom, so you're not all alone. See you.

Inside, Gaby was checking her watch. "Don should be here any minute to pick me up. We have this tedious doctors' dinner. They're honoring the new head of the hospital."

"He can at least stay for a drink, I hope. I could call George. Make it a party."

"I've got to go pretty soon also." There was a slight stammer to Nina's words. She paused and made an awkward gesture, fussing with a strap of her shoe. "Sam's wife is in Philadelphia for the weekend."

"Ah, visiting the aged parents? Thank heaven for aged parents. A whole weekend. I thought you seemed distracted."

"Don't be malicious, Lydia, please. It doesn't suit you. Or me."

"Right, right. No allowances. Do not under any circumstances permit Lydia to be bitter out of self-pity. She might even get like Esther. Keep her to her high standards." I went

into the kitchen again. Sure, George said over the phone, he'd
come right over—why didn't I tell him before that I was holding a reunion?—but he couldn't stay long. A date with a yoga
teacher. A new one? Yes, a new one.

I brought back another bottle of wine and handed it to Gaby
with the corkscrew. She could open bottles like a man.

"Esther always had a short attention span," she said, screwing it between her knees. "It's gotten even shorter."

Nina yawned and stretched one arm high, then the other, as
Gaby used to do in the dorm at night. "Oh, why not be
tolerant?"

"I'm doing my best." According to Gabrielle, though, Nina
was far too tolerant. Years ago she had begun to distrust Nina,
when it became apparent that their lives had somehow gotten
switched. Gabrielle was to have been independent, lean,
adventuresome, Nina the respectable wife and mother, maybe
struggling to hold a job as well—for that too was respectable
now. Gabrielle envies the independence; if Nina envies the
husband and children she doesn't let on. For all her affection,
Gabrielle finds Nina suspect, like a dear friend who might have
stolen something while your back was turned, or then again you
might have misplaced it yourself. And also, Nina lies. She has
to tell a certain number of lies because her lawyer lover, Sam, is
not only married but a public figure. (Of course Sam lies too.)
Gaby is quite aware that with someone as intricate as Nina,
further variables of which we know nothing may necessitate
further lies of which we know nothing. Scientists should not get
in the habit of telling lies, Gaby believes. (Of lawyers she
expects it.) It weakens their credibility, vitiates their work,
becomes a habit of mind. I tell her that's nonsense. Surely in
the lab and the classroom Nina is perfectly honest. Perfect,
maybe, Gaby replies; not honest. And I think how far we have
come from Aristotle's ideals of friendship. Friends pleasant and
useful, but loved really for something else. A mutual love of
character, which endures a lifetime as character itself endures.

"You didn't even tell Esther about Victor," Gaby said, the
bottle neatly uncorked. "Why not?"

"I don't know. It's too boring."

"Boring?"

"Not so much the facts, though they are boring enough. I

mean one's own emotions become boring. Don't you find that?
That's the trouble with Esther—she runs in the same old track.
Events keep changing, but we always react with the same
apparatus, in the same way. It's like cooks. You know how with
certain cooks, no matter what they fix, it comes out tasting
Chinese or garlicky or bland? I wish I could feel things the way
someone else feels them, for a change. Maybe that's why I don't
get bored with music. When you perform faithfully what someone else has composed, that's really what you're doing, taking
on another sensibility."

"You've always wondered what endures, Lydia," said Nina.
"So there it is. A style of experiencing. You can't escape it.
Look at those ridiculous people at Esther's wedding, trying to
change the ways they felt life. You might just as well try to get
a new body."

"But you," Gaby said to her. "You're almost a different
person now. Where's the continuity in you?"

"Oh, I've arranged for different kinds of things to happen to
me. That's simply a matter of taste. But inside, what Lydia
called the apparatus, the person to whom things happen, is the
same. We all are."

The doorbell rang, and Don, looking slightly untrustworthy
himself in his white three-piece suit, slightly like a professional
gambler, bent to kiss my cheek. Of course Don was quite
trustworthy, only showing off the results of a diet; he had
recovered his youthful shape and flair, and moved with the
grace of the young man who used to come and take Gaby out
on Saturday nights twenty years ago. He moved in the illusion
that he had recovered the actual youth as well as the trappings.

"I'm going to have a look at that ankle," he said as he
followed me down the hall. "You're still limping and I don't like
it."

"It's nothing. It barely hurts. Only when it snows. I mean,
rains."

"Hello, darling." He kissed Gaby, and kissed Nina too.

"Hello and good-bye," Nina said. "I must run."

Yes, speed home in her white Triumph (a new one; the old
had finally given out), shower, change, bedeck for Sam. Already as she gathered her purse, her jacket, her silk scarf, her
newspaper, a bemused languidness was taking shape in her

movements. Already she was feeling him. This love affair had not traversed the stages she had described to me at the race track. Through difficult, clandestine arrangements the fuchsia cloud had held for years; they found plenty to say without using each other up. But glory? Did he bring the world with him, and find it, this man who chose to sleep and shave and breakfast elsewhere? In the hall she said she was sorry to rush off. But clearly I had become an obstacle in the path of her need, just as Sam was an obstacle to mine, the pleasure of her company. We had become disturbances in that famous field of George's, where mobs of people jostled for their daily bread and occasional caviar, where far across, farther than I could see, were good times, peace, relief of want. I made myself an obstacle at the door—she had to brush past me. It's all right, dear. Go. I understand. Go get laid. But of course one couldn't talk like that to Nina, even at the sharp edge of want.

"I'll call you in the morning," she said. I could see it. She would call from the white and purple bedroom, with Sam beside her. "Just a minute," she would say to him. "I've got to call a friend." No, he must know who I am. "I promised to call Lydia. Wait." And as she speaks to me, kind and concerned, Sam will be teasing, stroking her here and there to distract her and make her laugh, make her brush him off with playful irritation so she can concentrate on me; at that moment Sam is less ardent than curious, one of those men whom sex truly interests, curious to learn exactly how far he can go, at what point Nina will be unable to keep up a rational conversation with her girlfriend. Ah, Sam! You don't know the history. You'll go far, and still she'll talk to me, I'll bet. She is after all a woman of formidable self-possession. You'll have your fingers inching up the inside of a bare thigh, and she'll talk to me. But briefly. She won't linger on the phone. Nor would I. You'll win soon enough, Sam. I waited with her till the elevator came.

While Gaby was in the kitchen mixing his martini, whose proportions only she could be trusted with, Don took off his white jacket to reveal a gold watch chain looped across his vest. My father neglected to tell me about vest pockets, even more secret places. Straddling a chair opposite me, he widened his eyes and attempted a leer. "Come now, my dear, let me have a feel of that luscious ankle."

I laughed. "Don, the philanderer image is just not you."

"No? Ah, what can I do? I try. Seriously now. Give me your foot." I did. "These are ridiculous shoes. You should wear solid ugly shoes for a while."

"Over my dead body."

"You're such a wonderful patient, Lydia." He was feeling around the ankle, pressing with his thumbs. "Does this hurt? Does that hurt?" I answered no. "Why are you making faces, then? Look, I really wish you would cooperate. I want to see this get better, to make up for what I did to Mr. Dooley."

"Who's Mr. Dooley?"

"Didn't I ever tell you that awful story? When I worked for the messenger service in Boston? Our mean old boss with the cane—we kept sawing bits off of it until he finally fell and broke his ankle."

"Ah, yes, I remember. So I'm your means to redemption?"

Gabrielle came in carrying the potion and three glasses. "Well, how is it?"

"My ankle is something like a pathetic fallacy. It corresponds to the weather."

"Weather?" said Don. "But look out the window. Today is a gorgeous spring day."

It was indeed. With no effort, though, I could see the snow. Two young policemen had come to the door that early evening, one black and one white, one tall and one short, their dark slickers dripping onto my doormat. They had their hats in their hands, and snowflakes glistened and melted in the black cop's thick Afro. They were solemn and nervous—I should have sensed it. But I was curt. I had been in the middle of a Bach toccata, and was sure they had come about the latest burglary, our building's third in two months. Hadn't I told the fellow who interrupted two days ago? I never heard anything—there was always music going. The white one said they'd come in regard to my children. Still curt, several beats behind, my ear lodged in a run of the toccata: *My* children? Some mistake. Big ones right here, little ones safely out of the city for the day. When the black cop leaned forward to say, "Please, ma'am, listen a moment," I drew back. At his next words, that word "bus," I crumpled like someone whose bones have suddenly disintegrated. Alan's yellow skateboard skidded down the hall to escape the news, and I with it.

It hurt but I hardly noticed. It didn't swell up till days later. Leaving the cemetery, Althea wanted to know why I was limping. No one else remarked. I was leaning on Victor's arm and listing like the *Titanic* in the film; to be expected. Only Althea knew sorrow would not make me list, but stand straighter. She stood very straight herself, like a child being measured. Thales could have calculated the height of the pyramid by the accuracy of her shadow.

Mornings I would wake at four or five, having slept briefly after our late-night talks and silences; for a moment I would know only the dark and the configuration of bodies and blankets. Then, oh yes. That pit. That ravine they fell in, now in me, snow-covered. And the ankle would hurt, a dull local throb, like a buzz, an insistent fly that you've given up shooing, that you tolerate. It was a minor sprain which should have disappeared quickly, but I kept on limping, reluctant to allow it full weight, and when it rains—for it no longer snows, the snowy season is past, the globe tilts farther every day from the time when they lived, carrying me farther from them every day, if only I could stop its revolving—when it rains, I get a twinge like a siren circling the ankle. It's not a bad pain; it soon settles into the dull throb, and with it I remember the slickers dripping onto the doormat, the melting flakes in the cop's Afro, the feel of bone collapsing in the damp air. I remember rainy nights in the dormitory when the four of us sat around eating cookies and smoking horrid sample cigarettes, backward girls, not yet dreaming of love, far less of loving children and losing them, but giggling over novels in which weather too blatantly expresses the emotional states of the characters; a pathetic fallacy.

"You have it backwards," Gabrielle said. "The term pathetic fallacy refers to the outside manifestation, to the weather and not to the person. Strictly speaking, your ankle is an objective correlative."

"Thank you."

"Once an English major," said Don, "always . . . Well, Lyd, hopefully it will clear up. If not I'll have to X-ray you again."

"Hopefully." Gaby spoke with distaste, and the finest trace of an accent. " 'Hopefully' is an adverb describing the way an action is carried out. The gladiators entered the arena hopefully. It is not a general term to convey the feelings of the speaker."

"I know that," Don said. "But it's passed into the language by now. It must fill some need. Don't you think you're waging a losing battle, love?" There was such a silken ease to him. Maybe she had foreseen it long ago—she did have an instinct for discerning potential. She told me once that she was trying patiently to draw the male supremacist teachings of the culture out of him, like sucking poison from a comrade's snakebite. It was unlikely that she would ever succeed completely, and I was glad: he might lose just that wry chivalry which made him charming instead of dull. Treacherous though it was, I wanted a drop of the poison to remain.

"We should still fight hopefully," she said. "It's wrong."

Don sighed with good cheer. "Try not to walk on it more than necessary, Lydia, and soak it in cold water. Don't neglect yourself, healthwise, that is."

Gaby's eyes flashed their two colors; her smile was immediate but grudging. "You use those words on purpose to irritate me."

"To aggravate you, do you mean?"

"You two could work up a terrific floor show. I've never heard you like this before. What's happened?"

"We have mellowed with age." Don reached over and took her hand. "Haven't we? We have forgiven and forgotten everything, so it's as if we just fell in love."

"Hopefully," said Gabrielle.

Forgiven and forgotten what, I was starting to ask, but the doorbell rang. George's warmth pervaded and changed the air. "It's wonderful to see you," I said, and I meant it. His shirt was half-open; a gold chain nestled in the hair on his chest. Still a dandy, and men's affectations, alas, appear sillier than women's. There clung to George the convivial, wistful aura of an organ grinder. He refused a martini—had to keep sober for his date tonight—but accepted a glass of wine with seltzer and a handful of cherries.

"You just missed Nina," Gaby told him.

"No, I met her outside. Her car was parked right down the street. We talked for a few minutes."

"All this coming and going," I said glumly. "It's like one of those French plays, a new scene every time someone walks in or out."

"I had the strangest walk over here," George said. "Twelve

blocks crowded with incident. First, right on my corner I saw two little boys, around nine or ten, steal four apples from the fruit stand and run off. No one seemed to notice. Then a few blocks up Broadway I saw two teen-aged girls steal some paperbacks from an outside rack. They tucked them under their sweatshirts. They didn't even run. I was beginning to wonder if something was wrong with me—I didn't have any urge to stop them or say anything. It wasn't that I identified with the kids particularly. I just observed. I remembered you once said I had no character, Lydia, and maybe you were right. Well, anyhow, crossing Eighty-eighth Street I happened to glance west, and down the block was a guy reaching into a woman's stroller. He pulled out her purse and ran. She yelled, the baby yelled. I started to run after him. It was automatic. I mean, I didn't feel the character stir within me or anything of the sort. I chased him across West End Avenue and all the way over to the Drive, and then he dashed down a flight of steps into the park. When I got down there he had vanished. I was really disappointed—I wanted to catch him. I didn't even go back to tell the woman. I just went on up the Drive. Maybe she thought I was in cahoots."

"I never meant you had no character in that sense."

"I know. I was only kidding. But how do you explain so many in one day?"

"It's probably always happening," Gaby said. "But the chances of seeing three—Nina would have to figure that out."

Don tapped ashes from his pipe. "Unless today is some secret thieves' holiday. A counterpart of Labor Day or May Day." He swallowed the last of his martini and stood up. "We'd better go."

"I hate to leave, Lydia, but . . ."

"If we don't show, Webster will have my head, sweetheart, not to mention my grant money. Think of all those hobbling children—"

"Okay, okay, stop apologizing. Oh, your groceries, Gaby—in the refrigerator. Hold it, I'll get them." But when I got into the kitchen something happened. I hadn't the will to move any more. I sat down and lowered my head to the table. Gaby came looking for me.

"Lydia? Oh God. What is it?" She bent and put her arm around me.

"It's nothing. Only everyone's going. This is the first night with no one. . . ."

"Where are the kids?"

"Althea's sleeping at a friend's. That was her on the phone before. Phil's in Boston at a rock concert. I won't get through the night alone, I know it. As it is, it's endless."

"You'll get through. Look, I must go—he needs me there. But I'll come back when it's over. It won't be that late—eleven."

"No!" I hadn't meant to shout it. "It's now! Everyone walking out the door!"

"Call Victor. What do a couple of insane weeks matter? He'd be here in a minute, you know that. You do know where he is, don't you?"

"Sure I know where he is. He's over in the East Sixties with some flabby old cunt."

"Lydia!"

"Oh, pardon my language. I forgot you're a purist."

"It's not that. You told me once how you hated that word. You said you could never use it for anyone."

"I was mistaken. I see now it has its uses."

"Well, call him anyway."

"No."

"Give me the number, then. I'll call."

"No."

George came in. "What's the matter?"

I was an idiot making this scene. I was certainly not imitating the better type of person. The better type of person would not cry uncontrollably in public over spending the night in an empty house. Gabrielle murmured to George and he groaned, a weary, drawn-out sound. "Go on. I'll stay."

I stopped as abruptly as an infant lifted up out of its crib, and went to wash my face. At the door as they left, George kept his arm around my waist, holding me up. "You'll be okay," he whispered. "Take it easy." Victor and I used to stand that way when guests left. " 'Bye. See you soon." Definitely no Job's comforters, those three pals. Job's comforters hounded him, wouldn't leave him alone, sat by his side day and night shredding logic. George's hand slid down my hip. Make it an accident, I prayed as I closed the door and moved off.

"So, what did you have in mind to do this evening?" he asked.

"What I planned to do was listen to Esther. She's as good as *Saturday Night Live*. I suppose I could work on the 'Trout.' "

"The least you can do is keep me company, kiddo. I'm here as your guest, not your babysitter." He was grinning but I could tell he was irked. "I'll play Monopoly if that's all you're up to. But first there are a few, uh, needs I have. I've got to make a phone call, for one thing."

"Oh God! The yoga teacher. I forgot all about her. I'm sorry. Honestly." Go, I should have said right then. Go in peace. But I didn't.

"Also I could use a pizza. A Sunday *Times*. A nice place to sleep—later, that is."

I straightened up. "Very well. We can call for a pizza at once. Immediate gratification. The *Times* isn't ready yet but at around ten we can go out to the corner and get one. So the gratification of that need will only be deferred a short while. It won't fester unfulfilled, in the field. As far as sleep, you can have your pick. My bed alone could sleep an army. What do you like on your pizza?"

"Not anchovies."

I ordered a pizza with green peppers and sausages, and then George called the yoga teacher and made his apologies. A sick friend. She must have offered to join him in his vigil. "Thanks, that's sweet of you, but it wouldn't work out. . . . Yes," he said, "she is, but it's not at all the way you think." True, but how is it then, I wondered. How? They didn't talk for very long.

"I am sorry, George."

"It's okay. You're a much older friend. I've only seen her a couple of times."

"Still she offers you something. I'm not offering much."

"No," he agreed.

The pizza arrived, and I locked the door after the delivery boy, feeling like a jailer. "Come in here. I've gotten to like eating in the bedroom. I'll get us some wine." We sat opposite each other on the huge bed, the box between us.

"Do you hear from Victor?" he asked.

"He called yesterday. He calls constantly. It's like his voice is here. The Shadow."

"He called me too, the other day. He didn't sound very good. He said—"

"Please don't tell me what he said, all right? I don't want to know."

He carefully extricated a slice of pizza from the pie. "I've been meaning to mention, I heard you last week at that Baroque Marathon thing. I happened to pass by at the right moment. I didn't know you played the harpsichord."

"You were there? I didn't even see you. That's nice. So what did you think?"

"Sounded fine to me. I'm no judge."

I smiled. "You're discreet. Competent but hardly inspired, is the best I'd say. The harpsichord is peculiar—the action feels totally different. Still, it was all right. Rosalie's trying to keep me busy. She and Carla were terrific, I thought. Weren't they?"

"Yes. Rosalie is always amazing. Why isn't she more famous?"

"She had a late start. She's not ambitious enough, either, in a commercial way, I mean. Listen, George. You want to be entertained? I can tell you a dream. I have the oddest dreams, since he left."

He tossed aside the crust. "That is what is called a busman's holiday."

"You don't have to analyze it. Just listen. I'd like to hear what it sounds like."

"Sweetheart, I'm a captive audience."

"Yes, you are, I guess. Well, I'm on this deserted subway platform at three in the morning, carrying a huge slab of raw meat in my arms. A whole side of beef."

George's mouth, surrounded by pizza, beard, and mustache, crinkled into a broad smile.

"If you're going to laugh at me—"

"Tough shit. You said not to analyze. You didn't say not to laugh."

"All right. I keep peering down the track for these two headlights that look like big eyes coming at you in the dark, but for a long time nothing comes. Finally one does, and another and another, but none of them are my train. I'm getting very anxious. The only other people waiting are a few heavy men in work clothes, back from working the night shift somewhere. They see me standing there clutching my side of beef, and not one of them bats an eye. Like this is quite an ordinary sight. Finally the right train comes and I get on, dragging my meat along with me. It's one of those old BMT cars. Remember, the kind with the pairs of straw seats all facing in different directions?"

"Mm-hm." He nodded.

"When I first came to New York there were still a few of those left. So I sit down on a straw seat. The car is pretty empty—the workmen, a couple of elderly ladies, the ones who clean office buildings at night, in flowered dresses and oxford shoes and funny pillbox hats, and a pair of teen-agers with that dazed sweaty look you get from necking too long at the movies. Nobody seems to notice me or my meat. But I notice something. The meat is smaller. It's about three-quarters of what it was on the platform. And—this is very weird—after each stop it shrinks a little more, till it's the size of, oh, maybe a ten- or twelve-pound rib roast."

"You're sure you're not making this up, Lydia?"

"No. What would be the point of that?"

"Some of my patients do. They think their dreams are too shocking, or too dull, so they do a little creative editing. Not that it makes any difference. What they invent is just as useful as what they dream."

"No escape, eh? Well, I'm not changing anything. I can see you don't like my dream, George."

"Baby, I love your dream. It's almost too good to be true."

"But I haven't even gotten to the best part. When it's about the size of a moderate rib roast I put it on the floor and get down on my knees—on that mucky subway floor, imagine! —and I take a cleaver, no, it was really more like an ax—I had it in my briefcase with some music—and I start to hack at the meat. The lights are very glaring. One or two people glance over, but with no real interest. I was hacking it into steaks—I've seen my butcher do it dozens of times. I always watch closely. I'm impressed by that kind of skill, how they manage not to chop their fingers off. I did a fine job, I must say. I hacked it up into about half a dozen steaks. That was all I had left from the original whole side of beef. Then I wrapped it in some brown paper and tucked it under my arm and got ready to go home. That's it."

George drank some wine and reached for another slice of pizza, his third.

"So what are you thinking?"

"Nothing," he said. "Nothing."

"But that I should be like that. It's so brutal and violent, isn't it?"

"Yes. But so was what prompted it. Here, you'd better have some before it's all gone."

We finished eating in silence. After the pizza and the wine I felt better. How infantile and selfish to make George break his date and stay with me. Needs conform to the available satisfactions, Gaby once said. Yes, I'd exaggerated mine, taken advantage of him. Probably all I had needed was another hour or two of company and some hot food. Everything seemed bearable now. The children—well, when I opened my eyes each morning I no longer felt a shock in my gut. And Victor? Women have died, but not for love. Maybe I'd never loved him all that much anyway. I'd never have made the kinds of sacrifices Gabrielle makes for Don. I didn't quiver every time he entered a room. There had been times when his touch left me cold. There were even things I'd never liked about him. Bits of curling hair in the bathroom sink. Forgetfulness. The way he made love when he'd had too much to drink, in a fumbling, drowsy way. Leaving the phone off the hook in his studio—that capacity to shut us all out. How he put away his things so deliberately, as if to secure them against . . . what? It was so unlike him to leave that book open, face down. If I had truly loved him would I have minded those things? Could it be I had never known real love at all? Almost forty-three years old and never known love! Ah, sad. Bad. "I think I'm a little drunk," I said. "That Gaby makes a mean martini."

"Don't you dream about them?" he asked suddenly.

"Uh-uh."

"You were never a good liar. Even I dream about them. I dream I take them to the zoo, to the beach. Once I even dreamed they were mine."

"Yours?" I whispered.

"I lost them at sea. The three of us were crossing the Atlantic in an open boat, like some man I read about in the paper, who took his kids. Just as we were coming to the harbor—we could already see the Statue of Liberty—they somehow fell overboard. I threw them life preservers but they couldn't reach them. And then—" He stopped. "This is the worst. I was afraid to jump in after them. I'm a lousy swimmer. I hated myself but I wouldn't jump in to save them. Even after I woke up I was ashamed, as if you could be responsible for what you do in your dreams."

"You knew even in the dream that they were not really yours. If they were yours you would have jumped, believe me. That bastard Victor certainly would have jumped." In his dreams, awake, anywhere. What is he dreaming these days? Empty rooms, it was, weeks ago. Room after empty room, he told me in bed.

"Maybe I did know, but I think it was worse than that. I think I would not risk my life for anybody."

"Well, you're here now."

"This is not much of a risk." He gave a small laugh. "No, I'm not saying I'm not useful. I can listen to anything and stay calm. I'm a regular vault of secrets, and I do keep them. But sometimes I feel a little removed from things. Maybe it's so many other people's secrets, blocking the way."

"I hate hearing you talk like this. It makes me feel bad."

"You see," and he laughed again, "you don't have the tolerance for it. Well, so much for the pizza. You don't want to go to bed, by any chance, do you?"

"Oh Jesus. Look, you know very well you could coax me and at some point I'd be susceptible. But I would really rather you didn't."

"I don't want to have to coax. I'm past that. I want someone who wants. . . . Lydia, didn't you ever notice that red ribbon on Althea's crib?"

I didn't answer for a while. "You did that?"

"Yes. When I was a kid everyone in our neighborhood did it. I had this urge. You never said a word, though."

"How was I to know? It never crossed my mind. I thought it was one of our mothers but that they were embarrassed to admit it. They told me what it meant."

"Did you mind?"

"No, only I was baffled. Well, why the hell did you stop? Why didn't you do it for all of them?"

"You never mentioned it, so . . . I just didn't. I'm sorry. But you don't really think—"

"Don't be silly." I drank some more, though my head felt perilously light. "I do dream. I dream . . . not that I lost them but they lost me. I mean couldn't find me. They were out together at . . . well, somewhere. They come home, come up in the elevator, get to the door. They can't get in because they've forgotten their keys."

"You're fading, baby. I can hardly hear you."

"I can't talk any louder. My head is spinning."

He pushed aside the pizza box and came closer. We sat cross-legged, knee to knee. "Okay. They forgot their keys," he prompted.

I spoke with my head down. "No, that's not right. Wait a minute, let me think. No. It's not that they forgot their keys. They have their keys. But they don't fit any more. They're the wrong ones." I looked up. "I did change a lock on the front door, just two weeks ago, after this kid broke in. I gave him a TV and sent him off."

"Wait, I'm mixed up. Is this part of the dream?"

"No, no, this is true. He came in through a window. What you would call a disturbance in the field. He wasn't violent or anything. I gave him an old TV we never used and he left, and I thought that was that. He didn't seem like a bad kid, really, but later when I was getting ready to go out I saw the little son of a bitch had swiped my keys from the kitchen table, so I had to have the lock changed. I told Althea and Phil that I lost them and it wasn't safe to keep the same locks."

"Did you call the police?"

"I didn't feel like seeing any more cops."

"Lydia!"

"Don't look at me that way, please. You didn't call the cops, did you, this afternoon when you saw all those things?"

"Oh, but that was—"

"Different? Yes, I know. Anyway, in the dream they come home and they still have the old keys. They ring the bell but no one answers. I'm not home."

"Where are you?"

"I don't know. Nowhere. Everywhere. I'm like a presence, not a real person. I'm watching the dream as though it's a movie. I'm there but outside it. I see them sitting at the door and I want to tell them I'll be home soon, not to worry, go across the hall to Patricia's, but I can't because . . . because I'm not in the movie. I'm only watching, they wouldn't hear me."

My eyes were streaming, but so calmly, as at the movies. George wiped my face with his dirty napkin. "So what do they do then?"

"They just sit on the floor in the hallway and think they've been abandoned. I know how they feel because I can see inside them, even though it's like a movie. It's as if I'm making up the movie as it goes along. The worst part is that I can't tell them I'll be home soon. They sit there for hours and it gets dark and no one opens the door for them. Their legs are all cramped. I can feel it, as if I'm their legs. I mean, I'm them and it's my legs. Oh, I can't explain it."

I stretched out on the bed, on my stomach. George stroked my back. I was shaking. "It doesn't make any sense unless you know where they were coming from."

"Well, where were they coming from?"

"Riverside Church. There was a disarmament rally, more like a religious festival, a pageant, I don't know how to describe it. I had been there too. They didn't lose me till after—we got separated somehow, in the crowd." I sat up again and looked at him. He seemed mesmerized. His eyes were shining wet, but calm, and calming. I felt quieter inside. I wondered if he shed tears for his patients too. "We were all actually at this thing, George, a year or so ago. In real life. It was a spectacle, almost something medieval. Thousands of people in the church, and music and singing and speeches, and in the middle of it all, the Bread and Puppet Theatre marched down the center aisle with huge puppets on sticks dressed up as skeletons and the devastations of war. And then the minister went up to the front—he lives in this building, it so happens; I see him all the time. All around him, up on the platform, were enormous Mexican piñatas in different colors hanging from that great ceiling. When he spoke it was magic. He has a theatrical presence: his gestures and his voice turn everything into theatre. The air around him gets charged. Even in the elevator. He spread out his arms as if he was being crucified, and he said, 'Suffer the little children to come unto me.' It was so rash—you know, he could have made an ass of himself, that's what I thought at the time. But he didn't. He was good. He said it right. He wanted all the children in the audience to come up to the front, he said, because they were the ones we had to preserve the world for. It was theirs. The future. He kept his arms stretched out, and children began to stream up from everywhere in the church. It was an amazing sight. He shook their hands and gave them big sticks to break the piñatas, and doves of peace came floating out. This I saw. In real life."

"Did Vivie and Alan go up?"

"No. You know what they were like. They were too . . . oh, self-conscious, and shy. A little too old, too. The kids who went up were younger. Phil, maybe, at six years old, could have done that. But in the dream . . . I dreamed it all over, the entire spectacle. And you see, in the dream . . . I see this man in the elevator all the time, George. It's hard to talk to him. We used to be very friendly. He must think—"

"Well, in the dream?"

"I just can't say it. It's too absurd. Oh, all right. He stood up there pretending he was Jesus Christ again, and everyone was under his spell. He said, 'Suffer the little children . . .' again, with his arms stretched out, and this time, in the dream, they went. They went! And then when they came home, they couldn't get back in. They thought *I* abandoned *them*, but it was the other way around. *They* went and left me behind. It's all wrong, don't you see? It's supposed to be the other way. I mean, even your mother—That was wrong, it shouldn't be like that, but not, not so wrong as this."

I bent my head and wept like never before. "Don't make me tell you any more. I can't. No, don't hold me. Leave me be." This is what you wanted, my love, and here I do it with someone else. Because to do it with you would be . . . Because it was delight, the radiant side, that bound us, the sun rushing on the world, the future. Not this dark. Spoiled. All spoiled.

George cleared away the food, then came back and sat on the edge of the bed. I smelled cigar smoke. This damn crying, worse than the last time, drugged years ago.

"How will I ever stop?"

"People always do."

"I'll be crazy again."

"No."

I lay down with my face in the pillow. I must have fallen asleep as crying children do, torn with longing and helpless. A dreamless sleep, at last. I woke with him nudging my shoulder.

"Lydia," he was saying softly. "It's almost eleven. I must have a paper. I'll be right back. Will you stay awake? or else give me your keys."

"I'll be awake. No, better take the keys. On the dresser." I sat up. "Do you have to do the puzzle?"

"Yes."

"Get two then. So do I."

"Aha! And you thought you were falling apart. You see? It's not so easy. You're still not ready."

"That's all very well, you and Freud and your abstract theories. But what will I do tomorrow?" My butcher, philosopher: What're you going to do?

"Tomorrow? Sunday. You'll find, oh, inner resources."

"Very funny. I mean *do*, specifically." Fold my hands and eat my flesh?

"Straighten up the place a bit, it sure could use it. The kids will be back—cook something. Balance your checkbook. Walk in the park. Run, that's even better."

"Sounds like a thrilling day. Anyway, I can't run with my ankle."

"Well, work, then. Work on—what was it again?"

"The 'Trout.' "

"Right. The 'Trout.' "

"You don't remember?"

"What?"

"I played it at school." I hummed a bit of the fourth movement. "We sang it together. You were helping me. You told me I certainly wouldn't die if I didn't get picked to do it. That you don't die of want."

"Ah . . . yes. No wonder I forgot. That was not my finest hour, was it?"

"No. You made your point, though. Wait, I'll give you a dollar for the paper."

"A dollar? You're a laugh a minute, Lydia. Forget it. My treat."

When he returned I was undressed and under the quilt. He tossed the papers onto the bed and began unbuttoning his shirt. "I trust you won't mind. I'm not planning to sleep in my clothes. That would be asking too much."

He sat up against the pillows on Victor's side with the

magazine section on his lap. On the cover was a photograph of
Central American guerrillas training for battle; they looked like
children. He leafed through till he got to the crossword puzzle.

"You'll find a pencil in Victor's nighttable. Top drawer."

"Thank you."

"Will you stay right there all night?"

"Yes, yes." He grunted. "I'd have to be nuts to walk around
this neighborhood in the middle of the night. Especially today.
Muggers' Day, was it?"

"I know it's childish. I know I'm asking too much."

"No. It's not asking too much." He put the magazine down
and turned to me. His eyes were subdued now, and amused.
"I've become interested in the possibilities of celibacy. I saw a
talk program on television last week where two women discussed what they called the new celibacy. They found it worked
well. It wasn't too difficult and it had excellent effects on their
concentration and energy levels."

"Really. They could have asked me too. I don't find it very
difficult either. It is a dimension missing, but the longer it goes
on, the less you miss it. I imagine it gets to feel natural."

"These women," continued George, "had been celibate for a
week."

We had a good laugh, like the old friends we were.

"Why is it that in the end I depend on you and not one of the
women?" I asked. "What does that imply about men and women?
I don't think I like it."

"I don't see that it implies anything. I'm not here because I'm
a man. I'm here because the others are busy with their own
lives and I'm at large."

"It used to be the other way. Men were busy, women were
available."

"Oh Lyd, come on. It's an individual matter—you can't make
a social theory out of it. It would have been just the same if
Nina or Gabrielle had stayed."

"Oh no. Not the same at all. We would have talked very
differently."

"How?"

"You'd have to overhear it to know. It would sound more
intimate in some ways—there's a common idiom, a sort of
native tongue, among women. More explicit detail, too. But less

intimate in other ways. You put up guards in different places. With a man you guard your soul—I realize you don't think there is such a thing—and with women you guard your pride. Men get to see that barrier down more than women do." It was true; I regretted breaking down in front of Gabrielle more than anything George might witness, and not simply because George and I were once lovers and witnessed much. Because men are more tolerant of weakness in women: It bears out their deep suspicions; it allows them to play their protective role. And perhaps because I cared more for Gaby's love, a reasonable love rooted in character and not sex. "In fact men may even be better, I mean more cost-effective, friends in a pinch—you can let your pride go and gratify them simultaneously."

"Somehow I don't feel flattered, sweetheart. Or gratified either, for that matter. You're so cynical. That's not quite what women have been saying lately, is it?"

"No, because they're speaking to other women, out of pride. Which is fine—everything they say is true." That in the long run, yes, you pay through the nose for indulging yourself with men. That a woman, however critical, would see weakness as your low moment, while a man assumes it's your true nature. "Except . . . except for these other truths we feel in the middle of the night, in the dark. . . ."

"I don't think there'd be a hell of a lot of difference with Gaby or Nina here. I think you're splitting hairs, Lyd."

"Maybe. You're probably a better feminist than I am. Maybe I could have slept with Nina."

"There goes the new celibacy! At this point you'd do almost anything, I see."

I laughed too. "No, I think there's always been something in the air."

"Well, she's awfully nice," said George.

"You should know."

"I do. Did you ever do that, though? I mean with anyone?"

"No. Did you?"

"No."

"Timid, both of us," I said.

"You are funny. I haven't thought of myself as sexually timid since I was sixteen. Uh, nor you, particularly, as I recall. . . . Oh, so you can still giggle like you used to. Do you really think that's what it is, timidity?"

"Well, yes, frankly. Also I never had the time. Even to find the inclination, that is."

"If an inclination is there you don't need time to find it."

"Yes, but don't you think some tastes can be acquired, if you're really an adventurer? Like squid or escargots?"

"Nina is an adventurer," he said. "I would guess Nina has been everywhere."

"I'm glad. I'm glad one of us has."

"And you wouldn't feel the same for Gaby?" he teased.

"Mm, no. Not that she's not attractive. I just don't—"

"Not your type, eh?"

It felt heady and strange, all this chuckling. There was suddenly the feel of a party. "I guess not."

"Do you know that's how Oscar Wilde messed things up for himself? At his trial, they asked him if he had held a certain boy on his lap, if he fondled him, if he kissed him. And he said, Oh no, he was much too ugly. He couldn't resist his own wit. But they took him up on it. They actually built a case on his little joke."

"Hoist by his own petard."

"Yes. I wonder what that means, literally," said George. "What is a petard?"

"I don't know. Something on a ship?"

"No, I think it may be something to do with war, fighting." We fell silent. When he picked up the magazine to return to his crossword puzzle, I saw he had an erection. He saw that I saw, and shrugged. "Why so surprised? You create a provocative situation, you say things, what do you expect?"

"I didn't mean to."

"You're quite sure about that?" He laughed, but in a distant, excluding way. "Didn't you ever hear those sirens on the radio, when they say, This is only a test, we are testing the emergency equipment?"

"Oh, good night!" I sank down and pulled the covers up to my chin. For about fifteen minutes I lay there unable to sleep, and then I said, "I was thinking before that maybe I should have stayed with you. We get along well. Then you say something—it doesn't even matter whether it's true or not, it's the way you say it—and I remember precisely why we broke up. It would never have worked."

George said nothing. He kept filling in his puzzle.

"It's not my duty as a woman to relieve you, you know."

"I never said it was. That's your notion. Go to sleep. You'll feel better in the morning. Do you mind the light on for a while?"

"No, I like it."

"Let's not go to sleep angry." He reached over to squeeze my hand.

Later, in the middle of the night, I felt his hands warm on my back. After all these years the touch was still familiar. In the dark I remembered everything about him.

"Lydie," he murmured, "I've been awake for hours. I even finished the Double-Crostic. Look, baby, if it's because of Victor, then never mind. But otherwise . . . Tell me if it is."

"It's not Victor, no."

"Then you're not playing fair. You knew this would happen."

"Don't talk to me about fair."

"I won't talk at all."

His lips brushed the back of my neck and my whole body trembled, proving Abelard was right. You can want what you don't want to want.

It was like long ago, only richer, and this time I felt virtuous. Now no one could call me ungenerous or conniving. A tease. What could be more absurd than a middle-aged tease? The best friend in the world, George; he would see me through the most abysmal moments. But unlike Nina or Gabrielle he demanded payment. He gave nothing for free—maybe that was why he was alone. What he gave, though, was lavish, and something they couldn't: he held me in his arms till the full light of day.

Modern Art

I was not exaggerating when I told George that Victor was like The Shadow. He calls two or three times a week. His reasons, in the order in which he presents them: First, to see how I am. Fine, I say. I would not complain to him if I were dying. Next, to see if the apartment needs any repairs that apparently only he is capable of making; when I say no, his doubtful "Oh?" is rimmed by a wistful halo, like a note captured by the soft pedal. To ask about mail from sources unaware of his change of address. I report the auto insurance bill, a bill for his father's new hearing aid, his alumni magazine, *Columbia*, a *Scientific American*, and flip through the junk: Project Hope, Push to Excel, Gray Panthers. His last chance to tell the National Rifle Association to go to hell. I omit the appeal from Zero Population Growth, which advises that if each family limited itself to two children a better world would ensue. I'm not sadistic. And finally, to see how Phil is. This last, far from being least, is the real reason for the frequent calls. Althea he sees: they go walking on weekends, through parks and galleries. Together they looked at Picasso's monumental (fat!) bathers. She told me he stared for a long time. And I always thought he preferred the more subtle figures of Matisse. Once they stopped for a drink; he bought her a Bloody Mary and she was thrilled. I thought it superfluous at her age. He does not need to resort to seduction. Young girls can forgive their fathers nearly everything, especially if the fathers are good-looking, witty, vigorous, and all the rest.

But Phil is unreconciled. He feels his father has done a dastardly deed, leaving his wife of nineteen years after a tragedy,

328

in her moment of greatest need. Leaving him—but this he does not say. It is easier to be angry on my behalf. He is puzzled that I do not show more indignation. Where is my pride? I suppose Phil's reaction is a "normal" one. I begin to see, after all my worrying, that he is a most normal boy, in the stereotypical way of his age: plays ball, keeps his room in chaos, is awkward but eager in pursuing his first romance, with Ilana, the trigonometry girl, enjoys the music of outrage (Rolling Stones, no satisfaction, anywhere; I rather like it myself), eats erratically, sulks, and disdains communication with me. Years ago, when he was more individualized, I thought I knew him, but this normality I find hard to penetrate. I know him only through the intimate declivities of his outgrown jeans, handed up to me—with each pair I stitch a wider hem. I am taller than average, but from his growth I get the illusion that I am shrinking.

I try to soften his heart towards his father. It is only fair, since I am the only one who understands why he left. Much of the time, now, I am able to regard Victor with a certain numbed objectivity. I no longer go about enraged. Since that one night with George—no, since that moment when he asked was it because of Victor and I saw that it was not—Victor seems distant, abstract. He is a sexy man who has suffered severe misfortune. This view, I know, is unfashionable. What is fashionable is not objectivity but self-help, with solipsism as its informing vision, and *realpolitik* for technique. However, Victor is a man who lost two children and I don't wish him to lose a third. I know what his devotion is like: he would not survive it. Look what he has had to do to endure the loss of Vivian and Alan—rush to the embrace of some fat old mama. For God's sake, his own mother had some class. She endured her goddamn cancer with class. Couldn't he imitate the better type of person? Still, he deserves his son.

Much of the time I am this paragon of fair-mindedness. Only one little rip in the screen of my objectivity: when I hear his voice on the phone—how am I, the apartment, the mail, Phil—then I become a fury. He becomes real and I become something savage out of myth, which is also unfashionable.

Summer is approaching. June, as the song says, is bustin' out all over. The children will be going away and I have a project to undertake. I will learn to live alone. A secondary project: I will learn to ride on buses again. City buses, to start with, in the hope that someday I will be able to look at those black-windowed, sealed long-distance capsules without turning away and rubbing my eyes. Not tears. They are a sliver of metal in the eye. Come winter I will work on snow, tramp in it, scoop it in my hands, make angels, and maybe someday ski. I may take a bus to a ski resort and plunge down a hill, then take the ride home on the dark road, simply to know its true measure, as Thales might have done. For the way that dark ride looms distorted in my head offends my sense of harmony.

And so I call Victor one afternoon at his studio. No more phone off the hook for the advancement of art. That is one habit shocked out of him. Soon he will break down and get a machine. ("But it rings, Lydia. That's the trouble.")

"Lydia, this is a surprise."

As soon as I hear his voice I feel furious. It comes on like a sudden siege of fever.

"I called to ask if you'd mind taking the car over the summer. I really don't need it and it's more trouble than it's worth. I'd rather take buses."

"Well . . . sure, if that's what you want. But it's much safer for you to have it at night. That walk from the bus stop."

"I can always get a lift from someone. Or a taxi."

"All right. I'll take it on Saturday. I'll be over to see Althea. Will you be home?" he asks hopefully.

"Victor, if you're in, I'm out. Oh, if you're coming up this time, ring the bell. I had to change one of the locks."

"Why?"

"It broke. It was old."

"Can you have a key made for me, then?"

"A key? Why? You're not living here." He waits, his silence sad, proud, and humble at once. He is appealing to my better nature. Also in the silence is something sexual, some reminder of intimate times, when we asked things of each other and received. A very heady mix. "Oh, all right. When I get around to it."

"I waited for Phil outside of school yesterday but he wouldn't even speak."

"You did? Well, I've tried to talk to him about it, but you know Phil. He doesn't like something, he removes himself."

Victor doesn't pick up that tossed-down glove. His response is silence, this time opaque, a wall. "He got a summer job as a lifeguard in a Y camp upstate. I assume that's okay with you?"

"I don't like all this secondhand information. I want to hear from him what's happening."

A pity I'm not the vindictive type: time was when I got my information about Phil secondhand from you, baby. "I don't like it any better than you do. Althea wants to work as a mother's helper. Some rich people out in the Hamptons with two little kids."

"First I want to know who they are, everything."

"I'm sure she'll tell you. When has Althea ever failed to give details?"

"What about you? Do you have any plans?"

Plans, you fucker. What do you think, Paris, Rome? Learning solitude is my plan. "Public transportation. And I've got lots of work. A lot of things are coming up in the fall."

"You're not short of money, are you? I'll make a deposit tomorrow."

"Why should I be short of money? I didn't retire when you left. But since you mention it, it's hard to balance the checkbook when I don't know what checks you're writing. I had to work on the last statement for an hour. Maybe we should have two accounts."

This sort of petty skirmish never interested Victor much. "I'm sorry. I'll keep you informed. You haven't even asked how I am."

"I can tell how you are. I've known you long enough."

"Tell me, then. We'll see if you're right."

"Victor, let's not do this. Let's just be civil."

"I don't want your kind of civility. The checkbook! What nonsense. You know very well there's a two thousand dollar credit line."

"Yes, but I don't like getting those little slips saying they had to put money in the account. I feel like I'm being reprimanded by Big Brother."

"It's not a reprimand. It comes out of a machine. I've told you a dozen times, they love to extend credit. That's how capitalism works. Think of it as a pat on the shoulder—we're good citizens."

"My father told me never to live on credit."

"Lydia, I am not going to talk about this kind of shit. What we need to talk about is them. We should sit down and go through every little detail we can remember. To try to understand. We are the only two people in the world who could do that together."

"I can do it alone." I do. It is sweaty work.

"Lydia."

Formidable man. Humbled and frustrated, he stands firm, like Phil. I did love him. Hearing his voice say my name like that—a bit hoarse; a cold, maybe—gives me a sexual pang in the midst of the fury. It feeds the fury. "I'll leave the car keys on the kitchen table. Let's not torture each other, okay? You left because it was too painful, so why are you creating more pain?" I hang up, and the fury and the sexual pang both subside. In a little while, through some obscure inner mechanism, he becomes distant, a man I once lived with, a sexy man who has suffered severe misfortune, now living with someone else.

Well, and what of her? The facts lie disassembled like pieces of a model airplane kit, defying you to fit them into a coherent whole. She is fifty-one. She runs that Montessori nursery school downtown. She is from Oregon and is a widow, childless. Conservatively dressed. Knows something about painting. She doesn't smoke and drinks only "a few drops" of wine (this from Althea). What does she think, then, when he swigs bourbon and rolls joints in the middle of the night? Maybe he doesn't need to, with her. Maybe she rocks him in her fleshy arms, crooning to her little boy not to cry. Yes, I can see how consolation from strangers might be an exotic spice, very tasty. Also from Althea, she has bamboo shades in her living room, an avocado plant, a finch she lets out of its cage (where is the white shag rug?); she has bifocals and big breasts; she is "slightly chubby and has a lot of gray in her hair, but is still attractive."

"Why 'but'?" I asked.

"Well—" drawled Althea. "You know."

"I don't know any such thing. You're supposed to be the feminist, but you have all the typical prejudices. You should say, 'She is slightly chubby and has gray in her hair, and is still attractive.' You probably don't need to say 'still,' either. Do you think girls with flat stomachs and dewy skin are the only people men could like? Do you think sexuality ends at forty, or thirty?"

"I can understand your bitterness, Mother."

Oh God, the voice of the helping professions is heard in the land. "I am not being bitter about her. On the contrary. I'm defending her."

"Well, if you're defending her," Althea flared up, "it's probably because you're glad it's her instead of some really young girl with a flat stomach. For your own pride."

Teen-aged daughters are not kind. Vivie was, she did not cut to the quick, but she was only ten. I mean nine—her birthday wasn't till April. No doubt she would have come to it too. Just as Althea will eventually temper justice with mercy.

"That may be," I conceded. ("That may be," I read in an assertiveness-training book in the drugstore, is useful for dampening critics or weakening adversaries before pressing on with one's own suit.) "But it so happens my stomach is quite flat. Look!" I stood up, sucked in my breath, and pulled at the waistband of Phil's jeans to show her how much room I had.

"Oh Mom! You're a panic."

"I try to keep you amused."

"But it shows that you're the one with prejudices."

I kept silent.

"Also," Althea went on, "she talks a lot but with long pauses in between sentences, and in the pauses she stares at you with these very searching green eyes. You're not sure whether she's done talking or not, or what she's searching for."

"I'd rather not hear any more. I didn't bring this up to begin with, remember?" I started clearing the table. Phil was eating with Ilana at Burger King.

Althea smoothed plastic wrap over leftovers, attacking each spontaneous wrinkle. "I can do the dishes."

"No, tonight's my turn. You do them often enough. You're altogether too helpful and domestic. Go out, live a little. Have another hole made in your ears, I don't know what."

"I'll keep you company." She shinnied up onto the washing machine, where she could keep an eye on me. "Mother, can I ask you a question?"

"Yes. Talk loud, the water's running."

"Does everyone have multiple orgasms all the time?. . . Can you hear me?"

"Oh yes, I can hear you just fine. That's loud enough."

"Well?"

"No. I don't know. Not all the time, I wouldn't think. At least . . . Where did you hear that?"

"In a book Diane loaned me. It says women have great unused potential. It sounds like everyone ought to be going around constantly . . . you know. I mean, what about from your personal experience?"

"I can't seem to recall. It feels like ages ago."

"Oh Mom, come on. You're being evasive."

I looked up from my dishes. "Althea, are you trying to tell me something?"

"Sort of."

"Well, well." I kept scrubbing, but I made sure to smile at her. What's done is done. "This is very interesting. Who . . . uh . . . that new one, Jeremy? Or is Darryl back on the scene?"

"Jeremy. Darryl is going out with someone else."

"So. Well, well."

"Mother." She laughed. "Is that all you can say, 'well, well'? Are you so shocked?"

"No. No, it's okay. I'll get used to it. I guess it had to happen sometime."

"It was long overdue."

"Oh, really?"

"I think so."

"So how is it? Is it all right to ask?"

"Oh, fine, fine," she said with labored cheeriness. "Except . . ."

There followed a technical discussion. I was pleased to hear myself strike just the right note of reassurance: light, almost breezy, but meticulously informative. Inside, though, accompanying my wise, motherly cadenza, was the same simpleminded *basso continuo:* Well, well. Well, well—so little Althea with her childlike face is having the orgasms I am not (except in my sleep; do they count?). Am I the retired dowager, having passed down the scepter? Are there not enough to go around? (As a matter of fact, the American Psychological Association once devoted several hours at a national conference to whether female orgasms during sleep were pathological. No! I said in disbelief.

You better believe it, George said. Male orgasms are never pathological.)

"Listen, though," I concluded, drying my hands on Phil's pants. "All this talk about orgasms is all very well. But birth control is the thing. At your age that's infinitely more important."

"Oh, I know all about *that*," she retorted. "We did *that* in school. I know where to get everything. Would you believe, there was a girl in my class who thought you might get pregnant by swallowing it?" She giggled. "Good thing you can't. I would have had Darryl's. Would you mind black grandchildren?"

"Althea! Coming from you, who were his close friend, that remark is in extremely poor taste."

For an instant she had Alan's deadpan look, fraught with mischief. "I wouldn't say it was such poor taste."

"Oh God!" I rolled my eyes to the ceiling. "Why couldn't I have had a daughter who was demure and reticent?"

Her face suddenly changed; in the silence she seemed to age. "You did." Then she put her head on my shoulder and cried, and said the bedroom felt so empty, there was no one to whisper to at night, she couldn't get used to sleeping all by herself. After a while she lit a cigarette and coughed. I had to give her a glass of water. I remembered how I had stopped nursing her—cold turkey—years ago, because I imagined she was sucking the life out of me. Now I am older, confident; I could nurse a baby easily but it is too late; there is no one left. I gave her water.

Slightly chubby, eh? Gray in her hair but still attractive. A finch? What am I to make of that? Nothing. It adds up to nothing.

When I tell Gabrielle about this peculiar blank distance I have come to feel in regard to Victor—the abstract Victor— how I cannot even work up any jealousy worthy of the name, only a weak curiosity, an insubstantial nastiness, she says that is quite natural: I am still disoriented over the loss of the children. My psychic energies are diverted elsewhere; for the moment I have none to spare. She discourses like a researcher who has just discovered the cure for cancer (something so obvious as to have gone unnoticed). I listen with respectful interest. What she is doing is called, in current argot, being supportive. I shouldn't knock it. It is well-intentioned and soothing, if you permit it to be.

"Be patient with yourself, Lydia. After all, you can't be expected to respond fully to more than one crisis at a time."

Who is expecting anything? That was not what I meant at all. We are having lunch in the sculpture garden of the Museum of Modern Art. It is a breezy, sunless early June day. Despite the bleak chill of the weather there is a crowd. Somewhere in forests the foliage is lush and green, but past the stone wall opposite our table, the tops of bare branches on trees either dead or retarded splay out like fingers against a sky white as bone. All I expect at the moment is to eat my lasagna in peace. More and more I love to eat. I love every hot sensation on my tongue.

"It's the women who believed their lives were in perfect order who get hysterical. The ones who took all the comfort and security for granted and never examined anything, never went through any real changes. Look how Ellen Kimberly carried on when Frank left. For ten years that marriage was a lie. A TV commercial. Everyone knew it except her. In your case it's very different. You had your hard times. And you do things, you have a life of your own. You never depended on Victor for every gratification. Very likely this numbness is a sign of strength. You're keeping it at arm's length for your own safety. You always had good instincts."

Yes, they do carry on, don't they? They have one-night stands with strangers, they tell off old friends, adopt a more flamboyant style of dress, take up radical politics. Yet Rosalie did that sort of thing long before her separation; maybe that was why her husband Karl called it acting out.

To Gabrielle's speech I replied, as to Althea, "That may be." She never used to bother to say the obvious, though. This reasonable, stylish analysis was never her style. Does it shake her security to see me shaken? Or do I drive her in desperation to clichés, as I did Victor?

"Besides, Lydia, I would not be at all surprised if he came back, and sooner rather than later. You two were so close. Going off to this woman is not a matter of rejection, or finding someone preferable. It's a way of coping with"—she lowered her lids for a moment and pushed on bravely—"the children's death. But it's a completely irrational act. A desperate act. He'll realize that."

I couldn't risk another "That may be"; Gabrielle was not stupid. While she theorized I became fascinated by what she was doing to her food. She was once again on the Scarsdale diet, revivified by scandal. She is always on some diet—their names and ideologies change. But this diet was clearly more serious-minded than the others; the intellectual sophisticate's diet, one that could exert a strong influence on an otherwise independent mind. At least Gabrielle seemed deeply committed. She had brought an extra, empty plate back from the cafeteria line. With a fork and spoon handled like surgical instruments, she took from the platter before her and placed bit by bit on the empty plate a scoop of coleslaw, three black olives, two slices of tomato, and several strips of Swiss cheese and ham cut julienne style. The only things left on her original plate were lettuce leaves, half a hard-boiled egg, and a radish. She then brought forth from her Channel 13 canvas bag a small can of Bumble Bee dark tuna, chunk style, packed in water, and a tiny can opener, which she wielded with the deftness of experience. She emptied the tuna onto the lettuce with a certain detachment, the way you dish out food for a pet, food that could have no possible connection with your own organs. Finally she sprinkled her meal with vinegar and raised her fork. I was overcome with compassion.

"There's no need to torture yourself like that. You're not fat at all."

"I feel gross."

"You may feel gross but you aren't. You have that feeling because you judge your body by a dancer's standards. The average person does not have, or require, a body like a dancer's."

"I can't help it. I danced for so long. You can't possibly know what it's like to feel gross. You can eat all day long and burn it up. Don't think it's easy to eat with you, Lydia."

"Yes, I fall upon the food of life! I burn!" We burst out laughing. "Is that really such a bad line? 'I fall upon the thorns of life! I bleed!'? Or were we just naive to laugh at it?"

"Well, I may be the wrong person to ask, since I'm not a Romantic. I don't go in for those great swings from the depths of suffering to rebirth. It strikes me as rather manic."

"Okay, with that caveat, is it a bad line? In your opinion."

"Yes, it's bad. It's pure self-pity. And the image is ludicrous. He took himself so seriously that he lost the critical faculty."

"I see. Would it bother you very much if I ate your cheese and olives?"

She gave me a wry look. "Go right ahead, what's the difference?"

"You have a very nice body," I told her, being supportive as I reached for the plate. "It's luxuriant. It connotes spiritual amplitude. Being a little rounded does not make you unattractive, you know."

"Oh yes?" Very French. "And how would you know?"

I didn't say how. The garden of the Museum of Modern Art is really an awful place to eat, crowded, noisy, overpriced, and especially prey to winds. The wind gets trapped between the concrete and the glass, battening at people and statues alike. Those massive stone figures are more than invulnerable and indifferent; they seem hostile to the chatting lunch crowd. Water ripples black and forbidding in the neatly squared trough, while the sage Balzac regards all with a sublime, avid scrutiny, amassing data for another human comedy. Usually a couple of people with semi-familiar faces come over to remind us of where we have met before, and after exclaiming at this coincidence, move on. This had already happened to each of us today and might again. Nonetheless we were eating here because it is near Gaby's office, and she likes to take quick looks at the paintings she has seen dozens of times before. In school she flexed her ankles and knees while she wrote her term papers; never a time-waster. Also, she chooses places lately that will distract me, get me "out of myself."

"Lydia, are you there?" She tapped my wrist—three rapid taps with the tips of her fingers. "You look like you're drifting off somewhere."

"I was thinking about the way we always talk about ourselves. That weekend when Esther was over, for instance. We used to talk about real things. And now the more we know about real things, the less we say."

"Well, what real things would you like to talk about?"

"I don't know. The state of the world. The state of the

subways. You sound so serene. Is your serenity for real? I've wondered for a long time. I can't make you out any more."

"It's real. I thought you didn't want to talk about us, though. I got the impression I was boring you." A muscle below her left (blue) eye twitched. Found wanting? Even at this late date she worried that if she were boring I might decide not to be her friend.

"No, no. You're not boring me. How silly. I meant the *way* we talk about ourselves. The worst things in our lives. Don't tell me that's what friends are for. I'd like to hear the good things. Remember Pascal? If all we can do to avoid the . . . the black hole is to seek diversion, if everything is ultimately diversion from—"

"Distraction is more like it," she corrected crisply.

"Do you translate it distraction? That's funny, I always thought of it as diversion. I guess because it sounded like it: *divertissement*."
"Technically you're right. But I've always wished he had used *distraction*. It seems more in keeping with the rest. It's more serious, after all. Anyone can seek diversion, without being in a state of dread. But distraction is something you need more desperately. Well, never mind, I know it seems pedantic. Go ahead."

"No, it's good to be precise. Anyway, we should share our diversions, or distractions. That way we each have more diversion. Surely that's better than sharing our black holes."

"Surely." She grinned with her old schoolgirl slyness. "So?"

"So tell me something. Tell me about the magazine. It's never dull or stupid. You must be awfully good to manage that."

"I am. People think it's glamorous, but I'm a drudge. To keep it in shape I run it like a dedicated housewife who goes around picking up every bit of lint on the rug every morning. You think that's funny. Well, I suppose it is. You don't want to hear about the day-to-day housework, though. I'll tell you about a burgeoning social trend I have discerned through my telephone contacts with eminent writers. The latest thing for a certain type of writer, a male writer, often a professor, somewhat over forty with at least two novels or books of poetry to his credit and two hairs on his chest, is to divorce his wife and take in a doting youngster. Most but not all of these men write about sex, alienation, and aging, and the male intellectual's Judeo-

Christian *angst* over these three items. Their tight interrelations. The girls, meanwhile, are talented literary types just out of college. Upon graduation they go into service, as it were, the way the same type became governesses in Victorian novels. They serve as housekeeper, muse, and concubine all rolled into one. Ellen Kimberly's daughter did it, in fact. Ellen thinks it's an honor, like being a page to a senator. Actually, if you took these fellows out of their jeans and cut their hair and put suits on them, they'd look not much more thrilling than a Senate committee. There ought to be a law."

"Shouldn't you at least call them women?"

"I'm not an ideologue, Lydia. If they were women they'd know better."

"Were we so different? Oh, I know the men we married were different, but in essence, what we did?"

"Me, you mean. I know what you've always thought. But I didn't sacrifice anything much when I stopped dancing. The fact is, I wasn't all that good. Don didn't really interfere. We do it to ourselves."

"Well, he certainly doesn't interfere now, at any rate. Did you make a feminist out of him, or what?"

"Oh, I gave that up. I realized it has to be done before age ten." She paused to eat her radish. I was relieved to hear her sounding more like herself. "He doesn't not interfere for the right reasons. I think it's a mixture of chivalry, laziness, even fear. But I can't quibble over motivation any more. As long as the situation is satisfactory . . ." She looked longingly at my lasagna. "I've never craved total communion, like Nina. I don't think I'd like it. I like privacy. But look, we're back to ourselves again. Let me see, what distraction can I offer you next?"

She assessed me with those shrewd eyes. As a girl she let her splendid auburn ponytail fan out over her back, but now her hair was cut razor-straight, not quite reaching her shoulders, framing her face. The fine lines of her face had grown less fine, it was true, but they still reflected for me her excellent mind of like refinement, which her Continental parents in the diplomatic corps trained her not to display too readily. It is a mistake to underestimate her. The opening clichés are mere distractions, while she busies herself observing, gathering data, weighing and measuring.

"Would you like to talk about Ronald Reagan?" she asked. "Cutbacks in school lunches? Have you heard ketchup may be considered a vegetable?"

"Enough." I laughed. "I want to hear about your serenity."

"Pascal always made me uneasy. True, you take up something to distract you from the emptiness and before you know it you need distraction from your distraction. It becomes self-defeating, an endless chain. Running the magazine is a bit like that. Not that I don't believe in it, or do it better, possibly, than anyone else could. But I also do it simply to do something, the way other women take courses or play cards. And yet with all that, I couldn't see believing in God to escape the chain. I suspect that's the biggest diversion of them all."

"At least you avoid the emptiness."

"It depends on what you consider emptiness. I enjoyed it when the babies were small and I sat in the park in the sun for hours, and then cooked dinner and waited for Don to come home. I didn't feel like a thinking reed."

"It's amazing how you've altered history to make it tolerable. You hated sitting in the park. I know because I sometimes sat there with you. Do you know how many times you said your brain cells were decaying? Why did you look for work in the first place? Anyway, you couldn't go back to that now, Gaby. Imagine, a woman your age sitting in a playground all by herself. Shocking."

"I guess not. I could take other people's babies to the park, maybe? It's such a pleasant image, in hindsight. Sitting on a bench in the sun. No phone calls or deadlines."

"That diet is making you light-headed."

"It's very possible. Give me some of your wine, would you? I could use it." She drank half a glass at once. "Look, I'll tell you about what you call serenity. It's simple. I just accept things." She smiled in an oracular and irritating way.

"Oh Gabrielle! You sound like that woman—what was her name?—who announced that she accepted the universe."

"Margaret Fuller, yes. The really good line, though, was Thomas Carlyle's response: 'She'd better.' "

"And you like that?"

"It's true, isn't it?"

"No. Some people enjoy fighting all the way. And it's also

lacking in charity. So besides the universe, what is it exactly that you accept?"

Gaby pulled her jacket around her shoulders. It was growing chillier, and the lunch crowd was thinning. She pushed away the plate of lettuce, gazed at the statues, and fiddled with an earring. When she spoke at last, she had that elusive, un-English rhythm of pauses between syllables. "I accept that no matter how hard I worked I would never have been a great dancer. I did better with words. I don't think verbal people make great dancers. I accept that I can't change the way I was brought up; those early things can't be eradicated and it's a waste of time trying. That my life is a patchwork of compromises and perhaps I like it that way, stitching together pieces that don't match. That no sudden revelations or great changes are going to—"

"Ah, I thought that once. You're mistaken."

"Are going to happen *in* me, I was going to say, not *to* me. This is who I'll be for the duration. Also that I got what I wanted, and God, did I regret it. I wanted Don to get off my back. For air. I even made inane remarks about his getting interested in someone else—remember?—so I wouldn't be the target of all that devotion. Well, he did, a couple of years ago, and it was not fun. We do shape things for ourselves, you know, lay the groundwork early on for certain events. Like plotting a mystery. Oh, I don't mean a freak accident, Lydia. That's different. But you have to be very careful what you long for."

"I never knew a thing about it."

"There wouldn't have been any point in whining. But it was awful. I don't mind saying it now. He knew exactly what he was doing and why, though we didn't talk about it at the time. We have a way of silently playing into each other's hands. We're very well attuned in many ways. For better or worse."

"So that's what he meant the other day, about forgiving and forgetting. And you weren't sorry then that you hadn't . . . Remember, that time years ago?"

"It's not a question of an eye for an eye. It just wasn't in me."

"That was before your women's group."

"A women's group can't undo your history. It wouldn't have

made any difference. I'm not one to lie and hide. Why, do you think you would have done differently?"

"If I had ever wanted to," I said, "sure, I think I could have. But then I'm more greedy than you."

"I don't see you dashing around now."

No. Thank you for staying, I had said to George as I kissed him good-bye the next morning, before the children came home. And when I told him it was the nicest thing that had happened to me in a long time, he understood perfectly that I could not make a habit of it. "I said, if I wanted to."

"Incidentally, Lydia—Don asked me to mention this but I've been hesitating. I didn't know how you'd take it. An old friend of his is in town for a few weeks on business, from Chicago. An awfully nice person, bright, pleasant. He does real estate, or something in that line. He's a bit at loose ends, not knowing many people. I'm sure he would love to go out to dinner with someone. What do you think?"

"Distraction, eh? I'm not such terrific company these days."

"You're very good company. You seem as lively as ever."

"Do I? That was one of the things that bothered Victor. Well, tell me, I've been out of it for so long, what exactly is expected on a date of this kind?"

"I imagine all that's expected is that you eat your dinner and converse. You certainly wouldn't have very much trouble there. Anything more should be optional."

"I don't know. I'll think about it. Let's get back to matters of consequence. How did you manage to accept Don's little fling?"

"It wasn't a little fling. It was a mess. He's such a romantic, he wouldn't know how to have a little fling. Everything he does is quite thorough."

"So?"

"You'll laugh at me," she said, and drank some more of my wine. "But I remembered that quote in Nina's kitchen, from Epictetus. 'Everything has two handles, one by which it may be borne, the other by which it may not. If your brother sin against you . . .' "

"Oh yes, yes, I know, don't pick it up by the handle of his injustice. After all, he's your brother, the comrade of your youth. That's the handle. Really, all that Christian charity is sickening."

"You were just mentioning charity, Lydia. And it's not Christian. It's Greek."

"Can't you stop being an editor for a little while?"

"You're a true friend," she said kindly. "Another self, was it? You're offended for my sake. But you needn't be. It passed."

"I am offended at how sanctimonious you sound! You're just too good to be true. Do you hope to be canonized? That was part of your upbringing too."

"You're missing the point entirely. I wanted him back. That was the truth of it." She looked at her watch. "I ought to head for the office pretty soon. Do you want to go in and see the paintings?"

"In a minute." I still had a bit of wine to finish. "Did George ever tell you about disturbances in the field?"

"No. What is that?"

"It's from some psychological theory about emotional needs and such. In an ideal world, let's say, you would seek what you need and immediately be satisfied, without any complications, and also, you would be able to satisfy people who need things from you. Of course in the chaotic actual world this rarely happens—thus we have neurotics and frustrated people—and what prevents it from happening is called disturbances in the field. The disturbances are, I guess, circumstances, other people, acts of God, whatever. It's derived from field theory in physics. A framework for looking at events."

She was tearing off bits of lettuce and munching them rhythmically, as Alan's old hamsters used to do. "What is the field, though? It sounds like Bloomingdale's on a Saturday."

For all her saintliness, I wanted to get up and put my arms around her. "Life. The whole works. I don't know."

Gabrielle shrugged and munched. "I was never good at broad inclusive visions. I see one thing at a time. I'm the hedgehog. Or is it the fox? I could never even remember which was which."

"This business with Victor, you see . . ." I knew I shouldn't, but she had touched me, and the wine prodded my tongue. "I need him, but I can't . . . when he's there it doesn't work. He needs, oh, maybe he needs this fat lady, but I doubt it. What he really needs is me. The disturbances are so thick, though, we can't begin to see each other through them."

"Lydia." She reached over to take my hand. "Maybe you could try to talk plainly to him."

"Plainly? Plainly, the disturbance is . . . What we both need is for that bus not to have crashed. We need *them*." I regretted it the minute the words were out and I saw the muscles of Gabrielle's fine face go slack with impotence and pity. Yet I didn't stop. "Remember that quote from Schopenhauer, when we lived in the apartment together, about the endlessness of desiring? Like the fisherman's wife—for every wish that's satisfied a new one springs up. God, he was so wrong. If I could have one wish I would be satisfied. I would not be like the fisherman's wife. I would never ask for anything again."

She murmured something sympathetic and squeezed my hand—what more could she do? It puts people in a terrible position, speaking like that. In bed with George was one thing, but over lunch at the Museum of Modern Art? No, this would never do.

Gabrielle was upset: she said she was going to give in and have chocolate cake for dessert.

"You might as well bring one for me too."

As we dug into the gooey frosting, I said, "I feel much better seeing you eat."

"Why, do you like to see me fat?"

"No, I like to see you uncontrolled. Gaby, I have a great idea. Take the afternoon off. We'll go to the beach. You can pick up your lint tomorrow."

"The beach! It's freezing."

We both looked up at the unpromising sky. "It won't rain, though. This is the best kind of day to see the ocean."

We went uptown to get my car (Victor's car, technically, and its farewell jaunt with me at the wheel), even though the indestructible green Volkswagen bus was parked less than half a mile away. Gabrielle did not drive. She did not ride a bike or ski, either. She no longer did anything that required traveling linear distances. She was superb at tennis, where you perform cunning maneuvers in a box.

There were more people on the boardwalk than I expected to find: mostly old people in slow pairs, taking the salt air, and a pack of kids on bicycles making the ancient planks grunt beneath them. Down below, the expanse of sand was dotted by soda cans and crumpled paper wrappers; the sea was greenish-black like an old crepe dress, with the breaking surf a crocheted collar; in the sky, gray shifted over gray, and way off on the horizon was a dark ship. From the cold railing of the boardwalk I might have measured just how far off, had I needed to. After Thales of old, that spacy, inveterate bachelor who believed all things had their source in water, I could have measured the angle of my line of vision to the ship, then rotated that angle around and projected a line that would touch earth, who knows, maybe not far from where I lived.

"It's terribly windy," said Gabrielle. Her hair was blowing everywhere, in her eyes, her mouth. She laughed and dug a barrette out of her bag to clip it back.

"Do you mind it?"

"Not really."

"When I was a kid and we went to the beach in the summer, I used to want the air to be very still, no wind at all. It can't be—there's always wind at the edge of the sea. Once in a great while for a few seconds it would stop, I could hear it stop, and I wished it would stay that way. But over on the bay side of the Cape, where my sister liked to go, it was very still. Not a stir in the air, sometimes. Some days hardly a ripple in the water. When we studied those Eleatic philosophers in school, that's what I was reminded of, those windless static days at the bay. And those few seconds at the ocean, that never lasted. Do you want to go down?"

"All right," she said.

We took off our shoes and walked down a rickety flight of stairs. There were no other people on the sand.

"I used to look at the beach from the top of a high dune and I saw three broad stripes. The sky, the sea, the sand. It was all so harmonious. I loved it." I smiled at her, huddled in her jacket, hands deep in her pockets. "I must have had the same sense of infinity and order that the Greeks were after. And it did seem static. Even the ocean, because that constant movement is really only one impulse, repeating infinitely. Did you ever have those sensations?"

"Yes, but not back then. We went to France every summer, to those green and rust-colored villages where we had family. It was all very close and cozy. Even the sky seemed low."

We sat down some yards from the edge. "I still have those absurd feelings about harmony and beauty and order," I said. "I expect to find them somewhere, holding up the world. Hah! That's one of the perils of a happy childhood. I'm sure Nina doesn't have any such expectations. It's like those principles you were brought up to feel were unalterable, and even though you've gone beyond them in your thinking, they're still in you, and you can't help measuring things against them. And when I see that the world is otherwise, I'm as stunned as a child. Music has harmony and beauty and order—it's the only place."

"You're lucky to have that. You were right, the sea is wonderful on this kind of day. Almost black."

Just as she spoke we heard garbled voices moving on the wind, then felt a rush of air. A group of eight or ten pale bodies in black bathing suits ran past us. Big sturdy bodies, men and women both; monumental, like Picasso's bathers. They dashed through the surf and gamboled in the breakers like overgrown children. The mood of the sea was rough but not dangerous. We watched, astonished.

"Who are those strange creatures?"

"They must be the Polar Bear Club," Gaby said. "Remember Esther told us about them? That time she came with Ralph. They swim all year round, in any weather."

"They are definitely a disturbance in the field."

"I think they're admirable. They are what makes it a field. Otherwise it's just a big black mass. It must be so cold, though. I wonder what makes them do it."

In less than five minutes they came racing out of the ocean towards the shelter under the boardwalk. As they passed us, water shook from them; I could see the goose bumps on their skin.

"Esther married that jerk Ralph because he took her to see the ocean," I said. "God only knows why she married the other one. Who ever has a sensible reason? If I hadn't married Victor none of this would have happened." You got married, I did not say aloud. You needed the apartment so I moved in with him. Holding me in his arms, after that first time, he offered to help me find a place but I said, No, now I want to live with you. Now? he said. As opposed to when? A half hour ago? "We set something in motion—I keep thinking that. Sometimes I wonder if I ever loved him. Or if I could have avoided it."

"Of course you loved him. You still do."

"They talk of falling in love, but there is a moment where it's voluntary, where you consent to fall. I liked him. And then I let it loose. I slept with him so much I got to love him. I mean, I loved what he made me feel."

"Love does not bear such close analysis," Gaby said.

"I never did before. When you don't have it is when you analyze it." I stood up and walked towards the water, rolled up my pants and got my feet wet. Not as cold as I expected. "Want to swim?" I called back into the wind.

"Are you crazy?"

"It's not bad. Come on."

"No." But she came closer. "You're not serious? What are you going to swim in, anyway?"

"Oh, in my scanty little undies, I guess. Do you find that too appalling?"

"You'll catch cold."

I laughed and took off my clothes. Gaby seemed distressed as she glanced around the empty beach. I went in quickly, the way I used to as a child, letting the first one splash me and diving into the next. I swam fast to get warm, heading for the stretch beyond the breakers as I had done hundreds of times before. The salt smell was wonderfully strong. Soon I was warm, but I kept on swimming hard, careful to stay parallel to the shore. The water was warmer than the air—I kept my head under as much as I could. Once I looked up to wave to Gaby. She was walking along the edge in the same direction, her eyes fixed on me. She waved back and called to me to come out. But I felt I had barely begun, and I knew that from the shore swimmers always appear frighteningly farther off than they are. I kept on because I was loving it, the strenuous, Lethean pleasure of it, and because it would be so deadly cold when I finally did come out and remembered everything. When I next looked towards shore I saw her walking into the water. She was in over knee-deep, holding up her skirt and calling. I veered round and swam to her. It took only a moment.

"What's the matter? Why'd you come in?"

She was shivering so hard her teeth chattered. "You were too far out."

"And *you* were going to save *me*?"

"I panicked, watching you. I just suddenly panicked. Let's get out. I'm freezing." We ran out. "I'm sorry. I don't know what I was thinking." She rubbed her eyes as if to awaken.

"Ah! Well, I do! Jesus Christ!" I shouted at her. "If someone wants to drown herself they swim out, *that* way." I pointed. "Not in the direction of goddamn Queens!" I hopped around and shook the water off me. "I was doing just fine! I happen to be a model swimmer. It's my only other talent. By the time you got out there I would have had to save you. Shit, we don't even have a fucking towel. Who comes to the beach without a towel!"

"What are you so angry for, Lydia? Can't you understand I meant well?"

"I'm angry because there I am endeavoring to persevere in my being and you think I'm a suicide! I'll go when I'm good and ready. I'm not ready. And anyway, I wouldn't leave you holding the bag. I haven't lost all sense of decorum, after all."

"Thanks. I'm delighted to hear it."

"It's lousy to be so misunderstood. When I really needed you two weeks ago, you had to go to a goddamn dinner, and now when I'm having a good time, you come to save me. Where the fuck are my clothes?"

"About a mile in that direction," she snapped.

We started walking.

"Oh, Gaby," I said softly, "it's more like a hundred yards."

In the car I turned the heat up high, and we sat for a while and warmed up. I told her I was very sorry for all I had just said, I did understand her gesture and would treasure it. Would she accept my apology? She answered, a bit distantly, that of course she would. Of course. She accepts everything, indiscriminately.

Transport

Happy families are not all alike; possibly, unhappy families are not all unhappy in different ways. Phil and Althea left for the summer. The next day, I began by studying the couple sitting opposite me on the downtown bus, some fifteen years older than Victor and I, in advanced middle age. The woman, a protruding-bone type, looked hollowed. She had strong wrists with long narrow hands, rather like mine, that clasped and unclasped jerkily. Her face was layered with make-up. Her stiff hair was artificially streaked, as though someone had emptied a bag of feathers over her head. She sat taut in the stifling heat, a bird of prey, while beside her sat her quarry: a smallish man who appeared to have recently shrunk, with waxen cheeks and wavy white hair that had a yellowish tinge. His face might have been mobile and expressive once, but it expressed nothing now except the most sullen indifference. Her face expressed much—irritation, scorn, most of all fear disguised as imperiousness. Words, in an unexpectedly rich and full voice, poured wetly from her red lips as from a pitcher.

"I don't know whether to have the wine or the champagne. If I have the wine I don't know whether to have red or white. They say white goes better with chicken, but it's not a hard and fast rule. I've served red with chicken and no one ever complained. I think I'll get the red on the way home. More people like it. It goes down easier. Champagne is too good for them in the first place and secondly it's expensive. Well, maybe in the long run not so expensive because they drink less of it. Still, it makes everything seem so elaborate. I don't want it to seem over-

350

elaborate. Besides, you can keep what's left of the wine but you can't save champagne."

She was glossy and animated, expensively dressed, but he was shabby, in loose dark pants and worn shoes. With effort he prepared to speak: breathed, swallowed, wet his lips with his tongue, raised his head but not in her direction. "Get the champagne." An asphyxiated voice, an accusing weariness.

"The champagne?"

The champagne? I was surprised too, after such cogent reasons. He didn't look like the sort who would want a party to seem over-elaborate.

"Yes, the champagne. Why not?"

"All right, all right. Champagne. If you say so." The right side of her mouth stretched over in the direction of her ear, exposing the row of molars, then snapped back into place as if on a rubber band. Twice. Pause. A third time. A tic. She sighed and her chin rose bravely again. Again she poured from her pitcher, and I drank, enthralled. "I have two kinds of salad, the potato salad and the bean salad. I have the potatoes all boiled, I just have to chop in some onions and peppers and add the dressing. I've still got to do the bean. I could use some help with the bean." Was there the faintest trace of coyness, supplication, desire in that imperious voice? Something sexual, a reminder of intimate times, when they had asked things of each other and received? He didn't commit himself; a meager nod. "So what do you think, should I use more of the red beans or the white? I think the white taste better." Tic.

"But the red," he brought forth slowly, "are more colorful."

Ah, an aesthete. A painter?

"The red it is then. Makes no difference to me. I have three chickens. Six legs. A chicken only has two legs, but the way they behave you'd think they expected them to have more. Everyone expects a leg. Did you ever notice? Especially Tom. It never fails. He grabs it. Well, I don't want him to have a leg this time. Let him see he can't always have exactly what he wants, like we owed it to him or something. Why should he always be the lucky one?"

He laughed aloud, one sharp "Ha," quickly over. It was impossible to tell whether he laughed at the prospect of Tom's not getting a leg, or in appreciation of her cunning, or in contempt of it, or at chicken dinners, parties, expectations in general. "You could buy an extra package of legs," he said.

A crowd of boisterous teen-agers entered and stationed themselves between us so I couldn't hear her response. I got off never to know what they were planning for dessert, though I was wildly curious. I was curious to know everything about them: what accidents or inevitabilities had brought them to such a pass. Whether Tom might be their grown child, and at what age he had started grabbing chicken legs. Could the other guests be their grown children too, maybe, safely traveled to adulthood, coming with wives and husbands and little ones? Oh, give them all legs! That's what my mother would have said. What the hell, let them enjoy themselves. Buy as many extra legs as you need. For Tom, above all, because he wants them so badly.

I worked all through the summer, and I traveled day and night, accumulating distance. Luckily our local buses are nothing like the futuristic kind that killed them. No, the older city buses, especially in warm weather, are open and airy and sociable, intimating long living rooms with picture windows and posters on the walls, a motley collection of guests. The motion, in fits and starts, is reassuringly dinky. Up in my neighborhood, which is like a town unto itself, new arrivals often spot a familiar face and rush over, in the manner of people at a large informal party. I half-expect the driver to get up and serve cold drinks. Strangers strike up conversations and exchange personal data. Occasional arguments erupt, conflicts of race or generation, but once in a while it is old ladies fighting with zest over an empty seat. The spectators listen eagerly, sometimes take sides. Everyone is engaged, silent or vocal. I am not lonely. I am part of a rapidly changing community. I glean, like Ruth in an unfamiliar land. No more dreams of classical order and harmony. Observation, empirical evidence, are the thing. I want to learn how ordinary people lead ordinary lives, something I have forgotten.

It was hot. People wore as little as possible; the buses were display cases for skin of all ages and colors. The weather drew out those who stay indoors in harsher seasons, old people with death in their eyes, pregnant women, mortality ripening in their bellies like juicy melons, cripples, amputees, and countless of the harmlessly deranged. The ex-mental patients who live in the neighborhood took to the buses as I did, their fantasies in florid bloom under the nurturing sun. The woman I had seen unroll a cylinder of paper towels to make a pillow to cry on climbed aboard early one morning, in much better spirits now, wearing a short red dress and high-heeled shoes, her shaggily cropped hair three shades of yellow. Addressing the empty seat beside her, she offered a running critique of the movies playing in the revival houses along Broadway. "Now, take *Guys and Dolls.* They don't make movies like that any more. What a cast! What a score! And that Marlon Brando! Sings, on top of everything else. Who ever suspected? There, my friend, is pure unadulterated what we used to call sex appeal. Believe me, he asks me to go to Havana overnight, I'd have my toothbrush packed in a second. I know a good thing when I see it and I saw it last night. And yet they say in real life he's a bastard. *Tant pis.*" It was good to see her feeling better. Nor was there anything very crazy about what she had to say, either. It happened Nina and I had seen *Guys and Dolls* that week too and made similar comments afterwards, licking our ice-cream cones and giggling like schoolgirls. Except the companion this woman giggled with was invisible.

She said her good-byes and made her exit. As I watched her strut into Dunkin' Donuts I glimpsed from the window a much younger woman, a pretty woman wearing a businesslike dress and old blue sneakers, pushing an empty baby stroller briskly up Broadway. My heart began to race. Poor thing. Really crazy lady, this one. Her baby gone and still she pushes the empty stroller. There but for the grace of God . . . Give thanks, Lydia.

I had to get off the bus and sit down in an air-conditioned coffee shop. Time stopped; I felt sick. Because the young woman, as I well knew, as any local habitué would know, had just left her baby at the day care center around the corner and was no doubt rushing home to deposit the stroller, change her shoes, and get to the office. A case of Ockham's razor, pure and simple. Esther, who said she observed the world from the windows of buses, found disappointment at the hands of nasty men. Perhaps you only learn what you already know.

But I drink a Coke and recover, and the summer moves along. One day scorches into the next; I stay alone and manage.

I appropriate a room at the school and practice there. Preparing
for the faculty concert series in the fall, for the "Trout" concert
at Lincoln Center, the tour in November, I am virtually never
home. That is one way of learning to live alone. I don't neglect
myself "healthwise," as Don warned. My ankle is too irksome
for running in the park, as George suggested, but I swim in the
midtown health club where my neighbor Sam is a lifeguard.
Under his boyish, awed gaze I swim so many laps that when I
return home I am too bemused to feel very keenly how empty it
is. And I sleep well in the empty apartment, but rarely in the
big bed he left me. Only when the heat is intense—since that
privileged bed comes with benefit of air-conditioner. Now and
then I meet friends in public places. Lots of movies. No more
reunions. I don't shop or cook. Burger King, Pizza Parade,
Aram's Falafel, Blimpie, Sabrett's frankfurter stands—like a
teen-ager or a bag lady, I have become a connoisseur of junk
food. No masochism trip, this: I was never a gourmet—it all
tastes fine to me. So long as it fills. How are you? Nina and
Gaby ask. Are you looking after yourself? and I say, just fine.
The children are fine too. Phil writes short uninformative letters weekly. I am pleased to find him literate—he has never
shown me his school papers. He says he is bored and has not
yet saved anyone from drowning. He's saving his money, though.
He doesn't mention his father. My chum Althea phones collect
from East Hampton. "How're you doing, Mom?" How're you
*do*ing, with a special lilting inflection, holdover from going out
with Darryl. I hope she remembers the calculus he taught her
as well. "I'm doing fine, dear. How are *you* doing?" She gives
excited rundowns of famous names spied half-naked in the surf,
and quotes in amazement the cost of summer rentals. "I'd love
to have a house on the beach someday. Do you think I'll ever be
able to afford it?" "Sure. There are plenty of cheaper beaches."
She is brief. Clambakes on moonstruck sands call to her. Bronzed
lifeguards. Althea, don't forget, birth control is the thing! I
restrain myself, say it only twice. The second time she is
understandably miffed.

My new chamber music group is going fine too. Twenty-odd
amateur pianists and string players from five boroughs want to
learn to play ensemble music under the guidance of Irving and
me. Irving is behaving himself and coaching the strings brilliantly.

He keeps his mouth shut about the pianists, thank goodness, for I have admitted a few who really aren't ready for the exigencies of classical trios—young housewives with babies, so eager for an evening's distraction, and my heart goes out to them. We meet Tuesday evenings at the Y across town, and naturally I go by bus.

The two spectacled women across the aisle are what my mother used to call "settled" and I never was. A bit younger than I, late thirties, plump, pastel polyester and sensible shoes types. Nothing more ordinary. How I crave the ordinary, all the more since I cannot seem to find it. Everything I glean seems to have a warp in it. I want to penetrate the ordinary, master it, like a rapist. I listen to these prospects with criminal intent.

"And how are the little cuties?"

"Oh dear. Oh dear. There's something wrong with both of them. The little one had so much trouble with a disc, she just lies in the playpen all day. And the big one just had a lump removed from her breast three days ago. I'm waiting for the biopsy."

"Tsk, tsk. How old are they again?"

"Nine and seven."

Nine and seven! Lump in the breast? Lies in the playpen all day? What hath God wrought this time? Yet the mother sounds so cheerful, speaks up so loud and clear. Inner resources. A moral exemplar.

"And how old is yours?"

"Mine is just five. Still in the prime of life."

"To tell the truth I'm more worried about the little one. She doesn't even stir when I come into the room any more. I'm taking her to the vet tomorrow."

I got off and walked the rest of the way, in a hot dusk that became a hotter night. The group broke up late and I was grateful for Irving's offer of a lift home. He pulls up in front of my building and sighs mournfully, as he has done often since his wife's death. She was a few years older than he, close to seventy.

"It was a good idea, this little group," he says, patting down his hair. "I wasn't so sure at first."

"I had a feeling they were out there. It's not so easy to find people to play with if you're not professional. And everyone loves it. We can keep it going in the fall. Get woodwinds and horns, make a real thing of it."

"What an entrepreneur."

I laugh. "Good night."

"Good night, Lydia dear." He kisses me on the cheek as usual, and God almighty, lingers an instant. Testing: will I turn my head? Well, I simply refuse to believe this. I move off. I will pretend it did not happen. Maybe it didn't. Maybe I am becoming one of those hungry women who see overtures everywhere.

"Thanks for the ride, Irving. See you Thursday."

In the apartment the phone was ringing.

"What's the idea of changing the goddamn phone number? What the hell are you up to? First the lock and now the phone. And I can never get you in. Where are you all the time?"

"Will you stop shouting, Victor? I just this second walked in. Hold on a minute."

I turned on the air-conditioner in the bedroom and took off all my clothes. I stretched out on the big bed, my side. "I didn't change the phone number. The phone company did it." I explained about Miss Fosdick and the technical reasons. "They called in May, right after you left. They said then that it would be in a few weeks, but as you see they didn't get around to doing it till a couple of days ago."

"Why didn't you protest?"

"I tried. It was no use."

"It doesn't feel right. I was used to that number."

"You'll get used to this one too. Or so she said. How did you get it, anyway?"

"When you dial the old number you get a funny click, and then a computer voice gives you the new number."

"Well, that's something, at least. Then I won't have to fill out all those postcards. They gave me about a hundred postcards to send people."

"Oh, were you planning to send me a postcard?"

"Actually I forgot about it. I've been very busy and I don't ever call here. I'd better let Althea know. She'll get scared when she hears that voice."

"Did you have a key made for me yet?"

"I keep forgetting. The kids are away, Victor. It's only me. Is it so crucial that you have a key?" He paid half the rent, but he would never say that. Leave me for the pillowy embrace of a mother, yes, but never stoop to mention the rent.

"Do I need to explain?" He turned ironic. "I get the distinct impression you're shutting me out."

"I didn't do either of these things on purpose, I've told you! Shutting you out! You're the one who left. Don't you remember?" Is she Circe? Does she cloud men's minds?

"Every word you've spoken to me in three months has been shutting me out."

"Well, what did you expect? You can't be here and not here at the same time."

"You know I'd be back in a minute if—"

"Don't give me conditions!"

"Conditions! When I was there, you were not. That's why I'm not."

"This is getting too metaphysical for me, Victor. I'm only a piano player."

He was silent so long I thought the line had gone dead. "You are the most exasperating person I've ever known," he said finally in a weary, tamped-down voice. It was like the voice of the shrunken man on the bus. "I sometimes wish I'd never started with you. But we did. We have unfinished business. I'm not through with you."

"No?" I asked quietly. The air in the room was more comfortable now. I raised my bare leg and did the exercise Don had shown me for my ankle. "I don't want to play Walter and Griselda. What more do you think you can take away?"

"Lydia!" The sound bruised my ear; I moved the phone a few inches off. "I didn't take those children! Those were my children too! What is wrong with you?"

I imagined he could see me, lying there all exposed. I pulled a sheet over me. "All right, I know. I know. I'm sorry. Only you started with her right before it happened. What'd you have to do that for?"

"It had nothing to do with it! You said so yourself. It's insane to think so. Primitive."

"I understand that. It just *feels* all connected. What I meant was your timing. If you hadn't done it right then you wouldn't have had such an easy place to go."

"That's how it was. I can't undo it. Look, we could try again, Lydia. We could try to—"

"I don't go for all this trying. It's a lot of bullshit. This is how I am. Take it or leave it."

"You stubborn bitch. I would have gone anyway. I'm not afraid to be alone."

Ah, that was a low blow. I was a bitch, we both knew that, but he was supposed to be a gentleman. I hung up and fell asleep with all the lights on.

The next day the mercury hit nearly a hundred degrees and clung there for a week, a waning, heavy August. I didn't mind the heat; it was deadening. To avoid the phone I stayed out every evening, and twice when it rang at midnight I didn't answer. It was the first week since he left that we hadn't spoken. Tuesday I got on a half-empty bus to go to the chamber music group, followed by two bearded men in their forties, in need of showers, dressed in limp white shirts with short sleeves hanging loosely around their arms. Not very nice arms, flabby, pale, sparse hairs. Professors of philosophy, that was soon clear from their talk of fall courses and schedules, and they set me wondering where Professor Boles might be now, and was her hair still flying with enthusiasm for the pre-Socratics? Did she still linger on obsolete cosmologies with only poetic value to recommend them?

"I'm going to try to prove to my seminar in ontological problems that death is not as bad as we think. Not something to be so dreaded, I mean. Simply as a demonstration in logic."

"Oh yeah?" The other fellow blows his nose in a crumpled handkerchief and looks incredulous. "How do you propose to do that?"

"Well." He warms to his task, rubbing a palm against his knee. "First I'll describe some real situation and get them to agree that it may be worse than dying. Physical torture, say. Concentration camps, shipwrecked with wild animals, whatever. They can think up their own—everyone has nightmares they'd rather die than live through. They'll begin to see it relativistically, as an option among others. Rational acceptance is the first step." His accents are so self-congratulatory, his eyes so glazed

and recessive, focused on the inner void. He outlines a series of
logical steps whereby death becomes quite tolerable, indeed
preferable to much else. Aren't the "negative" aspects of death—he
calls them loss of consciousness, fear of the unknown, cessation
of life, separation from loved ones—aspects we accept more or
less readily in other situations: sleep, travel? (Except cessation
of life. That we don't accept so readily. But he skims over that
one.) He has obviously not read Freud on the instinct of self-
preservation: the organism will fight off all obstacles to its
survival so that it can die in its own way, in its own time. Not
Eros over Thanatos. Just a kind of dumb, stubborn endeavor to
persevere in one's being.

The other philosopher has been listening with interest, nod-
ding from time to time. His eyes and nose are red and runny,
probably hayfever. I have been listening with interest too, yet
neither has taken the slightest notice of me, which on top of
their conversation is insult added to injury; after all, I am a
reasonably attractive female of their generation, skimpily clad.
"Nonetheless," the allergic one says, "you're going to find people hard to persuade."

"You think so?"

"Yes. You haven't taken into account the limits of logic. It's
beyond logic. So how are things going with Tina?"

The first one smiles evilly. "She's gotten me to agree to go to
a shrink for marriage counseling. I don't think it can do any
good but I figure, this way, when I leave, I won't have to feel so
guilty."

The friend probes the caving-in marriage. He tries to get the
first philosopher to put aside logic and state his "feelings." The
two philosophers have been affected by the 1960's and the
women's movement to the extent that they are aware of its
having become socially chic to acknowledge and articulate feelings.
They try, but their efforts are hapless. For one thing, the first
philosopher doesn't seem to know where his feelings are located.
As his friend inquires, he looks around vaguely at his fingernails,
his feet, his briefcase. "I only know the situation is completely
untenable," he concludes.

Is it? Is it one of those many situations to which death is
preferable? Have you thought of using it in your course? I bet I
could logically demonstrate that even this untenable marriage is

preferable to lots of other situations, but I too would be ignoring the limits of logic.

I got off and walked past the Metropolitan Museum, open late. There on the steps, serenading the evening crowd with violin, viola, and oboe, were three students from the music school. They were doing Vivaldi, and not badly, given the heat and the country-fair atmosphere, with hawkers of food and crafts their competition, and some yards off a white-faced mime cavorting with a hoop. I bought an ice cream and sat down for a moment to listen. They were ebullient. They exuded what Irving was always growling about, *joie de vivre*. I must remember to tell him; he would be pleased. The listeners were happily ensnared, their faces softened in the fading light. It was very much music of the daylight, tossing up its last gallant strength like a shower of fireworks. Yes indeed. This was a situation to which death was definitely not preferable. The violinist caught my eye and winked. I waved—I could have kissed them all— and threw a few quarters into the waiting violin case before I went on.

The heat was so heavy, with thick purplish clouds beginning to move in from the east, that only the most dedicated, the most in need of distraction, came to play chamber music. Our regular cellist was on vacation and a student was filling in. Irving's violin was as mellow as ever, but his temper was menacing, like the weather. He said little, but his sighs at every breakdown or false start were sufficient. The less able pianists faltered, while the best of the lot, a conceited, mustached young doctor who solemnly removed his beeper at the opening of each session, swore at the cellist, who had trouble keeping up a *prestissimo*. I found myself soothing the one and rebuking the other like a nursery school teacher; it was ludicrous. The last to play was one of those young mothers not ready for ensemble work. She stopped and started a sprightly Mozart third movement half a dozen times. At the end Irving rested his violin on his lap with tangible relief.

"Mozart is a wonder," he announced to the group of ten. "The resiliency of genius. No matter how he is mangled, he cannot be totally destroyed."

The woman's eyes filled with tears as she retreated. Even our young cellist Freddy's eyes widened.

"You did better than last week," I told her firmly. Ah,
supportive. "Everyone's hot and tired tonight. What you need
to do at home is count with a metronome. Now right here, for
instance, where the others join you, you have to wait two whole
measures after the chords before you pick up the theme. Listen."
I signaled to Irving and Freddy and we demonstrated. I had
meant to do only a few bars. But a wonderful thing happened.
The piece took off like a kite in a breeze; lyrical as well as
sprightly, it lightened the night's oppressive heat. Irving's face
lost its look of pain; the wound in his ear was healing. When we
came to the first natural stopping place he raised an eyebrow, I
nodded, and we went straight on. It was a moment of grace, too
good to stop. Freddy grinned and kept up. The others settled
back in their chairs. We were loose and hot and we indulged a
bit, made it witty and a jot more tender perhaps than it should
have been. There was a redemptive quality to our playing. The
young woman had mangled it, and we were redeeming it.
Everyone is redeemed tonight, Victor said at that Seder the
April before last. Everyone, the wise son and the simple, the
beyond simple, even the contrary. I had a fleeting vision of all
thirteen of us at the table, sloshing wine and laughing, and it
didn't make me sad. It was like a distant photo preserved under
glass. It made me play more willingly now, for this moment
that would take its place among other graced moments. The
piece was strenuous, and yet the pleasure I felt was easeful, as
when I swam hard against the wind on that cold day in June.
Midway I heard the click of the door and sensed heads turn.
The custodian sometimes came around entreating us to close up
shop; he could wait five minutes. Irving did a long and splendid
run of sixteenth notes; I echoed him and felt like laughing out
loud. It was the kind of performance we dream of, yet so often
happens spontaneously, in small rooms before small groups, as
this music was meant to be played. When we were done the
students clapped and cheered and began meandering out. I
turned. It was Victor who had entered in the middle, not the
custodian. He stood at the back looking damp and hot in old
jeans and sneakers, and thinner than when I last saw him, at
Althea's graduation. I braced myself for the fury but nothing
came. I went over to Irving.

"You're incorrigible. Don't do it if you can't take amateurs. This is my group and I won't have them intimidated."

"All right, all right. Don't get so excited. Didn't we do nice there? That was something, eh?" He patted my cheek. "Go, sweetheart, your husband's waiting."

Victor came up to the front and we stared. There was no ordinary greeting, kiss or handshake, quite right for us. I was stunned, seeing him, and still wide open from the music.

"It's funny," I said. "I just had a thought about you."

"What thought?"

"Oh, I don't remember any more." I moved off to get my things. I didn't even know how to speak to him. "What'd you come for, anyway?"

"It's pouring. I thought I could give you a lift home."

"You came all the way uptown to give me a lift?"

"I'll tell you in the car. Come."

On the main floor we found ourselves jammed in a tight crowd. A concert had just ended.

"What is a fugue?" a woman beside us asked her companion. "Is it a flat? Is that what it is?"

"No," the man said. "A fugue is . . . I think a sort of a shadow."

"You could tell them," Victor whispered.

"A shadow is not bad. It is something like a shadow."

He laughed and took my arm. The car, he said, was around the corner. He never carried an umbrella. We ran—I forgot about my ankle—and got soaked. Inside, I shook out my wet hair.

"I'm sorry about the other night," he said. "I really thought you had had the phone number changed. I didn't mean all those things I said. I tried to call after that but you weren't in."

"Is that why you came? To say you were sorry?"

"Partly. I wanted to see you. See how you are. Our phone conversations are, uh, less than satisfying. And at the graduation there were seven hundred other people. You were marvelous in there just now. I've missed it."

"Yes, it was a great moment. Let's get going. It's late." We drove a few blocks, then turned into the park. The smell of drenched leaves and grass filled the car. The silence was painful and I switched on the radio. Rain for several days was predicted.

"Tropical hurricane Boris," the announcer said, "has been downgraded to a tropical depression."

"Did I hear right?" Victor asked.

"I think he said that tropical hurricane Boris has been downgraded to a tropical depression."

"I thought so. That is a poem, isn't it?"

"Yes, what? A haiku?"

"Or Auden, maybe?"

We looked at each other. Seven months ago we would have laughed, or touched. He switched off the radio. "That show in November is on after all. I'll manage to get the stuff finished." His hands were tight on the wheel and he was staring straight ahead.

"That's terrific. I'm glad you got back to it."

"Some of it is work I had from before. Some new."

"What's the new?"

He stopped for a light but still didn't turn to me. We were in the middle of the dark park, alone. "Rooms. No people in them, but lots of windows, trapdoors, fire escapes. Odd things left lying around. There're a few with staircases in funny places. They're different from what I was doing before. You'll see. Will you come?"

"I don't know. It depends on when in November. I'm going out of town with Rosalie and Jasper. I'm not sure of the dates."

"I've never put on a show without you."

"Well, you may have to. I'm certainly not going to be an adornment at your opening, if that's what you mean."

"That's not what I mean."

"I'll come if I can. I'd like to see them for my own sake."

He drove on without speaking.

"All right, am I supposed to ask how you're getting along, Victor? Is that what you want, what you're waiting for? Is that what people do in these situations?"

"I don't know what people do. I wouldn't even know how to answer."

"So long as you don't tell me anything about her." No, don't even mention her name. Although now that it appears you've had nearly enough of whatever she offers, I can grant that she has a name: "Dorothy." I think of her that way, in quotes, someone I can't quite believe in, can't take seriously. She is not the issue. Any intelligent observer could safely conclude that in Dorothy's carpeted field Victor's needs are not satisfied, or are very likely oversatisfied—he never enjoyed being mothered. Dorothy will be a delayed casualty of the crash. How disaster spreads its net for victims.

"I wasn't about to. You know she's not the issue."

"So much the worse for her. I gather she'll be getting the short end one of these days?"

"I've never used anyone badly like that before. I always had contempt for men who did. Esther's men, you know. But meanwhile she's . . ."

"Happy," I finished for him. "You always did that well."

"I meant I haven't misled her. She knows what it's all about. Do you think I'm a total bastard?"

"I wouldn't say total. You have mitigating circumstances."

He parked in front of our building. "Lydia, what I want is a few friendly moments. Would you give me that much?"

"All right. I'll make an effort."

"When exactly is Althea getting back?"

"In a week. She had a great time. I think she was going out with a blond lifeguard."

"She leaves pretty soon after that. What is it, two weeks?"

"Mm-hm."

"I promised to drive her up."

"So I heard."

"She was planning to take a bus but I just couldn't— Would you have let her take the bus?"

"No. Not yet, anyway. If you hadn't offered to drive her, I would."

"So will you come, Lyd?"

"No."

"Why not?"

"What's the point? I can say good-bye at home. I'm not sentimental. And then there's that long trip back."

"With me."

"Yes."

"I need to talk to you. Be with you."

"You know where I live."

"Ah, I see. All or nothing."

"That's right."

"You were the one who said no conditions."

"I don't see that as a condition. It's how we lived before. Your way, in fact."

"And if I moved back what would you do?"

"Look, this is idle talk. If you wanted to be with me you'd be with me."

"I mean, how would you be?"

"Not on probation, Victor, I can tell you that much!"

No flash of anger ever alarmed him. He smiled in a bitter way. "But I have no key. Did you have the key made?"

"Oh Lord, I forgot. Honestly. It keeps slipping my mind." We sat for a few moments, listening to the tinny sound of rain on the car.

"I happened to be in Simon's the other day with a few people from the gallery. It looks exactly the same. They still have that suit of armor in the entrance, and the chocolate-covered mints. Do you know, for some reason we never went back there, after that time. . . ."

"Please don't." I remembered that dinner too, when I said let's try again, all the stages I missed, we'll do better this time, and he ordered a steak dripping blood. With it, all the perfumes of Arabia. We went home and had Alan. The memory hung there, enveloping us.

He took my hand. He kissed me. I didn't move.

"You used to like when I kissed you."

"I still do."

"We don't have to sit here in the car like teen-agers," he said.

"You have a hell of a nerve."

"Do I? It doesn't feel easy asking as if we just met. You're my wife."

"Oh. I would not have known. So what does that mean, I'm your wife? Easy access?"

"Don't play politics. You know exactly what I'm talking about. I planned to spend my life with you."

"Yes. I remember when you staked your claim. You ordered beer for me without even asking if I liked it."

"All right, I'm sorry about the beer, Lydia. Most people like beer. There's a statute of limitations for even more serious crimes."

"It's not the beer. You expected me to feel what you felt, to want you the way you wanted me. *Because* you wanted me."

"But you did," he said innocently.

"So then how did all this happen? You wanted me but you left me. I know it happens every day, but I can't fathom it. You still want me, but you're somewhere else."

"You make it sound so simple. Of course I want you. But it was so precious to you, your private tragedy, you couldn't show it even to me. You made everything about us seem superficial. Fragile. Like fair-weather friends."

"Well, maybe you were right to leave, then. Obviously we were fragile. Maybe we would have done even more terrible things to each other. I saw a couple on the bus last month who reminded me of us. I mean how we might become—they were older. Something awful must have happened to them along the way, too, and they had destroyed each other. Or maybe it wasn't anything awful. Just the usual attrition. I don't trust my judgment any more."

"What do you mean? What were they like?"

"Just a couple planning a dinner party. Nothing out of the ordinary. Only the way they looked and spoke was chilling. I haven't been able to get it out of my mind."

"Tell me what they said."

"What for?"

"Because. Because I like the way you remember every word verbatim and play it back. How do you do that?"

"It's just the ear." Clever Victor, courting my vanity. Last time he coaxed me into a story it was bedtime pornography— what was it like, with George? I wasn't very good at that, but I could be good at this.

"Come on, Lyd. I was always your best audience."

I fell. I told him how they looked, and repeated their talk about champagne, bean salad, and chicken legs. I started out in earnest but before long I was camping it up. "Oh, I left something out. With the bean salad, she asked him whether the red or the white beans should predominate."

"Life is full of hard decisions."

"It really wasn't funny. It was eerie." But I was smiling too, and I noticed my hand resting on his arm. I had done it unawares, out of habit. "Why should we be any different?

Wait, I'll give you a little test. Do you think red or white beans would be more effective in a salad?"

He assumed his deadpan, meditative air. "That would depend on what you aspired to effect."

"Attractiveness. Appeal. Good taste."

"Well, the white ones taste better but the red are prettier."

"You see? That's about what he said."

"That doesn't prove anything. Maybe he was a painter too."

"This is all very cute, Victor. But the fact remains you're spending your nights with someone else."

"I sleep at the studio, usually."

"Come on, that's not the point, where you sleep. You know hell hath no fury and so forth."

"I am the one scorned, Lyd."

"Oh, let's drop it. We sound like Althea and Darryl when they broke up. Look, you want to talk about them, right? Okay. There's something I can't for the life of me figure out."

"What?" He shifted eagerly in his seat and reached for my hand, but I lit a cigarette. Even this small display frightened me. The dimensions it could take: my grief and his poured into one pit—we could drown in it together.

"That night, about a year and a half ago—it was winter—she had to make up an experiment to weigh air and I couldn't think of one? I was going out to rehearse, do you remember? I told her to ask you."

"Yes, I remember."

"Well, the question is, how do you weigh air? I always meant to ask."

Victor smiled, not bitterly this time but with a terrible poignant sweetness. If that was what came over him when he summoned up his children, I wasn't sure I could stand it. It was purer, more distilled than what came over me. "I told her to weigh a jar filled with sand—there's not too much air between grains of sand. Then weigh the sand alone. The difference is the weight of the jar. Once you have that, you weigh the empty jar—filled with air, that is—and you can subtract and figure out the weight of the air. It's very tiny. You take the measurements of the jar, and do some arithmetic. Weight per cubic inch."

"How did you work that out?"

"I don't know. I thought about it for a good while. It's not very rigorous but it's probably the best you can do without lab equipment, beakers and rubber tubing and water and all that. It's a pretty stupid assignment to give a kid of that age to do at home, but you know those open classrooms."

"And did she do it?"

"Yes. Alan had a jar of reddish sand that he took as a souvenir from Colorado on that trip, and we borrowed Patricia and Sam's baby scale. They still had it from Samantha—this was before Bobby was born. It's a balance scale. It was such a small weight we could hardly see it on the scale. Air is very light, you know."

"Thanks. I just wanted to know." I opened the car door. "Good night."

"Hold it! Wait a second!" I ran towards the building. "Lydia," he shouted out the window. "Come to the show! Remember, I'm inviting you."

More than I was presently doing for him, was implicit. I raced to the dark apartment. Our pride, his mother had said, was insane. But it used to be for the world outside. Now we had turned it on each other like strobe lights that make you flinch in their glare.

I locked the door behind me with the relief of someone pursued. I couldn't afford to talk of how Vivian learned to weigh air. She was airy herself, and her breath, which the Eastern religions say is spirit, was sweet. It was cooler now after the rain, and when it was cool I slept in Vivie's bed. That was the saving grace about living alone. I could sleep in her bed. That was what got me through the summer nights. When the children came home I would smooth out the bed, erase all evidence of my body having lain there.

I stripped and fell onto her bed and listened as the remains of his voice faded. Talk to you. Be with you. Want you. Older snatches: Your face, Lydia, I could look at forever. . . . I could die in you, it would be all right. Don't ever fall in love with anyone else. Promise. You must never leave. Ah, that one was a joke. I shivered. My eyes throbbed, and a procession of colored streaks and blobs drifted by in the dark. I pulled the sheet around me and curled up against the wall like a mole, hiding from desire. The sheets smelled stale. I didn't care. He complained that I cleared out their things too hastily, but he didn't know I never took off the sheets. These are the sheets she slept on and they smell stale. Very soon I will have to remove them; they cannot stay here, rotting, forever.

If I really wanted him back perhaps I should have been more diplomatic? "Supportive?" Ah, no, I would stay alone forever rather than stylize my feelings to get him. No modern arts. No fashionable methods from the guidebooks on how to live. How to talk, how to listen, how to "communicate," how to "share your feelings," how to love—how to screw, that is: lying down, sitting, or standing, as it pleases you, my sweet, so long as I get mine. If I want him back it's as we were. I want the distance and the closeness zipping in and out like a yo-yo string; I want the frankness and the inability to compromise, and the passion born of radical identity—at the root—like seeking like, twining us. I want that raw scraping at each other as diggers scrape at treasure lodes, to excavate the Victor in me, the Lydia in him, till we fall apart exhausted, sated but not finished. That dig is never done. No, no fresh start on wholesome premises for me. I am all grown up. If I can't be my unregenerate self with him, I will manage without him.

I have learned to manage without him. Stripped. No man for the night, either. I had dinner with that friend of Don's. I did it to please Gaby and Don; friends must be permitted to help. They gave me this amiable businessman in a many-pocketed suit, who confided over an expensive French dinner his two ongoing goals in life: to make lots of money and to please a woman beyond her wildest dreams. ("Take a woman to the moon" was the expression he used. It was no crude offer, merely part of the *curriculum vitae*.) I muttered something about in getting and spending we lay waste our powers and he looked puzzled. What sort of commerce could I have with such a man? My babies gone, that is my business, the sweat for my daily bread. If Victor came back we would have to talk about them. He is so right. Only I fear catharsis may be overrated.

I have learned to manage, but oh yes, he can return when the time comes. When one of us has drunk enough gall. He used to say I tasted like salt and wine. I am still young; I would like to hear that again. (Not the moon; the earth will do.) He can return, this is where he lives. He was my brother, the companion of my youth, and by that handle it could be borne, not by the handle of his injustice, or mine. He can have me; I'm not afraid of that any more, and I never felt my body was something I needed to be stingy about. It doesn't run out, like salt or wine. I don't see how I can let him have my pain, though. That I am stingy about. It is my capital and I live off the interest. I don't want to part with a drop. No one can taste that, or even find the place I hoard it.

But he will, sooner or later. He will hunt till he finds the place, and suck it out and swallow, and then I will be more in him than ever and he will like that, since he is not afraid of taking in what life lays at his doorstep.

I will have to listen, with whatever forbearance I can muster, to his love affair. For he is also not a man who can use people badly with impunity. And whom can he tell but me, the companion of his youth? It was a mistake, he will say. How could I have done it? She is a person too. And I will be understanding. Forgiving? No. Understanding, yes, not forgiving. Only don't let him turn hangdog and contrite. It was his presumption I loved. His good-natured arrogance, the pleasure he took in his powers. His certainty that life must be good to him because he was worthy. God, he loved them so.

The Brown House Again

"I have indeed come to make an inventory," said
Giuseppino, "to round off your stock and collect it
into a unity—as you say, a cellar. I am going to turn
it into a story. That is what a second meeting does. It
is the story's touchstone, the last curve of the
parenthesis, which joins up with the first curve and
makes a unity of its contents."

ISAK DINESEN, "Second Meeting," *Carnival*

"Well, well, look who's here. What's the matter, you
got tired of eating garbage?" The fruit man's eyes
were troubled. He knew.

"Hi. Can I have a casaba melon, please, ripe?"

"Best melons in the world, right here." He waved two under
my nose. "You heard the latest?"

"What's that?"

"Oh, you're so fancy you don't read the papers any more?
They raided another kibbutz. Four children." His index finger
slid across his throat. "Like that. Two pregnant women."

"Yes, I did read about it."

"I suppose to you it's just a little nothing?"

"On the contrary. . . . I'll take half a dozen of those big navel
oranges, too." I was passing by on my way to rehearse the "Trout."
I had delayed as long as I could, but it was late September,
and Rosalie and Jasper were getting edgy, tired of my excuses.

The fruit man flicked open a paper bag. "Here, help yourself.
Animals. That's why they call them gorillas."

Guerrillas, I opened my mouth to say. Guerrillas is a totally different . . . But I thought of Vivian. Her advice: Smile sweetly and keep your thoughts to yourself. If I could manage to live alone, then surely I could manage Mr. Zeitlowitz.

"You don't got much to say for yourself today."

"No. I just came for some fruit."

"So tell me already, don't leave me in suspense, how come you came back?"

To put off the "Trout." Spur of the moment, thought I'd give you a treat! "Do I need an excuse? Maybe you'd rather I went elsewhere?"

"Ah! You see? I knew it. You're still one of us. Only a Jew answers a question with a question." With his back to me he muttered, "I was sorry to hear your misfortune. Terrible thing."

"Mm."

"I haven't seen your husband around lately. So how is he getting along? Nice fellow."

"Fine."

"You want a bunch of grapes? For you, only a dollar nineteen a pound." I shook my head, no. Suddenly his voice became a furtive whisper. "Now maybe you understand a little how it feels, huh?"

My hand tightened around a bunch of spinach—I could have shoved it in his face—and for an instant I wished this man had perished in a gas chamber or at least in the forests of Poland. But decent childhoods, alas, enslave us to decency and I repented, grudgingly. "It's not the same thing. I have no one to be angry at. Where are the McIntosh apples?" Phil was home, suntanned and taller, slightly less morose. Once more I was shopping in bulk.

"Hah!" He waved me to the apples. "If you worked here you'd have plenty! You wouldn't believe what I have to listen all day from *them*"—jerking his head towards the checkout counter—"about Jews. Jews, Jews. If it was up to them, back to the ovens. Poof."

"I think you must be exaggerating. They're always friendly to me and the other Jewish customers."

"And why not? They want your money, dummy."

"Don't call me names, will you, Mr. Zeitlowitz?" I handed him the apples to be weighed.

"Come on. What's the matter, you're so sensitive? Between *landsleute* it matters?"

"Yes, it matters." Wrong, Vivie, you were wrong. Sorry, my darling. "Esteban doesn't call me names and neither do the Koreans."

"Behind your back they call you. Worse."

"Well, then you can call me behind my back too. A bunch of bananas, please. No, not those. They're too green."

"Names you talk about—you heard the things they're saying about us in the UN? Starting all over. It was never finished."

"Uh-huh." I picked up the full basket.

"So have a happy New Year." He shouldn't have tried to smile; on his face it didn't work.

"The same to you."

"You can carry all that or maybe you want they should deliver?"

"I can carry it."

"So I'll be seeing you again?"

"If you're lucky."

When I arrived it was after six o'clock. The others were nearing the end of a Brahms quartet. I sat down to listen next to Howard Schor, the bass player, a man of prodigious memory and patience. Like his instrument Howard was built on a grand scale, with a firm comfortable body and a sanguine face. The absentminded haze in his eyes was misleading: he never failed to come in on time, and unobtrusively kept everyone on an even keel. Howard was always wiping his thick glasses on a handkerchief, tender, pensive daubs. He wiped them now, as he whispered hello and peered with interest into my bag of fruit.

"Do you want an apple?"

"That's too loud. I'll take a banana, if you don't mind."

His voice was like his instrument too, and he used it gently, as if hesitant to release its full breadth. His playing was not at all hesitant. Dense and witty. Last month we had toasted his seventieth birthday with champagne.

"How is this new violinist?" I whispered. "This is the first time I've seen him."

"Frank? Good. Young but very good. Listen."

Frank was plump and looked about twenty-two and he was good. Jasper had found him at Aspen during the summer and lured him back to New York. Jasper himself had gained weight as well as acquired a suntan in healthy Colorado. There was a new ease in the way he held his head; his brow was unfurrowed as he played, the tendons in his neck not quite so taut. Their violist was Carla Roby, a friend of Rosalie's I had played with at the Baroque Marathon in June. Carla was young also, wan and slender, with a wide-boned, expectant face. When the four of them finished, Rosalie pinned her streaming black hair back into its knot. They huddled together to talk; with every passionate toss of her head and wave of the errant bow, strands escaped again.

"Okay, we might as well get right to it and take a break later," Jasper said. "You ready, Howard? Lydia?"

"I guess."

Rosalie and Jasper and I took turns with the opening, slipping the temperate melody from hand to hand. A certain restraint in the strings gave it an exploratory sound—a snaking path. Rosalie's notes were rich as ever but slightly tense; Jasper was radiant. Soon he and I took up a dialogue, tossing the theme back and forth, chasing each other like shadows. Our timing and repartee worked perfectly. Except that beyond the accuracy, his notes were calling out to mine, eliciting, rousing them. It was not for nothing that Victor had imagined Jasper liked me: Jasper's sounds virtually yearned toward the piano like a creature with a mating call, or a great ship listing to slice the waiting surface of the sea. It had nothing to do with the flesh, though. It was another sort of yearning, selfless. I wished I could answer him in kind as I had in the past. But I couldn't afford to yearn towards anything with such abandon. Suddenly, just before she was due to pick up the theme, Rosalie stopped.

"I'm sorry, but something is wrong with the piano. Lydia, are you there?"

"Of course I'm here. What do you mean?"

"You sound awfully, I don't know, retiring. I think you need to be more forthright. It's a piano quintet, after all. Why include a piano if we're not going to hear it?"

Jasper passed a hand over his face as if to hide. "We're just running through to get it set, really. But as long as we've stopped . . . It's also a trifle fast, I think."

"I know," I said. "I started fast on purpose. When it's slow it starts to sicken and die."

"No, he's right, Lydia. I've heard it done at this tempo. Pretty soon it gets all tinkly and bright. It sounds like nothing."

At the slower tempo my solo, a simple unassuming bit, sounded moribund. As Jasper was about to take it up, Rosalie stopped us again. Howard emitted a few more turgid notes—perhaps he was hoping to charm us back. "I'm sorry, really. But, Lydia, this is the first time you really appear. So appear."

"Look, Rosalie, this is how I rehearse. I know exactly what's needed and I'll do it for real when the time comes. You keep stopping like this and we'll never get anywhere."

"This is not how you rehearse. You always go all out."

"Is this group therapy or are we playing music?" Carla Roby asked in her soft high voice.

"Quite right," I said. "Let's go."

"From letter D," Jasper murmured. There was a clumsy silence till I realized letter D was my part alone. While I played, Rosalie sulked for her nine-measure pause.

"Maybe we'd better take five minutes off," Jasper said at the end of the first movement. He went out to the coffee machine with Carla. Howard closed his eyes, practicing his bulbous notes. Rosalie removed the cello from between her legs and came to sit on the piano bench.

"This is not personal, Lydia. But a little feeling, you know, might help? Passion? Real, I mean, not Liberace. It gets us all down. What's the matter, are you sick or something?"

"I'm not sick. What's with you? We never get this way at rehearsals."

"I'm nervous. It's a big concert, we have a lot at stake. The ensemble has to mesh right. Otherwise it is trite. It might as well be a wine commercial. You know that."

"I'm tired. I worked on Stravinsky all morning at that church in the Village. It's a benefit for their draft-counseling program. Two years of festivals for poor Stravinsky—by the end no one will ever want to hear another note. But okay, passion. Feeling. I'll see what I can do."

"Jasper is weak. He should be taking over more."

"Jasper sounds fantastic. He has never played this well."

"Yes. I meant he should be getting the group in order more. I shouldn't have to do this."

"So don't," I said curtly. "Jasper has faith. He was never one to spell things out. He waits for them to happen."

The Andante was lyrical and wistful; I was spiteful. Feeling? I gave it to her with a vengeance. I let the notes drip from my fingers till they bordered on parody. Howard raised his formidable gray eyebrows. But no one stopped. I had gotten myself in a nasty bind—either they made demands or they made allowances. And in private, It's gotten to Lydia's playing, they would say.

The Scherzo was easier: short and glittery, all speed and color, controlled force and grace. Pianists can flaunt a kind of superficial verve that impresses an audience. Musicians are not impressed. I was overpowering the others, smothering their delicacy, without which the speed and color became crude fireworks. Jasper could have competed, fought fire with fire, but he was too good for that. He frowned, played with his eyes lowered.

The "Trout," for all its apparent ingenuousness, is a secretive work. When I first played it in college I was too ingenuous myself to confront all of its secrets—I played it as the lyrical, life-affirming piece it is reputed to be—and now I didn't choose to. One of the secrets is a strain of sadness—nostalgia, mourning—emitted covertly, like a leafy scent you have to bend close to catch. A great and magnanimous composer, but a composer of ambiguity, is asked to write a simple rosy evening's entertainment and tries to comply; despite his efforts the scent of ambiguity pervades the rosy entertainment. Another secret is the strikingly democratic meshing of the instruments, even the uncustomary bass. In all chamber music each voice speaks according to its abilities, but here each makes an equal contribution on its own terms, like the working of a perfectly ordered community. A utopia. No one stands alone for long; nothing individual is accomplished without the deferential support of the rest. Not that the five play much in unison. More often they play in contrast, sometimes in heated *mêlées*, with contradictions and digressions, one voice after another seizing the airwaves for a thrilling moment. But never tyrannically; it is a community of equals. The piano part is not technically difficult. The task is in the phrasing and the pauses, the pressure on each note that

yields the precise quality of sound the group needs to stay
buoyant, no more and no less. And then that harmony, that
clasping of hands like Matisse's dancers in a ring, gives the
quintet its irresistible vigor as well as its sweetness: love made
audible. That was what Rosalie was seeking; without it our
separate talents were barren.

It was the fourth movement I had been dreading all along,
the theme and variations using Schubert's song about the trout.
Jasper introduced the melody. His sound was pure and lucid, a
narrow band of light. I almost didn't come in on time, he so
captivated me. I had the first variation and it couldn't have been
simpler—single treble notes, an isolated melodic line. All any
pianist needed to do was allow it to emerge without impediment.
Some Chinese sage, I think, told a writer who aspired to write a
perfect book: First make yourself perfect, then write naturally. I
played but my mind was helplessly elsewhere: on that guileless
trout darting in the glistening brook, unaware of the angler on
shore who waited to trap him and finally, impatient for the
prey, muddied the water so the trout could not see his right
path. And on how I had longed to be chosen to play this in
college and George said you don't die if you don't get what you
long for, but I did get it in the end. And then Victor came in
during the rehearsal and we went to that bar near the unfinished cathedral. "You might get to like me. It's been known to
happen." I was not subtle, but the way I played the "Trout"
was, he said. "I loved the way you played it. I loved what you
kept back as much as what you put in." His hands shook but he
pressed on. "Do you think it's easy to talk to you like this?" I
played what I dreaded and it was far from perfect, or subtle. It
had a querulous sound.

"Now, Lydia," Jasper began, as we stopped by tacit consent.
"This is all yours. This is an opportunity."

"I'm not looking for opportunities."

"You have to!" Rosalie said. "We're not playing games here."

"I will when I have to. Just lay off."

"Wait a minute. Is there something going on here we two
should know about?" Carla asked. "Or is this how you three
always—"

"No. There's nothing." Jasper locked eyes with Rosalie. His
nod was barely visible and they began as one. I had to give

what they wanted this time. It was mere stubborn pride rising, a cold professional pride—what could Carla and Howard be thinking? I forced the naive, poignant melody inside, breathed it in like acrid air and breathed it out fresh and resplendent as it was meant to be, though it burned my chest like hell. The others took their turns with it, balanced and equitable as in a utopia. And for the rest of the movement we lovingly badgered that little melody, sent it up in the air and caught it, twirled it, twisted it and wrung it, squeezed every ounce of juice from it. Rosalie was elated. She wanted to do it all again so I could have my opening solo, but I refused. I didn't want to be out there alone. It was hard enough being in the group, being part of that audible love and putting mine in.

The last movement took the little utopia on Hungarian holiday; it was laced with dashing exuberance and my part was showy. I didn't mind brash romanticism—that didn't touch any of my untouchable places. I even enjoyed sweeping through a stretch of furious trills; during the brief lyrical calm that followed, I heard the click of the door behind me. Too early for any custodian to be rushing us. It was Victor again, I knew it. Uncanny how he could figure out where to find me. Come to replay history, correct the paths of atoms? Take me to a bar? Offer me a beer? I clenched my teeth and kept hold, finished my triplets with Jasper in a fine flourish. And then I made a mistake. I wasn't even sure what I had done but I was sure enough in the wrong key.

"Oh Lydia!" Rosalie practically flung the bow at me. "We repeated that already!"

"Shit. I'm sorry. That was dumb."

She wiped her forehead on her wrist. "And we were going along great.

"I said I was sorry. Those repeats are so confusing." I turned around. It wasn't Victor but Rosalie's ex-husband, Karl.

"Hi there, hon," she called. "Have a seat. just a few minutes, okay?" Karl made a gesture of all right with both hands, like patting down a billowy cloud.

"Twelve measures from the break," Jasper said mildly, raising the violin to his chin. "And then straight on. No repeat, Lydia. Carla, you could be a trifle louder with those thirds." He looked at me appraisingly and ten measures later whispered,

"No repeat here." Sixteen after that, "Repeat here." My protector.

"Well, praise the Lord," exclaimed Rosalie at the final chord. "We only have a week and a half more. The whole thing is balance. We must get that right."

Karl shook hands all around. He was dressed in a suit and tie; he must have been coming from his office. Karl, it struck me anew, bore a remarkable resemblance to Sigmund Freud, his spiritual ancestor, with the trim, graying beard, the kindly yet somewhat dismayed set of his features. He had a kindly stance too, leaning a bit forward as he greeted us.

"Nice to see you again, Lydia, and looking so well." The last time I had seen him was February—he came with Rosalie to pay a condolence call. They brought *marrons glacés*, which Victor and I finished in bed, watching some late movie. I noticed even then that they consorted a good deal for a couple who had ostensibly separated.

"Thank you. It's good to see you too, Karl." Unfortunately, thanks to Rosalie, I could not see Karl without an accompanying image of greasy pots and socks left on the floor, and yet he still appealed to me. He seemed right for Rosalie, ballast without which she might whirl off somewhere, hanging on to her bow.

"How's the 'Trout' going?"

"Oh, you'd better ask Rosalie that. She's afraid I'm going to ruin everything, even though I assure her I'll come through."

Rosalie approached, swirling a Mexican poncho over her head. We stepped out of range. "It's just that I don't get how you can withhold it or ration it out. Give and you'll have more. Loaves and fishes."

Besides the facial resemblance to Freud, Karl is also a Viennese Jew, one who managed to get to this country during the war as a teen-ager, all alone. It is possible that he too clawed his way through the forests of Poland, or rather Austria, leaving behind him a broken, doomed family, but he never speaks of it, at least not within my hearing. That journey is inside him, however, and may be why he once found the vagaries of Rosalie so alarming, as well as why he can now resolve to endure them.

"Are you ready, dear?" He is positively courtly. I can't believe it, about the raised bread knife.

"Lydia, want a lift?"

"I'm going with Jasper." I give a frosty glance. She shakes her head and mutters under her breath as we part.

Jasper and I drive in comfortable silence. He is probably hearing Schubert and hardly aware of my presence. Through the glasses his myopic eyes squint at the twilight streets. His profile is angular, the cheek concave like a medieval stone saint's.

"Want a cup of coffee?" I ask as he pulls up at my building. This is a formality. He never does.

"Thanks, but I'd better not. Frank is waiting for me. He cooks fancy dishes. Can't let them spoil." He grins boyishly. Jasper, lately, has begun to reveal details of his private life. Perhaps he didn't have one before.

"I thought you'd gained some weight. You look terrific."

"Thank you. How are the kids doing?"

"Fine. Althea's having a great time at school so far. Phil is coming to the concert. You'll see him. Are you worried too?"

"Lord no." He turns to face me. His mouth is stern, but I'm used to that by now. "How long have we been playing together, Lydia? Nine years? Ten? I'm not worried. Carla is very good, and Howard of course. It's a matter of trust, isn't it?" The stern lips relax into a wry smile. "I trust that if you need to collapse you'll have the good grace to do it afterwards."

"Jasper." I can actually feel my heart speed up in response. "Thanks." I lean over and kiss him on the mouth, close-lipped but sweet. God knows why I felt compelled to do that. We move apart and stare. He kisses me in return, the same brief way, and we start to laugh.

"Is Rosalie back with her husband?" he asks.

"Looks like it."

"You women. You certainly do flit around. It's beyond me."

"You're becoming a wonderful type, you know? You're going to be the most straitlaced middle-aged deviate anyone could imagine."

He makes a face of mock offense. "I beg your pardon, I'm only thirty-six."

"Oh God, a wit besides. What are we coming to?"

"So are you going to do the 'Spring' Sonata with me up in Massachusetts? We've been talking about it for two years. It's so gorgeous. And you know it's perfect for us."

"Why?"

"We're both such romantics underneath. What could be more romantic? All that ripply, sinuous stuff. What a chance to indulge."

"Oh, I don't know if I am any more. I played it with Greg Parnis years ago. We were not bad—I still have the tape. Well, maybe we should, why not? It'd be fun to work on."

Jasper whistles the opening theme of the last movement, a jaunty bit where the violin and piano echo each other half a slippery beat behind. I whistle my part too and for a few seconds we manage to keep the thing aloft, but it's awfully tricky, whistling to that funny, disjointed beat; our whistles start tripping and stumbling over each other and we end up dissolved in laughter.

"We'll do better than that, I trust."

"Thanks for the ride, my dear. Till tomorrow."

"Do you need any help with that?" He points to my bag of fruit.

"No, I can carry it fine. See you."

Before I even reach my door I hear it: not the usual early evening stillness I can't get used to, but a flurry of young voices. Jabbers and giggles. I hang my jacket in the hall and stand listening.

"Oh, but the way she said it. I thought I'd die!" A girl's bubbly voice.

"I honestly don't know how she can keep a straight face." Phil, loud and exhilarated.

"I don't think she *can* move the muscles of her face. I think she has paralysis of the face, if there is such a thing."

"Masturbation. No. 'Mas-tur-ba-tion.'" The girl's voice goes deep and nasal and takes on a pseudo-cultivated accent. "'This afternoon we will discuss mas-tur-ba-tion. I'm sure we all know what that is.'"

Howls, screeches, groans.

To deposit the fruit and get to the bottle of Scotch in the kitchen I have to walk through the living room. I don't want to spoil Phil's party. I'll glide through invisibly, wave if necessary. I make it to the doorway.

"Oh hi, Mom." Surrounded by allies, he's not at all abashed that I should come upon this secret face of his, the genial face

kept in reserve. I have to control my own face, smile back as if
he gives me this greeting every day with eyes wide open and
frank. It's I who feel bashful meeting them. "This is my mother,"
he declares without irony, in a voice that has shed its choked
constraint. "And this is—let's see, starting at the bookcase—
Nick, June, Toni. Ilana you already know."

"Hi, Ilana."

"Hi, Lydia." A pert, chorus-girl flick of a flat hand, palm
front. I like Ilana the informal, the gray-eyed, freckled, and
red-haired, bosomy in her salmon-colored T-shirt.

"David and Jose," he winds up.

"We have this sex education course," Ilana tells me. "We're
not sure we'll make it through, though. We might die laughing
first."

I sneak a glance at Phil, who doesn't even blink, but dips his
hand along with the rest into an immense bowl of gorp on the
floor in the center of their circle. The living room is strewn
with sweatshirts and knapsacks and sneakers. It is wondrous.
The kids themselves are a World Federalist's dream, a medley
of the races of the earth, drinking egg creams. George brought
over two bottles of seltzer the other day, but Phil must have
gone out and bought the extra milk himself. That too is wondrous.

"Don't mind the mess, Mrs. Rowe," Toni, the Oriental girl,
says. "We'll clean it all up before we go."

"I don't mind. I like it. Just . . . carry on." I leave them to
make my drink. I was afraid I'd inhibit them but my fears prove
groundless. From the kitchen I can see the black girl, June,
continue her impersonation.

" 'I'm sure you've all heard various myths concerning masturbation.' " She switches on a leering, mechanical smile. " 'Now,
what are some of the myths you've heard?' "

"Blindness? Rings under the eyes?" They inspect each other's
eyes.

"My dick-o will fall off?" the boy called Jose whines. "Oh
my God!" he gasps in falsetto, clutching himself.

A jumble of cries: "Oops! Catch it, quick! Over there!
Microsurgery can do wonders."

Convulsions of laughter. Rolling on the floor. How long since
Althea's friends sat there performing such antics? Long; Althea's
friends have been long past that. The gradations in those years

are subtle, the stages brief. I have forgotten how much I liked this barely-sixteen phase. I like the irreverence, the anarchy, the absence of control. Then it vanishes. They become proper, law-abiding citizens. They become us.

"That's nothing compared to menstruation. You missed it yesterday," Ilana says to Phil, beaming a sassy smile. "You cut, you delinquent youth. 'What myths have you ladies and gentlemen heard about mens-tru-a-tion?' "

"If I wash my hair it'll fall out?"

A boy reaches over to grab a clump of hair. "Look at this! Comes off right in my hand." Paroxysms.

I take my drink and slip quietly through the room, making an effort not to limp. I can walk right if I concentrate. The limp teeters on that line between voluntary and involuntary. Sometimes I worry that it will cross over to the wrong side and become a species of tic like the woman on the bus had. Or like Mr. Zeitlowitz.

"You'll poison any food you touch!"

"Help!" One boy grips at his stomach and pretends to retch, another tosses a fistful of gorp back into the bowl.

I shut the door of my bedroom. Happiness has come to Phil and I am glad. A fine thing, too, to be educated and to relish one's education so. *Brava*, courageous teacher of the nasal voice and the straight face. And *bravi*, boisterous outspoken children who can laugh away their discomforts. When I was a girl there were indeed whispers going round that it might be dangerous to wash our hair during menstruation. But could Phil even dream that his great-grandmothers in Eastern Europe probably visited a ritual bath after each period and had to show a bloodless white cloth to the guardian at the door before their husbands could screw them once again? Does June imagine that her ancestors in Africa shut women up in isolated huts every month for the duration? Does David understand that they bound his grandmother's feet so she would not run away from her biological fate, and as a result here he is, cozy in these United States?

They have a Beatles record playing now, Vivian's favorite—the *White Album*, whose theme she insisted was animals. "Blackbird singing in the dead of night"—so loud I can hear every word clearly—"Take these broken wings and learn to fly.

All your life, you were only waiting for this moment to arise.
You were only waiting . . ."

I was only waiting for this moment to lie down, after the
rotten rehearsal. I undressed and stretched out. Way across the
bed, on Victor's nighttable, was the book he had been reading
just before he left. Bronislaw Malinowski's *Magic, Science and
Religion*, opened and turned face down. Myths in abundance. I
had never touched it all these months but I did now, slithered
over the wide stretch of Victor's side and reached for the book.
Let's see, at last, what myths were on his mind. What put him
to sleep nights, after we lay silent or had our desultory talks or
made our grim love? Victor, it appeared, had been reading
about the ghosts of the deceased in the Trobriand Islands. The
ghosts go to an island called Tuma, where they enter the earth
through a hole especially made for that purpose, a passage
Malinowski coyly calls "a sort of reversed proceeding to the
original emergence."

Oh Victor! Is this what fed your dreams? While I slept, or
stole into Alan's room (not Vivian's, not to startle Althea, be a
mother at all costs) and stood in the dark fingering the furniture,
testing the bed to see what it had felt like to be Alan and lie
there safe, knowing parents lay right across the hall strong and
ready for any sort of rescue? While I lay there breathing in pain
you were dreaming about the souls of the dead crawling back
into the earth, a reverse proceeding? God, I wish you had told
me. No, you were right not to. I might have shrugged and said
something dismissive, told you to go to sleep. You were right to
leave, a reverse proceeding. Better than staying with me in a
snowy pit in the earth.

"Even more important," says Malinowski, "even more important is the fact that after a span of spiritual existence in Tuma,
the nether world, an individual grows old, gray, and wrinkled;
and that then he has to rejuvenate by sloughing his skin." Me.
You sloughed me like an old skin. "Even so did human beings
in the old primeval times, when they lived underground. When
they first came to the surface they had not yet lost this ability;
men and women could live eternally young."

They must have done something, committed some bodily sin,
masturbated or washed their hair during menstruation, to suffer
so huge a loss. For all the myths show self-indulgence punished

by a stripping away. Just look at them go! those treasured indispensables—penis, hair, eyesight, clear skin. Tough. Let the body have its way and you lose, you lose. Careless and pleasure-loving and greedy, having babies beyond your fair share . . . With all my schooling I should be above such superstition, but it seems I'm not. Reason has flowed in and out of me light as air, leaving no trace except an image of the flying hair of Professor Boles. So okay, tell us, Bronislaw, what did we do to lose eternal life? Since surely we all did it, in the person of the original offender.

They lost the faculty, however, by an apparently trivial, yet important and fateful event. Once upon a time there lived in the village of Bwadela an old woman who dwelt with her daughter and granddaughter; three generations of genuine matrilineal descent. The grandmother and grand-daughter went out one day to bathe in the tidal creek. The girl remained on the shore, while the old woman went away some distance out of sight. She took off her skin, which, carried by the tidal current, floated along the creek till it stuck on a bush. Transformed into a young girl, she came back to her granddaughter. The latter did not recog-nize her; she was afraid of her and bade her begone. The old woman, mortified and angry, went back to her bathing place, searched for her old skin, put it on again, and re-turned to her granddaughter. This time she was recognized and thus greeted: "A young girl came here; 1 was afraid; I chased her away." Said the grandmother: "No, you didn't want to recognize me. Well, you will become old—I shall die." They went home to where the daughter was prepar-ing the meal. The old woman spoke to her daughter: "I went to bathe; the tide carried my skin away; your daugh-ter did not recognize me; she chased me away. I shall not slough my skin. We shall all become old. We shall all die." After that men lost the power of changing their skin and of remaining youthful.

Foolish, negating creature. She refused to recognize the persevering life beneath the ravages of time. She didn't want the miracle; she turned away, intimidated by a vision of regeneration, dazed and cringing before an eternity of opportunities, when to recognize that simple gift was to be immortal. She was punished for her failure of nerve, and we shall all die.

The room had grown dark. I sank lower into the pillows on my side. It suddenly seemed very easy to die. Maybe the philosophy professor on the bus was right. Not as bad as we think. Not to be so dreaded. Fear had left me—it seemed the easiest thing in the world. All you had to do was give in. Yield and be taken. I was schooled for the opposite: to persist and to take. The world, they taught us, was ours for the taking. For the thinking. But I see now how to do it. You lie in a dark room and forget (I have made my bed in the darkness, Job said). You lie ready, you close your eyes, chase away will and desire like naked strangers. Easiest thing in the world. Like sleep. Like travel.

I woke in a pitch-black place, cut loose. What's the shape of the room, where are the windows and doors, what place is this? There's only me—not a body with a past but rather a sense of me, intrinsic and impalpable. Me, ageless, and a familiar ageless panic at the dark. For I cannot even tell how far the space extends, the darkness is so thick. I have to get hold. I am in a bed somewhere. My bed feels small, set in a corner perhaps, perhaps against a smooth, paneled wall? Just above it a window, overlooking a dark comforter of trees? And maybe, yes, twelve feet off diagonally, an open door. To my left, another small bed? My right hand fumbles along the wall behind my head for the cord. There was always a light there to scatter my fears, but no more. I thrash around in the void and knock something over. Reaching down—but the floor is wrong, a rug; it should be tiled—I find a switch on a fallen lamp and turn it on.

Ah, this. This big new bed. His side and my side. Cut loose by sleep I was almost elsewhere, in the room I shared with Evelyn in the brown house that idyllic summer, with a high window over the bed and a lamp above my head, and across from me my sister, and I was nine. If only I had not switched on the lamp. If only I could have tunneled through a hole in time to that room, that house, my parents, my sister, myself. Three broad harmonious stripes of sky, sea, and sand, and when we were lost all we needed to do was look for the yellow and white umbrella with the blue slipper hung on the broken spoke.

On the nighttable is my sister's latest letter, sent from Switzerland in its flimsy airmail envelope bearing her calligraphic writing in green ink. I pick it up but there is no need to reread it; I know it. She talks about her summer in the mountains, the radiant light. How she always loved heights. Yes, on the beach she claimed the enormous dunes as her own and now she is much higher, gazing down at the lands below, if she even cares to gaze down. She mentions that summer when we debated the merits of bay side and ocean side, and she was the Princess of the Beach while I struggled in the waves. She was afraid of the waves, she confesses, and she envied my rushing towards them on such intrepid feet. She thought then that unlike herself I could bear any turbulent tossing, and she thinks so still. She recalls the children, whom she saw only at wide intervals, with unbearable accuracy. She asks to be remembered to Victor and says we must make up at once. That is the term she uses, like a child, make up. Her husband René is well, traveling a lot. Anytime I want to come to Switzerland she will be there to receive me. Love, Evelyn. I did love Evelyn. She was my little sister. For a long time I felt deserted by her. Then when she came in February and slept in Vivian's bed and sat by my side for five days growing paler and quieter by the day I finally understood that she simply needed to breathe thinner air than the rest of us, and I let her go home.

I switch off the lamp, and after a while the room is not so dark any more. Not that dawn has come—dawn is still far off—but my eyes have grown used to the dark. If I close them I can feel myself in that old room with Evelyn sleeping nearby. Rich and strange, to have awakened in that room and that summer of a perfection so powerful that it endured in me and abided, dormant, ready to spring to life in the dark. For all at once the whole summer crowds around me, seeping into every sense—the briny smell of the air and the feel of the hot sand and our mother breaking off green beans from the vine for our breakfast and our father explaining that nature goes in cycles—even though I know this is the bedroom of now, which has sheltered the joys of love and its miseries, and I lie in it and weep. Not for my children and not over Victor, but in gratitude for the memory given me, a simple gift. It is incredible that in all our nights of whispering I never told him about the summer in the brown house—really told him, I mean, beyond the facts. I'll have to tell him now. Call him up. Not speaking is so silly, I told Phil. Didn't we love each other twenty years and he say he could look at my face forever and not tire of it? A quarter to one—I must have slept for hours—yet not so wildly late to call; I hear the soft pounding of Fleetwood Mac from Phil's room; none of us sleeps much these days. I'm crying and smiling together, feeling utterly silly and overcome. I don't even know what I'll say. I'll tell him I'm myself now, he should come back and be himself too; turning and turning we come round right. I'll tell him about Vivian singing that Shaker melody from *Appalachian Spring* in the shower in her pure steady voice; about sleeping in the brown house with Evelyn and how like Vivian she was then, born so full of grace; how she was not terribly articulate either but could hold long converse with flowers, and how I used to see Evelyn every time I watched Vivie running down a beach kicking up puffs of sand, clouds of glory trailing at her feet. That he should come home right away, I see it all now. I understand everything the way you do sometimes waking abruptly in the middle of the night, but then you lose it in the sharp light of day so I had to call now, right away. Tell him about simple gifts, turning turning, the valley of love and delight. And that Phil needs him.

I dial his studio but there's no answer so I hurriedly dig out the slip of paper with that other number, the one in case I needed him for anything, the one I almost tore up in fury but buried in the nighttable drawer instead. It rings three times before a voice answers, "Hello? . . . Hello?" The voice of a middle-aged woman, sleepy, heavy, capable, and good-natured. The voice of a woman getting on in years but very much alive, very game. Breasts like melons? Her inner thighs still sticky, maybe, from him? "Hello?" She sounds concerned and maternal, and rather nice. The breath I have been holding so long escapes into the receiver. Oh Christ, I didn't mean that, I would have spoken to her, but prudently she hangs up fast.

Ah, well. A pretty silly idea in the first place. Wipe your foolish face. Blow your nose. One of those middle-of-the-night ideas that turn out to be ludicrous in the morning. I lie back and try to breathe evenly. It's quite all right, nothing to be surprised at. Not as if you didn't know. Breathe. Remember to breathe.

Everything will be all right. And I do take some comfort. Because I still possess the brown house and all that went with it. That isn't lost; the memory is mine, and the vision, the myth, however mocked and contradicted by facts. I am still the person who lived it and made the mistake of trusting it. Anyway—and I light a cigarette to wait with—he'll call back. I give him five minutes. One minute to ask her about the call, four minutes to pour a drink, brood, and make up his mind.

All that went with it: I remember the one thing about the brown house that was anomalous, menacing. The one not idyllic thing. The toad in the garden. Down in the clearing bordering the stand of trees that became a comforter at night was the plank of wood about twenty feet long and raised off the ground like a seesaw, only it wasn't a seesaw. It didn't go up and down; it spun in a horizontal plane, describing a circle. And anyone in its path, anyone inside the circle, could get knocked over, or, as my father liked to warn, sawed in half. Our parents never let us go down there alone: we couldn't judge the extent of the circle. We would give the plank a push, then stand around nonchalantly, targets in a field, but they yanked us out of range in time. Riding it, either alone or with Evelyn, was the greatest of thrills. The world whipped around us and we kicked at its pebbly surface to make it whip faster. Our hair flew, we squealed, while our parents hung back near the surrounding trees. They were right—a dangerous toy, and it is curious that Mr. Wilson, the benevolent proprietor, should have set it in that hidden clearing in the idyll.

The telephone rings. The desire is gone but I can't not answer; he would soon come pounding at the door.

"Lydia? I'm really sorry to call at this crazy hour but I had to talk to you. Are you up?"

"I'm up, Rosalie. What is it?"

"I feel bad about tonight. I didn't mean to hound you, but—"

"That's okay. Everything you said was true."

"Ah!" She laughs with relief. "It's not that I want to take any of it back. I just hate to have bad feelings between us. We've been together so long. But this is so important."

"I don't have bad feelings. For a little while, maybe, but not any more. I know exactly how important it is, believe me."

"Well, good. I've been lying here thinking—the 'Trout' is . . .

oh, such a sort of communal work. You know what I mean. If we mess up that aspect we're betraying something more important than the music, even."

"God, Rosalie, only you could find a way to make a quintet into something political."

"Say what you like, Lyd, but you know I'm right."

She is always right. That's the trouble. "I suppose so. By the way, since we've gotten so critical with each other suddenly, there is something. . . ."

"What?"

"Could you not sing along? You sound like an extra instrument sometimes."

"Oh my! Was I that loud? All right, I'll try not to. Definitely not at the performance. Would it bother you if I wore the green gypsy dress again? I know it's a bit much but I kind of—"

"Why should that bother me? You look terrific in everything. It's only the singing."

"Okay, got you. I'm hanging up now. Karl is here. Right beside me, as a matter of fact. Sleeping."

"I figured as much. Well, have a good night. And listen— thanks for calling."

The moment I hang up it rings again.

"Lydia, are you all right? The line was just busy."

"I'm fine. It was Rosalie."

"Was that you who called a few minutes ago?" I say nothing. "It was, I know. What's wrong? Phil?"

"No, we're both fine, really. He had a gang of kids over tonight. It was nice."

"You must have called about something. Do you need anything?"

I can't stand that ragged edge in his voice, any more than I can answer that question. I'll try the plain truth, as Gabrielle suggested. "All it was, was . . . I was remembering a summer vacation up at the Cape when I was a kid, and 1 had an idiotic urge to tell you about it." There. He'll think I've gone off the deep end. The plain truth stinks, Gaby. Sucks, as Alan used to say. Decimals suck. Percents suck. Fractions.

"You're sure you're okay, Lyd?" God, am I tired of hearing that. And trimmed with guilt, not a pretty sound. "I'll come over if—"

"No, I'm quite sure."

"So what about your summer? Tell me."

"Oh, it's passed now. It was one of those moments. Nothing really. I guess I woke you, didn't I?"

"I'm sorry it happened this way."

"She has a right to answer her own phone. I should have thought first."

We say good night. The distance between us is awkward, weighty like a humid gray dawn, burdened with mutual remorse. Is this how separated couples talk long after, who've remained "friends"? Will he hold her close in bed now, or sit staring into the dark? Well, what difference can it make either way? I, for my part, am going to have something to eat. Either way, I'm starved. Either way, I will provide. Passing through the living room I notice that Phil and his friends have cleaned up, as promised. On the couch someone has left a copy of *Endless Love*. I fling open the door of the refrigerator and, I must say, I am dazzled. It is full of good things to eat, and they come from my very own providential hands: half a chicken steeped in soy sauce and wine, a lentil and sausage salad with fresh parsley and black olives, a casaba melon, six thick-skinned oranges, and more. I give it all a sly, intimate middle-of-the-night snicker, and like Gaby challenging her flesh in the dormitory mirror, like Rastignac to Paris, having buried his last naive tear, murmur, "*À nous deux, maintenant*."

Epilogue:
The Middle of the Way

Do you believe that every story must have a beginning and an end? . . . The ultimate meaning to which
all stories refer has two faces: the continuity of life,
the inevitability of death.

ITALO CALVINO, *If On a Winter's Night a Traveler*

The concert was a Sunday matinee. I went to bed
dutifully early the night before, but at three o'clock I
sat up in bed, wide awake. This happened often lately. I had
come to enjoy the dislocated hours, time unaccountable and
suspended. I would wander into the kitchen, turn on the radio
very low (*While the City Sleeps*), and cook, thinking of nothing
much, now and then murmuring in response to the cavalier
patter of the disc jockey, whom I liked and felt I knew intimately.
I cleaned up, checked to see that the oven was off, and was back
asleep before dawn.

Sunday rose crisp and clear, with a taste of change, of fall, in
the air. The hall was filled. From backstage I couldn't make out
faces in the crowd yet I knew well enough who was there.
Several who had heard me play the "Trout" twenty-three years
ago, though not my mother or father, and not Evelyn. Jasper
and I opened with a Poulenc sonata, spunky and wittily dissonant.
It could even be comical in a couple of places if it was done
right, with a certain panache. The classical repertory is not
known for its wit, so it was a treat to hear the audience laugh
aloud. Rosalie joined us for the Haydn trio, bedecked in her

gypsy dress, a red rose pinned in her hair. She kept her mouth closed; only once, during the Andante, did I hear a low hum, but a keen glance from Jasper aborted it. The Haydn was a delight to perform, like a child's ritualized game, forever fresh, forever the same. We lavished care on the details, the frills and trills and turns and elegant variations, and we whipped up a benign intoxication that spread through the audience. They streamed out happy, and I spent the intermission hunched in a corner smoking one Lucky Strike after another that I filched from Howard. "Since when did you become such a smoker?" he wanted to know. "Over the summer." He had to light them—my hands were shaking. "Come, it's time," he said.

There was no choice now. I had to do it—it was mine, work I had freely chosen. I walked onstage with the others and sat down and gave to our small and ephemeral utopia all it required. I let go of the impediments and of the past so bitterly dear to me and gave the whole spectrum: the lyricism and the control; the exuberance and the briskness; the beauty that pierced; and the scent of a terrifying ambiguity throughout. In that dreaded fourth movement with the innocent fluid melody, a melody that made my insides coil, a melody to which I once pressed my hand over the face of a howling baby, I gave with a free hand, loaves and fishes. Jasper was right—I could collapse later. Don't you dare angle after me; not yet! Plenty of time to die in! First this for my friends who have shown such forbearance. They were playing like souls exalted with the abundance of their own powers, showering gifts. So I too gave it everything that had happened to me, pure and simple. That was what the music, like a child, sweet but quite without mercy in its demands, seemed to be asking for.

When we finished I didn't move. I didn't hear another sound—my ear was blank. The others bowed once, twice; they seemed far away. Jasper walked over to fetch me like a boy at an old-fashioned school dance. He held me by the arm and we took a bow together. Three times he walked me offstage and back as you lead a child—I remembered not to limp—and then he left me behind because he had to do the Brahms quartet. I could rest; my part was done.

I found a small empty room back there and closed the door. In a moment there was a knock and Phil appeared.

"Mom? Holy shit, what are you crying for? You were terrific! Even I liked it!" He leaned down and patted me on the shoulder as he had patted Bobby when he cried.

"As good as the Rolling Stones?"

"Well . . ." He tilted his head and his lips curved slyly. Phil was showing the early signs of a debonair manner, as well as a mustache. "Let's just say it was very good. You're going to be a mess for the party. Your eye stuff is dripping."

"I'll fix it later. You don't have to watch. Wait outside. If you stand right near the curtain you'll see them at a good angle."

"Nah, I'll wait here."

He did until Victor walked in, looking gangly, awkward, his large hands hanging loose as if he didn't know where to put them. It seemed Victor was moving in the opposite direction from Phil, shedding the debonair. The three of us in one room again, and Phil got up to leave.

"Please don't go," Victor said. But he went anyway.

Victor sat down on an old couch, elbows on his knees, chin in his hands. "I've never heard you like that. All of you. It was . . . rare."

"Thanks. I know."

"I was right across the aisle from that guy from the *Times*. Even he clapped. You're sitting there so still and your eyes are like lakes, Lydia. I can't bear it."

"I thought it was what you wanted. I feel like I lost something out there. I feel naked. What is it, eight months? That's almost as long as it takes to make one."

"Eight months less four days." He took off his jacket and lay down on the couch. I hadn't seen him lying down for a long time. He looked muscular yet defenseless.

My eyes stopped their streaming. "It's the moments that you feel a little better that are the worst. Do you know what I mean? Because you're losing it."

"I know. But then it hits you again. Maybe each time with a trifle less force, I don't know. You don't really lose it."

"Cycles."

"Yes."

"I thought I could keep it full strength forever. It's like a . . . like a coat."

"But look at you." He smiled. "Some coat. And you're not even in black. Don't they wear black for classy concerts?"

"Only in the orchestra. You ought to know that." I was in red.

"I forgot. It's a nice dress."

"I feel very bare. I'm not used to it. . . . The idea that it really happened, Victor. I mean, that is the part— At the beginning I used to wake up in the morning and think maybe it was all a bad dream and everything would be the way it was before."

"I know."

"But what does it mean, that it happened?"

"Nothing. It was an accident. That's all there is to it. There's nothing to think about it. We can only think about them. A lot."

We sat without speaking. These many months, our chill nights in bed, our brutal love and his going, my disjointed life—they seemed like a dream. The children were real. Sitting together quietly in a room was real. We heard a burst of applause for the Brahms.

"Can I drive you home?"

"I'm not going home. There's a party at Carla's. The violist. She's right in the neighborhood."

We stood up and faced each other, Victor waiting for the invitation I could not give. Not after all the effort spent cajoling Phil: Come on, you'll have fun, shake hands with famous people! Champagne! Give me a break, I need a handsome escort. If Victor came, Phil would not. Nor was I about to give it up. I wanted to be made much of. I had damn well earned it.

"I'll see you soon, then," he said.

"Soon? Kiss me good-bye, till soon," I said.

"I'll tell you, I'm afraid to."

"Hah! You're afraid to kiss me?"

"You really want me to?"

"I said it, didn't I? Do you want it in writing?"

"You sound familiar. Have we met before?" He made an elaborate show of smoothing down his clothes, clearing his throat. "All right, baby, come over here and I'll kiss you."

"Why can't you come over here?"

His eyes measured the six feet between us. His eyes, uncannily gifted, perspicacious, cool but immensely tolerant. The look I had misinterpreted years ago as coldly critical. "We could meet," he said dryly, "at the apex of an isosceles triangle of which we are the points of the base."

"Oh God, Victor, it better be worth it."

We met near the door and he kissed me. "You were right to be scared. . . . Don't, I can't, I have to get to this party."

He stepped back. "Maybe Phil would like a lift home?"

"Phil is coming with me."

"Ah, I see."

Phil and I recuperated from the party in our living room. He was sprawled on the floor with a pile of *Sports Illustrated*s while from the phonograph the Rolling Stones once more clamored for satisfaction, followed by the Beatles' *White Album*, about animals. "Blackbird singing in the dead of night," they sang lightly, "Take these broken wings and learn to fly. All your life, you were only waiting for this moment to arise. You were only waiting . . ." Phil had discovered since the summer that he could read magazines and hear his music in rooms other than his own, rooms which even contained me. I was stretched out on the couch doing the Sunday *Times* crossword puzzle. I had changed from my ripply red dress to a loose brown nondescript thing, a smock, you might say, as Griselda had worn when she was ejected from her marriage and palace with nothing, a smock she was allowed in place of the innocence she had brought to that marriage but could not carry away. I would be putting on my fancy concert dress again, just as she would her royal garments, but my children would not be miraculously restored to me by their father. Still, I felt content to be slowly doing the puzzle in Phil's company. When it got worse again I would accept it; I couldn't be too proud to accept the better as well.

The phone interrupted. Happily I could reach it without moving from the spot. Nina congratulated me on the performance.

"Where did you vanish to? I looked for you right after but I couldn't find you."

"I was in hiding backstage. I wasn't up to a crowd. I don't mean you, but . . . Thanks for coming."

"It was a marvel. Every note. Like the last time, but so different. I'm sorry I never made it to the party but Sam is in awful shape. I had to sit and hold his hand. He's fallen asleep now."

"How is she?" Sam's wife was in the hospital again, in critical condition.

"She's not going to make it. I can tell from what he tells me. The complications are endless, like a chain reaction, and the kinds of drugs they would have to use to stop it would kill her. He's totally wretched. I didn't expect it would be this way. I feel pretty bad myself, strange as it seems."

Nina, so worldly, is so naive. "She's his wife," I said. I was doodling curlicues around the edge of the crossword puzzle. Vivian used to watch me sometimes as I doodled and talked on the phone. When I hung up she would say I couldn't have been truly paying attention—I seemed so intent, the little designs were so thorough and symmetrical. She was too young for me to explain it. People don't doodle till thirteen or fourteen, I've observed. Althea is a doodler.

"Well, yes, she is his wife, but . . . It's very odd, Lydia. Now that I know I can have him eventually, I'm not sure I want him. I keep brooding over all the negative points. Does that make any sense or is it purely neurotic?"

"Neurotic."

"You sound very sure."

"I can't help it. I am. You've had one of the longest illicit affairs on record and suddenly now . . .? It's simply guilt. This is a lousy stage of life to be alone, Nina." Phil, on the floor, raised his head from the magazine; his body stiffened.

"When isn't it? I never told you about my visit to Esther last weekend, did I? Do you know Esther's lost her job?"

"No. How come?"

"Budget cuts. This time it's malign neglect. She's working in a department store, men's socks or something of that ilk. Not quite her vocation. Have you ever seen her apartment?"

"No."

"At the moment she possesses three cats. Females, and they have Biblical names: Jezebel, Salome, and Vashti. The apartment is pervaded by essence of cat. A box in every room. Need I say more? You know how I feel about cats, Lydia. I get that from my mother, unfortunately. I once picked up a stray cat and held it on my lap and she immediately made me take my dress off and put it in the wash. Mothers are very powerful. Witness Esther's—you do remember all those cat stories? Anyhow, aside from the cats, who had the good sense to avoid me, her only friend is an older woman who sings in the Baptist church. There wasn't very much food in the house, except for cat food, that is. The stove is covered with antique grease. The bathroom—well, Sunday morning I couldn't find a clean towel after I took a shower. I had to use my kimono, supplemented by tissues. That is no easy feat."

"I can't believe it. The last time I saw her, that time she came up in May, things seemed to be going fairly well."

"Yes, well, not any more. We were out all weekend. We saw everything Washington has to offer. She was surprised that I'd turned so patriotic, but I couldn't stay in the apartment. It was too depressing."

"Did you make any suggestions?"

"I suggested that she clean up, for a start. Look for a decent job. But I'm not very good at it. I don't like to disapprove openly. I'd rather pretend everything is just fine. The milk for the coffee is sour, oh well, never mind. No clean sheets, never mind that either. But I do mind. You were right, way back then, about Clyde. I should have told her straight out what I thought of him, but I . . . it seemed so indelicate. And it was such a permissive time, too. Who could say what was right for anyone else? Now, of course, it seems so obvious, what she's done. . . . You ought to talk to her, Lydia. You have a . . . a certain influence over her."

"I'm not going all the way to Washington to sleep with cats and dry myself with tissues. No, thanks."

"You could call her."

"I'll see. I don't know how much good it would do."

"She did it for you, didn't she? Didn't you tell me that when you were moping at home with the babies she used to send you little inspirational bits about getting back to work?"

"Yes, that's true." I haven't told her about the more recent inspirational bits: The fool foldeth his hands together and eateth his own flesh. Say not thou, what is the cause that the former days were better than these? for thou dost not enquire wisely concerning this.

"Did they do any good?"

"Yes, but not in the way she intended. Not so much the messages themselves but the idea that it mattered to her. . . ."

"So there," said Nina. "What's the difference?"

We arranged to have dinner together in a few days, and why not invite George to join us? Perhaps he'd like to bring that yoga teacher I'd heard about? But Nina said no, didn't he tell you? "That's over. It seems she found him unreliable."

"George?"

"Yes. But it's all right. There's a new one on the horizon. She teaches scuba diving. He says they have a lot in common."

"George can barely swim."

"Ours not to wonder why, Lydia."

I went back to my puzzle, envisioning Esther and Esther's mother and the cats. As Nina delicately hinted, I could manage to be indelicate with very little effort. Nina's parents treaded cautiously through language like soldiers in a mined field. My parents were simpler people who said things straight, and from them I learned the better part of what I know. Since there was no one else for the job I would call Esther. It was time I did something for someone else, though all I could give her was a piece of my mind. Esther, for God's sake, do something about your slovenly life or you'll wind up like . . . Tomorrow, I would say that, at the risk of sounding like a simpleton. I've sounded like worse.

"The trouble with that kind of party," Phil said lazily, rolling over onto his back, "—what is it, like a cocktail party?—is that there's not enough to eat."

"Didn't you get anything to eat? There were lots of things being passed around."

"Yeah, but they were so little. Everything was in miniature."

"What time is it?"

"Five after ten."

"I guess we really should eat something, shouldn't we? Okay, come in the kitchen. We'll see what turns up."

Something always turned up these days, as if elves had been at work. But it was me, in the middle of the night, gliding around the kitchen like a somnambulist while the city slept. We found manicotti and a bowl of string beans sprinkled with dill. I hadn't any clear memory of stuffing the manicotti or sprinkling the dill, but there was no other explanation. Phil set out two plates, two glasses, two forks. "Napkins would be nice," I told him.

While we ate, Phil said he thought he needed a new mattress. His mattress had gotten soft. "But if it's too expensive—"

"I can afford a mattress if you need one. I'll go in later and take a look at it." I paused. "You know, before we go out and buy one, though, you might try Alan's. That was fairly new." I paused again, but he was calmly drinking his Coke. "Would you mind?"

"Nah," he said. "It's just a mattress." He gulped down some more. "Of course a lot depends on the shape of the body and the sleeping habits of the person."

"What do you mean?"

"Each individual person sleeps in a certain way and makes their, like, imprint on the mattress. Now, with different people settling into different places, each mattress develops its own bumps and slumps in different areas. That's why it's not good to keep a mattress too long, because you slump into the same places. It's bad for the bones." He put down his fork as he expounded earnestly, but when he saw me starting to laugh, his eyes crinkled too. He was reminding me of Althea, delivering her instructive speeches. Also of Alan, the tongue-in-cheek orator. Of Vivian, who reveled in the obscure and the absurd. And of Victor. "I'm not kidding—you must have noticed, if you ever slept in other people's beds, that the bumps and holes didn't fit your body. Like in some beds you roll towards the center and in others towards the edge? You're into someone else's . . . Come on, Mom, this is extremely serious stuff! Are you listening to me?"

I tried to stop giggling. "Yes, yes, I'm not missing a word."

"That's the reason hotel beds last much longer than regular beds, I mean beds in people's houses. It's a well-known fact. 'Cause the hotel beds get slept on by different people every night, so they don't ever develop the same . . . Hey, take it easy or you'll choke and I'll have to perform the Heimlich maneuver. What's with you?"

"I'm just feeling punchy. How did you pick up this wonderful information?"

"I know a lot of things." His eyes shot a triumphant gleam.

"You think I don't read enough, but you see? I bet I could tell you a lot that you don't know."

"If it's all this funny I wish you would . . . Wait, what is that noise?"

"What noise?"

"Shh." It was a key in the lock. I heard the first tumbler flip. The second wouldn't. How could he have forgotten?

"I'll go see." Phil got up.

I grabbed his arm. "No, it's all right. The new lock. It's one of two people. Just wait a second till I'm sure."

"Oh." His face was closed again. The pre-summer face, dulled eyes. "Who's the other?"

"Never mind that."

"Look, I better go see." He seemed to have grown since yesterday, as he took huge strides towards the door. I followed, limping. Before he got there the bell rang and Victor called my name.

"Shit, man! At least you changed the lock."

"I didn't change it because of *him*, Phil!"

"No? I thought you did. I never believed that story about losing your keys."

The bell rang again, long. I started for the door but Phil stood in front of me, blocking the way.

"You're not really going to let that motherfucker in, are you? Just like that? Don't you have any pride?"

"Don't tell me about pride, kiddo." Victor called again and pounded with the flat of his hand. "Not only am I going to let him in, but so are you. And be civil about it too."

"You think so, huh?"

"Yes. Sooner or later. So make it sooner. Save yourself a lot of time and trouble."

"Give me one reason—" His voice split, squeaked like a younger boy's. "One reason why I should!" He put an arm up to shield his eyes.

"Lydia," Victor shouted, "will you open this goddamn door since you never gave me the goddamn key!"

"Just one minute," I called back. "No reason," I said to Phil. "Some things don't need a reason. You just do them."

"Oh, Ma!" he wailed, and waved his hands helplessly through the air like a drunkard. Then he turned and slammed his body against the door, and as I watched him flail in misery I wanted to tell him so many things that rushed to me from time past, but they would mean nothing to him. Of that original fire descending in stages to smoke, vapor, cloud, mist, rain, earth, and finally rock—the way down. But then, oh, back again, the way up. The way up and the way down are one and the same, Heraclitus said, endless and, above all, reversible.

"Lydia!" Victor banged on the door. "If you don't open it I'm going to crash it open." He would, too. He had once before.

"*Please* wait a minute!" I called. How to tell Phil that Victor was my brother and the companion of my youth? He would choose the unbearable handle of his injustice.

"Please, try to understand," I whispered. Beneath the killing changes, I wanted to tell him, something abides, and if we don't hang on to that we are doubly doomed.

Phil turned around. His face was twisted in pain and wet. He clasped his hands and shook them at me like someone thrusting a weapon, or like someone pleading. Then he ran to his room and slammed that door so hard the floor quaked.

Victor's full weight hit the door, the lock rattled, I opened it.

He was ashen and in a sweat. "What was all that? What took you so long?"

"Your son. He's bigger than I am."

He tossed his jacket on a chair and gazed around at the room, and finally back at me. "It all looks the same." Then he started down the hall.

I followed. Not yet, I was about to say. Leave him be for now. But he didn't stop at Phil's closed door. He stopped at Alan's.

"Will you come in here with me?" he asked.

"What for?"

He opened the door and stepped inside, turned on the light, which was very bright, and we both blinked.

"Just come in." He sat down at the desk where Alan had wrestled with intractable fractions and scrawled disobediently on the wood with Magic Markers.

"All right. But just for a minute." I went in and sat on the edge of the bed.

"For a little while. Not forever."

He spun the chair around, leaned back with his hands locked

behind his head, and sat staring at the wall painted midnight blue, dotted with the constellations labeled in a clear, graceful hand. "I'm very tired," was all he said.

I watched him, still strong despite everything. The longer I sat, the more I felt I could look at him forever. I was tired too, but I was thinking that at last I might be able to sleep through the night. I was thinking that a time would come, maybe months, maybe years, when my ankle would stop feeling out of joint like Mr. Dooley's, the man whose supporting cane Don and his friends diminished bit by bit with a toothed saw. When I would be able to look at a chartered bus without feeling sick; when I could watch snow falling, when I could pass a class trip on the street, when I could see a magazine photo of skiers, without wanting to lie down and die. When all these ordinary things would resume their rightful proportions and places in a universe of ordinary things. The old bachelor Thales waited too, perhaps sipping wine with his friends in the marketplace, till that right moment when a person's shadow grows to the person's size, when the body and its image, its burden, its imprint on the land, come together in harmony, and at that perfect moment of equivalence, he could take the measure of anything in the universe.